THE PUPPET SHOW

PATRICK REDMOND

sphere

SPHERE

First published in Great Britain by Hodder and Stoughton in 2000
First published in Great Britain by Sphere as an epub in 2013
This paperback edition first published by Sphere in 2015

1 3 5 7 9 10 8 6 4 2

Copyright © Patrick Redmond 2000

The moral right of the author has been asserted.

A CIP catalogue record for this book
is available from the British Library.

ISBN 978-0-7515-6182-1

Typeset in Sabon by M Rules
Printed and bound in Great Britain by
Clays Ltd, St Ives plc

Papers used by Sphere are from well-managed forests
and other responsible sources.

MIX
Paper from
responsible sources
FSC® C104740

Sphere
An imprint of
Little, Brown Book Group
Carmelite House
50 Victoria Embankment
London EC4Y 0DZ

An Hachette UK Company
www.hachette.co.uk

www.littlebrown.co.uk

To my mother, Mary Redmond.

PROLOGUE

Bow, East London, 1984

'Where's Michael? Why isn't he here? I want to say goodbye.' Sean put down the bag he was carrying and stared at the ground. His face was flushed, his lip starting to tremble.

Susan Cooper, who had been following with his suitcase, took a deep breath. 'I told you, Sean, we can't find him.'

'But I want to say goodbye. I won't go without saying goodbye!'

The two of them stood on the pavement outside the Children's Home. It was a square slab of Victorian grey stone; the only detached house on its side of the street. Facing it was a council estate, a concrete maze that blocked out the sun and cast the narrow street into shadow.

Tom Reynolds, waiting in the car, now turned off the engine and made as if to get out. Susan shook her head. They were running late as it was. A few more minutes and there was no chance of avoiding the rush-hour traffic. A group of boys from the council estate played football in the road, trading insults with every shot, oblivious to the farewell scene that was being enacted before them.

She shivered. Though only early October, there was a sharpness in the wind that warned of approaching winter. An elderly couple walking by, laden with groceries, gave Sean a sympathetic look. Silently she cursed Michael. She really didn't need this now. 'I told you, Sean,' she said, more sharply than she intended, 'we can't find him. I'm sorry, but that's how it is.'

'Then I'm not going! I don't want to go! You can't make me!'

His gentle eyes were full of fear. Immediately she felt ashamed. Crouching down beside him, she brushed a lock of blond hair from his forehead. 'I'm sorry. I didn't mean to snap. We have tried to find him, really we have. You know what he's like. He's probably just got held up.'

'He doesn't want to be here.'

'Of course he does.' She kissed his cheek. 'He's your best friend. He wouldn't want to miss this.'

'He said he hated me and that he was glad I was going away. He said—' Sean's eyes were filling with tears '—he said that foster parents just act nice to trick you, and once I'm in their house they'll keep me in their cellar and pay the social worker not to say anything and ...'

Susan made soothing noises. 'He's just teasing you. The Andersons are kind people, Sean. You don't think I'd let you stay with people who weren't kind, do you?'

He didn't answer. She took his chin in her hand and looked into his face. 'Do you?'

Slowly he shook his head.

'They've got that lovely big garden and two dogs. You'll be happy with them, Sean. I promise you will.'

A horn blasted, followed by a raised voice: a driver cursing because the road was blocked by Tom's car. She couldn't delay any longer. 'Let's get you settled. Tom said you can sit in the front and listen to one of your tapes.'

Tom opened the passenger door and grinned at Sean. 'Ready then, mate?' There was another blast from the horn. Tom leaned out of his window. 'Hang on!' He ruffled Sean's hair. 'Let's see if we can break the land speed record on the motorway, eh?' Sean managed a smile while Susan helped him fasten his seat belt. 'You will come and see me?' he asked her anxiously.

'Try and stop me.'

He still looked worried. 'You won't forget about my photograph? You will keep looking?'

'Of course. We'll find it. Don't worry.'

She watched the car move away down the road. The boys from the estate let the vehicle pass, then continued with their game. As she watched, an unspoken prayer echoed in her mind. Oh God, please let this be a happy ending. He's only nine, and he's suffered enough. He deserves a happy ending.

Sadly, she turned and walked back into the house.

Michael stood at the end of the road, watching Susan hug Sean.

His school bag hung from his shoulder. He should have been back an hour ago. Instead he had wandered the streets, killing time. It should have been over by now.

He could tell that Sean was crying. Knew that he was frightened. Knew whose fault it was too.

Shame rose up in him, together with other, more complicated feelings he didn't want to acknowledge. Angrily he pushed them down. Sean was a baby and deserved to be scared.

He turned away, towards the tiny garage on the corner. The forecourt gate was unlocked, and he darted across it, jumped on to a crate and up on to the wall that ran along the back of

3

the houses. Behind him he heard an angry roar from the garage owner.

After walking along the wall, slowly to keep his balance, he dropped down into the back garden of the Home. A postage stamp with weeds. Entering by the back door, he moved through the storage room and past the kitchen. He could hear voices. Preparations had started for the evening meal. Bolognese, judging by the smell. Mince and tins of processed tomatoes, seasoned with wedges of onion, ladled on to spaghetti. They'd had the same dish four nights ago. But it was a simple meal, and there were twenty of them to feed.

He came to the main hall. The air was stale and tinged with the smell of damp. The paint on the walls was dirty. From the outside the house had a certain grandeur, but inside everything was shabby and in need of repair. The front door faced him. Beside it was a noticeboard and a pile of coats and bags. To his left was the television room. The older children were watching motor racing while the younger ones shouted in vain for cartoons.

The front door was opening. Not wanting Susan to see him, he darted up the stairs to the first floor, a hall surrounded by bedrooms. Someone was listening to Duran Duran behind one of the doors. Another door opened and Mr Cook stepped out. He was one of the members of staff who lived on the premises. He smiled at Michael, his cherubic face, pale beard and bright red cardigan making him look like an oversized teddy bear. 'Did you say goodbye to Sean?'

'Yes.'

'You must be feeling sad. Do you want to talk?' His voice was warm, his expression friendly. Michael felt his skin crawl. Everyone knew what Mr Cook's friendship was all about. Scowling, he hurried up to the second floor.

His room was at the front of the house, buried in the eaves

of the roof. It had a low ceiling, two beds and bare walls. When first he'd come here they had been allowed to hang posters, but not now. Something about damaging the paintwork. As if pieces of Blu Tack would make it any worse.

His own bed was a mess of sheets and blankets. What had been Sean's bed for the last year was now just a bare mattress. The bedding was at the laundry, being cleaned in preparation for the new occupant who would arrive next week. A boy of his own age whose name he couldn't remember, though Susan had told him. She had also told him that he must help the new arrival settle in. Show him the ropes. Just as he had done with Sean.

He sat down on his bed, facing the window. His only view was of the council estate. The views at the rear were better. From Brian's room, over the rows of houses, you could see the tops of the skyscrapers of the City of London itself. The City. The magic square mile. The financial heart of the country, so Brian had told him, where unimaginable fortunes were won and lost every day.

Brian was fifteen. Soon he would be leaving the Home, going to make his own fortune. Brian boasted that he would be a millionaire by the time he was twenty-five, with a big house in the West End and a mansion in the country, a fleet of expensive cars, a wardrobe of designer clothes, and servants to carry out his every command. Brian was full of dreams. Perhaps they would come true. In spite of everything he had experienced, Michael still hung on to the belief that sometimes dreams did come true.

He gazed out of his window but saw nothing. In his head he imagined himself as Dick Whittington, walking through the City, dazzled by the glare of streets that were paved with gold.

*

He was still sitting there half an hour later when Susan came to hunt for Sean's photograph. His presence startled her. She hadn't realised that he'd returned.

'What happened to you?' she demanded.

He ignored her.

'You should have been there.'

A shrug of the shoulders.

'Sean was really hurt.'

'So?'

'So, you should have been there. You're his best friend.'

'I don't care.'

The sight of his back was annoying her. 'That was a wicked thing to do. Telling him all those lies about the Andersons.'

'They're not lies.'

'You really frightened him. You know he believes every word you tell him.'

'Not my fault. Stupid baby. Stupid fuckin' baby!'

A reprimand was called for but she didn't have the heart. She understood the reasons for his anger, even if there was nothing she could do to alleviate them.

'It doesn't have to be the end,' she said gently. 'You can still visit each other.'

'Oh sure! Canterbury's just down the road. I can walk there after school!'

He turned to look at her. She studied his face: the thatch of black hair, the harsh features that seemed too old for a boy of ten, and the accusatory blue eyes that always made her feel guilty. An angry face, with nothing that could be called attractive. Jenny, one of the social workers, believed that one day he would grow into his looks and be quite the lady-killer. She hoped so. Good looks were an advantage, and children like Michael needed all the advantages they could get.

It had gone six o'clock. Her own family would be waiting for her. 'I have to go. Will you be OK?'

He turned back to the window. 'Course.'

She didn't want to leave it like this. He needed her, in spite of the show of bravado. But so did her own family.

Where are they, she thought suddenly, all the barren couples searching for a child to take into their homes and pour their love upon? She knew they existed. But she also knew that most wanted a newborn baby or a sweet child like Sean who was still sufficiently undamaged to be able to respond to that love. Few wanted a child like Michael, a child who had somehow fallen through the cracks and who stared out at the world with eyes that were centuries old, full of suspicion and the dark shadows of neglect.

'I can stay a bit longer if you want.'

Another shrug.

She felt bad, but not as much as she would have done once. She had learned long ago not to care too much. It would just break her heart if she did.

'I'll be here tomorrow. We'll talk after school. You haven't lost him, Mike. Canterbury's not that far away.'

'Don't care.'

'Yes, you do.'

She left the room. He remained on the bed, facing the window.

That night, while the rest of the Home slept, he ran away.

After gathering together some clothes and those few possessions he wished to keep, he crept downstairs. As he slid through the dark, he could hear the occasional sigh of someone's breathing, but otherwise all was silence. The Home was always so full of noise. Sometimes he thought it would drive him mad, but now he found its absence eerie.

In the hallway he searched through the school bags and crammed his belongings into one that was bigger than his own. Then he began to move from room to room. The front and back doors would be locked. The windows were supposed to be locked too, but he knew that this was often overlooked. He found what he was looking for in the television room and climbed out into the night.

He walked through largely empty streets, the houses packed so tightly together that they looked as if they might burst. He passed the corner shop, from which he'd stolen sweets and comics, and the old church with the derelict graveyard that he had told Sean was haunted. His way was illuminated by the weak streetlamps and the occasional light from a window. The night was cold and still. The few people about were mostly returning from pubs and paid him no attention, though one middle-aged man, walking his dog, did turn and stare. He quickened his pace, hurrying away towards the light and noise of Mile End Road.

The road itself was quietening now, the huge thoroughfare empty save for the last of the evening's traffic making its way home to Essex or down into the City and on towards the late-night drinking clubs of the West End. The pavements, too, were emptying as the pubs and restaurants had closed. What life there was now congregated around a handful of takeaways and late-night cafés.

It started to rain. He went into one of the cafés, a small but cheerful place full of the smell of greasy food, with pictures of film stars on the wall and jazz music playing softly from a battered loudspeaker. The smell made him hungry. Though he had eaten nothing at supper, he wanted to conserve what money he had, so he bought only a coke and a packet of crisps before sitting at a table in the corner by the window, waiting for the rain to stop.

*

8

As soon as he returned from the kitchen, Joe Green noticed the boy sitting alone.

He nudged his nephew Sam, whose head was buried in a music magazine. 'Did that kid come on 'is own?'

'What kid?' asked Sam, without looking up.

'How many kids are there?'

Sam raise his head, nodded and returned to his magazine.

The boy had finished his crisps and was now sipping from his can. The sight of him troubled Joe. He shouldn't be out on his own. Not at this time of night.

The café was virtually empty, the only other customers two youths who were laughing as they tucked into pizza and chips. Joe assumed they were students from Queen Mary College, on their way back after a party. The boy's eyes were continually drawn to them. Joe guessed the reason why. He went back to the kitchen, piled chips on to a plate, then approached the table in the corner. The pavement outside was covered in litter and he made a mental note to sweep it away later.

He cleared his throat. 'Mind if I sit down?'

The boy stared at him with eyes that were suspicious and hostile. Joe smiled. 'Well?'

No answer. Taking silence as consent, Joe sat down and pushed the plate towards the boy. 'My supper. Can't manage 'em all. Want some?'

The boy looked at the plate, then back at Joe. His eyes were still wary. Joe continued to smile. 'Go on. You'll enjoy 'em more than me.'

The boy reached for a chip. He ate it slowly and then reached for another. His eyes remained fixed on Joe. Unsettling eyes; troubled and full of anger. Joe gestured to the plate. 'Taste OK?'

The boy nodded.

'Don't want this place gettin' a bad name. Want ketchup?'

Another nod. Joe reached for the plastic tomato at the centre of the table and poured some sauce on to the side of the plate. 'What's your name?' he asked.

'What's yours?'

'Joe Green. To you, it's Joe sir.'

The eyes softened a little. 'Stupid name.'

'What's yours, then?'

No answer. 'The man with no name,' said Joe. 'Like Clint Eastwood. Where you goin', Clint?'

'Michael,' said the boy suddenly.

'Michael or Mike?'

'Don't mind.'

'Mike, then. Where you goin', Mike?'

The boy shrugged.

'Must be goin' somewhere. Gone midnight. No one's out this late 'less they're goin' somewhere.'

The boy lowered his eyes, reached for another chip and dipped it in the ketchup.

'Do your mum an' dad know you're 'ere?'

'Don't 'ave none.'

Joe whistled softly. 'Sorry about that, Mike. I really am.'

The boy gave another shrug. He had a spot of ketchup below his bottom lip. Joe fought an urge to reach across the table and wipe it away. 'It's late, Mike. Ain't you got somewhere to go?'

No answer.

'Shouldn't be out on your own. Not at your age.'

'There's some people. The Andersons. They live in Canterbury. Got a big house with a garden.' The boy stared down at the table. 'Want me to live there. Said I can 'ave my own room and anythin' else I want. I could go there.'

'Sounds good.'

'I could go there,' repeated the boy. He swallowed. 'If I wanted to.'

'Bit late to go tonight, though,' suggested Joe.

A nod.

'So what you goin' to do, then? Wander round on your own?'

'Maybe.'

'Yeah, maybe.'

Joe sat back in his chair and looked out of the window. The pavement was empty now, save for a lone figure in a dirty coat, shuffling along on the other side of the road carrying a collection of bags. A tramp, judging by the state of him. Someone with no home and nowhere to go. Joe turned back to the boy. 'It's a rough world out there. Too rough for a kid like you. Ain't you got somewhere to go?'

No answer. Joe took the boy's chin in his hand and looked into his face.

'Listen, Mike. I don't know where you've come from. What you're runnin' from. If you don't want to tell me, then that's your business. But believe me, anything's got to be better than being out there on your own.' He paused, smiling gently. 'Don't you think?'

At first nothing. Then slowly the boy nodded.

'So,' continued Joe. 'You got somewhere to go?'

For a moment the eyes were filled with a desperate longing. Just for a moment. Then they became as blank as glass. Another nod.

The plate was empty. Joe looked at his watch. 'Still hungry?'

'Yeah.'

'We don't close for half an hour. Think we've some chocolate cake left. What d'you say I get you a piece, and then I'll run you back to where you've got to go. Shouldn't be walkin' round on your own. Not this time of night.'

11

The boy nodded.

'You sit there. Back in a minute.'

Joe went into the kitchen. There was some cake left. He cut a large slice.

But when he returned to the table the boy was gone.

Michael let himself back into the Home through the window in the television room. He returned the bag to its place in the hall, then crept up the stairs.

He sat on his bed in the darkness of his room. In his hand was a small torch. He reached under his mattress, pulled out a small object and held it up to the light.

It was a shabby photograph of a much younger Sean, standing in a garden with his mother. She had been a tall, slender woman with the same blonde hair and gentle features as her son. She smiled for the camera, happy and healthy, before the cancer came and ate her alive.

Sean had had other pictures of his mother, but this had been his favourite, the one that could still make him cry. He had cried all the time in those first weeks. The other children, already conditioned to despise weakness, had victimised him. Sean, frightened and alone, had looked for protection from the person closest to him. The boy whose room he shared.

At first Michael had found Sean a nuisance. A shadow he couldn't shake. But as the weeks turned into months, annoyance had turned into affection. Sean had needed him to be strong and so he had been, burying his own fears and anxieties beneath a mask of confidence intended to reassure the younger boy, who rewarded him with an uncritical admiration he had never known before.

Now Sean was gone. Off to a new home and a new life. Sean had cried before he left, scared of what the future might hold. Sean had been a baby, always in need of protection. A millstone round his neck. He was glad to be rid of him.

He wondered what Sean was doing now. Perhaps the Andersons had locked him in a cellar, just as he had told Sean they would. He hoped so. He liked the idea of Sean in the dark, frightened and alone, with no one to care.

Just as he was now.

He stared at the photograph. Sean was terrified of its being lost. His hand tightened around it, ready to tear it into pieces.

But he couldn't do it.

Instead came the tears that he had been fighting against all day. He shed them in silence. Tears only mattered if there was someone to see, and there was no one here.

He returned the photograph to its place beneath his mattress. Tomorrow he would give it to Susan, tell her he had found it on the floor and ask her to send it to Canterbury.

Turning off the torch, he lay down on his bed and looked up into the darkness. In his head was a distant memory of someone in one of the countless foster homes telling him that he should never be afraid of the dark because God lived there.

He had been told a lot of stuff over the years. And all of it was crap.

In the still of his room he waited for sleep to come.

The next day he gave the photograph to Susan so she could send it on to Sean. But in the weeks that followed, when letters came from Canterbury, he tore them into shreds.

PART ONE

TRUST

ONE

The City of London: 1999

'Which one of you two has more capacity?' demanded Graham Fletcher.

The two occupants of the cramped office looked at each other. Stuart's desk was bare, save for the acquisition agreement he had just received, two days later than promised and in need of urgent review. Though Michael's desk was covered with papers, he had spent much of the afternoon sending emails to his friend Tim. The prospect of what lay ahead was a powerful incentive to keep quiet, but in the end Michael's conscience won out. He spoke up.

'I have.'

'Oh.' Graham looked disappointed. 'What are you doing, Stuart?'

'Project Rocket. The redraft's only just arrived and we have to get our comments to the client this evening.'

'I see. Michael, my office, two minutes. Bring a pad.'

'Lucky you,' said Stuart once Graham had left.

Michael sent a final email and rose to his feet. 'My heart soars.'

Stuart smiled. He was older than Michael – over thirty – and had come into the legal profession after years as a physics lecturer. The two of them had qualified six months ago and had shared an office ever since.

'Sure you don't want me to volunteer?'

'No, thanks. You stick with Project Rocket.' Michael rolled his eyes. 'Project Rocket! God, who thinks up these names?' Picking up his notepad, he headed for the door.

'Watch the body language,' Stuart told him.

Michael gave him the finger. 'How about this?'

Stuart laughed. 'Good luck.'

Michael walked along the corridor towards Graham's office. Secretaries sat in booths outside the doors of the solicitors they worked for. The air was full of the tapping sound of fingers on keyboards, discussions of last night's television, complaints about illegible handwriting and the constant hiss of the air-conditioning. Solicitors kept emerging from their offices to give tapes to their secretaries, to visit colleagues for advice on technical issues, to delegate unwanted work or simply to chat.

He approached Graham's corner office. One of the partners, Jeff Speakman, stood over his secretary Donna, dictating orally. Donna's mouth was a thin line. She hated Jeff's habit of doing this. Michael gave her a conspiratorial smile as he passed.

A group of trainee solicitors lingered by the coffee point, complaining about a boring lunchtime lecture they'd been forced to attend. A few weeks ago they would have been more circumspect, but as the latest rumour was that the commercial department would not be recruiting in September, the desire to impress was fading.

As always, Graham's office was a mess, with open files covering every available surface. Graham was speaking fast into his hand-held Dictaphone, a cigarette clenched between his fingers. In the corner of the room, Graham's trainee, Julia, worked quietly at her desk.

Sitting down, Michael gazed out of the window at the drab offices across the road. His friend Tim worked at Layton Spencer Black and had a panoramic view of the City. But, as Graham would have been quick to remind him, one came to Cox Stephens for the quality of its work, not its scenery.

Graham finished dictating and bellowed the name of his secretary. No answer. He swore. 'Julia, track her down. Tell her I need this urgently.' Julia took the tape and left the room.

Graham stared at Michael. He was a tall, thin man of about forty, with thinning hair, sharp features and aggressive eyes. He was renowned as one of the biggest bullies in the firm, notorious for giving his underlings minimal support and then blaming them for all mistakes, including his own. 'So,' he said. 'Not busy, then?'

'Not especially, Graham.'

'Well, you're about to be.'

'Yes, Graham.'

'A new takeover's just come in.'

'Really, Graham.'

Graham's face darkened. Cox Stephens operated on a first-name basis. 'We don't stand on ceremony here,' the senior partner had announced to Michael and his fellow trainees on the day they joined. Michael knew that Graham considered this policy demeaning to his partnerial status, and consequently made it a point of honour to call him by his first name at every opportunity. Last Thursday, at their fortnightly department meeting, he had managed to use it four times in a single sentence, forcing Stuart to fabricate a coughing fit.

'We're acting for Digitron. Heard of them?'

'No, Graham.'

'They're a software company. One of Jack Bennett's clients, but as Jack's frantic I'll be in charge.'

Michael opened his pad and began to make notes. In the background he heard Julia return to her seat.

'Digitron produce operating systems for businesses. Small scale at the moment, but they're looking to expand their presence in the market and want to buy Pegasus, which is a subsidiary of Kinnetica. They're paying a fortune. The assets are worth bugger all, but the trump card is Pegasus's long-term software supply contract with Dial-a-Car. That's really what Digitron are paying the money for. You have heard of Dial-a-Car, I take it.'

'Yes, Graham.'

There was a knock on the door. Jack Bennett entered. 'Sorry to interrupt. I've just had Peter Webb at Digitron on the phone. He wants a conference call at 8.30 tomorrow morning. Is that possible?'

Graham nodded, then gestured across his desk. 'Michael's going to be helping me.'

Jack beamed. 'Well, I'm very grateful to both of you.' He was a short, stocky man with a rugby player's build and a jovial face. He had joined the firm six weeks ago, arriving from Benson Drake with a client list of computer companies that was the envy of most of the competition. Still seeming to feel the new boy, he was extremely affable with everyone. As most of the partners had had to be forcibly restrained from shouting 'Hosanna!' when he arrived and covering the corridor with palm leaves, such behaviour seemed unnecessary. But it was an attractive trait.

Michael smiled back. 'No problem.'

'You can make the conference call?' asked Graham, once Jack had left.

'Yes, Graham.'

Graham took a drag on his cigarette. 'Of course,' he said slowly, 'I'll be doing all the talking.'

Michael understood the hidden meaning instantly. He nodded. 'OK.'

'In the circumstances, I think that would be best.'

Michael felt his shoulders tensing and tried to relax them. Rebecca was always warning him that what she called his 'sod off shoulders' were too much of a giveaway.

'These are important clients, after all. Don't want to get off on the wrong foot, do we?'

Graham kept staring at him, waiting for a reaction. He steeled himself, determined not to give him the satisfaction. 'Course not.'

'In the meantime I want you to organise company searches on Pegasus and Kinnetica. Review that acquisition agreement we did for Syncarta and identify the clauses we'll want in our document, and finally make a list of information we'll need Digitron to supply. And be sure to do it with reference to the client file. They won't be impressed if we ask for stuff we already have, and neither will I.' Graham raised an eyebrow. 'Think you can handle that?'

Still waiting. Well, you'll wait for ever, you little prick.

His body was as relaxed as if he'd just had a one-hour massage. He smiled sweetly, pouring all his contempt into his best fuck-you eyes.

'Of course.' A pause. 'Graham.'

He closed his pad and made his way back to his own office.

He ordered the searches and began to skim through the Syncarta agreement. Stuart went to the staff shop and bought them both ice-creams. Rebecca phoned to tell him a joke that was doing the rounds.

21

Half past five. Fetching the client file, he started on the questionnaire. The corridor was full of the sound of voices as the secretaries left for the evening. He worked quickly, as he was due to meet Rebecca at seven. As he did so, he sensed someone hovering. Julia stood in the doorway, looking anxious. 'I know you're busy, Mike, but could you look at these board minutes for me?'

'Sure. Hand them over.'

She stood and watched him. A quiet girl with mousy hair and nervous eyes. Less confident than the other trainees. He made one small correction then handed them back. 'These are great. Well done.'

Blushing, she lowered her eyes. He had long suspected that she fancied him. The idea seemed strange. Having spent most of his life accepting that he was ugly, he still found it hard to believe that he was now far from that. He smiled at her. 'Surviving?'

'Barely.'

'You're doing fine. Everyone thinks so. Don't let Hitler's twin bully you.'

'Maybe I should take lessons from you.'

'It's easy. Just chant the word "Graham" as if it were a religious mantra. Then he'll have a heart attack and the curse will be lifted.' He gestured to his desk. 'Better get on. Take care, OK?'

She left. After spending a further ten minutes tidying up the questionnaire, he switched off his computer. The lift was stuck in the basement, so he used the stairs instead. He walked through reception, stopping briefly to chat with the security man before heading out on to the street. The April air was warm, and sticky from the rain that had fallen earlier in the day. He considered catching the tube but decided against. Having been in the office all day, he wanted to stretch his legs.

He made his way through Broadgate Circle and on past Liverpool Street Station, loosening his tie as he did so. The streets were solid with traffic, while hundreds of commuters with tired faces and determined expressions marched towards their trains. It seemed as if the whole world was wearing suits, and his lungs were full of the smell of petrol fumes.

A street vendor stood on the corner, selling the *Evening Standard*. He bought a copy as he passed by. Interest rates were expected to fall. A celebrity marriage was breaking up. Nothing out of the ordinary. Just another day.

Continuing down Cannon Street, he crossed Ludgate Circus and walked along Fleet Street towards the Strand. The ratio of tourists to locals increased. An American couple with rucksacks asked him directions to Covent Garden. In the distance pigeons dive-bombed Nelson's Column.

He reached Chatterton's bookshop and made his way downstairs to the non-fiction section. A jolly-looking woman of about thirty sat at the till. She beamed at him then pointed to the art and architecture section, where a girl with short blonde hair was helping an elderly woman choose a book. The woman seemed uncertain as to just what she wanted, so the girl was making suggestions, showing her volume after volume. As he stood and watched them, the girl, sensed his presence and gave him a quick smile.

Eventually the woman made her selection and headed for the till. He went to take her place while the girl watched his approach. She was in her early twenties and beautiful. Slender and graceful with lively green eyes and a smile that always seemed on the point of toppling over into laughter.

'Hi, Beck,' he said.

'Hi, yourself.'

He kissed her. She smelled of soap and roses. 'I'm early. Want me to come back later?'

'No.' She gestured to a half-completed display of new books. 'Help me with this. Clare said I could go when I'd finished.'

They knelt together by the display. He started passing her books, while glancing over at the till. 'Clare looks happy.'

'She is. The hunky sales rep has finally asked her out.'

'So your hints paid off?'

'Yes, and about time too. Now Clare's panicking about what to wear, so I'm being dragged out tomorrow lunchtime to help her choose a new outfit.'

They both laughed. 'How was your day?' she asked.

He told her about the new takeover. She looked delighted. 'They must be really pleased with you.'

That didn't necessarily follow, but it made her happy to believe it so he nodded in agreement. 'Guess so.'

She continued to smile, but a sadness came into her eyes. He touched her cheek. 'What is it?'

'Nothing.'

'Tell me.'

'Later.'

'Promise?'

'Promise. Let's get this done.'

They worked together in companionable silence. When they had finished, he waited as she fetched her bag. The shop was virtually empty now. He looked at the books that surrounded him. Thousands of them. A drop in the ocean of the world's knowledge.

He noticed a new book about the artist Millais and thought how much she would like it. An idea for her birthday, perhaps. It was months away, but already there was a long list of things he planned to give her.

The weather forecast for the rest of the week was good, and as he waited he decided to surprise her at lunchtime one day, bringing sandwiches so they could sit together in Trafalgar Square and feed the pigeons. Once, a million years ago, he would have despised feelings like this. But that had been in a different life, the memories of which were now kept in a locked room in the darkest corridor of his mind.

He went to chat with Clare, teasing her about her forthcoming date. Rebecca returned and they made their way up the stairs and out of the shop.

As they walked along the Strand, heading towards Leicester Square and their dinner date in Gerrard Street, she pointed to a poster promoting a new exhibition at a Piccadilly art gallery. 'Patrick Spencer. He was only one year ahead of me at St Martin's. Look at him now.'

Now he understood her sadness. 'Yeah,' he said quietly, 'look at him now.'

'I don't mind. He was good. He deserves it.'

'So do you.'

'Maybe.'

'Definitely. You'll have it too.'

'In my dreams.'

He stopped, put his arms around her and stared down into her face. 'You know what I reckon? That ten years from now, when Patrick Spencer is a big celebrity and in all the papers, the one question that every journalist will be asking him will be, "What was it like to be at college with Rebecca Blake? *The* Rebecca Blake. The biggest noise in the art world for decades." That's what I reckon.'

She smiled. 'Sure.'

'Sure. It's going to happen, Beck. Just you wait and see.'

They hugged each other, there on the street, with people jostling past them, all with their own destinations, their own lives, hopes and dreams. A middle-aged woman smiled at them as she passed. He smiled back and thought to himself: *This is what love means. Wanting someone else's happiness even more than your own.*

'Come on,' Rebecca told him. 'We'll be late.'

Arms draped round each other, they made their way towards Gerrard Street.

Dinner was not going well.

Mr and Mrs Blake adored Chinese food. On their frequent visits to London from Winchester they always insisted on having dinner at the Oriental Pearl in Gerrard Street. 'Wonderful stuff,' Mr Blake would proclaim as he tucked into his Peking duck. 'Why can't our national food taste like this?' Mrs Blake would nod her agreement and then observe that one day they really should make a trip to China itself. At this point Michael always had a vision of Mr Blake standing in the middle of the Forbidden City, that glorious monument to China's extraordinary history, haranguing a street vendor because his chop suey didn't taste the way it did in the Oriental Pearl. But as Mr and Mrs Blake were Rebecca's parents, he kept these thoughts to himself.

'And how are things at work, Michael?' asked Mrs Blake as she finished her soup.

'Fine, thanks.'

'He's just got involved in a really good project,' Rebecca told her mother. 'It only came in today, didn't it, Mike?'

He nodded. The restaurant was crowded. A waiter was hovering, waiting to clear their plates. The others had finished their starters so he tucked into his final spare rib.

'Well, that's wonderful,' said Mrs Blake. She turned to her husband. 'Isn't it, John?'

'Let's see how it pans out before we start a standing ovation,' he replied caustically.

'Dad!' exclaimed Rebecca.

'Well, after what happened last month …' began Mr Blake.

'That wasn't Mike's fault,' said Rebecca quickly.

Mr Blake wiped his mouth with his napkin. 'So whose fault was it?'

Rebecca looked annoyed. 'I thought we'd agreed not to talk about that.'

'Anyway,' added Michael, 'it won't happen again.'

Mr Blake snorted.

'Your father's just concerned, Becky,' said Mrs Blake. 'For both of you.' She smiled at Michael. 'I'm sure you'll do very well.'

He smiled back and found himself wondering, as he often did, which one of them he disliked more.

The table had been booked for five people. Rebecca's elder brother Robert had had to cancel at the last minute. 'An important meeting,' Mrs Blake had announced proudly. Robert was a surveyor, and doing staggeringly well if his parents were to be believed. Rebecca had been disappointed at the news. Michael had expressed disappointment, too, while taking it as proof that God had not yet forsaken him.

The waiter reappeared. Mr and Mrs Blake stared at Michael expectantly. Both had heavy, fleshy faces and the demanding eyes of those whose lives had held so little in the way of disappointments that the slightest setback could send them into a rage. They resembled each other in that strange way that so many long-married couples do. There was nothing of Rebecca in either of them. Her looks had been inherited from one of her grandmothers.

He still hadn't finished, but it was inhumane to expect Mr Blake to continue waiting for his Peking duck so he put the last rib back on his plate. A pool of juice had gathered there. He wanted to pick up the plate and lick it, just to see the shock on their faces. Instead he nodded to the waiter.

Mr Blake refilled their wine glasses. Rebecca nudged

Michael's arm. 'Forgot to tell you. I think I've found us somewhere to live. It's only temporary, but it sounds really good.'

'Temporary? What do you mean?' The two of them were renting a small furnished flat in Camberwell, but the lease was about to expire.

'It's another rental. Clare told me about it. Clare's my friend at work,' she explained to her parents. 'She has a friend called Alison. Alison's husband Neil works for one of the merchant banks. He's just been seconded to their Singapore office, and they have to leave in a couple of weeks. There's four months left on the lease of their flat, so they're looking for someone to take it over. It's fully furnished, so we wouldn't have to rush out and buy everything.'

'Where's the flat?' he asked her.

'South Kensington.'

'Jesus! We're supposed to be saving money. How much is that going to cost?'

'Not much more than we're paying now. The flat's very small, apparently, and the landlord is some work contact of Neil's father, so they're not paying the full market rate. But they are liable for the whole period.'

'South Ken!' exclaimed Mrs Blake. 'Oh, Becky, that would be wonderful!'

'But we're not looking for another rental,' Michael pointed out. 'We want to buy. Get settled in our own place before the wedding.'

'But our lease expires in a couple of weeks. We're not going to buy anywhere in that time, which means we'll have to extend for another six months. This way we're only committed for four. Most people wouldn't want such a short lease, but for us it's ideal.'

'And what fun to live in such a smart part of town,' added Mrs Blake.

'So how much extra rent are we talking?' demanded Michael.

'It would only be for four months.'

'How much?'

'I'm sure,' said Mrs Blake, 'that Becky's father would help out if it's a problem.'

Mr Blake smiled indulgently at his daughter. 'Of course I would, sweetheart, if that's what you want.'

'Yes,' said Mrs Blake. 'It would be lovely for you. But of course, if Michael is so set against it ...'

'I didn't say I was against it,' Michael told her.

Mrs Blake sighed. Rebecca and her father were staring at him: Rebecca hopefully, Mr Blake coldly. He realised that Rebecca had not forgotten to tell him but had picked her moment carefully, knowing that her parents would back her up. He took a deep breath, trying to swallow down his anger. 'OK.'

Rebecca kissed him. 'We'll just go and look. We may not even like it.'

'I'm sure you will,' her mother told her.

'And if you need help with the rent ...' her father began.

'We won't,' said Michael, more aggressively than he'd intended. He softened his tone. 'It's kind of you to offer, and I'm really grateful, but we can manage ourselves.'

The main courses arrived. The waiter stood over the table, preparing the Peking duck. Mr Blake's eyes were shining. 'That looks wonderful.' Mrs Blake asked Rebecca for news of their friend, Emily. Michael reached for his wine glass. The rest of the evening stretched before him like an assault course. Smiling at no one in particular, he waited for the food for which he had no appetite.

They left the restaurant at ten o'clock and headed towards Leicester Square. The streets were full of people and the heady smell of exotic food. They said their goodbyes, and Mr and Mrs Blake headed for the tube station and the train that would take them to Robert's flat in Clapham. Michael and Rebecca made their way to the bus stop on Regent Street. The bus arrived just as they did, ready to take them south, across the Thames and home to Camberwell.

Disembarking at Camberwell High Street, they walked up the hill, hand in hand. The air was cooler now, and Rebecca had no coat. He offered her his jacket. She said she was fine.

They reached the apartment block: a huge slab of red brick built at the end of the 1980s. Their flat was on the second floor: a functional unit of stone floors and neat surfaces. Michael walked into the kitchen and poured himself a glass of water. Rebecca stood watching him. 'You'll like the flat,' she said. 'I'm sure you will.'

'Yeah, I'm sure I will.'

'It's only for a few months. Just enough time to find somewhere to buy. A place that's really our own.'

He turned to face her. 'Why did you have to tell them?'

'Tell them what?'

'About work. What happened last month. They didn't need to know that.'

She lowered her eyes. Said nothing.

'Why?'

'Because I was worried. I wanted someone to talk to.'

'Why didn't you talk to me? It was our problem, not theirs.'

She sighed. 'They're part of my life, Mike. That doesn't stop because we're together.'

'I know it doesn't. But I'm your fiancé and this was between us. I told you there was no need to worry. Why didn't you believe me?'

'I did believe you.'

'No, you didn't. You told them. Gave them more ammunition to use against me.'

'They're not against you. They're just protective.'

'You don't need protecting from me.'

'I know I don't. I didn't mean it like that.'

He put his glass down on the table. 'It doesn't matter. Let them hate me if they're so desperate to do so.'

'They don't hate you.'

'Like hell they don't.'

They stared at each other. She looked upset, and the sight made him feel ashamed. 'I'm sorry,' he said quickly. 'Don't take any notice of me. Today was hectic, and I'm just feeling strung out.'

Her face relaxed into a sympathetic smile. She walked up to him and began to massage his neck. 'Then why don't I make some hot chocolate? We can watch the rest of that Humphrey Bogart film and you can tell me all about it.'

He wanted to agree and make her happy. But the evening had left him full of nervous energy that he needed to dispel. 'Better if I go for a walk.' He kissed her cheek. 'You go to bed. I won't be long.'

But it was past midnight when he finally returned.

He crept into their bedroom. She was asleep, lying on her side, her breathing so soft that he could barely hear it.

She rolled on to her back. A piece of her hair stuck up like an exclamation mark. Gently he stroked it down.

She opened her eyes and smiled up at him. 'What are you doing?'

'Watching you sleep.'

'I'm not asleep now,' she said, reaching out and pulling him down to her.

*

After they had made love, they lay in each other's arms. Quickly she drifted into sleep. He remained awake, his mind leading him on a journey he did not want to take, across space and time, to a grey-stone house in Bow.

He had lived in that house for six years. It had been his home, his world. It had always been full of people, full of noise and life. He had never lacked for company. But he had always been alone.

All his life he had been alone.

Until now.

He tightened his hold on her, wrapping himself around her, as if trying to fuse the two of them into a single being that could never be parted.

TWO

The following evening Michael saw his friend George for a drink.

It could only be a quick one. Rebecca had arranged for them to go and see the flat later. They met at a wine bar at St Paul's: an underground cellar with barrels for tables and sawdust on the floor. The wine bar gave free bowls of cheese crackers to its patrons, and when Michael arrived George was already sitting at a barrel in the corner, a wine glass in front of him, chewing furiously.

Michael sat down. The cracker bowl was virtually empty. 'Glad to see you eating. You need to build yourself up.'

George reached for more crackers. 'Frightening, isn't it? If I get any thinner I'll snap.' He had taken off his jacket, and his shirt struggled to contain his huge stomach. He was short and round, with a plump, babyish face. 'I got you a glass of white,' he said. 'Is that OK?'

Michael nodded. 'Thanks. How was your day?'

'More important, how was yours?'

'Don't ask.' A candle stood on the barrel between them. He

moistened his finger and began to move it through the flame.

George watched him. 'Are they still giving you a hard time?'

'Some of them, and it pisses me off. One mistake, that's all it was. It's typical of that place. You make a single slip and everyone forgets all the positive stuff. I'm good at my job. I'm the one that the trainees come to when they want help. People my own level too. I did that printing company acquisition virtually single-handedly, and it wasn't an easy one either. The client sent me champagne when it was done. Everyone was delighted, all looks wonderful, then one bloody phone call and it all goes pear-shaped.'

'It was a client,' said George awkwardly.

'So? It wasn't like I swore or called him an idiot or anything. I was just—' he paused, reaching for the right word '—a bit short. I was hassled. It happens. He didn't even sound that bothered. Then suddenly I'm hauled into the managing partner's office and given a formal warning, and now it feels like they're watching me all the time, waiting for me to mess up. A new merger's come in. I'm doing it with this wanker called Graham Fletcher who's going to dump all the work on me and try to get me fired if I make the slightest error.'

He stopped. His face was flushed, his breathing heavy. 'Sorry. You didn't come here for this. Rant over.'

George's expression was understanding. 'It doesn't matter.'

Michael leaned back in his chair and stared up at the ceiling. 'It just seems like I spend my whole life trying to fit in and not rock the boat for fear that all that's good in my life could be snatched away. Like last night. We had dinner with Becky's parents. Her father spends all evening looking at me like I'm dirt and her mother tries to cause friction and I just have to sit and smile and look like I'm happy to be there.' He took a deep breath. 'Sometimes I feel like I'm just going to explode.'

'Better at them than at work?' suggested George.

'Is it? Results could be catastrophic either way.'

His finger was hot from the flame. He sucked on it, downed his drink and managed a smile. 'Enough of my angst. You look mellow.'

'Naturally. We had a revision afternoon. Four hours reading the paper and *Loaded* magazine. You definitely picked the wrong profession.'

George was a trainee accountant with a small firm in the West End, trying and failing to pass his professional exams. Michael smiled. 'Are you saying that accountants are better than lawyers?'

'Of course. What are lawyers but glorified penpushers? It's accountants who make things happen. We're the movers and shakers.'

'Is that right?'

'Absolutely. Accountancy is the new rock'n'roll. We're so hip it hurts.'

They both laughed. Michael had a sudden image of the two of them sitting in a classroom at school, arguing over whether Nirvana were as good as the Stone Roses.

'How's Becky?' asked George.

'Fine. She'd arranged to see our friend Emily or she would have come along. She says you must come for dinner soon.'

'You're lucky,' said George suddenly. 'Having someone like her. I know how tough it's been for you. You make me feel ashamed sometimes, when I think how I take my parents for granted. But you struck gold when you met her, and though I'm jealous as hell I'm happy for you too.'

Michael felt sudden affection for the plump young man who faced him. 'I'll get the next round. Some more crackers too. Can't risk you wasting away.'

Again they laughed. He made his way towards the bar.

*

He met Rebecca at eight o'clock at Embankment tube. She was poring over her battered London *A to Z.* 'I don't know which is the best station,' she told him. 'Let's go to High Street Ken and walk down.'

They passed through the ticket barrier and make their way down to the platform. There were delays on the Circle Line and the platform was crowded. 'How was George?' she asked as they waited for a train.

'Fine. How was Em?'

'Not too good, actually.'

He was concerned. 'Why? What's happened?'

'Nothing in particular. She was just feeling a bit down about things. I felt bad about not being able to stay long, so I'm taking her out for lunch tomorrow. I know she'd like to see you. Will you come too?'

'Course I will.'

The platform continued to fill up with people, while the overhead display gave no indication of when the next train was due. The atmosphere was tense. They pushed their way through the crowds, towards the far end, trying to improve their chances of getting a seat when a train finally did arrive.

'Liz called me today,' she said.

'Liz from college?'

She nodded. 'Her new boyfriend's cousin owns a tiny gallery in Crouch End, and she suggested that a group of us put on an exhibition there and try to get some important journalists and dealers to come.'

'Sounds good.'

'You think?'

'It's a chance to get your stuff seen.'

'It won't be seen, though. Not by anyone who matters. Crouch End is hardly the centre of the art universe.'

'It might. We can phone around. Talk the show up.'

She sighed. 'We tried that for the show in Camberwell. A journalist from the *Guardian* promised to come but then didn't.'

'So? We try again and maybe this time he will.' He stroked her cheek. 'No one said this was going to be easy. Nothing worthwhile ever is. But it's going to happen. You just have to keep believing.' Suddenly he laughed. 'God, listen to me. I sound like a self-help manual.'

She laughed too. 'Just a bit.'

'All I'm saying, Beck, is that something good may come of it. So don't just say no, OK?'

'OK.'

They heard the sound of an approaching train. When it entered the station, everyone on the platform moved forward, only to see that the compartments were already packed. Groans of disappointment filled the air. The doors opened and a couple of passengers fought their way off. In the resulting confusion, Michael grabbed Rebecca's arm, elbowed his way through the people in front and into the resulting space. He heard someone shout abuse and smiled sweetly as the doors closed.

The train started to move. He grabbed a handrail, and Rebecca hung on to his neck. The air was hot and thick with the smell of bodies crammed against each other, sweat soured with vexation.

Half an hour later they walked out into the hum of Kensington High Street. It was nearly dark now. Rebecca studied her *A to Z* and led him down a side road. They wandered past tall, severe apartment blocks and smart white houses on quiet streets. The noise seemed to fall away behind them. The streets were wide and comfortable, with taxis and cars sliding smoothly along them. Peaceful but alive.

They made their way to Pelham Gardens, a large square,

lined with sleek, four-storey houses of grey stone that had all been converted into flats. The houses, which had huge porches supported by pillars, all looked out on to a small walled garden at the centre of the square.

They reached number thirty-three. Rebecca pressed the intercom for flat six and they were buzzed in.

After crossing a tiled hallway they made their way up the staircase. The flat was on the second floor. A small, pale woman in her late twenties and the mid-stages of pregnancy stood in the doorway, smiling a greeting. 'I'm Alison. Come in.'

They walked into a small, carpeted hallway with a low ceiling. To their right was a sitting room that ran into a tiny but well-furnished kitchen. 'Neil sends his apologies,' explained Alison. 'Something's come up at work. Let me show you round.'

It didn't take long. At the end of the hallway was a good-sized bedroom. Next to it was a comfortable bathroom and a tiny boxroom, empty save for a couple of suitcases. 'I suppose it could be used as a spare bedroom,' observed Alison, 'but there wouldn't be room for much except a bed.'

They walked into the sitting room. Like the other rooms, its ceiling was low, but the effect was intimate rather than oppressive. The furniture was plain but comfortable. Alison pointed to the settee. 'That's a sofa bed,' she explained, 'so you can have people to stay.' A small dining table stood in a corner by the window. The curtains had not yet been drawn. Outside was a tiny balcony, looking out at a row of small but well-tended gardens and the backs of the houses that faced on to Cromwell Road. Though right in the centre of the metropolis, the atmosphere was surprisingly tranquil.

'It's a lovely flat,' said Rebecca.

Alison smiled. 'We've been happy here. Shame we have to leave, but it's a great opportunity for Neil.'

'What do you do?' asked Rebecca.

'I was in banking too.' Alison patted her stomach. 'But my career's on hold for a while.'

'What's the landlord like?' asked Michael.

'Mr Somerton? Very nice. At least I think so. I've never met him, though we've spoken on the phone a couple of times. He's a work contact of Neil's father, which is how we got the flat.'

'Will he want to meet us?' asked Rebecca.

'Doubt it. To be honest, I don't think he's that bothered. He's very wealthy, so this flat is small potatoes. I'm sure he'd have let us terminate the lease early, but we wanted to see if it could be of use to someone else.'

'Well, we really like it,' Rebecca told her. 'Don't we, Mike?'

He nodded.

Alison beamed. 'Why don't I make some coffee and you can ask me any questions.'

Half an hour later they made their way back to the tube – Gloucester Road Station this time, as Alison had told them it was nearer. They passed a huge Sainsbury's. 'That's handy,' observed Rebecca.

'Incredibly so. How can we live without Sainsbury's?'

'And there's a sofa bed.'

'I know. Your parents can book their train tickets now.'

'You hated it, didn't you?'

He shook his head. They had crossed Cromwell Road and were approaching the tube. A row of expensive grocery shops stood opposite. 'It just seems a bit upmarket for us.'

She looked anxious. 'It's only for a few months.'

He tried to scowl but couldn't manage it. 'OK. Let's take it. But I warn you: turn into a Sloane Ranger and it's all over between us.'

She kissed him. 'I won't.'

In the distance he could see a Mexican restaurant, all bright colours, full of noise and energy. He gestured towards it. 'I'm hungry. Let's eat out while we can still afford to.'

They moved in ten days later, on an overcast Sunday. Alison and Neil had already gone, flying out to a new life in Singapore. Alison had left a box of Thornton's chocolates and a card wishing them a happy stay and giving them a contact number for their new landlord.

They unpacked the basics, then went for a walk in Kensington Gardens, to watch parents help children sail boats on the pond and to hunt for the statue of Peter Pan that Rebecca had visited with her grandparents on a trip to London years earlier. The reality disappointed her. 'It's smaller than I remember.'

'You were only five,' Michael pointed out. 'A Pekingese would have seemed like the Hound of the Baskervilles back then.'

He had brought his camera. A man took a picture of the two of them standing in front of the statue, arms round each other, smiling, happy to be together.

Later they phoned for a pizza. They ate it surrounded by their suitcases, listening to old tapes, sharing the memories resurrected by each song.

The following morning Michael was phoned by Alan Harris.

Alan worked at a law centre in Bethnal Green, providing free legal advice to people in the area. While at university, Michael had spent a summer at the centre as a volunteer, and occasionally Alan phoned him with emergency queries which he dealt with himself or referred to a handful of trusted allies scattered through the various departments of the firm. As Cox Stephens took an extremely dim view of its staff providing free advice, the whole thing had to be carried out in complete secrecy.

Alan explained that he was advising a distraught woman who was going to be evicted by her landlord that evening. 'The lease is only a couple of pages long. Could you have a look at it and see if there are any arguments we can raise to help her?'

'Sure. Fax it through right now. I'll go and stand by the machine.'

He arrived there only to find a fifty-page document coming through for one of the partners. As he waited he heard someone call his name and looked up to see Graham Fletcher striding down the corridor brandishing a huge document of his own.

'Michael, the revised acquisition agreement on the Digitron deal has just come through. Digitron want a meeting tomorrow morning to discuss it.'

'Tomorrow?' His heart sank.

'Is that a problem?'

'It doesn't leave us long to review it ourselves.' Behind him the fax machine whirred away.

Graham frowned. 'You're the one who'll be reviewing it. I'm far too busy.'

That figured. He nodded, while the fax machine began to whine. Clearly it had jammed.

Graham handed him the document. 'The meeting is at their offices at eight.'

'I'll handle it. You don't have to worry about a thing.'

'I should hope not,' Graham retorted, before striding off towards the coffee machine. Hastily Michael fixed the jam, grabbed the lease and returned to his room.

He tried to phone Nick Randall in the property department only to be told that he was on an external course all day. That meant he would have to deal with the problem himself. He studied the lease, hoping for an easy solution, but one did not present itself.

Turning his attention to the acquisition agreement, he realised that it was completely different from the first version. Clearly the review was going to take hours, and he also had urgent work to do for a partner in the banking department. He considered phoning Alan and conceding defeat, but he knew a woman might end up homeless if he didn't come up with something. Picking up the lease, he headed for the library.

As Michael read up on landlord and tenant law, Rebecca continued unpacking.

She had taken a day off from the shop, determined to get the flat just how she wanted it. Chris de Burgh played as she worked. Michael loathed his music, but for her it was a guilty pleasure, and she took advantage of his absence to indulge.

Their framed movie posters now hung on the walls. Both of them adored old films. Rebecca's passion was the dramas of the 1930s and 1940s; Michael's the silent epics. On their first date he had taken her to see Abel Gance's 1927 master-piece *Napoléon*, and she, eager to impress, had spent the whole time bombarding him with facts about Charlie Chaplin and other silent greats that she had read in a book that afternoon. The first present he had ever given her was a poster for Alfred Hitchcock's *Rebecca*. She hung it next to his *Napoléon* poster, both taking pride of place above the television.

Her cookery books were stored on a shelf in the kitchen. She had over a dozen, but *A Taste of India* was the only one she used regularly. Michael adored curry, and she made him one every Friday evening. After they had eaten, they would curl up together on the sofa and watch an old movie: a silent one week, a talkie the next. This Friday it was her turn to choose.

She made a note to check out the local video stores.

The phone kept ringing. Her mother called to ask about the move, as did her brother and two of her aunts. She phoned Michael to inform him of her progress, but he sounded harassed and couldn't talk for long.

In the afternoon she went to the shops, introducing herself en route to an elderly man with a warm smile whom she met in the downstairs hallway: a retired pianist who lived in one of the ground-floor flats and who wished her a happy stay. On her return she discovered that a plant had been delivered: a house-warming present from Emily. She placed it on the table in the sitting room beside Alison's card.

The unpacking was virtually finished and already the flat was starting to feel like home. Picking up Alison's card, she reread the message inside. An impulse seized her. Walking into the hall she picked up the phone.

Quarter to nine. Michael returned home, the Digitron file clutched under his arm. Though he had managed to find a temporary solution for Alan's tenant, it had taken much of the afternoon and he was only halfway through his review of the agreement for the following day's meeting. He would have to finish it after supper.

He was greeted by the smell of chilli con carne. Rebecca appeared from the kitchen, smiling in welcome. 'Hope you're hungry.'

He nodded, rubbing his temples, feeling the first rumblings of a headache. In the background, U2 sang about a place where the streets had no name. 'Do I have time to change?'

'Not really.'

He walked into the sitting room and saw their possessions set out everywhere. She followed him in. 'What do you think?'

'Looks great.' He took off his jacket and sat at the tiny

43

dining table. A bottle of wine, unfinished from the previous night, stood at its centre, next to a plant that had not been there that morning. 'Who's the plant from?' he asked.

'Em.'

'Oh, right. She called me today for a chat.'

'I hope you were nicer to her than you were to me.'

He smiled sheepishly. 'Sorry about that.'

She laughed. 'Doesn't matter.' After pouring them both some wine she sat beside him. 'Guess who I spoke to today?'

'Your mother?'

'Mr Somerton.'

The name didn't register. He waited expectantly.

'The landlord.'

'Why did he phone?'

'I called him. Wanted to say how much we liked the flat. He was really friendly, asking about us and what we did.'

She was starting to look guilty. 'And?' he prompted.

'I've invited him over for a drink tomorrow night.'

He groaned.

'It seemed like a good idea. I mean, this is his flat.'

'And we're paying him rent. He doesn't need the red-carpet treatment too.'

'He's not expecting that.'

He arched an eyebrow.

'He sounded really nice. I'm sure you'll like him.'

'Things are really hectic at work. I've got meetings tomorrow. They may run on.'

'He's not coming until nine. You'll be finished by then.' She smiled encouragingly. 'Please, Mike. We were really lucky to get this flat, and I just think it would be a nice thing to do.'

He exhaled. Managed a smile himself. 'OK.'

'Thanks. The food's ready. I'll bring it through.'

She walked back into the kitchen. He remembered the work he still had to do and his headache arrived with a vengeance.

For Michael, Tuesday proved to be a particularly bad day.

Most of it was spent at Digitron's offices in Docklands, sitting in a room with no windows, going over the revised agreement. It was surprisingly acceptable, and the meeting should have taken only a couple of hours. Unfortunately Digitron's financial director was in a bullish mood, complaining about virtually every provision, and it wasn't until four o'clock that a realistic list of objections had been compiled.

On returning to the office, Michael was cross-examined by Graham Fletcher, shouted at for not paying sufficient respect to Digitron's concerns, and told that three boxes of Pegasus contracts had just arrived and needed to be reviewed and reported on by Friday night. 'I'm not impressed with the way this deal is going,' Graham told him. 'You don't seem to be on top of things.' Michael was on the verge of replying that things would be going a damn sight better if Graham deigned to do some work himself, but managed to bite his tongue. He restricted himself to a cheerful, 'Yes, Graham. Of course, Graham. Don't worry about a thing, Graham,' before returning to his room.

He was met by his secretary Kim, full of apologies. 'You know I'm off to Greece tomorrow. Well, there's been a mix-up in the cover rota. I'm trying to fix something up, but I've got to go in five minutes.' He told her it didn't matter and wished her a happy holiday.

Sitting down at his desk, he began to wade through the contracts, checking them against the list Pegasus had sent. Two were missing. The covering letter was dated a week earlier. Graham had sat on it for days. He swallowed his resentment, established which departments should review which documents, then tried to call the relevant people, only to find that they had all left for the evening.

He located the all-important contract with Dial-a-Car and began to look through it. Digitron's financial director phoned. More objections to the agreement, all of them ridiculous. He spent a frustrating hour trying, as diplomatically as possible, to make him accept this.

As soon as he put the phone down, Jack Bennett charged in, looking stressed. 'We've just had new instructions. Computer maintenance company called Azteca, looking to sell a subsidiary. A rush job. I know you're stretched, but I really need your help. Can you do a meeting first thing tomorrow? Possibly all day.' Michael looked at the pile of contracts in front of him and managed a smile. 'Sure. Why not? Give me the details ...'

When Jack had gone he looked at his watch. Eight o'clock. He needed to leave now if he was going to be home in time. Work lay piled up in front of him. When on earth was he going to get it done? The last thing he needed was a visit from the landlord.

For a moment he considered phoning Rebecca and telling her that he couldn't get away. It would be for the best. The mood he was in, it was doubtful he could go a whole evening without saying something he might regret.

But it was what she wanted. And he had agreed.

Switching off his computer, he made for the door.

Five to nine. Rebecca heard a key in the lock.

She had spent the first part of the evening making sure that the flat was spotless before showering and changing into a new dress. Now she was in the sitting room, pacing restlessly.

Michael stood in the hall. 'Where have you been?' she demanded.

His face was flushed. He looked bad-tempered and irritable. 'Don't start,' he told her.

She ignored the warning. 'He'll be here in a minute. Go and get changed. I've ironed your blue shirt and it's on the bed. Wear it with the chinos.'

He smiled provokingly. 'And how was your day, dear?'

'Hurry up!'

The smile turned into a scowl. 'This was a bloody stupid idea!' He marched off to the bedroom. She removed the wine from the fridge. A Chardonnay. The man at the wine shop had assured her that it was delicious. It had better be at that price.

The buzzer went. Suddenly nervous, she pressed the entry button. In the last moments, as Mr Somerton made his way up the stairs, she checked, for the hundredth time, that everything was tidy.

There was a knock on the door. She took a deep breath and opened it.

The man who stood in the corridor was in his late forties, tall, like Michael, and well built, with light brown hair that was starting to grey, a strong face and shrewd dark eyes. He was dressed smartly but casually: wool jacket, dark shirt, cotton trousers, good shoes. He smiled at her. 'You must be Rebecca.'

She nodded. 'Mr Somerton?'

'Max, please.'

'And I'm Becky. Won't you come in?'

He walked into the hallway. 'Did you find it all right?' she asked politely.

'It was difficult, but I just about managed.'

She realised what she'd said and blushed. He laughed good-naturedly, moved into the sitting room and gestured around him. 'The flat looks wonderful,' he told her. 'Your possessions have made all the difference.' He spoke slowly and easily. His voice was really beautiful: deep, rich and resonant. Like velvet. The telephone did not do it justice. She smiled shyly, liking him already. 'Thank you. Mike's just coming. Won't you sit down?'

There were footsteps behind them. Michael walked into the room. Her heart sank.

He was wearing jeans and a scruffy sweatshirt. His hair was uncombed, his smile unenthusiastic, his body language hostile. Max held out a hand. 'You must be Mike.'

He nodded, shook the outstretched hand. And then said, 'It's Michael, actually.'

For a split second a strange expression came into Max's face. Not anger exactly. Something Rebecca couldn't identify. She started to panic, convinced that the evening was ruined before it had even begun.

Then the expression was gone, replaced by a warm smile. 'Of course. A name is the most important badge we have to define ourselves. It shouldn't be shortened without permission. Forgive me.'

Michael had the grace to look embarrassed. 'Doesn't matter,' he said awkwardly.

They sat down, she and Michael on the sofa bed, Max on a chair facing them. Michael poured the wine. Max gazed about him as if looking for something. 'Do you mind if I smoke?' he asked.

'No. We don't, but please go ahead.' Rebecca fetched a saucer to be used as an ashtray. Max produced a silver case and removed a thin cigar. He lit it, inhaled, then blew a cloud of smoke into the air. The smell was strong but not unpleasant, making her think of the scent of trees after rain. She noticed he had a tiny cut on his neck, a shaving scar. He did not wear a wedding ring. 'We love the flat,' she told him.

Max sipped his wine. 'I hope it's not too small.'

'It's perfect, isn't it, Mike?' She hoped Michael would say

48

something, but he just nodded. She wished she'd thought to put on a CD. They could use some background noise. She smiled nervously at Max. 'I'm glad you could come.'

'I'm delighted to have the chance to meet you both.' He tapped ash from his cigar and turned to Michael. 'Becky tells me that you're a lawyer.'

Again Michael nodded.

'Which firm are you with?'

'Cox Stephens.'

Max thought for a moment. 'Jack Bennett's just joined them, hasn't he?'

'You know him?'

'We've had a few dealings.' Max sipped his wine. 'This is delicious,' he told Rebecca. 'You have excellent taste.'

She felt relieved. 'Not me. The man at Oddbins. An exciting wine: unusual and challenging. Those were his words.'

'They always say that,' observed Michael, 'so they don't have people complaining when they realise they've spent a fortune on something that tastes like piss.'

Rebecca flinched. But Max looked amused. 'You weren't ripped off this time,' he reassured her. 'Quite the contrary.' Again he turned to Michael. 'I also understand,' he continued, 'that we hail from the same neck of the woods.'

'You're from Richmond?'

'Bow.'

The revelation took her by surprise. As it did Michael. 'I see,' he said.

'Bassett House to be precise. In Lexden Street. A Children's Home, which closed down soon after I left. Do you know Lexden Street?'

Michael turned to stare at Rebecca. She felt guilty, as if she had been disloyal. Max had been so easy to talk to on the phone that she must have said more than she'd intended. She gave Michael a nervous smile. 'Small world,' she said. He nodded.

'Where was the Home you stayed in?' Max asked him.

'Thorpe Street.'

Max thought for a moment. 'There's a pub. What's it called? The Feathers?'

'The White Feather.'

'Yes, I remember the sign now. White feather against a black background.' Max smiled. His eyes remained fixed on Michael. 'Do you know Lexden Street?'

Michael nodded. 'There's a corner shop.' He didn't return Max's stare.

Rebecca, wishing she'd been more circumspect, tried to lighten the mood. 'Not the one you and your friends used to nick sweets from?'

Max smiled at her. 'I think we used to do that too.'

'It was a long time ago,' said Michael suddenly.

Rebecca decided it was time to change the subject. 'Where do you live?' she asked Max.

'Arundel Crescent. Do you know it?'

She shook her head.

'The other side of the Old Brompton Road. Up towards Knightsbridge.' He laughed. 'Very handy for Harrods.'

'It sounds lovely,' she told him, then added: 'I don't know the area at all.'

'Then why not come and see it? I'm having a drinks party on Saturday night. Starts at seven. Quite informal.'

'That's very kind. Thank you.' She turned to Michael, not sure how to answer. 'Saturday night. We don't—'

Max came to her rescue. 'I'm sure you have plans already. But you'd both be welcome if, by any chance, you do find yourselves free.'

His glass was empty. Michael refilled it, while Max pointed

to a painting that hung above their heads. Two ships in the moonlight. 'You mentioned that your degree was in fine art. Did you paint that?'

She shook her head. 'My grandmother did. My style is very different.'

'Have you always wanted to be an artist?'

She nodded. He smiled encouragingly, so she began to tell him about her work and the factors that had influenced its development. Of her love for mythology and legend. Of her discovery of the Pre-Raphaelites whose works were steeped in those old stories, and her desire to become a painter herself. She found herself talking on and on. He was a good listener, possessing that rare gift of appearing totally focused on the words of another and inspiring confidences as a result. The smell of cigar smoke filled the room. It made her feel light-headed. As she spoke she was aware of Michael sitting beside her. She wished he'd contribute. But he said nothing.

Half past ten. The wine bottle was empty. 'I've kept you long enough,' Max announced. 'Thank you for your hospitality. I must go.'

They rose to their feet. Shook hands again. 'Would you like us to call you a cab?' she asked.

'No, thank you. It's an easy walk.'

They stood by the door. 'Tell me,' Max said to Michael, 'have you been back?'

Rebecca didn't understand the question. Michael did. 'Yes,' he said. 'Once.'

'When?'

'Last year.'

'Visiting someone?'

'No. Just delivering some papers for work.'

'Was the corner shop still there?'

51

'Yes.'

'Did you nick a Mars bar? For old times' sake?'

For the first time that evening, Michael smiled. A rueful smile, meant more for himself than for the others. 'Something like that,' he replied.

Max kissed Rebecca's cheek. 'It's been a pleasure,' he said, giving her a card with his address.

Half an hour later she sat in bed. The overhead light was off. All illumination came from her bedside lamp.

A travel book on the South Pacific lay in her lap. As a child she had been enthralled by a novel about sailors who had been shipwrecked in the Fijian islands two hundred years ago, only to be mistaken for gods by the local cannibals. Since then she had always wanted to see the islands. Perhaps they would honeymoon there if funds permitted.

Michael appeared from the bathroom, naked save for his boxer shorts, and climbed into bed beside her. His dark hair, still damp from the shower, hung over his forehead. She brushed it back. 'I wonder if Sean has been back,' she said.

He didn't answer. Just looked thoughtful.

'You wonder too, don't you?'

'Maybe.'

'We could try to trace him.'

He shook his head.

'Don't you want to see him again? There was a time when he was the most important person in your life.'

'That was fifteen years ago.'

'But you still think about him. I'm sure he thinks about you too. And if you ever decide that you want to trace him, then I'll help you look. I'm sure that we can find him together.' Gently she stroked his cheek. 'I just wanted you to know that.'

He took her hand and kissed it. 'I do.'

'I'm sorry,' she told him.

'For what?'

'For telling Max about the Home. I didn't set out to. He'd been asking about me and then he started asking about you. I mentioned Bow. He asked if your family were cockneys, and it just came out. I didn't tell him anything else. Honestly.'

'Doesn't matter.' He put his arm around her. She leaned against him, feeling warm and safe. They sat together in silence. Comfortable. Familiar.

'I liked him,' she said eventually. 'Did you?'

'Yeah. He was OK.'

'We don't have to go to the party. Probably wouldn't be our sort of thing anyway.'

'Maybe we should, just to see the house. I know you'd like to, and it's not as if we'd have to stay long. I've got an early start tomorrow. Let's go to sleep.'

She put out the light. They lay together, she draped across his chest. His breathing was slow and deep. The darkness was strange to her: a new room in a new flat with its own sounds and shadows. Ten minutes passed. Twenty. Half an hour. She sensed he was still awake and whispered his name. He stroked her hair. Smiling, she allowed her eyes to close.

THREE

Thursday lunchtime. Rebecca sat in a cheap and cheerful pasta bar on Fleet Street with her friend Emily Fielding.

The place was packed, the customers primarily young professionals and secretaries. The air was humid and full of the sound of dozens of conversations. They had to share a table with two earnest-looking men in suits who were talking loudly about bond issues as they attacked their plates of lasagne.

Emily ate slowly and neatly. She had a mask-like face that could be plain in one light and quite beautiful in another. Pale skin and dark, shadowed eyes, surrounded by long, luxuriant chestnut hair. An old-fashioned face that reminded Rebecca of the heroines in the Pre-Raphaelite paintings she loved so much.

Once she had asked her brother Robert if he thought Emily attractive. Robert had just laughed. But Michael hadn't.

As if reading her mind, Emily said, 'It's a shame Mike couldn't make it.'

Rebecca nodded. 'He sends his apologies. When we had lunch the other week his workload was manageable, but now things are manic. He didn't get in until eleven last night and was off at dawn this morning.'

Emily looked sympathetic. 'Poor thing.'

Rebecca swallowed a mouthful of pasta. The sauce was spicy and left her mouth feeling dry. 'Thanks again for the plant.'

Emily smiled. 'My pleasure.'

Rebecca felt guilty. Emily worked as an assistant at a literary agency and didn't earn much money. 'There was no need. It must have cost a fortune.'

'Not really. Are you settled in yet?'

'Yes, which is just as well as Mum and Dad descend on Sunday. It's the first place we've had with a spare bed.' She laughed. 'Robert says he feels spurned!'

'Are you taking time off?'

'No. Mum's dragging Dad round the shops. She'd love to see you. Can you do lunch on Monday?'

'Wouldn't you rather spend the time on your own?'

'It's only lunch. Go on.'

Emily nodded. 'All right, then.' She reached into her bag and pulled out a card and a beautifully wrapped present. 'These are for your father.'

'Em!'

'It's nothing special.'

'You shouldn't have bothered.'

'It's no bother. Besides, I wouldn't want him to think I'd forgotten his birthday.'

'He wouldn't care.' Rebecca stuck her fork into her pasta and realised what she'd said. In her head was an image of her father and Robert sniggering about Emily while her mother scowled her disapproval. 'I mean, he wouldn't expect you to get him anything. But he'll be pleased that you did. And Mum's really looking forward to seeing you. She says she wants to hear all your news.'

'That should take all of twenty seconds.' Emily prodded her food unenthusiastically; her plate was almost as full as it had been when they had sat down. Rebecca watched her, feeling the old unease. Emily realised that she was doing so. Momentarily they stared at each other, then each gave an embarrassed smile. Emily began to eat. Beside them, the two men laughed raucously at a shared joke.

'Have you heard from David?'

Emily shook her head.

'Good. He was a complete jerk.'

'Perhaps I was the jerk.'

'No, you weren't. It was all his fault, and you're well rid. Someone special will come along soon, Em. Just you wait and see.'

Emily lowered her eyes. 'Maybe.' She sipped her drink. 'So how did it go with the landlord?'

'Fine. I was nervous beforehand but there was no need. He was really charming.'

Emily stared at her closely. 'Good-looking?'

'Not really. But attractive. Turns out he's from Bow originally. A Children's Home, just like Mike.'

Emily looked concerned. 'How did Mike feel about that?'

Her expression put Rebecca on the defensive. 'How should he feel?'

'Strange, I expect. I mean, it's not a part of his life he talks about much.'

'He talks about it with me.'

'I know that,' said Emily quickly. 'I only meant ...' She paused, clearly struggling for the right words. 'His life has changed so much since then. Bow must seem like another world now. I know it's a different situation, but sometimes when I think about my mother it's like I'm remembering someone else's life rather than my own. And that's horrible.'

She stopped suddenly. Looked sheepish. 'Sorry. It's none of my business.'

Again Rebecca felt guilty. The way she always did when she thought of Emily's mother. 'I didn't say that.'

They sat in silence for a couple of minutes. The two men got up to leave, and Rebecca saw a chance to lighten the mood. 'I hope you feel honoured,' she said, raising her voice. 'Sharing a table with two masters of the universe.' One of the men turned and gave her a funny look. She started to giggle. Emily smiled, and the tension eased.

She found herself thinking of Michael's friend George. Chubby, chaotic George. The Tinky Winky of the accountancy world. She knew he was lonely and wondered whether to introduce him to Emily. He was hardly, to use one of her mother's expressions, the answer to a maiden's prayer. But he was funny and he was kind and Emily deserved something decent and dependable in her life. She decided to raise it with Michael and see if he thought it a good idea. Hopefully he would.

She watched Emily put down her fork, her plate half-empty. Not a brilliant effort, but better than it could have been.

'Finished?'

'Yes.'

'Then we're off to that espresso bar near the law courts for large hot chocolates with cream. It's my treat, so no arguments.'

For the first time Emily laughed. 'I wouldn't dare.'

Rebecca laughed too. Arm in arm they headed for the door.

Michael sat with Rebecca on the sofa bed watching *Sunset Boulevard*. The room was in darkness. The only illumination came from the flickering screen.

A large Toblerone lay on the table in front of him. Another

key ingredient in their Friday night rituals. Rebecca stretched out her hand towards it. He slapped her arm. 'Greedy.'

'I'm not.'

'You've just eaten a huge curry.'

'You ate the curry. It was too hot for me.' She broke off two chocolate triangles and handed one to him. He bit down, and sweetness filled his mouth. She did likewise and both chewed contentedly.

'You eat too much,' he told her.

'I don't.'

'Yes, you do. Last time we had lunch in Trafalgar Square you bought the entire contents of the sandwich shop.'

'Only because you made me.' She tried to imitate his voice. 'Go on, Becky. Buy that chocolate cake. You know you want it. Then you ate half of it yourself and forced me to feed the rest to the pigeons. I went back to the shop as hungry as when I'd left it.'

He started to laugh.

'It's not funny! We were so busy that afternoon that I couldn't go and buy anything else to eat. The only reason I didn't pass out from hunger was because Clare let me share her cough sweets.'

'Now that's what I call healthy eating.'

They were both laughing now. She put her legs over his and he wrapped his arms around her. 'That was a great curry,' he told her. 'Thank you.'

She kissed him. 'I'm glad you enjoyed it.'

On the television screen Norma Desmond sat with Joe Gillis watching one of her silent films. 'We didn't need dialogue,' she told him. 'We had faces.' They spoke the words with her. 'Great line,' Michael said.

Rebecca nodded. 'You have to feel sorry for Norma Desmond. It must have been terrible suddenly to lose your career and then have to sit and watch yourself become extinct.'

'At least she didn't lose her money. Think what happened to Mae Murray.'

She thought for a moment. 'Was she the one who ended up on the perfume counter at Macy's?'

'No, that was Louise Brooks, and she wasn't that big a star anyway. Mae Murray was a millionairess superstar in the 1920s who lost her career to the talkies and her money to the Wall Street crash. A few years later she was found sleeping rough on a bench in Central Park and arrested for vagrancy.'

The scene shifted to a bridge table where Norma Desmond sat with her chain-smoking has-been friends. They cheered when the camera focused in on Buster Keaton. 'The video shop has some of his films,' said Rebecca.

'Ones we haven't seen?'

'I'm not sure. But even if we have, I'd sit through them again. I think he's better than Chaplin.'

'So do I.'

She broke off more chocolate. 'William Holden's sexy,' she announced.

'So's Gloria Swanson.'

Her eyes widened. 'Do you think so?'

'Of course. She's a complete babe. Pamela Anderson, eat your heart out.'

More laughter. 'It's true what she says, though,' he observed. 'She can say anything she wants with her eyes.'

She kissed him again. He felt intensely happy. Of all their times together, these were the ones he loved the most.

They sat in companionable silence, watching the story unfold. After ten minutes the phone began to ring. He waited for the answerphone to kick in but it didn't. 'I thought you'd put the machine on,' he said.

'I thought I had, too.'

'Let it ring.'

She shook her head. 'It might be important.'

After stopping the tape he switched on a nearby lamp. She walked out into the hall. He sat, blinking in the light, listening to her talk to her parents about their forthcoming visit to London. In the pleasures of the evening he had forgotten that they were coming, bringing the inevitable friction with them.

Time passed. Rebecca kept trying to hang up, but her parents weren't having it and the conversation dragged on. Eventually she returned to the room and resumed her place beside him. 'Sorry about that,' she said. 'The machine's definitely on now.'

He switched off the lamp and started the tape again. The film continued to roll. Norma Desmond made a grand return to Paramount Studios. Rebecca made some jokes about the fashions of the period. Smiling, he held her close, trying to pretend that the moment had not been spoiled.

The following evening Michael walked with Rebecca towards Arundel Crescent.

They were dressed simply, Rebecca in a blue dress with a short skirt, Michael in a denim shirt and cords. He had insisted that they were not dressing up. 'Max did say it was informal.'

They walked along the Old Brompton Road. The air was muggy, the crispness of spring now turning into the sluggish heat of summer. The road swarmed with life: young people, on foot or pouring out of taxis, meeting in groups, drifting into restaurants and cafés, laughing with that easy confidence that comes with money. They walked past a bar with salsa music blaring from its windows. 'I'm sure we should have brought a bottle,' said Rebecca.

'Relax. It's not that sort of party.'

They passed South Kensington tube, leaving the noise

behind and entering the peace of the residential streets. Cool white houses that had not been divided into flats. Michael had always associated wealth with the colour white.

They came to Arundel Crescent, a row of early-Victorian houses that looked more like villas, built of creamy white stone, four storeys high. They were grander than he had expected.

Number seven stood at the centre of the row. Through a bay window they saw two couples, both well dressed and middle aged, sipping what looked like champagne from crystal glasses.

'I think this was a mistake,' Rebecca told him.

He nodded. 'Let's go and see a film instead.'

One of the women noticed them standing there. She said something and Max appeared in the window. He waved in greeting. Michael did likewise. 'Shit. We've been spotted.' He looked at his watch. Quarter past eight. 'We're leaving at nine.'

'We can't. It's too obvious. Ten.'

'All right. Compromise. Five past nine.'

They knocked on the door and were admitted by an elderly man with a bow tie, a central European accent and a dignified manner. They waited in a long hallway. Max appeared in a doorway, smiling. 'Delighted you could make it. Come in.'

They entered a double drawing room with a deep-pile white carpet and pale green walls, full of people, most in their forties and fifties, the men in blazers or expensive suits, the women in evening dresses. The harsh buzz of conversation was softened by the sound of Mozart playing quietly in the background. Waiters and waitresses moved between the guests, carrying trays laden with champagne and canapes. The air was thick with the smell of smoke and perfume.

A woman stepped out of the crowd towards them. A strikingly beautiful woman of about thirty whom Michael was sure he had seen before. Max smiled at her. 'Lavinia, this is Michael and Rebecca.' She nodded perfunctorily before whispering something in Max's ear. He nodded. 'But first, some introductions.'

He led Michael and Rebecca to the corner of the room, towards one of the couples they had seen from the window. Hugh and Valerie Harper. Hugh was from New York, a partner at one of the American law firms that were springing up all over London. Valerie, like Rebecca, was from Winchester. Max explained these connections, exchanged a smile and a joke, then slipped seamlessly away. The perfect host.

A waiter approached with champagne. They each took a glass while Valerie asked Rebecca which part of Winchester she was from. Michael gazed at a clock on a mantelpiece. Twenty past eight. He smiled at Valerie and thought, *Oh God, get me out of here.*

Quarter to nine.

Valerie was charming. She had been to the same school as Rebecca, and the two of them now swapped anecdotes while Michael tried to look interested. Hugh had gone to join another group.

His eyes drifted over the room. The furnishings were tasteful and had the obvious simplicity that denotes huge expense. Too tasteful almost, like an advertisement in a glossy magazine.

His eyes came to rest on Lavinia as she glided from group to group, tall and willowy, as elegant as a Greek sculpture. She was wearing a strapless, backless dress of pale gold that looked as if it had been made for her. Her chestnut hair was cut short. Her eyes were deep blue, her skin flawless, and tight over high, delicate cheekbones.

Suddenly he realised where he knew her from. A poster for a perfume that had been plastered everywhere about five years before. A simple poster, showing a face of extraordinary loveliness gazing wistfully at nothing in particular.

The face was still lovely, but there was a hardness in its flawless lines that the camera had not shown. Perhaps because then it had not then been there to reveal.

She approached Max, who was talking with two men in suits. He smiled and held out a hand. As he talked he stroked her bare arm, while she leaned against him, her head inclining slightly on to his shoulder. The movements of each were fluid and easy with familiarity.

She realised Michael was watching her. Her eyes moved over him with the lazy arrogance of one who had been admired all her life and took it as her due, then turned back to the group she had joined.

He made his excuses to Rebecca and Valerie and slipped away. Asking directions from one of the waiters, he then made his way to the lavatory. Anything to kill time.

Standing in the hallway, he felt reluctant to return to a gathering where he was underdressed and out of place. Instead he walked in the other direction, taking this brief moment of privacy to see some more of the house.

He descended a short flight of stairs. To his left, a door stood half-open. Curiously he went inside.

The room he entered was very different from the one he had left. Smaller, with a wooden floor and oak-panelled walls lined with shelves that were heavy with books on all manner of subjects: history, politics, religion, philosophy. In front of him was a fireplace. To his left was a comfortable chair; to his right a walnut writing desk, facing a window that looked out on to a walled garden. It was a comfortable room, snug and private. A room that had nothing to do with show and served no purpose other than to be lived in.

Above the fireplace was a painting: a man in Regency

costume standing on a path in the moonlight, staring up at a ruined castle on a hill. He moved closer, trying to identify the artist.

'Do you like it?'

Max stood behind him, studying him coolly. He remembered his rudeness the first time they had met and felt exposed.

'What are you doing here?'

'Went to the gents. Got lost on the way back.' He tried to sound convincing.

For a moment the dark eyes remained frosty. Then they warmed and Max laughed. It was an attractive sound: warm and welcoming. Michael began to relax. 'Sorry,' he said sheepishly.

'Don't apologise. Is the party that terrible?'

'No, it's great. I just—'

'Don't like parties?' suggested Max, finishing the sentence for him.

He nodded.

'Something else we have in common.'

'Honestly?'

'Can't stand them. Complete waste of time.'

'So why are you holding this one?'

Max looked thoughtful. 'I don't know,' he said slowly. 'Actually, I don't remember organising it. Must have done so during one of my blackouts.'

It was Michael's turn to laugh. He looked about him. 'I like this room.'

'But do you like the painting?'

'Very much. Who's the artist?'

'No idea. Stumbled across it in an antique shop in Suffolk. I liked it so I bought it.'

Michael shook his head.

Max looked concerned. 'Was that a mistake?'

'Yes.'

'How so?'

'You never buy a painting because you like it. You buy it because it's good.'

'I see. And how do you know if it's good?'

'Simple. If it looks like it was painted by a five-year-old, then the artist has talent and you'll double your investment within a month. But if it looks like it was painted by a monkey, then the artist is touched by genius and is going to start slicing his ear off before you can say what a load of Jackson Pollocks.'

They both laughed this time. Max took a cigar from his silver case, lit one and inhaled. 'Clearly this is a subject close to your heart.'

'Absolutely. Becky has me well trained.'

'When did she leave St Martin's?'

'Nearly two years ago.'

'And no success yet, I take it?'

He shook his head. 'She's displayed in a few exhibitions. Showcases for new artists. But they were in places like Camberwell and Tooting and no important reviewers or dealers came. Just family, friends and people looking to scrounge a free drink. To get noticed you need to show somewhere high profile, like a big West End gallery.'

'She's passionate about her work.'

Michael nodded.

'But is she any good?'

The question took him by surprise. Momentarily he was offended on Rebecca's behalf. But the dark eyes were sympathetic rather than judgemental. 'I think she is,' he said. 'But having all the talent in the world is worth nothing if the right people don't see your work. We haven't managed that yet. But we will.'

Max looked thoughtful. 'I'm sure.'

Silence. Max took another drag on his cigar. 'Is all well at the flat?'

'Yes, thanks.' Then, for no particular reason he added, 'Beck's parents arrive tomorrow.'

'And are *they* permitted to call you Mike?'

The question threw him. Again he regretted his earlier rudeness. 'I'm sorry about that,' he said.

'It doesn't matter.'

'Yes, it does. I can be an idiot sometimes.'

'Don't be too hard on yourself,' said Max kindly.

He smiled, feeling self-conscious. 'They are allowed to call me Mike. But they don't make use of the privilege. I'm pretty sure they have their own pet names for me.'

'And what would they be?'

'Waste of space. No-hoper. Destroyer of our daughter's future happiness.' Again he laughed and suddenly thought: *Why am I talking to him about this? This is nothing to do with him. Nothing at all.*

'How long are they staying?' asked Max.

'Until Wednesday. It's her father's birthday on Tuesday so we're having dinner at a Chinese restaurant in Gerrard Street. Me, Beck, her parents and brother.' He grimaced. 'One big happy family.'

Max tapped ash into a tray. 'May I ask you something?'

'Of course.'

'Where did you get that posh accent?'

Again he was taken by surprise. 'There's nothing posh about it.'

'But there's not much Bow either. Just the occasional trace.'

'Yours doesn't even have a trace. Where did you get it?'

'I asked first.'

'I left Bow when I was thirteen. Went to live with foster parents in Richmond. They were wealthy; they sent me to a good

66

school, and the accent just rubbed off. What about you?'

'Elocution lessons.'

'Really?'

'Why are you surprised?'

'I don't know.' He thought for a moment. 'It just seems ...'

'Excessive?'

'Well, yes. I mean, accent isn't the big deal it used to be.'

Max smiled. 'You're right. No one cares where you're from any more. We live in a classless society. Talent and determination can open any door.'

Michael nodded.

'Are you really so naïve as to believe that?'

For the third time he was taken by surprise. He felt embarrassed, as if he'd tried to be clever and ended up looking foolish. 'I'm not naïve,' he said quickly.

'Aren't you?'

'No.'

The dark eyes continued to study him. 'No,' said Max slowly, 'I don't think you are.'

Michael knew some sort of apology was called for, but the comment had stung. 'I'm not naïve,' he said again. 'I know exactly how the world works.' He paused, then added defiantly: 'And I'll make my mark in it.'

'I don't doubt it. I'm sure you'll make your foster parents very proud.'

He shook his head. 'That would be difficult. My foster father dropped dead of a heart attack when I was eighteen, and my foster mother sold up and went to live in the Bahamas. I haven't seen her since the funeral.'

Max whistled. 'I'm sorry,' he said gently. 'That's awful.'

He nodded, expecting Max to move on to another subject. But he didn't. Instead his expression became curious. 'You don't agree?' he asked.

'I said so, didn't I?'

'In a manner of speaking.'

'They were in my life for a while, but now they're gone and my life goes on. What else is there to say?'

'What, indeed?'

Michael sensed that he was being judged, and the realisation made him angry. 'You probably think I'm callous. Well, what if I am? What does it have to do with you?'

Max said nothing. Just stared at him.

'Who are you to judge me? You know nothing at all about my life.'

'That's right, I don't. But I'd like to.'

He softened his tone. 'I'm sorry. This is your house. I had no right to speak to you like that.'

Max shook his head. 'You had every right. I made a judgement about you without the facts on which to base it. I'm the one who should apologise. Not you.'

The eyes continued to study him. Sympathy combined with curiosity, making Michael feel vulnerable somehow, as if he were a child again. 'Perhaps,' he said, 'one day we'll manage to have a whole conversation without needing to apologise to each other.'

'Stranger things have happened.'

There were footsteps in the corridor. Lavinia appeared in the doorway. 'People are asking for you,' she told Max, speaking quickly, her tone nasal and flat. She reminded Michael of Norma Desmond, whose career had died with the coming of sound because her voice could not match up to the splendour of her visual image.

Max stubbed out his cigar. 'Natives getting restless, are they? Thanks for the warning, darling. I'll be through in a minute.'

Lavinia left. The two of them faced each other.

'Look,' said Max slowly, 'if things become too grim with your future in-laws, then why not give me a call? Perhaps we could have a beer.'

Michael smiled. 'And talk about art?'

Max smiled too. 'Or stores from which we've shoplifted.'

'It wasn't true, what I told you. About when I went back to Bow.'

'Wasn't it?'

'An old couple ran the corner shop in Lexden Street. The man had a bad leg. Maybe you remember them?'

Max shook his head. 'After my time, I think.'

'They weren't very observant and there were no security cameras. We used to nick stuff all the time. When I was eleven, the old man caught me stealing a carton of cigarettes. Usually we were too quick for him, but this time he grabbed me and got his wife to call the police. But when they came he told them that it had all been a mistake. That I hadn't tried to nick anything after all.

'When the police had gone I just laughed. Called him a wanker or something, then ran off. I didn't understand it then, but I do now. I think that he and his wife felt sorry for us. They knew we had no families and that our lives were messy enough without a police record to further complicate things.

'So when I went to the shop that last time it was to thank them for what they'd done and to show them that I had made something of my life. And the sad thing was that they weren't there any more. The new owner told me that the old man had died and the old woman had gone to live in a retirement home in Essex. So it was all for nothing.'

'Not for nothing,' Max told him.

He shrugged. 'Perhaps.'

'I'd better get back. Stay here if you want. I meant what I

said, Mike. Phone me, OK?' Max continued to smile. 'Mike. Am I allowed to call you that now?'

'You are.'

'Good.'

Max left the room. Michael remained where he was, but in his mind he was back in the corner shop, walking between the shelves, full of tins and packets and rows of sweets in jars, watching the old man who sat at the counter, his tired face lighting up as his wife appeared from the storeroom carrying a cup of tea, coming to exchange a smile and a loving word. Theirs had been a hard life, with little in the way of material reward, but it had not been without joy.

He made his way back to the party.

'Where did you go?' demanded Rebecca as they walked along Arundel Crescent.

'Had a nose around the house.'

'Mike!'

'Relax. I didn't go upstairs or anything. Just checked out the books in Max's study.'

'What were they like?'

'You'd have hated them. Nothing on Rossetti or Millais. So how did you get on with Valerie?'

'Great. You might have looked interested.'

'I did try. But you have to remember I've already read *A Portrait of the Artist as a Young, Hip Winchester Chick*.'

She hit him with her elbow. He laughed and put his arm round her. They left the quiet of the residential streets and reached the Old Brompton Road. Back to the traffic and the sounds of life. 'Lavinia's stunning, isn't she?' she said.

He nodded half-heartedly. She looked surprised. 'Don't you think so?'

'She's lovely to look at. But she's too perfect. It's like

comparing Cindy Crawford with Julia Roberts. They're both stunning, but Julia Roberts looks real.' He kissed her cheek. 'Just like you.'

She leaned against him. 'I wonder if Max thinks she's too perfect.'

'Probably not. You can't expect everyone to have my taste.'

'Do you think he enjoyed the party?'

The question surprised him. 'Why do you say that?'

'I don't know. As I was talking to Valerie, I kept watching him. It was difficult not to. He was the focal point of that party. The star, if you like. He's the host. He's rich and charming and everyone wanted to talk to him. He was always smiling and friendly, but there was something in his manner. Like he was keeping people at a distance. Even Lavinia. Didn't you notice that?'

He opened his mouth and then shook his head. 'I didn't notice anything.'

They approached the bar with the salsa music that they had passed earlier. The windows were open. They heard people shouting over the Latin beat. He thought of the week that had just passed and the one that loomed, and felt a sudden need to unwind. 'Let's have a drink,' he told her. 'I have an urge to get completely blitzed.'

She laughed. He led her inside.

FOUR

Tuesday afternoon. Michael entered his office carrying two cups of coffee. He handed one to Stuart and sat down at his desk. 'How long do you have to talk for?' Stuart asked him.

'An hour. How am I going to drag out company formation for that long?'

'By speaking very slowly?' suggested Stuart.

'Ha bloody ha.' Michael took a sip of his coffee. Still too hot to drink.

'Who's your audience?'

'All trainees across the firm. It's one of those monthly lunchtime lectures.'

'And who's landed this on you?'

'Kate Kennedy. What really pissed me off was the way she tried to make out that she was doing me a favour by giving me an opportunity to enhance my presentation skills. Why doesn't she just admit that she can't be bothered and is looking for someone to dump on?'

'Well, it could have been worse,' Stuart told him.

'How?'

'It could have been me.' Stuart laughed apologetically. 'Sorry. I'll give you a hand preparing it, if you like. Two heads and all that.' His phone rang. His financial analyst girlfriend, bored and wanting to chat. Michael watched him. Stuart had been out of the office last week on a professional development course. It was good to have him back.

Susan, their temporary secretary, entered, carrying the main acquisition agreement for the Digitron deal. She was a plump, nervous-looking girl of about eighteen. He suspected this was her first job.

'I've flagged a couple of places where I couldn't read your handwriting,' she told him.

'Are you saying my handwriting's bad?'

She looked horrified. 'I'm only joking,' he said quickly. 'Thanks for your help. I'll check through it now.'

She left the room and he picked up the document. In spite of Graham Fletcher's prophecies of doom, the deal was progressing smoothly, and he had even managed to negotiate a reduction in the purchase price. They expected to sign on Friday, and he couldn't wait for it to be over. Anything to avoid having Graham breathing down his neck.

It was five o'clock. He'd promised Rebecca that he'd be home by half past seven. He considered asking Stuart whether he wanted to knock off early and go for a drink but decided against. After two days of Rebecca's parents, he was feeling dangerously belligerent. Alcohol would only make things worse.

Jack Bennett entered and stood by Michael's desk, looking awkward. 'How are you?'

'Fine.'

'Digitron going OK?'

He nodded, and remembered Max saying that he'd had dealings with Jack.

'The thing is, Mike, Azteca have moved the timetable forward.'

'How far forward?'

'A week, which means that we have to put the disclosure bundle together by Monday. The earliest we'll have the papers is tomorrow afternoon, so it looks like we'll have to work over the weekend. Does this bugger your plans?'

It did. One of Rebecca's countless cousins was having a twenty-first birthday party in Winchester on Saturday. Another was having her baby christened on Sunday. They were going to both events and would be spending the weekend as guests of Rebecca's parents. Forty-eight hours of relentless joy. Except that now the demands of his job had got in the way. Proof that every cloud did have its silver lining.

He managed to damp down his smile. 'No. No plans at all.'

Twenty past seven. He had just returned home and stood in the archway between the kitchen and the sitting room.

Rebecca sat with her parents on the sofa bed, all drinking tea as they listened to her brother Robert brag about how well he was doing at work. A pile of birthday presents and cards lay on the table between them, due to be opened over dinner at the Oriental Pearl.

Robert was a couple of years older than Rebecca and had the same heavy features and demanding eyes as his parents. 'Mr Young says,' he announced, 'that if I carry on the way I'm going then we could be talking partnership in a couple of years.'

His father beamed at him. 'Well done!'

Robert glanced at Michael and a mischievous light came into his eyes. 'He also said that though I'm very good on the technical side, my real strength is the way I strike up a rapport with clients. He said that's the biggest trick in building a successful career.'

Michael gave a self-deprecating smile. 'Maybe you should give me some tips.'

Robert's face fell. 'Yeah, maybe I should.' He sounded disappointed. Clearly he had been hoping for a rise. No chance. Rebecca smiled at Michael sympathetically.

'Do you think we should have invited Emily?' asked Mrs Blake.

'God forbid!' Robert exclaimed.

'That's a bit harsh, darling,' his mother told him.

'It's not. This is a birthday party, not a wake. The last person we want is the little match girl.'

Mr Blake burst out laughing. Robert followed suit. Rebecca glared at her brother while Mrs Blake's mouth was a thin line. An image of Emily came into Michael's head, stirring feelings of protectiveness. He rushed to her defence.

'Who are you to sneer at her?' he demanded. 'You know what her life has been like. You should be thankful you're not in her shoes, and I'll bet that if you were, she'd be far less eager to sneer at you.'

Mr and Mrs Blake looked uncomfortable. Rebecca, her eyes anxious, shook her head.

But for the second time a mischievous light came into Robert's eyes. 'Better watch out, Becky,' he said to his sister. 'Sounds like you have a rival for Perry Mason's affections.'

'Shut up,' she told him.

'Why? If you ask me, they're very well matched. You know how much Emily loves to play the martyr. She'd be in her element if she had to visit her beloved in prison.'

'Robert!' cried Rebecca.

'That's enough, Robert,' said Mrs Blake forcefully.

Silence. Rebecca continued to glare at her brother, her face flushed. Mr and Mrs Blake eyed Michael warily. And Robert grinned at him. Michael forced his features into an approximation of a smile, while vowing silently that one day he would wipe the smirk from Robert's face for ever.

He took a deep breath. 'What time are we leaving?' he asked Rebecca.

'Eight o'clock.'

'I'd better shower and change.'

He walked into the bedroom. In the background he could hear Rebecca arguing with Robert while her father muttered and her mother tried to make peace, all four keeping their voices as low as possible. He opened the window and breathed in the warm evening air. The prospect of the forthcoming meal made him feel sick. The three of them aligned against him, with Rebecca caught in the middle, her loyalties torn.

Suddenly he felt terribly alone. He looked up at the sky and wished that just once there could be someone in his life who had no other loyalties. Someone who was there entirely for him.

But it wasn't going to happen. The sky was still light and there were no stars to wish upon.

Closing the window he made his way to the shower. He didn't bother to soap himself; just stood still, letting the hot water pound his face, breathing in the steam that built up around him until his lungs felt raw. He heard the telephone ring, followed by the sound of Rebecca's voice. Another relative probably, calling to wish her father many happy returns.

An upset-looking Rebecca was waiting for him back in the bedroom. 'That was someone called Jack Bennett. He said to tell you that Azteca have called a crisis meeting. It's at the office and he needs you there.'

Relief swept over him. He began to dress. 'What time does it start?'

'As soon as possible. He said that you should jump in a cab immediately.'

He reached into the wardrobe and pulled out some trousers. 'So, no dinner for the future jailbird. What a calamity. Are your parents bearing up?'

'Don't—' she began.

'Why not? Did Jack tell you about this weekend? I have to work then, too, so I won't be able to come to Winchester. You can tell your parents. Really make their evening swing.'

She looked hurt. 'And what about *my* evening?'

He felt ashamed. 'Sorry. I shouldn't have just sprung that on you. But you know how it is between them and me. You'll enjoy it more if I'm not there.'

There was a knock on the front door. She looked surprised. They weren't expecting anyone. 'I'll go,' she said.

He fastened his belt, reached for a jacket and heard Max's voice. Startled, he walked out into the corridor.

Max stood in the hallway, holding a bottle of champagne, explaining to Rebecca that people had been leaving the building when he'd arrived so he'd not needed to use the buzzer. 'Michael mentioned that today was your father's birthday.' He handed her the bottle. 'I thought this might aid your celebrations.' As he spoke, he noticed Michael and gave him a friendly nod.

Rebecca, clearly taken aback, smiled nervously. 'That's really kind. Would you like to meet my family?'

'I'd be delighted.'

She led him into the sitting room and made the introductions. Mr and Mrs Blake, both beaming, gave him profuse thanks, which he accepted graciously. He asked Robert about his job and offered congratulations on working for such a good firm. Mr and Mrs Blake now looked like a pair of Cheshire cats. Michael skulked in the background.

'This is a beautiful flat,' gushed Mrs Blake. 'Becky and Mike are very happy here.'

'I'm very happy to have found such good tenants.' Max looked at his watch. 'I must go. I'm meeting friends for dinner on Kensington High Street. I hope the five of you enjoy your evening.'

'Four, actually,' explained Rebecca. 'Mike's been summoned to the office.'

'What a shame.' Max looked at Michael. 'Why not walk up to the High Street with me? You should be able to pick up a cab there.' He turned to Mr Blake. 'If it's any consolation, I know some of the powers that be at Cox Stephens, and they all predict that Michael has a dazzling career in front of him. You must be tremendously proud of your future son-in-law.'

Mr Blake's eyes widened. Max stared at him expectantly. Mr Blake managed a strained smile. 'Yes, we're very proud.' He turned to his wife. 'Aren't we?' She nodded in agreement. Michael, feeling a need to laugh, bit down hard on his lip.

'It's been a pleasure to meet you,' said Max. He turned, gave Michael the most fleeting of conspiratorial winks, then made for the door.

'That was an evil thing to do,' said Michael as they walked down the stairs.

'How so? I merely gave them the opportunity to express delight at your glittering prospects. Though now you mention it, your future father-in-law didn't seem overly keen to do so.'

Michael started to laugh. 'Too right! What you made him say was blasphemous. Like forcing the Pope to recite a black mass!'

They reached the front door. Max laughed too. 'So,' he said, 'how would you like to spend the evening?'

'I'm sorry?'

Max looked amused. 'I asked Jack to call you. There's no urgent meeting, and I'm not having dinner with friends. You told me how much you were dreading this birthday celebration, so I thought I'd give you the opportunity to avoid it.'

For a split second Michael felt indignant at not having been consulted. Then the feeling was gone, replaced by immense pleasure that Max should have gone to so much trouble for his sake.

As if reading his mind, Max began to look apologetic. 'Perhaps I was presumptuous. I should really have checked with you first. Please spend the evening with your family if you'd prefer. If you like, we could have a quick drink, after which you could go on to the restaurant and say the meeting's been cancelled.'

Michael shook his head. He thought back to their conversation at the party and felt suddenly awkward. 'I'm sorry I didn't call you, as you suggested. I did want to. I was just worried about imposing.'

'You wouldn't have been imposing. I'm sorry if I made you feel you would have been.'

'You didn't,' he said quickly. 'I didn't mean—' He smiled. 'God, will the apologies ever end?'

'So, what would you like to do?'

'I don't mind.'

'Let's have something to eat first. Gerrard Street is clearly out, but apart from that the city is our oyster. We could try Langan's. Or San Lorenzo. The Savoy Grill.' Max paused. 'Or we could have a cheap and cheerful curry down Brick Lane.'

He beamed. 'Sounds good to me.'

'Me too.'

Michael sat with Max at a private drinking club in a Soho basement.

Above their heads, the streets were full of light and the noise of a million people, their voices made sluggish by air that was sticky with heat. But the club itself was cool, dark and quiet, with stone walls and a low ceiling that held the shadows thrown up by the candles that stood on the mostly empty tables.

They sat in a corner, drinking cognac. They had been here for an hour, continuing the conversation they had started in a crowded restaurant on Brick Lane.

Except that it wasn't really a conversation. In those few moments when he stopped to think about it, Michael realised that he was doing all the talking.

It wasn't deliberate; just that it was difficult to stop. There was something about Max's smile, and the soothing quality of his voice, that drew information out of him as easily as a needle drawing thread through delicate silk.

'Do you ever think about your mother?' Max asked.

He shook his head. 'Not now. To think about someone, you need clear memories of them, and I have none of her. I was only three when I was taken into care. To me, she's just a jumble of vague images. Like bits of a dream that don't make sense.'

'But you used to think about her?'

'When I was in the Home I thought about her all the time. I hated her because I had to grow up there. I hated her for not being strong enough to cope. I remember this social worker telling me that she was dead, and I told him that I was better off without her.' He gave a harsh laugh. 'God, what must he have thought? An eight-year-old kid saying something like that. But that's the point. I was just a kid, too busy trying to make sense of my own life to try to make sense of hers.'

He swallowed a mouthful of cognac, felt it slide down his throat and become a comforting warmth in the pit of his stomach. Max smoked a cigar and studied him with eyes that were curious without being intrusive. Michael continued to speak.

'But I have made sense of it now. In a strange way, my time in the Home did help me do that.'

Max smiled but said nothing.

'So many of the teenage girls there, girls who, like my mother, had been in care all their lives, had this overwhelming desire to get pregnant. It didn't matter who by. They didn't want a lover, as they didn't trust adults. They just wanted a baby. Someone to give them the unconditional love that nobody had ever given them before.

'But when they'd had a baby, many found they couldn't cope. They were still children themselves, in spite of all their attempts to pretend otherwise. In the end, the baby would be taken into care, just as they'd been. Some of them fought to get their child back. But others, like my mother, just gave up and turned to drugs to dull the pain. And so it became a vicious circle.'

He looked up at the ceiling, watching shadows slide along it. 'You know,' he said quietly, 'sometimes I wish that I could see her once more. Have the chance to tell her that I understand what her life must have been like, and that I don't hate her for what happened in mine.'

'And if you did have the chance,' asked Max gently, 'do you think you would be able to tell her that?'

'I don't know,' he said honestly. 'I hope so.'

He picked up his glass and rolled it round in his hand, watching the thick liquid catch the light from the candle.

'What about you?' he asked. 'Do you ever think about your parents?'

Max shook his head.

'Not at all?'

'I was so young when they died. They're not real to me. Just vague images, like your mother is to you. All my childhood memories are of Lexden Street.' Max smiled. 'And its corner shop.' His eyes were warm. The air was full of the smell of cigar smoke, which Michael found soothing. Behind him he could hear the sound of other conversations, all spoken in low voices.

He knew it was late and that he had a busy day ahead of him tomorrow. But he liked this place, and he wanted to stay and talk. 'It's a terrible thing,' he said slowly. 'The need for love. It makes you vulnerable. It can make you do things you don't want to do.'

'Like what?'

'There was a man at the Home called Mr Cook. He had a baby face and a ginger beard and looked like a big teddy bear. He knew all about the need for love. Knew how to use it. He liked kids, you see. Liked doing things to them. But he never forced himself on them. He was too clever for that.

'Most of the kids at the Home were like me. We'd been moved from foster home to foster home and been disruptive in all of them. We'd been labelled as troublemakers, and the Home was our last resort.

'But you'd always get a couple of misfits, kids who shouldn't have been put there. Kids who'd just lost their parents, or who'd had years with the same foster family. Kids who'd known what love was and then suddenly been deprived of it. They were the ones Mr Cook used to target. He'd make a fuss of them. Give them presents. Encourage them to tell him their problems, like a cuddly uncle.

'Then, when he had their trust, he'd start asking them to let him do things. Intimate things. And if they said no he'd never get angry. He'd just turn cool towards them. And because they were lonely and wanted someone to care about them, they'd usually end up letting him do what he wanted.'

His hand tightened round his glass. His voice darkened as he remembered.

'There was a kid called Sean. He was eight when he came to the Home, a year younger than me. His mother had died of cancer and he had no other family. The two of us shared a room. Sean used to cry all the time and the other kids picked on him. Then Mr Cook started to befriend him, or at least he tried.

'But I wouldn't let it happen. I don't know why. Normally you let people fight their own battles, but there was something about Sean that made me feel protective. I wouldn't let him go anywhere without me. I made sure that he and Mr Cook were never alone together. Then, one day, Sean was sent away to foster parents, and I didn't need to protect him any more.'

'Didn't anybody say anything?' asked Max. 'Make some sort of complaint?'

'Some girl did once. But nobody believed her. This was in the early 1980s, and there wasn't the awareness of child abuse that there is now. All the other adults who worked at the Home thought Mr Cook was an angel. If you'd met him, you'd have thought so too.'

He sighed. 'And anyway, to most of us, adults were just part of the system, and we'd stopped trusting that a long time ago.

'Then, when I was eleven, this girl called Sarah Scott came to the Home. She was about my age. I can't remember what her background was. She was really quiet. Wouldn't say boo to a goose. Inevitably Mr Cook started on her. Poor kid. I remember seeing her once, sitting in the corner of her room, just crying quietly. I should have done something. Tried to help her. But I had my own problems. I just left her to sort out her own.'

Michael swallowed, thinking of what came next.

'One day she decided she couldn't cope any more. She climbed up on to the roof of the house and threw herself off.

She wasn't killed. The roof wasn't that high. But she was crippled. She'll spend the rest of her life in a wheelchair.

'Naturally there was a huge scandal, especially when they understood why she'd done it. The Home had been privately run. The authorities used to send kids there but never made proper checks on how the place operated. Once this happened, of course, they waded in and took the Home over. There was an investigation, and Mr Cook was sent to prison. And when the investigation was over, do you know what the authorities did?'

Max shook his head.

'They took us to Alton Towers for a day.' He started to laugh. 'Five hours at a fucking funfair, followed by fish and chips on the way back! As if that could make up for what had happened to Sarah Scott.'

He stopped suddenly, staring at Max, looking into his eyes. *Why am I telling him this?*

Feeling self-conscious he gazed down at the table. Someone had scratched the letter 'R' into the wood. He traced its outline with his finger. The surface was smooth and cool.

He looked at his watch. Quarter to twelve. He should be leaving now. But still he made no move to go.

'The Home wasn't a last resort for you, though,' said Max quietly. 'It all changed when you were thirteen.'

'Yeah, it all changed.'

He looked up. Max continued to study him with eyes that were sympathetic and non-judgemental. Again, for reasons he didn't really understand, he began to speak.

'Do you remember, during the war in Yugoslavia, there was a spate of books written by soldiers who'd rescued an orphan and brought it back for a better life in England?'

Max nodded.

'In the book you'd always have photographs. The before

84

and after shots. A picture of the child looking wretched in its Bosnian hellhole, followed by one of the same child holding a puppy in a Berkshire garden, beaming like one of the Ovaltinies. An extreme version of those lifestyle makeovers you get on daytime TV.

'I'm not saying those people didn't love the child. But sometimes I used to wonder why they needed to write a book about it. Why did they need to broadcast their generosity to the nation unless the adoption was motivated more by a desire to be seen as generous and giving than by a desire to give a damaged child a new start in life?

'My foster parents were like that. He was a merchant banker. She didn't work. He didn't need to either, as both had inherited money. They'd had a privileged life, and I think it made them feel guilty. Made them feel they should give something back to society.

'So they decided to foster a child. A difficult child from a rough background. Someone whose wretched, deprived life they could be seen totally to transform. I was the one they selected, and my life *was* transformed totally. I lived in a lovely house by the river. I went to a good school and wanted for nothing. All they asked of me was that I never bothered them with my problems, and that I make token appearances at their parties and dinners to tell everyone how well I was doing and how incredibly grateful I was.'

'Did they never try to adopt you?' asked Max.

He shook his head. 'Safer to foster. That way the ultimate responsibility isn't yours. They could still give me back if I became too difficult, and the threat of being sent away was a great way of keeping me in line.' He smiled. 'Like buying a washing machine with a guarantee that allows you to return it at any time if you're not completely satisfied.'

'It must have been difficult for you,' Max suggested.

'Why? I was thirteen when they took me in. I wasn't naïve. I knew what was going on. It was a business transaction, with both parties getting something. For them it was massive kudos with their friends for their astonishing generosity. For me it was an expensive education, a cultured accent and a place at Oxford. Who's to say I didn't get the better deal?'

'Who, indeed? Now you even have a grave you can go and visit.'

He shook his head. 'You visit a grave because you miss the person buried there, and I was never allowed to know my foster father enough to miss him.' He sighed. 'I should probably go, though. If it wasn't for him and his wife I wouldn't be where I am now.'

'And where is that?'

'The holder of a first-class degree. A qualified lawyer with good prospects.' He smiled. 'And paying rent to a Rachmanite landlord for a short-term lease in the smart part of town.'

Max smiled too. 'Don't you mean an extortionate rent?'

'That goes without saying.'

'It doesn't have to be short-term,' said Max suddenly. 'Not if you want to stay.'

'Thanks.'

Max lit another cigar. 'Be careful,' Michael told him. 'Those things will kill you.'

Max inhaled and breathed smoke into the air. 'But what a wonderful way to die.'

A comfortable silence. Max finished his drink and pointed to Michael's glass. 'Another?'

He looked at his watch. It was nearly midnight. 'Shouldn't this place have closed?'

'Extended licence. We have hours yet.'

'I've got work tomorrow.'

'That doesn't have to be a problem. I asked Jack to tell

people you had an early-morning meeting and wouldn't be in until noon.' A pause. 'So do you want to stay and talk a bit longer?'

He nodded.

Max rose to his feet and made his way to the bar.

The following afternoon Michael made himself a coffee and went to see Jonathan Upham.

Jonathan was a six-years-qualified solicitor who had come with Jack Bennett from Benson Drake. Shortly before Jonathan's arrival, he had been taken out to lunch by two members of the department who had been qualified for a similar period. Over lunch, Jonathan had described in detail all the transactions he'd ever been involved in, and then expressed the view that if you were going to do the job properly you really should be willing to work all the hours God sent. His audience had nodded in agreement before rushing back to the office to tell everyone that the new recruit was a total prick.

However, in the two months since Jonathan had joined, this view had been revised. On the negative side, he was formidably hard-working and wouldn't have recognised a joke if one had walked up to him and said 'Bite me'. But on the positive, he was completely lacking in arrogance and always happy to give advice to more junior lawyers on technical problems they encountered.

Michael knocked on Jonathan's door. 'Are you busy?'

Jonathan looked up from his desk, his earnest eyes made even smaller by the thick glasses he wore. He was only thirty but looked considerably older. 'As always. How goes it on Digitron?'

'Signing on Friday, thank God. Can I ask you something?'

Jonathan nodded. Michael sat down. 'Do you know someone called Max Somerton?'

Jonathan nodded. 'Why? Do you?'

'He's my landlord.'

'Oh, right.' Jonathan looked impressed.

'He said he'd had a few dealings with Jack Bennett, so I was just curious.'

'A few dealings?' Jonathan seemed surprised. 'Well, that's one way of putting it.'

'What do you mean?'

'Max got Jack most of his clients.'

'Seriously?'

Another nod. 'If it wasn't for Max, Jack wouldn't be the star he is today.'

Michael started to laugh. Jonathan looked confused. 'Sorry,' explained Michael. 'I just had an image of Jack in a top hat and tails doing a Fred Astaire routine.'

Jonathan still looked puzzled. 'Jack isn't into ballroom dancing.'

'I know. Forget it.' He sipped his coffee. 'So how does Jack know Max?'

'Well, about ten years ago Max instructed Jack to do some work for him. Max had shares in a computer company and wanted some licensing agreements drawn up. Jack was just starting to make a name for himself in the computer sector. Max was impressed with his work and began to introduce him to people he knew in the industry who could be potential clients. And there were lots of them. That's the thing about Max. He knows everyone. People with money usually do.'

'How did he get his money?'

Jonathan looked thoughtful. 'Not sure exactly. I think he started off as a stockbroker. Made a pile. Invested it wisely. Made more money and did the same. That would make sense.'

'Sense?'

'I remember Jack saying once that Max's great strength was

his ability to predict approaching trends, both economic and social, and to make money from them. For example, he used to have interests in all sorts of companies, but he liquidated most of his assets at the end of the 1980s, just before the recession kicked in, which meant of course that he was sitting on a pile of money when everyone else was panicking and trying to sell everything for half what they'd paid. And he was one of the first people to realise just how massive the computer industry was going to be, and that the real money was going to be in software, not hardware. Some of his shareholdings must be worth a fortune.'

'Do you like him?'

'Difficult to say. I only know him by reputation. I've said hello to him once or twice, but we've never met properly.'

Michael was surprised. 'How come?'

'Whenever we get instructions from Max, Jack deals with them himself. Sure, I do most of the donkey-work, but I've never been allowed to go to meetings or anything high profile like that.' Jonathan smiled. 'Jack's a great bloke, but he's funny about Max.'

'Funny?'

'Funny's the wrong word. What I mean is, he's possessive. The way some partners are about their most important client. Are you and Max friendly?'

'Sort of.'

'Then be careful, OK?'

The phone went. Jonathan looked at the display. 'I need to take this. Talk to you later.'

Michael walked out of Jonathan's office. As he made his way down the corridor he saw Jack Bennett standing by the coffee point talking to Kate Kennedy.

Jack saw him approach. For a split second a strange expression came into his face.

Then it was gone. He smiled.

Michael smiled back. Feeling slightly uncomfortable, he made his way back to his office.

Thursday evening. Nine o'clock. Rebecca stood in the box-room of the flat.

The room was empty, save for her easel and a box containing her oil paints and brushes. Michael had suggested that she use the room as a temporary studio. When first she'd left college she'd shared a studio in Bethnal Green with three friends, but as the months had passed, and two of them had started to achieve a small measure of success, she had found it increasingly soul-destroying to work alongside them.

A blank piece of canvas stood on the easel. Michael had been urging her to start something new, and she had meant to do so that evening. But instead she had tidied the flat, phoned some of her friends and packed a bag for the weekend, so that when eventually she did make her way to the boxroom she had convinced herself that it was really too late to begin.

The window was open. The May night air was warm and still. The huge houses in front of them acted as an effective barrier to the sound of the traffic that flowed constantly along Cromwell Road.

Hearing a key in the lock, she called out a greeting. Michael came and stood in the doorway. His collar button was undone; his tie hung slack around his neck. 'You look tired,' she told him. 'Are you hungry?'

He shook his head, then pointed to the canvas. 'That looks good.'

'I've been busy.'

He looked sceptical. 'Well, maybe I haven't,' she admitted. 'Sometimes I wonder what the point is. Nothing's ever going to happen. Why fool myself?'

'It will happen. It just takes time, that's all.'

'And what if it doesn't? There are so many talented people out there. So much competition. How will I ever stand out?'

'Because you're good.' He smiled. 'And because I believe in you.'

She smiled too. 'I'm glad you're home.'

'So am I.'

'And I wish you were coming tomorrow.'

His expression became troubled. 'Do you?'

'You know I do.'

'Even though my presence would just cause friction?'

She sighed. 'It'll get better, Mike.'

'No, it won't. It'll only get worse. As far as your family are concerned, I'm the biggest mistake you've ever made.'

She stared levelly at him. 'I don't think I'm making a mistake.'

Suddenly he turned away. 'Maybe you should,' he said quietly. 'They're your family, Beck. They've always been there for you. Families are the most important thing in the world. No one knows that more than me.'

'You're important too.'

'You say that now, but if we stay together it'll just drive a wedge between you and them. Are you willing to risk that?'

'It won't happen,' she told him.

'It might. What if they forced you to choose?'

'They wouldn't.'

'But what if they did? What would you do then? You might choose them, and even if you didn't you'd hate me for what I'd made you give up. Either way it would be the end for us.'

'What are you saying?' she asked. 'Do you want to break up?'

'No. Of course not. I just get scared sometimes, that's all. I really love you, you know.'

91

He turned back towards her, close to tears.

'Oh, Mike . . .'

He shook his head, managing to smile. 'Don't take any notice. I'm just tired. I always talk rubbish when I'm tired.'

'No, you don't.'

He lowered his eyes. 'I know I can be difficult. I know I'm not the easiest of people. But you're everything to me. I don't know what I'd do if I didn't have you.'

She stared at him. Found herself remembering the first time they'd met.

It had been eighteen months ago, at a party in Chiswick given by her school friend Jennifer and boyfriend Paul. As she chatted with Jennifer, she had watched a striking young man with jet-black hair and unsettling blue eyes who stood alone in the corner, nursing a drink, talking to no one.

'His name's Michael,' Jennifer had told her. 'He was at college with Paul.'

'He looks arrogant,' she had observed.

Jennifer shook her head. 'But he is contained. Impossible to know.'

At that moment he had turned and made eye contact. His stare had been direct and confrontational, and she had whispered to Jennifer, 'I bet I can make him smile.'

He had been hard work. Exasperatingly so. In the months that followed she had often been close to giving up. It would have been easy to do so. There were other men in the world and she had never been short of admirers.

But she hadn't. Instinct had told her that this was something really special, and that she would always regret it if she walked away.

And slowly he had allowed her to penetrate the walls he had built around himself and see the angry, lonely, frightened person who hid behind them. The person who had come to love her with an intensity that was sometimes frightening because it was an emotion that had never had a proper outlet before. The person who, in the intimacy of their bed, would hold her to him as if his life depended on it.

She walked up to him now, put her hands around his face and began to stroke his temples. Early on in their relationship she had realised the soothing effect that simple touch could have on him. 'Why me?' she asked. 'You could have had anyone. What is it you see in me?'

His face softened. He smiled down at her. 'Nothing.'

'Nothing?'

'Everything.'

They hugged each other, there in the empty room.

FIVE

Friday. Twenty past five. Michael, who had just returned from the offices of Kinnetica's lawyers, sat at his desk, staring at his computer screen, checking through the afternoon's e-mails.

Stuart entered, carrying a file. 'You're back. Did Digitron sign in the end?'

'Only just. We're in the taxi and the client announces that he's not happy with two of the warranties.' Michael raised his eyes to heaven. 'Those warranties were absolutely fine. I went over them with him twice last week, and he was happy enough then. But not now.'

'Did you talk him out of it?'

'Couldn't. Graham Fletcher was there, so he takes charge. You can guess the rest.'

Stuart nodded. 'Yes, sir. No, sir. Three bags full, sir.'

'Exactly. Consequently we get to Forrest Hardwicke's offices twenty minutes late. We're taken into this huge conference room to be greeted by the lawyers and half of Kinnetica's board, all smiles and backslaps and let's put this goddamn deal to bed. Then Graham announces that the agreement has to be amended.' He started to laugh. 'Kinnetica's chairman started shouting that he wasn't changing a word and that if we didn't sign immediately the deal was off. Our client got uptight, too, and it looked like the whole thing would collapse. Fortunately the partner at Forrest Hardwicke calmed everyone down and asked what the changes actually were. Then he took Kinnetica off to another room, and when they came back they said they'd agree one but not the other. So we accepted that and signed after all. Then they all went to a wine bar in Smithfield to get completely pissed.'

'Why didn't you go with them?'

'Are you kidding? Now it's done, Graham's taking all the credit and doesn't want me around to steal his thunder. He suggested, forcefully, that I had things to do back at the office. I was tempted to deny it, but then thought what the hell. The client's such an arsehole that he and Graham are welcome to each other.'

Now Stuart was laughing too. Michael sat back in his chair and stretched his arms above his head. The room was stuffy. They were not allowed to open the windows – something about interfering with the air-conditioning.

He took a deep breath, let the air out slowly, and had a sudden image of Rebecca sitting in her brother's car as it drove down to Winchester. He looked down at his desk. The thought of a weekend alone depressed him, and momentarily he wished he was with her. Then he remembered the fiasco of the one and only Blake family party he had attended and realised that for the sake of their relationship it was safer if he stayed away.

But was it really safer? In his absence, her parents and brother would have free rein to try to poison her mind against him. They could whisper their fears into her brain, scattering dark seeds of uncertainty in the hope that one would take root and grow.

He couldn't win, whatever he did.

He sighed. Stuart looked quizzical. 'All right?'

'Just tired. Anything exciting happen when I was away?'

'Kate Kennedy was asking whether there were any clients we could bill. Catherine Chester from the property group phoned with some question for you, but she said it could wait until next week. That's all.'

Michael rose to his feet. 'Do you want a coffee?'

'No, I'm leaving now. Helen and I are off to Bristol, and we have to catch a train at six. See you on Monday.'

Michael went out into the corridor. Around him, the secretaries were switching off their computers and reaching for their bags. Their conversations were more animated tonight, charged with excitement at the thought of the forthcoming weekend. Hearing someone call his name, he turned to see Jack Bennett approach.

He felt uneasy, just as he had the last time their paths had crossed. He smiled. 'Hi.'

'All well on Digitron?'

'Yes. We signed this afternoon.' He was on the point of adding 'thank God' but decided against.

'Well done.' Jack smiled, too, but his eyes seemed strained. Perhaps he was also tired. Perhaps.

Michael stood, waiting, feeling an uncomfortable mixture of expectation and apprehension.

'Thing is, Mike, I've been through the papers Azteca sent over, and in spite of my earlier panic there isn't actually that much to do. So rather than ruin your weekend, I'll make a list of what we need to disclose, and perhaps you'd come in early on Monday and draft something up. Is that OK?'

He nodded. Again he had an image of Rebecca sitting in her

brother's car and wondered whether he should follow her down to Winchester. 'Are you sure?'

Jack nodded.

'Thanks.'

'No problem.'

There was no need to say any more. Yet they continued to stand, facing each other. One of the secretaries walked past them carrying her bag and humming a Spice Girls song.

Michael cleared his throat. 'Thanks for Tuesday night. For phoning me at the flat. It was kind of you.'

'Pleased to help,' Jack told him. A pause. 'How was Max?'

'Mr Somerton?' He felt awkward about referring to Max by his first name. 'Fine. We just had a drink and a bite to eat.' Pausing, he then felt obliged to add, 'I mean, we hardly know each other.'

Jack nodded. Again they stood in awkward silence, each waiting for the other to speak.

'Well, it was no problem,' said Jack eventually. 'And thanks again for your help on Digitron. They're not the easiest client, and it sounds as if you did an excellent job.'

'Hope so.'

'There weren't any problems with the Dial-a-Car contract, were there? We didn't need Dial-a-Car to consent to the change in ownership of Pegasus?'

'No. I checked. There were no specific change-in-control provisions. I'd better let you get on. See you Monday.' He turned to go.

'Change-in-control provisions can sometimes be buried in the miscellaneous section. You did check that, didn't you?'

He stopped. Turned back, smiling, trying to ignore the sinking sensation in the pit of his stomach. 'Of course.'

Jack nodded, then walked away. Michael watched him until he was out of sight.

Then he rushed back to his office.

It was empty. Stuart must have left already. He scanned the files in his cabinet, his heart starting to race.

Finding the Dial-a-Car contract he turned to the miscellaneous section, the dumping ground for trivial provisions: notice periods, acceptance addresses for faxes.

The section that, in the mad rush of the deal, he had not thought to check.

There won't be anything. There won't, there won't, there won't.

But there was.

A crisp, three-line paragraph stated that if ownership of Pegasus changed without Dial-a-Car's written approval, then Dial-a-Car had the right to terminate the contract at any time without liabilty, such right to be waived in writing.

His throat felt dry. His stomach was churning, making him feel that he could vomit and soil himself at the same time.

The Dial-a-Car contract had been the whole reason for the deal. It was the contract Digitron expected would help establish them as a major player in the market: a contract for which they had paid a fortune and signed a binding agreement, less than two hours ago.

A contract which, because of his carelessness, could now be snatched away from them whenever Dial-a-Car saw fit.

He knew what he had to do. When a catastrophe like this occurred, there was only one thing to do. Find a partner and confess everything. It was a dreadful prospect but he had no choice. He rose to his feet.

Then, slowly, sat down again.

He couldn't confess to this. It was the end if he did.

It was less than two months since he'd been given a formal warning. He was skating on thin ice already. A mistake like this would send him crashing down into the icy waters beneath. Graham Fletcher would see to that. He might as well start clearing his desk now.

And even if they didn't sack him, it would still be all over for him at Cox Stephens. Digitron would bring a claim for negligence, and though the damages should be covered by the firm's professional indemnity insurance, the claim would put their premiums through the roof and everyone would know that he was the one responsible. It would be like a black cloud above his head, destroying any chance of partnership or a long-term future at the firm.

He could leave, of course. But even that wouldn't solve the problem. People would find out. They always did. Someone would tell someone and the word would spread, following him around like a bad smell, jeopardising his prospects wherever he went.

No, he couldn't tell. The best thing was to keep silent. To say nothing. To hope that it would all just go away.

But it wouldn't. All it needed was for someone to spot the provision. Someone at Digitron. Or, worse still, at Dial-a-Car. From this day forward he would be living under the constant dread of exposure.

He clenched his fists and hammered at his temples, giving physical expression to the rage he felt at himself. Pain filled his head, momentarily dulling the thought that was pounding at his brain, just as his fists had done.

What am I going to do? Oh God, what am I going to do?

Two hours later he switched off his computer and rose to his feet.

He had told no one. The weekend would be spent trying to decide what action to take.

He walked out of the office, through Broadgate and on towards Liverpool Street Station. The streets were full of life:

people in suits pouring out of wine bars, their faces slack with alcohol, all smiling at the prospect of the weekend ahead.

He entered the station and crossed the forecourt, pushing his way through the crowds who made their way towards the mainline trains and their homes in Essex and beyond. Passing through the ticket barrier, he headed down into the Underground and the Circle Line to Gloucester Road. There were no delays that night, just people with the same smiling faces and air of cheerful expectancy. He hated them all.

The flat was in darkness. Rebecca would be in Winchester now, able to relax and enjoy time with her family because he was not there to spoil it for her. He walked into the sitting room. The air was stale, so he opened the glass door that led out on to the balcony. She had left a note on the dining room table. He picked it up:

Will phone tomorrow. Don't work too hard. Please come down if you get the chance. I love you. R.

He sat down on the sofa bed. Laughter echoed down from the flat above. It sounded as if Richard and Suzanne were having a dinner party. Richard and Suzanne were fund managers in their early thirties. Rebecca had introduced herself and found this out. She was good at things like that.

He wanted to be with her and considered catching a late train to Winchester. A problem shared was a problem halved, and she was the one person in the world he would trust to tell.

But could he really trust her? What if she panicked and told her parents? It would not be the first time. And in doing so she would supply them with more ammunition to use in their battle to steal her from him for ever.

No, he would not go to Winchester. It was safer to stay here and try to resolve this himself.

The telephone in the hall began to ring. Rebecca probably,

just to let him know she had arrived safely. She would know by his voice that something was wrong. Best not to answer.

But it wasn't her. The machine cut in, then a deep, resonant voice drifted into the room.

'Mike, it's Max. Hope all is well. I'm calling from Suffolk. I've got a place here. Did I mention that?' A pause. 'Well, no matter. I'm here with Lavinia. We're staying the weekend. I had to call Jack about something and he told me that you don't have to work after all. I imagine you'll be heading down to Winchester tomorrow morning, but if not, then why not come and join us? You'd be very welcome. Let me give you the telephone number ...'

At first he sat and listened.

But the voice was warm and inviting. It drew him like a moth to a light.

He picked up the phone. 'Hello.'

'Mike!' Max sounded delighted. 'Thought I'd missed you. Did you hear the message?'

'Yes.'

'Are you going to join us?'

'Um ... I don't know. Where are you in Suffolk?'

'Cottleston. It's on the coast. Do you know this part of the world?'

'No.'

'Good. No excuse not to come, then. When can we expect you?'

His head was still full of work and he couldn't think clearly. 'I'm not sure. It may not be possible. I'll have to find out about trains.'

'No need. I'll send a car for you. There's a chauffeur company I use. Shall I book one for tomorrow morning?'

The question was asked in a way that suggested agreement was taken as read. He played for time. 'Who's we?'

101

'Lavinia and myself.'

This didn't sound like a good idea. He struggled for a polite way to refuse and said the first thing that came into his head. 'I don't have anything smart to wear.'

'My God, what do you think we're doing here? Shooting grouse and sipping cocktails?' Max started to laugh. 'Relax. The whole thing is very low key. Wear whatever you feel comfortable in.'

He thought back to Max's party, remembered Lavinia's indifference that had bordered on disdain. 'I don't want to intrude.'

'Which you would be if you'd invited yourself. But I'm inviting you. You should come, Mike. It's beautiful up here. Maybe I could show you some of the countryside.'

He realised that he was still holding Rebecca's note. 'It's really kind of you to invite me, but I think it would be better if I went to Winchester.'

'Are you sure?'

'Yes.'

'Good choice. A weekend with the in-laws. The perfect way to unwind after a hard week.' Another pause. 'Is that what you really want?'

At that moment in time, there was only one thing he wanted: a solution to his problems at work. Some clue as to what he should do.

Max would know what to do.

The idea was rejected instantly. It was stupid. Madness.

He tried to put it out of his mind, but it would not go.

'Is that what you really want?' asked Max again.

'No.'

'Didn't think so. What time shall I send the car?'

Still he hesitated. This felt all wrong. 'Look, I'm not sure ...'

'Ten o'clock. Is that too early?'

So there was nothing for it. Max was not taking no for an answer, and he was too beset with anxieties to argue.

And just possibly, it might work out for the best.

'Ten is fine.'

'Good. Look forward to seeing you.'

As he put the phone down he thought of Rebecca and told himself that he was doing the right thing. He would only ruin her weekend if he went to Winchester. His was ruined, whatever he did.

For the rest of the evening he sat in front of the television, his mind so full of worries that when he went to bed he had no recollection of what he had watched.

Michael sat in the back of a Jaguar as it made its way out of the city.

It was a drizzly, grey London morning. Drops of rain slid down the windows. The journey was taking longer than expected. An accident at Stratford meant that the traffic moved at a snail's pace.

Steve the chauffeur, cockney and bald as a billiard ball, was chatting away cheerfully. 'Nice bloke, Mr Somerton. Driven for 'im loads a' times. Lovely house 'e's got. Been there before?'

Michael's answers were friendly but short. The stuffy air was giving him a headache.

He was tired. He had lain awake most of the night, his mind continually replaying the events of the previous day. A solution had yet to present itself but he would think of something. He had no choice.

But it was not just his fears that had kept him awake. He had also been plagued by a question to which he did not yet have a satisfactory answer.

Why is Max singling me out? What does he want from me?

He couldn't deny that he found the attention enjoyable. But it was also unsettling.

They reached Stratford, and the traffic ground to a complete halt. Steve put on a tape of New Age music, soft and relaxing. Michael sat back and allowed his eyes to close.

When he opened them again the car was moving quickly. He felt a draught against his face. The air was cooler now. The rain had stopped, and Steve had opened a window to let in the wind. Stretching, he looked around him.

They had left London far behind. Dense woodland hemmed them in on both sides, then suddenly fell away to be replaced by grassland, gleaming with the remnants of the early-morning rain, rolling away into the distance like waves on an emerald sea. Its surface was smooth, save for the occasional tree, branches twisted like the limbs of a soul in torment. Beautiful but stark.

'Are we in Suffolk?' he asked.

'Yep. Be in Cottleston any minute.'

He thought back to his history lessons and remembered that three hundred years earlier Suffolk had been one of the hunting grounds for Matthew Hopkins, the Witchfinder General. It seemed an appropriate setting. He imagined a terrified woman being dragged across the fields by an angry mob to be hanged from one of the trees that sprouted from the earth like a harvest of gibbets.

This was not the England of chocolate boxes. But he liked it.

They drove through a gate and along a tree-lined drive that opened up to reveal a beautiful Georgian house of white stone, all clean lines and large windows, symbolising a time when England believed in its future. It was surrounded by lawns, the grass battered flat by the wind. As they approached, he saw the door of the house opening.

He climbed out of the car into a wind that was tinged with salt, blowing with a ferocity that would never have been possible in the congested streets of London. Steve handed him his bag. 'Have a good weekend.'

'Thanks. You too.' He made his way towards the house.

Lavinia stood waiting for him. Without saying a word, she led him inside, across a hallway with a marble floor and into a large drawing room with creamy-white walls and sofas you could sink into and be lost in for days. She gestured to one. He sat down.

She perched elegantly on the arm of a chair, lit a cigarette, inhaled and breathed smoke through her nose. She was dressed simply in jeans and a jumper, but she wore them with the instinctive grace of one who had spent half her life as a professional coathanger. He listened for sounds of life but heard none. 'Where's Max?' he asked.

'On the phone.' Her eyes were as hard as two chips of cobalt.

'This is a lovely place,' he said awkwardly.

She nodded but said nothing. He smiled in an attempt to disguise his nervousness. 'I was supposed to be working this weekend. Fortunately my boss decided he didn't need me.'

'Not exactly,' she told him.

'What do you mean?'

'Max phoned your boss and *told* him that he didn't need you. He wasn't very pleased, apparently, but you know how persuasive Max can be.'

Her words threw him completely. He felt both indignant and flattered, an uncomfortable combination which did nothing to alleviate his sense of unease.

She continued to stare at him. He managed to resurrect his smile. 'Lucky me.'

For the first time she smiled back, a predatory expression

that did nothing to thaw the ice in her eyes. 'Yes,' she said slowly. 'Aren't you the lucky one?'

'I'm sorry. I didn't want to intrude.'

She raised an eyebrow. 'You mean you didn't want to come?' She breathed smoke in his direction. 'Max will be disappointed to hear that.'

Her eyes were making him uncomfortable. He rubbed at his nose. 'That's not what I meant.'

'So what did you mean?'

'That three can be a crowd.'

'Four, actually. I have a friend arriving soon.'

'I didn't know that.'

'Why should you know? Or should I have asked your permission?'

'I didn't mean that.'

Again she smiled. 'Do you ever mean what you say?'

He heard footsteps. Max walked into the room, smiling. Feeling immense relief, Michael rose to his feet. Max clapped his hands together. 'You've arrived! Sorry I wasn't here to greet you. I hope the journey wasn't too grim.'

Michael smiled back and thought to himself: *You shouldn't have spoken to Jack; you had no right to do that.*

'Let's take your bag to your room,' said Max. 'Then I'll show you round.'

Lavinia stubbed out her cigarette. 'Yes, we'd better give you the grand tour.'

'No need for both of us,' Max told her.

Her face darkened. 'If you're sure,' she said sulkily.

'I am. You stay here, darling.'

Momentarily her eyes fixed on Michael. Then she turned away.

Max led Michael across the hallway and up a stone staircase. They walked along a corridor with a deep-red carpet before entering a large, well-furnished bedroom with a huge window and an en suite bathroom. Michael put down his bag and went to look at the view of the long lawn at the back of the house, running down to a cliff and the cold grey expanse of the North Sea.

Max came and stood beside him. 'Is the room all right?'

He nodded but said nothing.

'You don't like it?' Max sounded concerned.

'What's not to like? It's all great. This house. Everything.'

'But?'

He didn't answer. 'But?' repeated Max.

He breathed out slowly, his eyes still fixed on the view. 'You shouldn't have done that.'

'Done what?'

'Told Jack he didn't need me. It wasn't fair. Things are busy and he did need me.'

Max looked surprised. 'How did you know about that?' Then he sighed. 'No, don't tell me. I can guess. I'm sorry. You weren't supposed to find out.'

Michael turned towards Max. 'It doesn't matter that I found out. It matters that you did it. I have to work there. Jack's an important partner.'

'And I'm an important client.'

'That's why I'm here, is it? To draft a loan agreement?'

'No, of course not. You're here because I didn't like the thought of you having to work the weekend.'

'I need Jack on my side. I don't want to piss him off.'

'You don't need to worry about Jack.'

'That's easy for you to say. You're the client. You're the powerful one. I'm just a grunt on the ground. Jack has power over me, and if he decides he doesn't like me, he could screw my career.'

'Jack likes you.'

'Oh, sure he does. Just like Lavinia. God, I've never had such a warm welcome. She puts Becky's parents to shame.'

He stopped suddenly and turned back to the window. Wind pounded the glass. In the distance he could see a fishing boat, tiny as an insect, bobbing on the surface of a great grey beast that was waiting to swallow it whole.

'I'm sorry. I shouldn't have said that. Told you I could be an idiot.'

Silence.

'I probably shouldn't tell you this,' said Max slowly, 'but Lavinia was up for a high-profile cosmetics contract. This morning she heard that it had gone to another model. Someone younger. Yet more evidence that her career is drawing to its inevitable close. That's what your reception was all about. Personal feelings didn't come into it.'

Michael continued to stare out of the window. In his head was an image of the perfume poster he had seen all those years ago. Unexpectedly he began to feel sympathy for Lavinia. Her face was her fortune. All her life she must have taken it for granted. Now, every time she looked into the mirror she would have to watch that fortune fade.

'Do you want to leave?' Max asked him.

A part of him did. This felt even more wrong than it had last night.

But in spite of everything he was pleased to see Max. And it seemed an awfully long way to have come just to turn round and go straight back.

He shook his head. 'I just wish you'd asked me, that's all.'

'I'm sorry. I will next time.' Max looked at his watch. 'Lunch will be ready now. Let's go and eat.'

When they got back downstairs, Lavinia's friend Suzanne had arrived.

A buffet lunch had been laid out in the drawing room. A collection of cold meats, fish and salad. As he ate, Michael chatted with Suzanne, a striking Eurasian woman of about thirty. She had met Lavinia during a brief stint as a model but now lived in Norwich with her recording engineer husband and worked as a freelance translator. 'I was glad to leave the fashion world behind,' she told Michael. 'All that backstabbing. I don't know how Vinnie stands it.' She was warm and friendly, with an ease of manner that made him feel he had known her for years.

Max and Lavinia stood together on the other side of the room, conducting an animated conversation in whispers. Eventually they left the room. Michael, sure that he was the cause of their disagreement, watched them go, again wishing that he hadn't come. Suzanne asked him about his job and he turned his attention back to her.

They returned half an hour later. Lavinia came and sat next to Suzanne, her expression warmer than before. She gave Michael a half-hearted smile, then began to ask Suzanne for news of mutual friends. Max remained by the door. He caught Michael's eye and gestured for him to follow.

They walked out of the house and towards a silver Porsche parked in the drive. 'I told you I'd show you the countryside,' said Max. 'Climb in.'

They drove for miles, with no apparent destination. The sky had cleared now, so Max opened the sunroof and put on a CD. The sound of Elgar floated above the soft purr of the car's engine. He seemed preoccupied, and Michael sensed that he was pleased to have left the house. For the most part they sat in silence, but one that was not uncomfortable. Slowly the car filled with the rich scent of cigar smoke. It was a smell that he was coming to associate with Max, and to like.

Eventually they made their way to Southwold, a beautiful coastal town with an old hotel in its central square and sweeping views of the sea. They sat together at a table in a crowded pub on a cliff above the beach, drinking the local beer. Max asked him about work and told him some anecdotes about Jack. As always, he spoke slowly, his voice warm and soothing. Listening to it, Michael longed to tell him about the disaster of the previous day and to ask his advice as to what he should do.

But he remained silent. He could not share this problem with Max. He could not share it with anyone.

It was evening by the time they returned to the house. Before dinner, he phoned Rebecca to explain where he was. Not wanting to admit that he had chosen Max over her, he said that others from the office were there too, that Max's guests were potential clients, that the visit was simply a PR exercise for the greater glory of Cox Stephens and that he'd had no choice but to come. She believed him without question. Her trust made him feel ashamed. He told himself it was for the best.

They ate dinner in a spacious dining room, the only light coming from the candelabra on the sideboard and on the mahogany table at which they sat. The food was served by Mr and Mrs Avery, a middle-aged local couple who lived in a wing of the house and acted as its permanent caretakers.

The meal lasted two hours, the wine flowing freely with each course. Max was at one end of the table, Lavinia at the other. The sea air had given Michael an appetite, and he ate and drank freely. Suzanne did most of the talking, describing some of the hopeless bands who had recorded at her husband's studio. Lavinia laughed along with the rest of them, seeming relaxed and at ease. Occasionally Michael would catch her staring at him, but the room was so full of shadows that he could not determine what emotions lurked within her eyes.

Later, they took their coffee into the drawing room. He sat on a sofa, his head spinning from the alcohol he had consumed. The others floated around him, carrying on a conversation that he no longer had the energy to join. Stifling a yawn, he decided to make his way to bed.

Before he could do so, Lavinia came to sit beside him.

She was smiling. Though his senses were sluggish, she still made him uneasy. Slowly she stirred her coffee. She drank it black without sugar. 'Where did Max take you this afternoon?' she asked.

'Southwold.'

'He took me there once. We had dinner at a hotel. The Swan, I think it's called. Suffolk's beautiful, but too quiet for me. I prefer London.' She sucked on her spoon. 'Don't you agree?'

He nodded politely.

'You mean, you're bored here?'

'I didn't say that.'

She laughed, a soft, cat-like sound. 'Relax. I'm just teasing you.' She continued to stir her coffee. 'You're very easy to tease. Does Rebecca tease you?'

He wanted to tell her that it was none of her business. Instead he nodded.

'I don't believe it. She seems too sweet.' Her tone was provocative. 'She's very pretty. Do you think she's prettier than me?'

His hackles rose. Unease gave way to anger. He looked into her face and said, 'Yes, actually I do.'

He waited for her smile to fade, but it didn't. Instead she laughed again and touched his arm. 'How chivalrous you are. So true to your lady love. I admire that. I wasn't very nice to you this morning. Did you think I was a bitch?'

He was too tired for this conversation and wished she would leave. He shook his head.

She continued to smile. 'Liar.'

111

'All right. I did at first. Then Max explained about the contract.'

'I'm sure he did. Dear Max. A wonderful man. The two of us make a wonderful couple, don't you think?'

Another nod. He wanted to be somewhere else.

'So do I.' Again she sucked on her spoon, then licked dark drops of liquid from her lush red lips, sighing contentedly. 'Lovely. Not too hot. Otherwise I might burn myself, and I'm sure you wouldn't want that.'

He opened his mouth to answer. She threw the contents of her cup into his face.

Momentarily he was blinded. Steaming liquid filled his nose and mouth. His skin felt as if it was burning. He began to choke.

She jumped to her feet. 'You filthy pig! You think I'd let you touch me? What do you take me for?'

His eyes were stinging. He rubbed at them, blinking, trying to focus.

'I suppose you'd like us to do it on the sofa with the others watching? Is that what gets you off, you little freak? You're Max's guest, for God's sake! How could you talk to me like that?'

He shook his head, not believing what he was hearing.

'Don't try and deny it! It's bad enough you talk to me like some whore without trying to make me out a liar too!'

He rose to his feet, his heart pounding. Coffee had sunk through the fabric of his shirt and was stinging his skin. Lavinia backed away from him. Suzanne put a protective arm around her.

He managed to find his voice. 'You're lying—' he began.

'No, she's not,' Suzanne told him. 'Or are you going to call me a liar as well?'

He stared at her in bewilderment. 'What?'

Her eyes brimmed with scorn. 'You heard.' She turned to Lavinia. 'I'm sorry, Vinnie. I wasn't going to say anything. I didn't want to spoil the weekend. The little creep came on to me, too, over lunch, but I was too embarrassed to speak up.' She snorted. 'God, I wish I had now.'

The room was starting to spin. He struggled for words, but shock and alcohol dulled his ability to think. Mutely he shook his head. His legs were trembling beneath him. He stumbled backwards, knocking into a table. A china figurine toppled to the floor. It fell with the surreal, slow-motion quality of nightmare.

He turned towards Max. Their eyes locked.

Max's face was dark with a multitude of emotions, none of which he could identify.

Then suddenly it cleared and became a mask.

They all wore masks. All three of them; actors in a twisted charade that he didn't understand, and of which he was the unwilling star.

He fled from the room, up the stairs, to the sanctuary of his bedroom. Locking the door behind him he leaned against it, his stomach heaving.

In the distance, faint as a sigh, was the sound of laughter.

Sunday morning. Half past seven.

Michael, his bag packed, crept downstairs to the telephone on the hall table.

A card beside the phone gave details of a local taxi firm – an unexpected stroke of luck. He picked up the receiver and dialled the number. Six rings, then an answer.

'Hello, thank you for calling Renton Cabs. We're closed at the moment, but if you leave a message after the tone we'll call you straight back.'

Frustrated, he put down the receiver.

'They don't open until ten on Sundays.'

He turned. Max stood in the hallway, wearing strong shoes and a sports jacket, as if ready for a walk.

Michael felt cornered, just as he had in Max's study at the party.

Max gestured to his bag. 'You're leaving.'

He nodded.

'Without saying goodbye?'

'Is there any point?'

'And without breakfast too.'

'Looks like it.'

Max looked at his watch. 'The others are still sleeping. Mrs Avery won't be serving for a couple of hours. There's a hotel a couple of miles up the coast. They do the full English spread.'

The very idea of food turned his stomach. 'I'm not hungry.'

'The walk will give you an appetite.' Max's tone did not allow for disagreement. 'Leave your bag. Come on.'

They walked in silence along the beach.

It had rained during the night. Their feet sank into the wet sand, which was littered with clumps of seaweed and the occasional piece of driftwood. To their left was a shallow cliff; to the right, the sea, almost invisible under a thick blanket of mist. The wind, so strong yesterday, was now just a faint breeze. Seagulls swooped overhead, their cries a plaintive lament that did little to fill the stillness around them.

Michael struggled for something to say. In the end it was Max who spoke first.

'I was eight when I first came here. An excursion from the Home, on a May morning rather brighter than this one. I'd been in the Home for two years by then. Two years of being buried alive in those narrow streets. I'd almost forgotten there was a world outside Bow.

'They piled us into a coach and drove us to Southwold. We had to sing songs all the way to show them how happy we were and how lucky we felt. When we arrived they marched us down to the beach, gave us buckets and spades and told us to build sandcastles. It was a competition: a chocolate bar to the child who built the best one.

'I waited until they stopped watching, then walked off by myself along the beach. I walked for miles and miles, until I was too tired to walk any more. Then I climbed the cliff and just stood there, looking out to sea and up at the biggest sky I'd ever seen in my life. I couldn't believe how big it was. I felt like God, with the whole world laid out before me.

'And I vowed to myself that one day I'd have a house here. A beautiful house by the sea, bigger than the Home, and mine entirely. My world. A place where I'd make all the rules, and anyone who broke them would be banished for ever.'

'Now you've got the house,' Michael told him, 'and you make the rules. You have money and you have power. Everything you could ever have wished for.'

'Yes, I have,' said Max rather sadly. 'All my dreams came true.'

'Are you going to banish me?'

Max said nothing, just carried on walking. His silence hurt Michael, who kicked at the sand with his shoes as if trying to punish it for his own weakness.

'I didn't do anything. They're lying. I don't expect you to believe me, but that's the truth.'

'I do believe you.'

'You do?'

Max stared in front of him. His stride was slow and measured. 'Try not to think badly of Lavinia. Jealousy is a terrible thing. It can bring out the monster in all of us.'

'Jealousy? What reason does she have to be jealous of me?'

'What reason, indeed?' echoed Max, his voice as soft as if he were talking to himself.

'And what of Suzanne? Why would she lie?'

'She's Lavinia's oldest friend and wants to help her fight to keep something alive which, if it ever had life at all, was dead long before this weekend began.'

The sand was now covered in stones. Michael picked one up and hurled it out to sea, watching it vanish into the mist. In the distance he heard a splashing sound. 'Is it really over between you?'

'Yes.'

He picked up another stone. In his head he saw a beautiful face on a million posters. He told himself that she did not deserve his sympathy, but still he felt it.

'She said the two of you made a good couple.'

'We do.' Max smiled ruefully. 'Wealth and beauty. It's an unbeatable combination.'

'Do you think she'll be OK?'

'I'm not the only man in London with money, and looks such as hers will open most doors. She won't be alone for long.'

'I don't know what I'd do if Rebecca told me it was over.'

For the first time, Max turned towards him. His eyes were sympathetic. 'Don't you?'

He shook his head.

'You're braver than me,' Max told him. 'You've risked more, emotionally. But it was a gamble worth taking. There's something very special between you two. I could see it the first time I met you. It's nothing I could ever define. But it was there.' A pause. 'I envy you that.'

Michael thought of Rebecca. He wanted to be with her. But he wanted to be here too.

'When I was a kid,' he said, 'I was scared of dying. It was the most terrible thing I could imagine. But not now. Now the most terrible thing would be for her to die and leave me to go on living without her.'

He rubbed at his neck with his hand. In his other hand he still held a stone. He let it fall.

'Until I met her I'd always been alone. Nobody had ever cared about me, and I hadn't cared about anyone else. It's awful to live like that, but in a strange way it's easier. People could hurt me, but I could fight back and defend myself.

'But I can't fight her. That's what happens when you love someone. You give them power over you. They hold your feelings in their hands. They can hurt you again and again, and you can't do anything to stop them.' He breathed heavily. 'Sometimes I hate her for that. Sometimes I want to hurt her really badly before she gets the chance to do the same to me.'

He stopped walking and looked down at the ground. His shoes were thin canvas and the stones beneath hurt his feet. Just as the thoughts that jostled inside his brain were causing his head to ache.

Why am I exposing myself? This is my life and it has nothing to do with him. Nothing at all.

He looked up. Max was watching him, his eyes that comforting mixture of interest and sympathy. They made him feel vulnerable. He lashed out.

'What is it with you? I don't talk to people like this. I wouldn't even tell Rebecca some of the things I've told you. I don't know what you want from me. I don't even know what I'm doing here!'

'You're here because I wanted the pleasure of your company. I'm sorry for what happened last night. I'm the one you should blame. I hope you can forgive me.'

He remained silent, too choked to speak.

'And now,' continued Max, 'you have two choices. Either

you accept my apology and we go on with the weekend. Or you refuse it, in which case I'll arrange for a cab to take you to Winchester, or to London, or wherever else you want to go.'

The two of them stood facing each other. Behind him, Michael could hear the hiss and crash of the waves. In his mouth he tasted salt.

'You can't call a cab. It's not ten o'clock.'

Max smiled. 'They open at eight, actually. I was playing for time.'

Michael's own expression remained serious. 'I do forgive you, but I can't stay. Not after last night. I'm sorry.'

'Why? Because you feel embarrassed? Then I'll ask the others to leave.' Max reached inside his jacket pocket and pulled out a tiny mobile phone. 'I'll phone Mrs Avery now. They'll be gone by the time we return.'

He felt alarmed. 'You can't do that!'

'Can't I? As you said yourself, it's my house and I make the rules. You're my guest. If the others make you uncomfortable, then they leave.'

Michael shook his head. 'You don't need to do that.'

'Does that mean you'll stay?'

For the first time that morning he smiled. 'Yes.'

'Good.'

Max put the phone back in his pocket. 'And now,' he continued, 'as I seem to bring out the confessor in you, why not tell me what's been troubling you since you arrived here?'

'I can't.'

'Then let me guess. I doubt it's a personal problem. Perhaps I flatter myself, but I think you might have told me. I suspect it's something to do with work.' A pause, an eyebrow raised quizzically. 'A mistake that you're not sure how to rectify?'

'I don't make mistakes,' he said defensively.

'Then you're a better man than I am, Gunga Din.' Max

smiled reassuringly. 'We don't have to use names. Company A is buying Company B. You know how it goes.'

He thought of Jack Bennett. Digitron was Jack's client, and Max was Jack's friend.

It was too dangerous. He couldn't risk it.

But he wanted to risk it. He had always wanted to risk it.

'You won't tell anyone?'

'You don't need to ask that. You can trust me, Mike. You know that, don't you?'

At first he didn't respond. Then, slowly, he nodded.

'I'm hungry. Tell me as we walk.'

Together, they continued along the beach.

The Crown Hotel was a grim Victorian edifice of red brick overlooking the sea.

The dining room was half-empty. Max and Michael sat together at a table in the corner. Most of the other guests were elderly couples, all talking in soft voices. Middle-aged waitresses in old-fashioned pinafores moved between the tables taking orders or distributing food on the type of overly decorative bone china favoured by Rebecca's grandmother.

Max speared his last piece of bacon with a fork. Michael, who had finished eating, sipped his tea. It tasted as if the bag had been left to stew for days, so he reached for the orange juice instead.

'You're positive you didn't misread the clause?' asked Max.

Michael nodded. 'I just don't understand how I missed it.'

Max swallowed his mouthful. 'You were under pressure. Mistakes happen.'

'It's not just a mistake. We're talking monumental fuck-up. The clients have paid a fortune for a company that will be worth a third of the purchase price if that contract is terminated. We should have got the waiver before exchange. At the very least, it should have been a completion condition.' He exhaled. 'Christ, what a mess.'

'Don't be too hard on yourself,' said Max kindly.

'That's easy for you to say. This is professional negligence. The clients are bound to sue, and it'll be my reputation that goes down the toilet. Graham Fletcher will see to that. I can kiss partnership goodbye at Cox Stephens – or anywhere else.'

Max had finished eating. He lit a cigar. 'And that's the summit of your ambition, is it? Partnership at a big law firm?'

Michael hadn't expected this. 'Well, what's wrong with that?' he asked.

'Partnership is a poisoned chalice. It ties you to others and leaves you exposed. There's no limited liability. You could lose everything you own, and all because of someone else's carelessness. Take my advice, Mike. Never put your fate in the hands of others, and never risk more than you can afford to lose. That's always been my policy, and it should be yours too.'

Michael shrugged. 'Maybe.'

'And why waste your life in the legal profession? What is a lawyer but a hired gun? Someone whose function is to solve the problems of others. Wouldn't you rather be creating problems of your own?' Max shook his head. 'No, you should be aiming much higher. I would, if I were you.'

'But you're not me.'

A strange expression came into Max's face. 'I was once,' he said quietly.

Michael sipped his orange juice. Max breathed smoke into the air and sighed contentedly. Then his eyes became businesslike. 'Enough of my pearls of wisdom. Let's decide what you're going to do.'

Michael felt a sudden warmth inside his stomach.

'No one else at the office knows about this, do they?'

'No.'

'Then you have two options. Just as you did on the beach.'

Michael waited expectantly.

'The first is to remain silent.'

He nodded. 'I can't think what else to do. But if I keep quiet, then I'll spend every day panicking that someone's going to spot the provision.'

'Why should someone spot it? From my limited experience of the law, I know that in transactions such as this it's customary to alert the other side to any consents they'll need. Failure to do so is usually due to oversight rather than malice. You said that this contract has been running for five years already, that there's never yet been a change in ownership, and that the relevant clause is buried where no one would think to look for it. Odds are that everyone, including the other party to the contract, has forgotten it exists.'

'You really think so?'

'Yes. I'd bet you a sizeable sum of money that no one is ever going to notice your oversight. Or if they do, it will be years hence when you've left the legal profession far behind you.'

'Assuming I leave the profession. You don't know that.'

Max smiled. 'Not for sure. But I have my suspicions.'

Michael smiled too, ruefully. 'If someone does find out, I might be forced to leave.'

'Why so? Would the other party really wish to end the contract? The terms are more than fair, aren't they?'

He hadn't considered this. 'I don't know ...' he began.

Max shook his head. 'You misunderstand. I wasn't asking a question. I was stating a fact.'

'What do you mean?'

'You see, Mike, five years ago, when Pegasus signed its contract with Dial-a-Car, I was a shareholder in Pegasus's parent company, Kinnetica. I was even involved in the contract

121

negotiations. I am right, aren't I? We are talking about Kinnetica's sale of Pegasus to Digitron?'

His jaw dropped. 'You can't know about that! It's not been announced yet. The press release isn't even issued until tomorrow.'

Max continued to smile. 'Jack Bennett's a good man, but indiscreet – with me, at least. Likes to let me know about the high-powered deals he's involved in. An attempt to impress me, I suspect. A dangerous policy, what with client confidentiality, but as Jack has yet to anger me I don't see any reason not to keep his indiscretions secret.'

Michael whistled softly.

'And that,' continued Max, 'leads us to option two.'

'Which is?'

'That I contact Henry Marshall, the MD of Dial-a-Car, and ask him to send you the necessary waiver, dated before exchange. He's on holiday at the moment, at his place in Devon, but he can draw it up there. All that's really needed is his signature on a piece of paper.'

Instinctively Michael shook his head.

'Why not? Worried about letting the cat out of the bag? Scared that Dial-a-Car will use it as an excuse to demand even better terms?'

He nodded.

'Don't be. Another pearl of wisdom for you, Mike. Everyone has their weak spot. Real power lies in uncovering that spot and turning it to your advantage. Henry's weakness is gambling. He's lost a fortune over the last few years. Not just his own – company money, too, and you know about the penalties for that. I've bailed him out financially on more than one occasion. He owes me and he knows it. Now it's time to call in the favour.'

This was all moving too fast. Again he shook his head.

'The waiver could be with you tomorrow. Peace of mind, which is what you really want. You've trusted me with your mistake, Mike. Trust me with this too.'

He stared down at his plate. Empty, save for a small piece of tomato. 'I have trusted you,' he said slowly. 'Now you know my weak spot. Now you have power over me.'

He looked up. Again Max's expression was strange. 'You don't have to worry about that.'

'Just like Jack doesn't have to worry about disclosing confidential client information. As long as I don't make you angry, all my skeletons stay underground.'

The expression remained. 'You're not Jack, and he's not you.'

Embarrassed, Michael watched the waitresses moving between the tables. From the kitchen came the sound of a plate smashing. 'Someone's going to be for the high jump,' he observed.

'But that someone isn't going to be you.'

'Isn't it?'

'No. As I said, you have two choices. If you keep quiet, I doubt anyone will find out about your error. Your reputation will remain unblemished, though you'll have to live with the fear of discovery. If you want the waiver, I can get it for you, and you'll have obtained a crucial document without having to bother your client and superiors, and without having to make any concessions to Dial-a-Car. Peace of mind and an enhanced reputation. The choice is yours, but I know which one I'd go for.'

He stared at Max. 'You'd do that for me?'

A nod. 'You can trust me. I won't let you down.'

Again he felt a warmth in his stomach. Stronger this time. 'Thanks.'

'No need to decide now,' Max rose to his feet. 'I'm off to the gents. Now stop worrying, because everything will be fine.'

Michael sat alone, watching the steam rise from his teacup. He felt light-headed, as if a huge weight had been lifted from his shoulders. A couple of elderly women at a nearby table were each insisting, with typical British politeness, that they should be the one to pay.

An idea came to him. He beckoned a waitress over. 'Could I have the bill, please?'

She smiled at him. 'No need. Your father's already paid.'

'Who?'

Her smile faded. 'The man you were with. I'm sorry. I just assumed.'

Out of the corner of his eye he saw movement. Max had re-entered the room, passing easily between the tables. A strong, contained figure. At peace with the world and himself.

And suddenly all that had passed between them – the confidences he had told without understanding why, the complicated and unfamiliar emotions he had experienced – all began to make sense.

He felt vulnerable. Just as he had on the beach. But this time the feeling was far more intense. He tried to disown it, but it clung to him like a leech.

Max sat down. 'Ready to go?'

'I've changed my mind. I want you to phone the house and ask the others to leave.' His tone was harsh and demanding.

Max looked surprised. 'I thought we agreed there was no need.'

'So you're not going to do it? Fine. I thought it was rubbish anyway.'

Max pulled out his mobile and tapped out a set of numbers. 'Mrs Avery, I'm sorry, but you must ask Miss Carlisle and her friend to leave.' He paused, his eyes fixed on Michael. 'As soon as possible. We'll be back within an hour and I'd like them gone by then.'

Michael reached out a hand and took the phone. A flustered female voice was speaking on the other end. 'Mrs Avery, it's Michael Turner. There's no need to disturb anyone. It was just my idea of a joke. I'm sorry to have bothered you.'

He switched the phone off and handed it back to Max.

'Why?' Max asked him.

'Because I needed to know that you'd do it.'

They stared at each other.

'Do you play golf?' asked Max.

'What?'

'Do you play golf?'

He found his composure. 'Do I look old and sad?'

'None of that. It's a useful game. You wouldn't believe the number of deals struck over eighteen holes on a Sunday morning.'

He smiled. 'You're going to teach me how to swing a stick?'

'Why not?' Max smiled too. 'I'm a member of a club near here. We'll have a knock around, then lunch at the club restaurant. The food is disgusting, but the wine cellar's excellent.'

'What about the others? Shouldn't we go back?'

'I'm in no rush. Are you?'

He shook his head.

'Good. Golf it is. Prepare to be humiliated.'

Michael rose to his feet. 'You're the one who's going to be humiliated. I am Ozymandias, king of greens: look on my drives, ye Mighty, and despair.'

'You're quoting poetry,' Max told him. 'Now that really is old and sad.'

Laughing, they walked out of the restaurant.

Late that evening, Max dropped Michael outside the flat.

The two of them had driven down from Suffolk alone. Having spent most of the day at the golf club, they had returned to the house only to find that Lavinia and Suzanne had already left.

The flat was in darkness. He had expected Rebecca to be back, but instead she had left a telephone message that she had flu and didn't feel up to travelling. He phoned her parents and managed to have a reasonably civilised conversation with her father, who agreed to pass on his love.

Taking a beer from the fridge he went to stand on the tiny balcony. The night air was warm and still. He watched the lights in the windows of the houses opposite, wondering who lived behind the curtains and what their lives were like.

His problems were solved now. He should have felt happy.

But instead he felt uneasy. The solution Max had proposed amounted to a form of blackmail. Was it wise to allow himself to be used in a power game that had begun years before he and Max had even met?

And now a new game had begun. One between Max and himself, in which Max held all the power. A man about whom he knew virtually nothing, and one who had no compunction in using the frailties of others to advance his own ends. How could he trust a man like that?

But he did trust him. That was the bizarre thing.

He pushed his fears to one side. Everything would be all right. Of course it would.

Finishing his beer he made his way to bed.

SIX

Monday morning. Half past eleven. Michael sat at his desk, checking amendments to the disclosure letter he had started to draft first thing that morning. Jack Bennett wanted it by one o'clock, and he was well on schedule.

The office was quiet. Half the department were out at meetings. In the corridor, the secretaries sat discussing the weekend's television or telephoning their friends. Kim, his secretary, now returned from Salonika, came in to show them her holiday photographs. Most were of a handsome Greek waiter. He and Stuart teased her about it and she smiled good-naturedly, her tan helping to disguise her blush.

The phone went. It was Max. 'I've spoken to Henry. He's agreed to draw up a waiver, and I've told him that it must be faxed through to you today. He's promised you'll have it early afternoon at the latest. Is that OK?'

'You bet. Thanks, Max. I'm really grateful.'

'My pleasure. Can you transfer me to Jack? I need a word with him. See you soon, yes?'

'Definitely.' Smiling, he made the transfer.

An hour later he finished the disclosure letter. Stuart asked if he wanted to grab some lunch. He agreed, then made his way up the corridor to Jack's office. It was empty. The relief he felt would have been unimaginable ten days earlier.

Leaving the letter on Jack's desk, he headed back to his own office. Graham Fletcher emerged from the gents as he passed and called his name.

Then everything began to go wrong.

'I spoke to Jack earlier,' Graham told him. 'He said he was surprised we didn't need any waivers from Dial-a-Car and suggested I just make sure that you'd carried out all the necessary checks. You did, didn't you?'

Michael felt uncomfortable. 'Actually we did need a waiver. There was a consent clause in the miscellaneous section. I forgot to tell Jack.'

Graham looked horrified. 'Oh my God! It's not in the bloody completion conditions!'

'No need. We've got the waiver already.'

Momentarily Graham relaxed. Then his eyes narrowed. 'How?'

Michael began to improvise. 'I contacted Dial-a-Car direct. Spoke to their MD, who sent it through.'

'Why didn't you tell me?'

'Thought I had. Sorry.'

Slowly Graham nodded. 'All right. Make sure you give me a copy, and next time keep me fully informed.' He didn't look entirely happy.

Michael returned to his office to collect Stuart. The two of them ordered chicken Kiev in a greasy spoon café near Liverpool Street Station. Stuart chatted cheerfully about his weekend in Bristol. Michael ate little and said less, wishing he hadn't bumped into Graham. He knew that everything would be all right, but still he had a nagging sense of unease.

*

Two o'clock.

They returned to the office. Michael saw a fax on his chair. The waiver. He felt relieved.

But it wasn't the waiver. Just a general enquiry from the Hong Kong office.

It didn't matter. It was only two o'clock. Max had talked about early afternoon.

Graham Fletcher strode into the office. 'I told Jack about the waiver and he thought we should tell Digitron. Now they want a copy. Fax one through to them.'

Lunch was sitting heavily in his stomach. He began to feel queasy. 'When? Tomorrow?'

Graham looked at him as if he were retarded. 'Today, of course.'

'No problem.'

And it wasn't a problem. It would be with him early afternoon. Max had said so.

His phone rang. Someone from the litigation department with a query. He tried to concentrate on what was being said.

Three o'clock.

No sign of the waiver.

Graham reappeared. 'Sent it yet?'

'No.'

Graham scowled. 'Well, get your finger out, then!'

'Sorry. Been on the phone. I'll do it now.'

Graham left. For the fourth time he checked the departmental fax. Nothing.

Suddenly it occurred to him that Max might have given Henry the general fax number instead. He phoned the fax room. They checked their records and said that nothing had been received.

He called Max. The phone was answered by an elderly-sounding man with a central European accent. Mr László, one half of the Hungarian couple who kept house for Max in London. Mr László explained politely that Max had just left and would be out for the rest of the day.

'Can you give me his mobile number?'

'There would be no point,' Mr László told him. 'He does not have it with him.'

He swallowed down his frustration. 'Can you tell me where he's gone? This is very urgent.'

'This evening he is having dinner at the Sugar Club in Warwick Street. His reservation is at eight o'clock. I do not know where he will be before then.'

'If he phones, will you ask him to call me. It's extremely important.'

'Of course.'

As he put the phone down he cursed under his breath. Stuart looked up from his desk. 'Everything OK?'

He nodded. A terrible suspicion had taken root in his brain which he tried to ignore. It was still early afternoon. The fax would come. Max wouldn't let him down.

Half past four.

Still no waiver.

Michael, now beside himself with worry, paced up and down the office. Stuart stared at him. 'Mike, what's going on?'

'Nothing. Don't hassle me.'

Graham stormed into the room. 'I've just had Digitron on the phone. Why haven't you sent the waiver?'

He played for time. 'I can't find it. We've had a temp for the last ten days. She must have put it on the wrong file.'

Graham's eyes threatened to pop out of his head. 'You can't find it?'

'Don't worry. I will.'

130

Graham jabbed a finger at him. 'I want a copy on my desk in twenty minutes. No excuses!' He marched out.

Stuart looked concerned. 'Do you need help?'

'No.' He ran a hand through his hair and changed his mind. 'Yes. I have to make a phone call. Can you go to the fax machine and check nothing's come through?'

Stuart left the room. Michael called Max's house. Again Mr László answered. No, Max hadn't called. His whereabouts were still unknown.

Stuart returned. 'No faxes. Sorry.'

A call to the fax room yielded the same response. Sweat was making his shirt stick to his skin.

Kim appeared. 'Graham Fletcher's phoned. He wants to see you immediately.'

He made his way to Graham's office on legs that felt as if they were made of lead. The door was open. Jack Bennett stood beside Graham. Jack looked agitated, Graham apoplectic. Michael felt sick.

Bluff it out. You've done it in client meetings. You can do it now.

'Digitron have just phoned,' Graham told him. 'Someone at their office has spoken to Dial-a-Car to thank them for the waiver, and now it turns out that nobody at Dial-a-Car has a fucking clue what they're talking about!'

Michael swallowed, trying to keep his voice steady. 'The managing director knows.'

Graham's face was purple. 'The MD's on holiday. They spoke to the financial director, who said he had no knowledge of any waiver having being given.'

'He also said,' added Jack, 'that the MD would never have issued a waiver without consulting him, and that if ownership of Pegasus had changed without their consent they'd take it ill and at the very least would want some improvement in the terms and conditions.' He shook his head. 'This looks bad, Mike.'

Bluff it out. Bluff it out.

'He's wrong. They should speak to the MD. He'll back me up.'

Again Jack shook his head. 'The MD's assistant has already spoken to him. He told her that he'd never heard of you, and that no waiver exists.'

Michael felt as if he'd been punched in the stomach. He took a step backwards. The floor seemed to be sinking beneath his feet.

Graham was shaking with rage. 'What the hell are you trying to do? Isn't it bad enough you missed the consent clause without coming up with this cock-and-bull story to try and cover your arse? The clause was buried in miscellaneous, for God's sake! No one would have spotted it! Why couldn't you just keep your mouth shut? You fucking incompetent! Well, believe me, your days at this firm are numbered!'

Michael's head was spinning. This couldn't be happening. He looked at Jack, whose expression was as grave as if he'd just heard that someone had died. In a way, he had.

And yet, buried deep within the contours of his face was the faintest hint of a smirk.

In his head he heard Max's voice. The sound was smooth and velvety. Seductive and deadly.

Everyone has their weak spot. Real power lies in uncovering that spot and turning it to your advantage.

His head cleared. Suddenly he understood everything.

Max had said that he knew Lavinia had been lying. That, too, had been a lie, a ploy to inspire trust. And it had worked. He had trusted Max and had revealed his own weak spot.

As Jack has yet to anger me, I don't see any reason not to keep his indiscretions secret.

He had thought his own indiscretions would remain hidden, but he had been wrong. For he had already angered Max. And now Max had his revenge.

Max had spoken to Jack that morning to tell him of Michael's mistake. But mere betrayal wasn't enough. Michael must be seen to dig his own grave: manipulated into proclaiming the existence of a fictitious waiver so that the world would see him as not only incompetent but as someone who would tell dangerous lies in an attempt to hide his failings from others.

Jack would have done what he was asked. After all, he had his own reasons for not wanting to anger Max. He had not been the responsible partner for this transaction, so his own reputation would not be damaged. And he could not help but be pleased at the discrediting of someone he was starting to view as a rival for Max's favour.

It had all been lies. Everything that had passed between them yesterday. He had trusted Max and had paid the price.

Graham continued to shout, but Michael wasn't willing to listen any more. He turned and marched from the room. The corridor was silent, everyone standing like statues, watching him pass. He ignored them all. His rage was so great he felt he would explode.

He marched up Warwick Street towards the Sugar Club.

The first part of the evening had been spent in the corner of a crowded pub in Piccadilly, sipping beer and nursing his resentment. He should have been drunk, but anger had boiled away the alcohol before it could dull his senses. A good thing too. For what lay ahead he needed to be very clear.

He walked through the door, exchanging the unfocused noise of the street for the concentrated buzz of the restaurant.

Striding past the bar at the front, he entered the main dining section. The tables were packed tightly together. All seemed to be occupied, the guests primarily young and fashionable. Waiters in black uniforms with white aprons slid between the tables bearing trays of food. The air was thick with voices and the crash of cutlery on plates. The lighting was low and intimate, all spotbulbs and candles, adding to the sense of proximity. The perfect place to make a scene.

Max sat a table at the centre of the restaurant. His companions were two Japanese men of about forty, both smoking the same elegant cigars as Max himself. Max was leading the conversation, his smile animated and charming. His two guests nodded admiringly as he spoke.

A waiter appeared with their starters. They extinguished their cigars and prepared to eat.

It was time. He began to make his way through the tables, his heart beating like a drum buried deep in his chest.

Max saw him approach. Momentarily he looked surprised, then he smiled. 'Mike, what an unexpected pleasure. Will you join us?'

He smiled back. Then, raising his voice, said, 'Hell will freeze over before I'll ever share a table with you.'

Max's eyes widened. 'I'm sorry?'

'I trusted you. Well, more fool me. It's worked out better than you could have ever hoped.' As he spoke he was aware that all other conversation was dying away.

'I'm afraid,' said Max calmly, 'that I don't know what you're talking about.'

Michael continued to smile. 'Oh, you're good, aren't you? All smarm and charm. Nobody would guess what a really vicious cunt you are.'

He turned to Max's guests, both of whom were staring at him, their faces rigid with shock. He was glad they were Japanese: a race in front of whom one should never be seen to

134

lose face. 'Don't trust this man,' he told them. 'He'll screw you over the first chance he gets.'

'There appears to have been some sort of misunderstanding,' Max told him. 'I think it would be best if you left now.' His voice remained calm. Under any other circumstances Michael would have applauded his composure. But not now. Now he just wanted to destroy it.

Reaching across the table he picked up a plate. Scallops covered in a creamy sauce. He threw the contents at Max, splattering his face and clothes. Behind him he heard a woman gasp. Picking up a glass of red wine he hurled that too.

'You bastard! You think you can just mess around with people's lives? Well, you made a big mistake trying to mess with mine!'

Then he turned on his heel and marched out of the restaurant.

He reached the corner of the street and stopped, leaning against the wall, ignoring the people who walked past him, staring over the rooftops of the buildings and up into the thin strip of London sky. The blues and reds of early evening were fading now as the day died: greyness replacing colour like reality eclipsing hope.

His anger was gone now, replaced by hurt and intense self-hatred. He had always believed that the life he had led had made him strong. That he could never be fooled by others. But he had been wrong. Max had offered him the illusion of emotional intimacy, and he had rushed towards it like a blind man, unable to see the trap that lay in his path. And though he hated Max for his treachery, he hated himself even more for his weakness in being deceived.

A young couple, both drunk, were making their way unsteadily down the street. The man collided with him. An apology was offered. Ignoring it he moved off into the night.

*

Nine o'clock the following morning. Michael lay in bed staring up at the ceiling. The curtains were still drawn. On a normal day he would have been at his desk half an hour ago. But today was not a normal day.

It was all over at Cox Stephens. Of that he was sure. If he'd kept quiet about his mistake he would probably have survived. But of course he hadn't kept quiet.

Rebecca had called last night. He had left the machine to answer her call. She was feeling better now and would be returning that afternoon. When she did, he would have to tell her what had happened and hope that it wouldn't make any difference to their future together.

And it wouldn't. They loved each other. That would be enough.

Wouldn't it?

Rising from the bed he made his way to the bathroom. He showered and shaved, then put on his suit. His shirt was creased. It didn't matter any more but still he ironed it, acting out a routine that he had performed every working day for nearly three years.

He made himself a coffee and stood on the balcony, looking out on to the grey city morning. The sky was filling with dark clouds. There would be rain before lunchtime. He wondered if he would still have a job by then.

Leaving the flat he made his way to the tube. The rush hour was over and the platform was virtually empty. When the train arrived he sat in a compartment that was silent save for the rustling of papers and the hiss of personal stereos. A copy of *The Times* lay unopened on his lap. He stared in front of him, steeling himself for what was to come.

As he walked up the steps of the office he told himself that whatever happened he would show no regret or remorse. He would not give them the satisfaction.

He made his way across the entrance hall, giving the man at the reception desk his most brilliant smile before summoning the lift. When it arrived he stepped inside and pressed the button for the fifth floor.

The corporate department went about its business. Secretaries worked at their desks, solicitors moved between offices and telephones rang all around. A few people looked up as he passed, but most carried on as if nothing had happened. The smile remained glued to his face. He had worked hard for Cox Stephens and he would be a great loss. He knew it, and one day they would know it too.

He walked into his room. Stuart beamed at him and held up a piece of paper. 'Where have you been? The waiver came through.'

'What?'

'The waiver's here. The one you were panicking about. It came through to the fax room yesterday while we were at lunch.'

This had to be a joke. 'That's not possible. I checked with the fax room and they said nothing had come through.'

'I know. Blame it on Personnel and their stupid policies.'

'What policies?'

'Of having to use people's initials all the time rather than their full names. One of those efficiency drives that ends up making things even less efficient than they were before. The fax room noted your initials down and then sent the waiver off to Matthew Taylor in the property department. He was at an all-day meeting yesterday and his secretary was off sick, so they've only just realised. The fax room changes shifts at two o'clock, so by the time you spoke to them no one there would have remembered that a fax had come in for you.'

He snatched the fax from Stuart.

And there it was. The waiver, dated before exchange. Just what he had wanted.

Just what Max had promised to deliver.

Feeling dizzy, he sat down at his desk. 'But that doesn't make sense. Dial-a-Car's MD said he'd never heard of me.'

Stuart started to laugh. 'It gets better. Jack Bennett was in earlier. The MD phoned him about an hour ago. Very apologetic. Apparently his assistant has a complete phobia about disturbing him on holiday. He shouted at her once when she called about something trivial, so now she won't ever contact him unless the company's about to go into liquidation or there are terrorists in the boardroom. She assumed, because the FD had never heard about the waiver and there was no copy of it on file, that you must have been talking out of your backside. Now she stands corrected.'

Michael laughed too. A shrill, hysterical sound. It was wonderful news, but its implications made him feel sick.

'Jack was asking where you were. I think he wanted to apologise about yesterday. Apparently the MD was singing your praises, saying what a huge asset you were to the firm.'

There were footsteps in the corridor. Graham Fletcher entered, looking rather uncomfortable. 'You've heard, I take it?'

He nodded. His phone rang, but he ignored it. Kim would take a message.

Graham breathed out slowly, his mouth a thin line. 'Well, all's well that ends well. Be sure to send the client a copy.' He left the room.

Again Stuart laughed. 'I think that's what you call an apology. Do you want a coffee?'

'No, thanks.'

Stuart left the room, almost colliding with Kim. 'Mike, I've got Becky on the phone. Shall I put her through?'

He nodded. Kim made her way back to her desk and his phone rang again. He picked it up. 'Hello?'

'I told you to trust me.'

He swallowed. His throat was as dry as bone.

'Are you still there?' Max asked him.

'Yes.' It came out as a whisper.

'I've booked a table at Cadogan's in Seething Lane. Twelve-thirty. Be there.'

The line went dead.

Michael made his way towards Cadogan's.

Reaching Monument, he turned left towards Tower Hill. To his right was London Bridge and the great expanse of dirty water that was the Thames. The streets were crowded; people were moving quickly, trying to avoid the rain that had started to fall. In the distance he could see the grim edifice of the Tower of London. An appropriate setting. He felt as if he were going to his own execution.

Cadogan's was on the left-hand side of Seething Lane; a private dining club, situated underground. He made his way down the stairs and into an empty bar with stone walls and a low ceiling, where he was stopped by an officious-looking man in a bow tie. He explained that he was meeting Max, declined the offer of a drink and took a seat.

To his right was the dining room, the tables packed together just as they had been in the Sugar Club. It was nearly half full. All the diners were male; most were over forty and in pinstripe suits. The atmosphere was discreet and exclusive, the buzz of conversation soft but heavy with self-importance. Another good place in which to make a scene.

Half past twelve. He began to play with his cufflinks: a pair of silver shields emblazoned with the initials 'MT'. They had been a present from Rebecca. He wished he was with her now. He wished he was anywhere but here.

Ten minutes passed. The bar filled with people, but there

was still no sign of Max. Perhaps he had decided not to come, to make his absence an unspoken expression of anger. Michael dared to hope, but in his heart he knew that he would not escape so lightly. After what he had done, there would need to be some form of closure between them.

Quarter to one. Max entered the bar and began to make his way over. He had no coat and was soaked from the rain. Michael rose to his feet, opening his mouth to speak the apology that he knew would do no good.

And realised that Max was smiling. The wry, amused smile that was his trademark.

'Sorry I'm late. Had to park miles away and then got caught by the rain.' Suddenly he took a step backwards and held up his hands in a gesture of surrender. 'You're not going to throw anything, are you?'

The warm reception threw Michael completely. Mutely he shook his head.

'Thank God. I'm fond of this shirt and I don't want it ruined by flying seafood.' Max wiped his forehead. 'I'd better dry myself off. Come and keep me company.'

They walked through the restaurant, towards a small flight of stairs that led to a corridor and the lavatories. As they moved, Michael tried to swallow down his fear and to focus on the tiny part of his mind that wondered whether he would ever manage to have a conversation with this man without needing to apologise for something.

They reached the gents. Max held the door open. Michael walked through. The room was bigger than he had expected: urinals and basins to the left, stalls to the right. It seemed to be empty. He heard Max closing the door and turned. 'Look, Max, I'm really, really—'

Max struck him across the face.

For a well-built man he moved with astonishing speed.

140

Michael barely had time to register motion before it felt as if an iron bar had slammed into his skull. He was already off balance and was now knocked backwards, tripping over his feet, collapsing against the far wall and cracking his head as he fell. His vision blurred. Max moved towards him. He tried to back away but there was nowhere to go.

One of the stalls opened. A frightened-looking man stepped out then stood still, as if uncertain what to do.

'Get out!' roared Max.

The man ran from the room. Max strode from stall to stall, kicking the doors open. All were empty. He secured the main door with a chair, then turned. Michael, his back to the wall, felt like a rabbit caught in the headlights of an oncoming juggernaut.

Max stood over him, his face black with fury. His whole body was shaking. He raised his hand, as if to land another blow. Michael flinched and covered his face.

But the blow was never struck. Instead Max moved suddenly away, going to stand by one of the basins. He rested his hands on the sink and stared at his reflection in the mirror. His breathing was ragged and raw.

Michael touched his face. The whole left side felt numb. He, too, was shaking. 'I'm sorry ...' he began.

'Don't,' Max told him.

'But I am. You have to understand—'

'Understand what?'

'I thought it was lies. Everything you said. All that stuff about trust. You made it sound so easy. Well, it's not that easy for me.'

'You think I don't know that?'

'I did trust you. Then it went wrong. I thought it was all a trick, a way to get back at me.'

'You think I would do that to you?'

Michael was close to tears, and the realisation made him feel ashamed. 'Well, why not? What reason do I have to trust you? I don't know anything about you! I don't even know who you are!'

'Don't you?'

Max turned towards him. The anger was fading from his face, and his eyes were full of pain.

Michael hung his head.

'Then let me tell you.'

Max turned back to the mirror and reached out a hand. Gently he touched the glass, as if caressing his own reflection.

'I was born in Budapest on Christmas Eve 1950. My real name is Istvan Selymes. My father's name was Tibor, my mother's Ilona. Istvan Selymes, son of Tibor and Ilona. I was their only child.

'We lived in a tiny flat in a huge concrete block. Hungary had been occupied by the Soviets since the war. My parents worked in a factory. They were nationalists who wanted independence for the Magyar people. Their friends wanted the same. They used to come to our flat in the evening and talk about a free state and how it could be achieved only through a national uprising. I used to creep from my bed and listen to them dreaming their dreams. The way they talked, you'd think an independent Hungary would be a new Eden. That's what they believed. That's what I believed too. Every night I'd ask God to send an uprising so that all our dreams could come true.

'In October 1956 the uprising took place. The glorious event we'd all prayed for. And it wasn't a dream, but a nightmare. People took to the streets, waving Hungarian flags, trying to fight the Russian tanks with nothing but their bare hands.' He laughed suddenly, a harsh sound, full of bitterness and impotent rage. 'They were cut down like flies. Thousands of them, slaughtered indiscriminately by the Russians as they sought out the ringleaders. My mother was shot dead as we ran from the guns. She was still holding my hand when she fell.

'My father and I fled the country, like thousands of others. We crossed the border into Austria, paying a professional guide to show us the way. He took what little money we had, so we were destitute by the time we reached the refugee camp. My father had been wounded in the fighting, and the journey took the last of his strength. It wasn't enough that I'd lost my mother. I had to sit by his bed in the camp and watch him die too.

'My uncle was in the camp with us. My mother's brother. His name was Michael, just like you. He still had some money left. My father made him promise that he'd take me far away. He didn't want me to stay in Austria, as it was too close to the Russians and their reprisals. He wanted me to be safe. Just before he died, my uncle promised him that he'd always take care of me. He swore that I'd never be alone as long as he lived.

'So we made our way to England. My uncle spoke a little of the language, and he wanted to make a new start here. We reached London in February 1957. We spent a few days in a boarding house in Shoreditch. Our money had virtually run out by then. Sometimes my uncle would stare at me with a strange look in his eyes, but when he'd see me watching him he'd always smile and tell me that everything would be all right.'

Again he laughed, but by now all the rage was gone. His fingers continued to stroke the glass.

'One evening, he told me to pack my few possessions. He said we were going to a new home. We walked through the streets for what seemed like hours, until we reached Lexden Street and a big grey house that looked like a prison. He told me that it was a place for children who didn't have any families, and that I was going to stay there for a few days. Just a few days, until he found some more money.

'I wept, of course. I begged him not to leave me. But he told me not to be afraid. He said that it would be an adventure, and that he'd return for me before I knew it. But the days turned into weeks, then months, and he never came back.

'He just left me there, in that godawful place. I couldn't speak the language. I couldn't communicate. I was six years old. I'd lost everything that had ever mattered to me. I was completely alone, in an alien country. I had no one to depend on but myself.'

Michael looked up. Max turned away from the mirror. The two of them stared at each other.

'And now you talk to me about trust.'

Again the tears were near. Michael shook his head. 'I didn't mean—'

'You think I would do that to you?'

'I just—'

'You think I would do that to you?'

Again Michael hung his head. 'I know you must despise me, and you have every reason. But I am sorry.'

His heart was slowing now. Closure had been achieved. He expected Max to leave.

But he didn't. He remained where he was. And when he next spoke, his voice was soft.

'I'm the one who should be sorry. I had no right to hit you. Neither do I have the right to ask you to forgive me. But if you do, I give you my word that I'll never hurt you again.'

'Why?' whispered Michael.

'Why what?'

'You have everything. Why does my forgiveness matter to you?'

'Because I understand you. I understand what your life has been about. I know how it feels to grow up alone, without love and hope and all the things that give life beauty and meaning. I know how much that can damage you. I know how it can turn the whole concept of trust into the hardest and most frightening thing in the world.'

Michael shook his head. 'You're not me. You don't know how I feel.'

'You're wrong. When I look at you I see myself. I see the person I was more than twenty years ago. The person who was still learning how to fool the world with a smiling mask when all he felt inside was resentment and rage. I couldn't believe it, the first time we met. It was like meeting a ghost.' Max sighed, a sound that ached with regret. 'It's extraordinary.'

Michael took a deep breath. He didn't trust himself to speak, but still there were things he needed to say.

'I'm sorry. For what happened in the restaurant. For making you look a fool in front of everyone.'

Max looked genuinely pained. 'I don't care how you made me look. This isn't about that.'

'I know it's not.'

Max crouched down and stared into his face.

'Oh Michael,' he said slowly. 'Can you imagine the doors I can open for you? Doors you'd have to hammer at for years before they'd even move an inch. Just like I did.'

Michael swallowed. 'It's not about opening doors. Maybe it was once. But it's not now.'

'I know it's not.'

At last the tears came. They fell easily, no longer hindered by shame. Max put a hand on his shoulder. A simple gesture of affection and support.

They remained like that for some minutes. Slowly Michael became aware of a noise in the distance. Someone was banging on the door, demanding to be admitted. He wiped his eyes and leaned back against the wall. 'It sounds as if we have company.' His voice was shaky with emotion.

'Forget them. They don't matter.'

'They might break down the door.' He managed a smile. 'I'm sure Cadogan's would look very ill on that. You might be blackballed.'

'I'll survive. The food here is even worse than at the golf club. Christ knows why I've stayed a member for so long.' Max smiled too. 'I expect the rain has stopped now. Let's grab a sandwich somewhere, sit by the river and watch the world go by.'

They rose to their feet. Michael realised that they would have to walk through the restaurant. 'I don't want people to see I've been crying. I'd better wash my face.'

'No need,' Max told him. 'They'll be too wrapped up in their own self-importance to notice a young man with a crumpled suit and the whole of his life before him. But one day they will. Ten years from now, when you've left them far behind and they're running just to keep sight of your shadow.'

He shook his head. 'Sure.'

'Sure. It's going to happen, Mike. Just you wait and see.'

Together they made for the door.

Rebecca, carrying her weekend bag, let herself into the flat.

She heard the sound of music. The Cranberries were singing 'Be With You'. It was her favourite record: a glorious three-minute ode to being in love. When first she'd heard it, she had simply enjoyed its energy. But then she had met Michael, and suddenly it was as if the lyrics had been written especially for her.

She had been looking forward to their reunion all day. Though she adored her family, her home and her life were with him now. She hated it when they were apart.

He was standing on the balcony wearing jeans and a T-shirt, staring out at the late-afternoon sunshine. He had not heard her enter. She called out his name. He turned, smiled and walked towards her.

'I didn't think you'd be here,' she told him. 'Not at this time.'

'Came home early with a blinding headache.' He smiled. 'At least that's what I told them at work.'

She smiled back. 'So what's the real reason?'

'I wanted to be here to meet you.'

'And why was that?' she asked teasingly.

'Because I love you. And because sometimes, in spite of everything, it's wonderful to be alive.'

He began to laugh, seeming excited. 'What is it?' she asked. 'Has something happened?' He didn't answer. 'Mike?'

He opened his mouth to speak. Then suddenly shook his head. 'No, nothing's happened.' He paused. 'Except that work is going well. The bad stuff is in the past now. You don't have to worry any more.'

'I wasn't worried.'

His smile was one of sceptical amusement. 'Oh, really?'

Now it was her turn to shake her head.

'And why was that?'

'Because I believe in you, Michael Turner. I know you'll never let me down.'

His expression became serious. 'No, I never will.'

Then the smile was back. He gestured towards the balcony. 'It's going to be a beautiful evening. Let's go out.'

'And do what?'

'And be with you. Like our song says. What else matters but that?'

Love for him swept over her like an adrenaline rush. 'Nothing,' she told him. 'Nothing at all.'

She put her arms around his neck. They kissed each other,

slowly and tenderly. She felt needed. She felt complete. His eyes were two pools of perfect blue with deep, dark centres. She gazed into them, and in her head a voice began to whisper.

Your love is a house of cards, built on sand. A single breeze and the whole structure will collapse.

For a moment she felt uneasy. As if someone had walked on her grave.

But only for a moment. It would never happen. They were halves of a single whole. Their foundations were made of stone that was as old as the earth, capable of withstanding any weather.

So she continued to smile up at him, while in the background their song reached its end and was replaced by another.

It was long past midnight. Michael lay beside Rebecca in their bed.

They had lain awake for hours, talking about everything and nothing, their bodies wrapped around each other, like vines that had become so tightly entwined that they had no choice but to grow in tandem or choke each other in the attempt.

Rebecca slept, her breathing smooth and easy. For Michael, sleep remained a stranger. He stared up at the ceiling, waiting for the demons that came in the still, empty hours to torment him with visions of his darkest fears.

They came that night. Just as they had done so many times in the past. With voices soft and sweet, they poured their venom into his brain like drops of poisoned honey.

But this time it was different.

He was different.

The loss of Rebecca was the worst thing he could imagine. Without her, he would be nothing. He would be destroyed. But he would not be alone.

His life had changed that day. A change that he had never dreamed of, and one that he welcomed with joy.

He lay in the darkness, listening to his demons. Slowly their voices faded away, as if frightened of his new-found power.

PART TWO

DIVISION

ONE

Wednesday morning. Eleven o'clock. Michael sat with Stuart in their departmental progress meeting.

These meetings took place on alternate Wednesdays. The whole department would gather round a huge table in one of the downstairs conference rooms, drinking bad coffee and taking it in turn to describe their current workload, so that those who were overburdened could be relieved by those who were not.

That, at least, was the idea. A fine idea save for one basic flaw. To admit that you were less than half-dead from over-work was to land yourself with administrative jobs tedious enough to render the most excitable of brain cells terminally inactive. Consequently, each member of the department made even the most basic task sound like a labour to daunt Hercules. In practice, the meetings were little more than a vanity exer-cise, a chance to flex one's corporate muscles to gasps of awe from mere mortals.

Michael was finding this morning's meeting particularly galling. He had to give his talk on company formation to the trainees at lunchtime and had yet to finish his slides. The conference room had no windows, and the artificial light was giving him a headache. He sat doodling on his notepad, listening to Jonathan Upham drone and trying to contain his irritation as precious time ticked away.

Jonathan finished his five-minute monologue and passed the baton to Belinda Hopkins. Belinda was the most senior assistant solicitor in the department: five feet eight of aerobicised ambition, now homing in on partnership like a heat-seeking missile in Armani. She viewed Jonathan as her biggest rival and had no intention of being outdone. She began to spit out client names with the rapid fire of a machine gun.

Julia, Graham's timid trainee, grew pale. She was responsible for taking the minutes but could never keep up with Belinda's formidable pace. Two weeks earlier she had been publicly reprimanded by Graham for her failings, and it looked as if another dressing-down was on the cards. Michael, who was familiar with Belinda's workload, began to make a list which he would pass to Julia at the end of the meeting.

As he did so, he realised that he was being watched.

Jack Bennett, sitting at the other end of the table, was staring at him.

He began to feel uneasy. The way he always did with Jack now. It was nine days since the drama with the Dial-a-Car waiver and he had not forgotten the way that Jack had gloated at his impending ruin.

But had it really been gloating? Could he have misread the signs? Jack had spent most of the last week out of the office, visiting clients, but on the few occasions when their paths had crossed he had been perfectly affable and given no sign of bearing any ill will.

Belinda continued to bombard them with evidence of her

industry. For a second Jack's expression remained serious, then he rolled his eyes conspiratorially. Michael gave a quick smile. Jack smiled back, then looked away.

Yes, he could have misjudged Jack.

Could have done.

Belinda finished speaking. Stuart took over. Michael stared at his notepad, trying to think about what to put in his slides.

As Michael's departmental meeting drew to its close, Rebecca sat alone behind the checkout in the non-fiction section of Chatterton's bookshop. Clare, her usual companion, was in the back office, ordering new stock.

It was proving a slow morning. So far, no more than a dozen people had ventured downstairs, and only one of them had actually bought anything. A new travel book on Fiji lay on the counter before her. She wanted to phone Michael but couldn't do so until there was somebody to cover for her.

She had been thinking about him all morning. He would be giving his talk soon, and she knew that he was nervous.

Not that there was any need. He would do a fine job. He was good at what he did. Provided he kept his temper under control, his future was secure. Six years from now, if Cox Stephens didn't offer him a partnership, there were plenty of firms that would. And that would just be the start. She had complete faith in him. He had talent, drive and ambition and would achieve great things. He would be a success.

And what would she be?

A middle-aged man in a shabby sports jacket made his way down the stairs, giving her a shy nod before crossing the floor towards the history section. She watched him, twisting her engagement ring round her finger.

What will I be?

She knew the answer already. A famous artist. Everyone

believed that it would happen: her parents, her brother, Michael. Michael most of all.

There had been a time when she had believed it too. Implicitly. Before the rejections had started to arrive. She looked at the rows of bookshelves. They surrounded her like the walls of a coffin from which she might never escape. This wasn't the future she had planned for herself. This wasn't the way her life was supposed to be.

Fleetingly, the man in the shabby jacket caught her eye. She smiled at him. All day she wore a smile, but there were times when she wanted to scream.

Her college friend Liz had phoned the previous night to say that the Crouch End exhibition was looking doubtful. In spite of her initial lack of enthusiasm, she had become increasingly excited at the prospect of showing her work, and the news had left her feeling depressed. She told herself that she just had to be patient. It was going to happen. The shop was simply a transition period before her real life began.

If it ever did.

But it would. The big break was on the way. She was good, and she knew it. One day the world would know it too.

Yes, she was good. She was really good.

So why haven't you painted anything new for weeks?

She wished Clare was here. Being alone gave her too much time to think. Gave her mind the chance to wander down avenues of possibility that it was safer not to explore.

That evening Emily was taking her to see some foreign film at the Swiss Centre. She wasn't really in the mood but knew that Emily was looking forward to it. And Emily was her best friend. Had been since they were born. Sometimes, when she thought of Emily, she would remind herself of this, repeating it like a mantra as if frightened that otherwise she might forget.

The man in the shabby jacket was approaching, holding a book. Still smiling, she prepared to make her second sale of the morning.

Half past two. Michael walked into his office. 'How did it go?' asked Stuart.

'Fine.' He sat down at his desk. 'Except for that little prick with the Hugh Grant hairstyle who sits with Karen Clark in tax. He kept sniggering.'

'Did you say anything?'

'No. I just picked him to lead on my practical exercise, and he made a complete pig's ear of it! Revenge is sweet.'

Stuart laughed. Michael checked through his messages. All were marked 'urgent' but it didn't matter. Now the talk was done, nothing could worry him.

Julia entered, carrying a piece of paper. She smiled nervously. 'You forgot the attendance list.'

'Thanks. Wasn't too boring, was it?'

'No, it was great. Everyone said so.'

'You don't have to flatter him,' Stuart told her. 'He's not the one who writes your appraisal.'

'I'm not.' She realised he was teasing her and flushed. 'It was really good, Mike. You'll have loads of trainees phoning you now with company law questions.' She made as if to leave but then turned back. 'And thanks for your help this morning. I can never keep pace with Belinda.'

'No problem,' he told her.

'I think Belinda's an android,' said Stuart. 'She's got the most robotic voice I've ever heard and she never seems to draw breath. She must have lungs the size of Africa.'

They all laughed. Stuart asked Julia about the latest trainee gossip. Michael picked up his phone to call Rebecca.

There was a bleep from his computer and an e-mail came

through on his screen. It was from Max. *Hope the talk went well*, it began. He read it through then typed a reply.

Half past seven. Rebecca, carrying a video, walked with Emily along Pelham Gardens.

The cinema trip had been aborted. They had arrived at the Swiss Centre only to discover that the projector had caught fire and destroyed the print of the film.

They entered number thirty-three. Rebecca's pianist downstairs neighbour was in the hallway, checking the post. She introduced him to Emily, while praying that Emily's plant would look healthier than it had that morning. Michael's idea of caring for it was to pour on so much water that it ran the risk of drowning, and she had taken to leaving it out on the balcony all day in the hope that fresh air and sunshine would act as a tonic.

They entered the flat. The door to the sitting room was closed. Through it, she could hear the sound of the television: a sports commentator exclaiming about the extraordinary atmosphere. She remembered that some important football match was taking place that night. Michael had planned to go to the gym that evening but had clearly changed his mind. 'Looks like Mike's home,' she said, and opened the door.

Immediately her nose was assailed by a rich, vaguely familiar smell. Behind her, Emily said, 'I didn't know he'd started smoking.'

Max Somerton sat on the sofa. A bottle of what looked like Scotch, together with two half-empty glasses, stood on the table in front of him.

He rose to his feet, his smile relaxed and easy. He was dressed as casually as he had been the first time they'd met. 'I'm sorry,' he said, gesturing to a cigar that was smouldering in an ashtray. 'Mike said it would be all right.'

She felt startled, just as she had when he'd brought the

champagne for her father. What was he doing here? Her eyes scanned the room, hoping to find it tidy. She did and felt relieved. The plant, looking slightly less limp, stood in the centre of the dining table.

'It's lovely to see you,' she told him.

'Likewise.' He glanced over her shoulder. 'This must be Emily.'

Emily, who had been hovering in the doorway, now entered the room. She nodded shyly. 'This is Mr Somerton,' explained Rebecca. 'Our landlord.'

'Friend, too, I hope,' added Max, still smiling.

'Yes, of course.' She felt embarrassed.

Max turned to Emily. 'I understand that you work in a literary agency.'

Again Emily nodded. Rebecca wondered how he knew this. Presumably Michael had told him. Where was Michael? As if in answer, she heard the lavatory flush.

'Do you write yourself?'

Emily shook her head while fiddling with a lock of her hair. Then, unexpectedly, she spoke. 'But I used to when I was a child. I had so much imagination then. I still have it now, but not the talent to back it up.'

'Imagination is a talent in itself,' said Max kindly. 'Most people have it sucked out of them by the grind of daily life. Don't let that happen to you.'

Momentarily Emily's face lit up. She smiled hesitantly, then lowered her eyes.

Max turned to Rebecca. 'I hope you're feeling better now.'

'Better?'

'You had the flu.'

'Oh. Yes, much better.'

'Forgive my delay in asking. You must have thought me very remiss.'

'Not at all.'

'I've been away for a few days,' he explained, reaching for his cigar. She heard the bathroom door open then the sound of footsteps. Michael entered the room. 'Hi. What happened to the film?'

She explained about the fire. 'We were going to watch a video.' On the television screen, thousands of people were doing a Mexican wave. 'But we don't want to disturb you.'

Michael looked at Max. 'You're not,' he said hesitantly. 'It's just—'

Max came to his rescue. 'The game doesn't start for a few minutes. Let's watch it at my house and leave the others in peace.'

'You don't need to do that,' said Rebecca, not wanting to appear inhospitable. 'Why not stay?'

'Wouldn't dream of it.' He gestured to the video box. 'What's the film?'

'*Elizabeth*.' She risked a joke. 'We got it so Em can drool over Joseph Fiennes.'

Emily looked horrified. 'I don't drool over him.'

'My mistake. I meant Daniel Craig.'

Emily blushed. Michael put a protective arm around her. 'Ignore Beck. She drools over Sir John Gielgud.'

Max extinguished his cigar, picked up the bottle of Scotch and made his way to the door. He kissed Rebecca's cheek. 'See you soon,' he told her. It sounded more like a statement than a wish.

'You didn't tell me about his voice,' said Emily, once the two of them were alone. 'It's beautiful.'

'You think so?'

'Don't you?'

'Yes, I suppose so.' She put the video into the machine.

Emily sat down on the sofa. 'It's nice that he and Mike are close,' she said.

'They're not. They hardly know each other.'

'They must be friendly if they're watching football together.'

The comment made her defensive. 'You're an expert on Mike's friendships, are you?' she said sharply.

Emily looked uncomfortable. 'No, of course not.'

Immediately Rebecca felt guilty. 'Sorry. Didn't mean that. I was just a bit fazed to walk in and find my landlord sitting there. All I could think about was how lousy I am with a duster.'

Emily laughed. Rebecca did the same.

The room was still full of the smell of cigar smoke. She opened the door to the balcony so it could escape, but the evening was still and the smell remained.

It was after eleven by the time Michael returned.

Emily had already left. Rebecca sat up in bed, reading. 'Who won?' she asked as he entered their bedroom.

'Do you care?'

'Not excessively.'

He started to undress. 'It's a great film,' she told him. 'You'd enjoy it.'

He walked into the bathroom. She shut her book and listened to the sound of him brushing his teeth. There was still no breeze, and it was close in the bedroom. She fanned herself with her hand. 'When is George back from holiday?' she called out.

'Next week.'

'Then I'll organise a dinner party so Em can meet him. I thought we could ask Clare and her new man as well. See if we can help that romance along too.'

He walked back into the bedroom. 'Matchmaker,' he said with a smile.

'Can't stop myself, can I?'

He climbed into bed beside her. 'He called you Mike,' she said.

'What?'

'Max called you Mike. I thought he wasn't allowed to do that.'

'Only at first. I don't mind now.'

She touched his arm. There were drops of perspiration on his skin. 'Are you having a shower?'

'Thought I'd wait until tomorrow. Do I stink?'

She kissed him. 'I like your stink.' His breath smelled of mint, and his hair hung low over his forehead. She brushed it back. 'I didn't know you two were friendly.'

He rubbed her shoulder. 'We talked a lot during that weekend I spent at his house. He's a nice bloke. Quite private, really. Not the social animal you might think.'

She nodded.

'He wants to take us out to dinner next week. He suggested the Savoy Grill. I told him you'd always wanted to go there. How about it? You'll like him.'

'He might decide he doesn't like me.'

'Of course he'll like you. What's not to like?'

She remembered the way she'd spoken to Emily. 'Yeah, what's not to like?'

'Is that a yes?'

'OK.'

Tuesday evening. Six days later. Michael and Rebecca made their way to Max's house.

They moved slowly through the crowded streets. Rebecca's feet hurt. She was wearing new shoes that had fitted like a dream in the shop but now seemed too tight. She wished she'd thought to put on a more comfortable pair.

There would be another guest at dinner. Caroline, Max's

new girlfriend, was joining them. 'She runs a PR company,' Michael had told her. 'I haven't met her, but she can't be as bad as Lavinia.' Rebecca, who had not warmed to Lavinia on their one meeting, felt grateful to be spared her presence.

They reached the house. Mr László showed them into the same drawing room where the party had been held. 'Mr Somerton will be with you shortly,' he told them. There was a large television in the corner which Rebecca had not noticed last time. Perhaps it had been moved to make space. 'Is this where you watched the match?' she asked Michael.

'Yes.'

'It seems a bit grand for football.'

Shrugging, he began to pour himself a Scotch from the drinks cabinet.

'Mike! This isn't our house. You can't just help yourself.'

He looked surprised. 'Max won't mind. Want one?'

She shook her head. He reached for the television control and switched on a news programme. She stared at him. 'God, make yourself at home, why don't you?'

Again he looked surprised. 'What's the problem?'

Shaking her head, she watched the screen. A politician whose teenage mistress had just sold her story to the tabloids was proclaiming his devotion to his wife. Her feet continued to ache.

Max entered the room. He kissed her cheek. His skin was hard and smelled faintly of cologne. 'You look lovely,' he told her, 'but you don't have a drink. May I get you one?' Politely she declined.

'Caroline's on her way,' he explained. Michael excused himself. Max turned off the television and the two of them faced each other.

'Thank you for inviting us,' she said. 'It's very kind of you.'

He smiled affably. 'A pleasure. Did your father enjoy his birthday?'

'Yes. He loved the champagne. You shouldn't have gone to so much trouble.'

He waved a hand dismissively, his eyes remaining fixed on her. 'I'm sorry we're eating so late. Caroline had a meeting she couldn't cancel. I hope your day wasn't too taxing.'

She shook her head. 'Except for first thing. An author came to sign copies of his book and we couldn't find any. He became quite objectionable.' She gave a laugh. 'The delights of the job.'

'But not a delight you'll enjoy much longer. Not once the art world embraces you.'

'I hope so.'

'I'm sure of it.'

His gaze made her self-conscious. In the distance she heard the doorbell. 'Will that be Caroline?'

Max nodded. 'I should warn you. She's quite apprehensive.'

'Of what?'

'Meeting you.'

'There's nothing frightening about me.'

He continued to smile. 'You'd be surprised.'

Caroline was a tall, elegant woman in her late thirties, bringing with her the scent of flowers and an air of quiet efficiency. Max made the introductions. Caroline smiled, her pale blue eyes warm but appraising. She had a fine-boned beauty that reminded Rebecca of the actress Alice Krige. 'I'm delighted to meet you,' she said in a voice that was low and throaty. 'Max tells me you're an artist.'

'Not yet. But watch this space.'

'I will. One day I'm sure I'll be able to boast that I've had dinner with you.'

Rebecca wondered if she was being teased. She flushed slightly, while hearing footsteps approach. 'I don't know about that,' she said.

But Caroline was no longer listening. She stared at the door expectantly. When Michael reappeared she held out her hand, her smile suddenly dazzling. 'You must be Michael. Max has told me all about you.'

Michael smiled sheepishly. 'I hope you didn't believe it all.'

'Only the bad stuff,' Max told him.

Michael laughed. Rebecca did, too, glad that he was back. She slipped her arm through his.

'None of it was bad,' Caroline assured him. 'Far from it. You work at Cox Stephens?'

Michael nodded. Rebecca did likewise. She thought she could detect the faintest waver in Caroline's voice. Perhaps Max was right and she was apprehensive. But she didn't seem the type to be unnerved by strangers.

'I have a friend who's a lawyer,' continued Caroline. 'He says your firm is one of the best in the City. You must be very good.'

Michael looked embarrassed. 'Not really.'

'Don't believe him,' Rebecca told Caroline. 'Cox Stephens have a star in their midst.'

'Hear, hear,' agreed Max. Rebecca smiled at him, while giving Michael's hand an affectionate squeeze.

'Do you plan to stay there long-term?' Caroline asked Michael.

'Maybe. It's OK for now.'

Max nodded. 'It'll do until we plan the next move.'

Rebecca was taken aback. This was Michael's future. What did it have to do with Max?

She stared at Michael, waiting for a reaction. But there was none.

She must have misheard.

Max looked at his watch. 'We should leave.'

They made their way to the door.

*

The Savoy Grill was three-quarters full.

Rebecca sat between Max and Michael at a circular table in the corner of the restaurant. Her beef was rare, just as she liked it. Michael preferred his meat well done, but to her it was like chewing leather. She ate slowly, savouring the flavour.

'You enjoy living dangerously,' observed Max.

'I do?'

'After the BSE scare.' He speared a piece of salmon. 'I know people who won't even eat beef-flavoured crisps.'

'My mother being one of them. She'd have a heart attack if she could see me now.' To her right, Caroline quizzed Michael about his job.

Max's face was in shadow. The lighting was subdued and intimate, so that at times it seemed as if they were the only diners in the restaurant. A uniformed waiter glided by, moving so elegantly that he might have been on skates. The background hum of conversation was little more than a whisper. The tables were so well spaced that there was no need to raise even the softest voice.

She sipped her wine, a French red that Max had assured her would complement the dish. It did.

'You approve?'

'Definitely. You're very knowledgeable.'

'Actually I interrogated the wine waiter on the way to the gents. If it was up to me, we'd all be drinking cider.'

She laughed. He refilled her glass. 'Are you happy in the flat?'

'Very, but we're trying not to get too comfortable. I'll be phoning estate agents this week.'

He looked surprised. 'There's no need. The flat's yours for as long as you want it. I did tell Mike but he must have forgotten.'

She felt awkward. 'We wouldn't want to outstay our welcome.'

'That won't happen, I assure you.'

His eyes remained fixed on her. She stared into his face, remembering the first time they'd met. He had put her at her ease almost with the first word he spoke. His eyes had been warm and his manner charming. He had wanted her to like him, and she had done so.

The eyes were still warm, but something in his manner was different. She could not put it into words, but she knew it was there.

'Mike tells me,' he said, 'that you're using the spare room as a temporary studio.'

She nodded, then added quickly: 'Unless you'd rather I didn't.'

'Why would I do that?'

'I might make a mess.'

'It doesn't matter. I want you to feel at home.'

'I do,' she assured him.

'Good.'

She cut into her beef while listening to Michael tell Caroline some anecdote about one of the partners he worked for. Caroline laughed enthusiastically. A little too enthusiastically perhaps. There was something in the sound that Rebecca found familiar. She tried to place it but was unable to do so.

'Last time I was over,' continued Max, 'Mike showed me some of your pieces. You're very talented.'

'Me and a million others.'

'That's right. There's so much competition. You can have all the talent in the world, but the only thing that really matters is knowing the right people.'

Nodding, she reached for her glass.

'Have you heard of Hampton Connaught?'

'No.'

'An art gallery in Cork Street. Quite sizeable. Caroline's done PR for them in the past and is a close friend of the owner, Richard Markham. Richard's planning a showcase for new talent in the autumn. It would be a proper exhibition, running for about a month. Each artist would show half a dozen pieces. He has five artists lined up and is looking for a sixth. What if that artist were you?'

Momentarily she was lost for words. She put her glass down. 'Cork Street . . .'

'I understand your hesitation,' he said quickly. 'It has become rather stuffy of late. But increasing numbers of new names are exhibiting there, and it's still a highly prestigious West End address. It would definitely get you noticed.'

She shook her head. 'I didn't mean to seem reluctant. It would be fantastic. But would they want me? My work might not be suitable.'

'There's no theme to the exhibition. Just a chance to show the pieces you're most proud of. What about your paintings of people looking into mirrors and seeing their true selves? Mike said they were wonderful. Caroline's meeting Richard tomorrow. She could show him those.'

A multitude of emotions swept over her: excitement at what could be the breakthrough she'd dreamed of, fear that it would surely end in rejection, and bewilderment at the speed at which it seemed to be happening.

Suddenly she saw a problem. 'The originals are in Winchester. I've only got slides here. Mr Markham might not be able to tell enough from them.'

'Slides will be fine,' Max told her. 'Please say yes. I know how much this means to you, and I really want to help. We both do.'

Her heart was racing. She took a deep breath, trying to slow it down. 'OK. Yes.'

'Splendid!'

Caroline and Michael both turned towards Max. 'Becky's agreed,' he told Caroline. 'You can talk to Richard.'

'If you don't mind,' added Rebecca quickly.

'I'd be delighted,' Caroline told her. 'I know how difficult it is for new artists to break through. Obviously I can't guarantee that Richard will want you to take part, but I'll do my best to persuade him.' She glanced fleetingly at Max, then back at Rebecca. 'I really will.'

'Of course he'll want her,' announced Max. 'I'd put money on it.' He raised his glass. 'To success.'

The others followed suit. Rebecca clinked glasses with Michael. He laughed. So did she. Max and Caroline were smiling at her. Caroline's eyes were warm. So were Max's. Warm and sympathetic. Wanting her to like him.

He was asking her a question. She concentrated on what was being said.

'Have you ever been to Suffolk?'

She shook her head.

'Caroline and I are spending this weekend at my house there. It's an artist's paradise. To see it is to feel inspired. At some point you must come and judge for yourself.'

'I'd like that.'

'I would have invited the two of you to join us, but I knew you had plans.'

Michael looked surprised. 'We don't have plans.'

Max frowned. 'Sorry, I must have misunderstood. Then why don't you both come?'

Michael's face lit up. 'How about it, Beck? You're not working this Saturday.'

'I know, but wouldn't we be intruding?'

'Not at all,' Max assured her. 'We'd love to have you.' He turned to Caroline. 'Wouldn't we?'

Caroline's eyes had widened very slightly. Her smile faltered, but only for a moment. 'Of course,' she agreed.

'Then we'd love to come.'

They had all finished eating. A waiter arrived to clear their plates. Max began to tell Rebecca about the house. She sipped her wine, trying to ignore the feeling that, in the nicest possible way, she had been manipulated.

Midnight. Michael poured himself a glass of water. Rebecca stood in the doorway, watching him. The kitchen light was on. The rest of the flat was in darkness.

'You knew, didn't you? About the gallery.'

He nodded between swallows.

'When did he tell you?'

'Over lunch, on Friday. He asked me not to say anything. He wanted it to be a surprise.'

'It was certainly that.'

He turned towards her. 'I thought you'd be pleased.'

'I am pleased.'

'You don't sound it.'

'I am. It was just unexpected.'

His mouth was still wet. He wiped it with his hand. 'I didn't know you'd had lunch together,' she said.

'It wasn't a big deal. He was in the area and phoned on the off chance.'

'What did you talk about?'

He shrugged. 'Stuff.'

'What stuff?'

'I don't know. Work. The meaning of life.'

'And me.'

Momentarily he looked awkward. 'Well, yeah. He was interested in how you were doing and he wanted to know if he could help.'

'You really like him, don't you?'

'Don't you?'

She hesitated. He looked concerned. 'Why not?'

She shook her head. 'I do like him. But this weekend feels like a bad idea. I'm sure Caroline doesn't want us there.'

'Yes, she does. Max wouldn't have asked us if he thought it would upset her.' He put down his glass. 'We can't pull out now,' he told her. 'It would look rude. Especially when they're trying to help you.'

She nodded.

He looked relieved. 'If you really hate it we'll make an excuse and leave. But you won't. It'll be fun. I promise.'

She managed a smile. 'And it's just a weekend, after all. It's not like it's going to be a regular thing.'

'Of course not.'

She looked down at the floor. Outside she could hear the wind blowing. Rain was battering the patio doors. A storm was blowing up. Terrible weather for the start of June.

She wondered if there would be storms in Suffolk.

'What did you think of Caroline?' he asked.

'You were the one who talked to her all evening. What did you think?'

'I liked her. She's not a gold-digger, like Lavinia.'

'You don't know that.'

'You think she is?'

'Maybe. Maybe not. It's none of our business either way, is it?'

A strange expression came into his face. There for a second, then gone.

He shook his head. 'I'm off to bed. Are you coming?'

'In a minute.'

He walked towards their bedroom. She remained where she was.

She wondered if Caroline really was a gold-digger. Possibly. That was Max's problem. It didn't matter to Michael or to her.

She turned out the kitchen light and made her way to bed.

TWO

Wednesday morning. Quarter to twelve. Michael waited at the coffee point for the kettle to boil. Two secretaries stood beside him, discussing forthcoming holidays, talking over the background buzz of typing and the ringing of telephones.

He was lost in thought. A client had faxed him a draft shareholder agreement to review. 'I'm sure you'll give it a clean bill of health,' the accompanying message had read. Not a chance. The non-compete clauses were clearly illegal, and the voting provisions would have baffled Einstein. Major redrafting was needed. In his head he began to compose suitable wording.

Julia appeared beside him. 'I've been looking for you everywhere. You have to hide.'

'Why?'

'Graham's had a phone call from some corporate client in Hull called Addletons. A complete nightmare, apparently. They want a junior assistant to go to Hull immediately and spend the rest of the week renegotiating their supply agreements. Graham's on the hunt for someone capable to send, and you're the obvious choice.'

'Shit!'

'Go and hide in the library. I'll come and tell you when it's safe.'

'Will you warn Stuart?'

'Yes. Hurry up.'

He rushed towards the door that led to the back stairs, expecting to hear someone bellowing his name. He didn't. Offering up a silent prayer of thanks, he began to descend.

And walked straight into Graham.

His heart sank. It was all he could do to stop himself cursing. 'Where are you off to?'

'The library.' His tone was surly, but he was too fed up to care.

They faced each other on the staircase. The top button of his shirt was undone and his tie was loose around his neck. Graham hated sloppiness. He waited for the lecture.

Graham scratched his face. He had just returned from a ten-day holiday in Cyprus and his skin was peeling. 'I've been with Keith Harper in banking. Had a regulatory question and needed a yes or no answer. Didn't get it, though.' A snort. 'Be easier to get blood out of a stone.'

Michael knew better than to agree. Graham would just tell everyone that he was badmouthing partners. He waited for the blow to fall.

Graham looked at his watch. 'Well, better press on.' He moved past Michael, heading towards their department.

Michael remained where he was, hardly daring to believe his good fortune. He began to laugh to himself.

And then stopped.

Why wasn't he being sent? It was a lousy job, he was suitably junior and Graham hated him. He had even done work for Addletons in the past. No one was better qualified.

Did Graham think him incapable?

No, that wasn't possible. After all, he had been trusted to run with the Digitron deal virtually single-handedly.

He was on the point of dismissing the idea when he remembered something.

First thing that morning he had seen Jack Bennett disappear into Graham's office. The door had remained shut for about half an hour.

What had they been talking about? Had they been discussing him? Could Jack have cast aspersions on his ability?

Was Jack trying to sabotage his reputation?

He told himself that he was being paranoid. Jack would never do that. But the suspicion persisted.

Tell Max.

The idea came out of nowhere. Slowly he turned it over in his mind, studying it carefully, as if examining a precious stone.

His anxiety began to ease. He decided to wait and see how things developed. In all likelihood, nothing was amiss. But if there was a battle to be fought, it was good to know that he was not obliged to stand alone.

He made his way back up the stairs, hoping that Julia had managed to warn Stuart.

One o'clock. Rebecca let herself into thirty-three Pelham Gardens.

That morning Michael had delivered her slides to Max. She had dug them out first thing, only to become convinced that the gallery would be able properly to judge her ability only if she sent actual canvases instead. Michael had managed to re-assure her, but in her panic she had gone to work without her purse.

She made her way upstairs to fetch it. When she reached the flat she found a beautifully wrapped package by the door. Attached to it was an envelope, marked with her name.

She let herself into the flat. The air was stuffy. She opened a window, then the package.

Inside was an expensive, lavishly illustrated coffee-table book on the Pre-Raphaelites. The cover showed one of her favourite paintings: Millais's romanticised vision of the Princes in the Tower. Two blond innocents, clasping hands on a dark staircase, frightened by the shadows that surrounded them.

The book had only recently been published. They had just received copies in the shop, and she had considered taking advantage of her staff discount and treating herself to a copy. Now there was no need.

She opened the envelope and read the note it contained.

Becky,
   It was a pleasure to see you last night. The first of many such evenings, I hope. Please accept the enclosed as a small thank-you for making Caroline feel so welcome.
   Looking forward to showing you Suffolk.
   Affectionately
   Max

His handwriting was beautiful. Elegant and persuasive. Just like his voice.

She had hardly spoken to Caroline. Michael deserved this, not her. It was a lovely present, though. Just what she wanted.

Perhaps Michael had suggested it.

The first of many such evenings.

Was that such a terrible prospect? He was wealthy, he was charming and he wanted to be their friend. Michael liked him. She wanted to like him. There was no reason not to like him.

But still the idea troubled her.

The book was still in her hand. She put it on the table by the sofa. It blended in perfectly yet still seemed out of place.

An intrusion that disturbed the established order in her home.

She went to fetch her purse.

Saturday afternoon. Five o'clock. Rebecca stood by the window of her bedroom at Max's Suffolk house running a comb through hair that was still damp from the shower.

The window was open. It was a beautiful day: the sun was bright and powerful, but the air was cooled by a faint breeze that blew in off the sea. She watched sailing boats sliding over the surface of the water, rising and dipping with the waves. Max kept a boat at a marina up the coast and had suggested they take her out the following day, if the weather stayed good. Rebecca had tried to appear keen, but sailing had never held much appeal for her. She hoped her lack of enthusiasm had not shown.

The four of them had travelled up the previous night, stopping for a leisurely dinner en route and arriving close to midnight. That morning Max had taken them for a drive through the surrounding countryside, ending up at the coastal town of Aldeburgh, where she had walked with Michael along the pebble beach and bought postcards to send friends and family. The sea air was invigorating, but she had spent happy childhood holidays in Cornwall and found the Suffolk coastline stark and desolate in comparison.

That afternoon they had played tennis on a court hidden in the trees that surrounded the house. She had partnered Max, who played a fast, tactical game that suited her own. They had proved more than a match for Caroline and Michael, the former clearly no athlete, the latter preferring the power game of squash and regularly belting the ball out of the court. 'We make a good team,' Max had told her as they raced through the final set. 'Future opponents will tremble before us.'

She heard footsteps behind her. Michael appeared from the bathroom, a towel wrapped round his waist.

'Feeling better?' she asked.

'After that humiliation?'

She smiled. 'You weren't humiliated.'

'Who are you trying to kid? We didn't win a single game in the last set.' He smiled too. 'My manhood is in ruins.'

He took off the towel and began to dress. Her eyes roamed over the huge four-poster bed, the sofa and chairs, the antique writing desk and the deep, cream carpet. It was like a room in an exclusive hotel where they were staying free of charge.

An electric fan blew cool air towards her, lifting the hair away from her face. 'Did you sleep here last time?' she asked.

'Yes.'

'It's grander than I expected. I keep worrying I'll break something.'

He pulled a shirt over his head. 'Even if you do, Max won't hang you for it.'

'Won't he?'

'Can't afford to. If you were dead he'd have to partner Caroline.'

Her hair was dry now. She put down the comb. 'I don't think Caroline likes me.'

'Why do you say that?'

'Because of the way she acts.'

He fastened his belt. 'How does she act?'

'Fine, when it's just her and me. When you're around I might as well not exist.'

He frowned. 'I don't think that's true.'

'It is. You're the one she wants to talk to. You're the one whose jokes she laughs at.'

'Perhaps your jokes aren't funny.'

She felt alarmed. 'Did Caroline say that?'

Quickly he knelt beside her. 'Hey, I was only teasing. Of course she likes you. If she didn't, then why would she offer to talk to Richard Markham about you? Maybe she's just more comfortable with men. Like some men are more comfortable with women.'

'Yeah, maybe.'

He rubbed her arm. 'Do you want to leave?'

She did. But it was his weekend, too, and she didn't want to spoil it. 'No.' She managed a smile. 'You know me. Just want to be the centre of everyone's world.'

He kissed her cheek. 'You're the centre of mine. Come on. Let's go downstairs.'

They rose to their feet. He squeezed her hand. 'It'll be fine,' he said. She returned the squeeze and told herself that he was right.

But he wasn't.

No one was rude to her. No one made her feel unwelcome. On the surface it was a perfectly pleasant evening.

It was what was going on beneath the surface that troubled her.

There were other guests now: Caroline's business partner Sarah, her merchant banker husband Tom, and a friend of theirs called Alan, who worked as an illustrator for an advertising agency. All three were in their late thirties. Their presence surprised Rebecca, who had thought Caroline wanted a quiet weekend with Max. Then she remembered that the inclusion of Michael and herself had already put paid to that.

They gathered in the drawing room before dinner. During the introductions she discovered that Tom worked at the same bank as a friend of her brother's. She asked about his progress. As Tom answered, she watched Caroline and Sarah laughing together with the easy intimacy that came from years of close friendship. Perhaps Caroline really was more comfortable with men, but it didn't look that way.

They made their way to the dining room. Max sat at the head of the table, flanked by Michael and Caroline. Rebecca, still talking to Tom, found herself seated opposite Sarah at the other end. The French windows looked out on to the sea, soon to turn from grey to black as the light faded from the sky.

She sipped her wine: a delicate white, perfect with trout. Outside, the wind was rising, whipping across the smooth surface of the water, making it churn. She wanted to watch the storm develop, but Sarah, an aggressively friendly woman, kept dragging her into the conversation at their end of the table. Someone lit the candles, and shadows appeared on the walls. Alan told her that he had attended the same art college as herself. Her eyes wandered towards the other end of the table.

Michael was telling Max and Caroline about a disastrous holiday to Greece that he'd taken as a student. Max was smiling, his expression benevolent. Caroline was laughing out loud. There was something in that laugh she found familiar, just as she had at the Savoy.

She remembered a long-ago afternoon when Robert had brought a new girlfriend home to meet the family. Her name had been Kathleen: a quiet, pleasantly pretty girl who had sat on the sofa, smiling nervously and saying little. The conversation had been light-hearted, full of jokes and affectionate teasing. Kathleen had laughed regularly, the sound just a little too eager as she strove to please and gain their acceptance.

Just as Caroline strove to gain acceptance from Michael.

Something caught in her throat. A tiny fishbone. Not big

180

enough to choke her, but still a cause of discomfort.

She swallowed it down and continued her meal.

Time passed. Conversations fragmented. Max spoke with Michael, Tom with Caroline. Alan told Rebecca about his new house in Ealing. It was close to one that friends of hers had just bought. She even knew the street. 'How do you like your flat?' Sarah asked.

'Very much.' She cut herself a piece of Wensleydale, the cheese crumbling under her knife.

'Where is it?' enquired Alan.

She told him. 'Expensive area,' he observed.

'We're lucky. Our rent's very reasonable.'

Sarah smiled. '*Very* reasonable.'

'Really?' Alan looked interested.

'Max is our landlord,' explained Rebecca, 'so it's not full market rate.'

'What Becky means,' added Sarah, 'is that they don't pay rent.'

Rebecca was taken aback. 'Who told you that?'

'Caroline.'

'Well, she's wrong.'

'Oh.' Sarah's smile faded. 'Sorry. I didn't mean anything by it.'

Rebecca felt embarrassed. 'Doesn't matter,' she said quickly.

'It's just that that's what Max told her.'

She felt a tightening in her forehead. At the other end of the table Michael was drawing something on a piece of paper. She couldn't see what but guessed it was some sort of company tree. When he had finished he looked anxiously at Max, as if eager for approval. Max studied the drawing, then shook his head, pointing to the paper and making an observation. Michael looked downcast. Max smiled encouragingly, his expression reassuring. Like that of a father trying to reassure a son.

Brightening, Michael picked up his pen and began to make corrections.

Max seemed to sense her eyes on him. He smiled at her. Warmly, as always. She managed to do the same.

There must be some mistake. Of course they were paying rent.

So why had Max told Caroline that they weren't?

She sipped her wine while Alan continued to describe his house. Outside, the storm was building.

She cornered Michael in the corridor. 'What's this about not paying rent?'

He looked uncomfortable. 'Who told you?'

'That doesn't matter. Is it true?'

'Yes.'

'Since when?'

'A few days ago.'

'I don't believe it! You had no right to agree that without telling me!'

The others were drinking coffee in the drawing room. Michael pulled her away from the doorway. 'I didn't agree anything,' he told her. 'Max decided he wasn't taking rent from us and instructed his bankers not to accept my standing order. He said that if we feel strongly we could give the money to charity each month, and that's what I'm going to do. There's a new charity helping underprivileged kids in the East End, and I'm going to have the standing order changed to—'

'Or we could just move out.'

He stared at her. 'Why would we do that? I like the flat. So do you.'

'Mike, we can't stay there if we're not paying rent.'

'Why not?'

'Think of the obligation it puts us under.'

'Obligation?' He looked genuinely taken aback. 'Look, you've got this wrong. It's not like that at all.'

Max emerged from the drawing room. She bit her tongue. 'Has Mike told you?'

She nodded. 'And it's incredibly generous but I don't think—'

'No, I haven't,' said Michael suddenly. 'I thought you should be the one.'

She was confused. 'Tell me what?'

'Caroline had a phone call just before dinner,' Max explained. 'From Richard Markham, the gallery owner. He loves your work and wants you to be part of his exhibition.'

The issue of rent vanished from her mind. She gasped. Michael gave her a hug. 'Congratulations. Didn't I tell you to have faith?'

Euphoria swept over her. She started to laugh, feeling giddy with excitement. Max looked amused. 'I take it you're pleased?'

'Are you kidding?' It came out as a virtual shriek. 'This is fantastic! I don't know what to say.'

Max held up a hand. 'You don't need to say anything. This is the reward your talent deserves. The exhibition is scheduled for October. You'll meet Richard soon to discuss commission charges and other such things. I've told him that your lawyer—' he pointed to Michael '—will be handling all the negotiations.'

She was still laughing. Max's expression was indulgent. She remembered her earlier ambivalence towards him and felt ashamed. Impulsively she hugged him. His arms enfolded her, drawing her to him. He felt solid and safe. Just like her father.

He released her and smiled, his eyes as comforting as Christmas lights.

Then, pointing to Michael, he said, 'Can I borrow him for a while?'

And she replied, 'No, he's mine.'

Her tone was sharp and defensive. Michael's eyes widened. She felt herself blush and wondered what had possessed her to say that. 'I was only joking,' she added quickly. 'Of course you can.'

Max continued to smile. 'It'll only be for an hour or so, and I promise to return him in good condition.'

She laughed nervously. 'That would be nice.'

'Why don't you have coffee with the others?' he suggested. 'We'll be back soon.'

They strolled off down a corridor on the other side of the hall. She watched them go, trying to swallow down the jealousy that was building up inside her. She didn't like sharing Michael. Even if it was only for an hour or so.

She walked into the drawing room. Caroline's smile of welcome dimmed slightly on realising that she was alone. Quickly she expressed her gratitude. Caroline accepted graciously, but her eyes kept flitting towards the door.

The others offered their congratulations. She sipped her coffee and felt out of place. They tried to involve her in the conversation, but having known each other for years inevitably they kept returning to topics that meant nothing to her. After half an hour she'd had enough. Pleading tiredness, she made her escape.

She stood in the hallway, looking about her. The house was beautiful but unfamiliar, and she did not want to go to bed alone. She went to find Michael.

The floor of the corridor was tiled, and her heels clattered on its surface. In the distance she could hear billiard balls slamming into each other. She remained still, not wanting to announce her presence too soon.

She could not make out their words, only their tones. Max's was soothing and reassuring, Michael's hesitant and confiding, revealing the vulnerability that hid behind the mask of confidence he wore for the world. A vulnerability that he showed to no one.

Except her.

She walked into the room. The two of them stood on either side of a huge snooker table, a light hanging over its surface. Both smiled as she entered. She knew instinctively that neither wanted her there.

'Who's winning?'

'I am,' Michael told her.

She waited for Max to add something. Instead he just stood there, chalking his cue and watching her with eyes that gave nothing away.

'I'm tired,' she said. 'I'm going to bed.'

'Then we should finish,' volunteered Max.

'There's no need. Carry on with your game. I just came to say goodnight.'

'Are you sure?' Michael asked.

She nodded.

'I'll be up soon,' he told her.

As she walked up the corridor she heard the game start up again.

The light was off in the bedroom. Wind and rain lashed at the windows. She lay in bed, listening to the storm, breathing in air that was stale and muggy. She was naked, covered only by a thin sheet. Her skin felt slick with sweat.

She thought about the exhibition. The lucky break of which she'd dreamed. A chance to be noticed. A chance to shine. She told herself these things as she tried to recapture the initial euphoria.

But the feeling was lost now, consumed by emotions of a darker hue.

In her head was a picture of her family. Her parents were at its centre, her brother standing just behind them, the three of them surrounded by a mass of grandparents, uncles, aunts and cousins. All were smiling at her. All loved her. She took that love for granted, treating it as a comfort blanket to wrap around herself whenever the need arose.

When Michael talked about his childhood, she tried to imagine growing up in a world where you mattered to no one. But she couldn't. It was beyond her comprehension.

That childhood was in the past now, and he had her to love him. She was the only person who did. Sometimes the realisation made her sad, and she would embrace the feeling as it helped her ignore the sense of pleasure that he had no other attachments to dilute the intensity of his devotion to herself.

Until now.

Lightning illuminated the room. It looked like a set from an old black and white film. That evening an arts cinema in Chelsea had been screening Erich von Stroheim's silent classic *Greed*. She had read about it in *Time Out* and had planned to surprise Michael with tickets. Before Max's invitation had come and got in the way.

Warm air pressed down on her like a blanket. She felt as if she were suffocating, surrounded by luxury in a gilded cage.

It was good that Michael was close to Max. She was glad he had found someone else to trust and confide in. Someone who could act as the father he had never known.

Yes, she was glad. She really was.

Which was just as well.

Because there was nothing she could do to stop it. Not when Max had been so good to her. Not when she was beholden, and had to smile and show gratitude as he began to force himself into their lives.

These thoughts crawled across her mind like spiders, spinning webs of resentment and suspicion. They made her feel ugly, so that when Michael finally came to bed she feigned sleep.

By next morning the storm had blown itself out, leaving a dull, exhausted sky. She opened the bedroom windows, letting in air that was refreshingly cool.

Michael showered first and was already dressed when she emerged from the bathroom. She sat down on the bed and began to rub her hair with a towel.

'Go down,' she said. 'I'll follow.'

'Are you sure?'

'Of course. You don't have to hold my hand, Mike.'

He smiled. 'See you in a bit.'

His footsteps faded away. She dressed in jeans and a blouse, in keeping with the informal tone of the weekend, before making her way to the dining room.

Caroline sat with Alan, the two of them reading the Sunday papers over coffee and toast. There was no sign of the others.

'Michael's gone with Max,' Caroline explained.

'Where?'

'A hotel up the beach. It does a full English breakfast.'

She felt snubbed. 'I didn't know they'd planned anything.'

'It was Max's idea. Spur of the moment.' Caroline gestured to the table. 'Mrs Avery didn't have the right food in. The rest of us don't eat much in the morning, and I gather you're the same.'

She was. So it wasn't a snub after all. But it felt like one.

She wondered if Caroline felt snubbed too.

As if by way of answer, Caroline gave a brittle laugh. 'Well, let them block their arteries with all that fried stuff. Why don't you sit down?'

She had lost what little appetite she'd possessed. After exchanging pleasantries she took a pile of colour supplements through to the drawing room, flicking through them as she drank her coffee. She read a feature on a forthcoming celebrity wedding. Their own wedding was scheduled for May of the following year, at her local church in Winchester, followed, she hoped, by a honeymoon in Fiji. The guest list had yet to be finalised. She wondered if she'd be sending an invitation to Max.

There was movement behind her. Caroline stood in the doorway. 'Am I disturbing you?'

'No.' She rose to her feet. 'Do you want the papers back?'

Caroline shook her head. Her pale blue jumper matched her eyes, which were friendly but anxious. 'I came to check you weren't feeling too abandoned.'

'I'm not.' She hesitated. 'Are you?'

'A bit.'

'I'm sorry.'

'Don't be. Blame Max's stomach.'

'Actually I was talking about this weekend. Mike and I didn't want to intrude.'

'You're not.' Caroline looked concerned. 'Have I made you feel that?'

'No, I just meant—'

'Please don't think that. I'm really glad you both came.' Caroline paused. Her tone became apologetic. 'I'm sorry you and I haven't had more chance to talk.'

'It doesn't matter. We're talking now.'

Caroline's face relaxed. 'Yes, we are.' Her features softened, making her look much younger. Rebecca sensed that in a different setting this was a woman whose company she could enjoy.

'Anyway,' she added, 'it gave me the chance to meet your friends.'

'Do you like them?'

'Very much,' she said politely.

'Max thought you would.'

The comment surprised her, but she gave no indication of this.

'Well, they keep me entertained,' Caroline observed.

'How did you meet Max?'

'Through mutual friends. We've known each other for about a year, but only as acquaintances. Then, a couple of weeks ago, he called and asked me to dinner.'

'And I take it you were pleased.'

Caroline blushed, ever so slightly. 'Very.'

Rebecca smiled. 'When Mike first asked me out I was ecstatic. I never thought it was going to happen. But it was worth the wait.'

'Except for the panic about what to wear.' Caroline smiled too. 'Men are so lucky, aren't they? They can throw on anything and smarten it with a jacket. It's us women who have to make the effort.'

'And then, if the men are anything like Mike, they don't even notice.'

Caroline laughed. Rebecca did too.

'It's nice,' remarked Caroline, 'that Max and Mike get on so well.'

Rebecca nodded, wondering just how pleased about it Caroline really was.

'Well, it's nice for Max, anyway. I think he sees Mike as a younger version of himself. Someone on whom he can bestow his pearls of wisdom.' Another laugh. 'Men and their egos!'

Another nod.

Caroline looked at her watch. 'Sarah's suggested that we go for a walk. Would you like to come?'

Rebecca remembered how unsuccessfully they had tried to involve her in their conversation the previous evening. 'I think I'll wait for Mike.'

'Are you sure? You'd be very welcome.'

'I know. But I'd rather stay. Thanks, anyway.'

She returned to the papers. When she had finished she phoned her parents to tell them about the exhibition. They were thrilled for her. Her mother was almost in tears. She managed to sound thrilled herself.

The house was silent now. She walked slowly through its corridors, listening to the sound of her shoes on the tiles and feeling like a tiny fish that had been swallowed by a whale.

She came to the snooker room. Its walls were oak-panelled and hung with prints of Hogarth's more colourful works. It made her think of an old-fashioned gentlemen's club where men came to smoke and share their secrets.

The balls were set out on the table, ready for another game. She rolled the white ball towards the triangle of reds, but her aim was poor and it thudded harmlessly into the soft felt, leaving the existing order undamaged.

From the window she could see the back lawn, running down to a cliff and the sea. Max and Michael were walking towards the house. Concealing herself behind a curtain she watched their approach.

They moved slowly, their steps so in unison that an innocent observer might think they had known each other for years. Michael was talking, his expression the anxious one he wore when asking for advice. The one he showed to no one except her.

Max began to speak. Michael's face relaxed. He started to laugh. Max did too.

Jealousy flared up in her. A black seed of resentment took root in the pit of her stomach and began to grow.

They walked on towards the house. She remained where she was, staring up at the sky. The clouds were clearing now. The sun broke through, shining its light on the water, making it gleam. A beautiful view that would make a good painting. And there would be no shortage of weekends to capture it on canvas, of that she was convinced.

Someone was calling her name. She made her way along the corridor, wearing a smile to mask the hostility that lurked beneath.

THREE

The Baker Connolly Literary Agency was on the fourth floor of a grey-stone building facing St Paul's Cathedral. Three agents worked there, supported by two assistants, a secretary and a receptionist. One of the assistants was Emily Fielding.

Emily sat in her tiny corner office reviewing Susie Sandelson's Italian contract. Susie was a new client, represented by Kevin Ashford, the most junior agent and the one for whom Emily did most work. Kevin was marketing Susie's first novel as 'Bridget Jones with attitude', which was another way of saying that the Bridget character had a pierced tongue and a marked enthusiasm for recreational drugs and went through men like Kleenex. Last month he had secured a lucrative British publishing deal, and though the Americans remained lukewarm the European rights were going like hot cakes. Secretly Emily thought the book predictable, but she liked Susie and was glad that things were going so well for her.

It was warm in the office. There was no air-conditioning, and a small fan swung half-circles on her desk. From the open window she could see a party of Japanese tourists squinting in the midday sunshine as they photographed each other in front of the cathedral. Kevin had told her that they might be moving to new premises in the West End. She hoped not. She would miss the view.

She looked at her watch. Quarter to one. Michael had phoned earlier to say that he had a meeting in the area and suggested lunch. He'd expected to be finished half an hour ago, so it didn't look as if they would meet after all. She was disappointed but resigned, knowing how these things could run on.

She studied the contract. The paperback royalty rates seemed excessively low. After checking the file, she made the necessary corrections. As she did so she thought of the novel she herself had written two years ago and submitted to agents and publishers, only to have it turned down by everyone. The memory made her feel sad. Though she was pleased for Susie, she couldn't help being envious too.

There was a knock on the door. She looked up and her spirits lifted.

Michael stood in the doorway, his suit jacket slung over his shoulder and a briefcase in his hand. 'Made it! Ready to eat?'

'Do you still have time?'

'I've got a mobile. They can call if there's an emergency.' He took it from his pocket and pressed a button, his eyes widening in fake alarm. 'Oh, no. I've switched it off.'

'Mike!'

He grinned. 'Don't worry. Things are quiet anyway. Let's grab a sandwich and sit in the Temple.'

They made their way towards Ludgate Circus and crossed into Fleet Street, stopping at a takeaway to buy lunch. 'The chocolate cake looks good,' he said. 'Why not have some?'

'So you can nick it, the way you do with Becky's food?'

He smiled. 'Perhaps.'

She smiled, too, and bought a slice.

The Temple gardens looked out on to the Thames. Dozens of young professionals sprawled on the grass, devouring expensive sandwiches and complaining about bosses and workloads. The air was still and the sky cloudless, so they took shelter in the shade of a tree. She saw drops of perspiration on his forehead. 'I don't envy you having to wear that suit.'

'The tube's a nightmare at the moment. It's like travelling in a mobile sauna.' He opened a can of Diet Coke and gulped down half the contents. 'Still, it could have been the New York subway.'

She bit into her sandwich and licked spicy Thai sauce from her fingers. She hadn't realised how hungry she was. He watched her eat while trying to pretend that he wasn't. The realisation made her feel self-conscious yet pleased at his concern.

'Why do you mention New York?' she asked.

'They're looking for someone to send to the New York office. Last week Jeff Speakman, one of the senior partners in our department, asked me if I was interested.'

'Are you?' She kept her voice neutral.

'Told him I was.' He wiped drops of dark liquid from his mouth. 'Not that it did me any good. Turns out they want someone more senior. Typical Jeff. Always gets his facts wrong.'

She masked her relief. 'You must be disappointed.'

He shook his head. 'I don't really want to leave London. Not now things are starting to happen for Beck.'

'And for you,' she suggested.

'Yeah, I suppose so.'

'How was the weekend?'

'I enjoyed it. Beck said she did, too, but I'm not sure. I spent a lot of time with Max and she may have felt ignored.'

A faint breeze cooled her face. She leaned back against the

trunk of the tree, listening to the leaves rustle overhead. 'You like him a lot, don't you?'

'Well, what if I do? It's no big deal.' His tone was defensive.

'It wasn't meant as a criticism,' she said quickly. 'I'm pleased for you. I know Becky is too.'

His face lit up. 'She said that?'

'We haven't actually talked about it,' she admitted. 'But I'm sure she is. I'm seeing her this week. I could sound her out if you like.'

'Yes, please.' He finished his sandwich and crunched the wrapping into a ball. 'What day are you meeting?'

'Tomorrow. We're having lunch with Lorna.'

He grimaced.

'She's not that bad,' she said, but without much conviction.

'No, she's great. I love her dearly. I love all Beck's friends dearly.' He rubbed her shoulder affectionately. 'All except one.'

She remembered the first time she'd seen him. It had been at the party where he'd first met Rebecca. She had stood and watched the two of them talking, wishing she had had the courage to approach him first. Wishing, as she had so many times in the past, for some small portion of Rebecca's unquestioning self-belief.

She had lost out that day. But she had gained too. For he had proved an unexpectedly good friend, and one whose importance in her life was ever growing.

'I'm glad you're not going to New York,' she told him.

'So am I.'

They sat in the silence that can only exist between those who are truly comfortable with each other. Her eyes roamed over the gardens and came to rest on a young couple who sat nearby, their arms draped around each other. The man was whispering something. The woman smiled up at him, her nondescript face made beautiful by the joy of requited love.

She felt an emptiness in the pit of her stomach.

Michael was staring at her. His eyes were sympathetic, as if he could read her thoughts.

She gave him a small smile. 'Do you need to get back?'

'No.'

'Neither do I.'

'Good.' He picked up a twig and began to scratch at the earth.

'If you find any treasure, will you share it with me?'

'Of course.'

The tree trunk felt cool against her skin. She wished they could stay here all day. Just the two of them. Not needing to talk. Happy just to be together.

'Have you called him yet?' he asked.

Her daydream collapsed. She wished he hadn't asked that. Though she said nothing, his eyes remained expectant. She shook her head.

'You said you were going to.'

'I know.'

'So why not do it?'

'Why do you think?'

'He's your father, Em. He always will be, in spite of what's happened.'

A lump came into her throat. She swallowed it down. 'I know that too.'

'So call him. You can't keep putting it off.'

'Can't I?'

He didn't answer. Just stared at her. She knew he was right, but she was frightened and the fear made her sharp. 'You're a fine one to talk. When was the last time you called your biological father?'

She regretted the words as soon as they were spoken. He flushed slightly, as if she'd slapped him.

'Touché,' he said.

'I'm sorry. That was a stupid thing to say.'

He breathed deeply. 'No, it wasn't. You're right. I must sound like the world's biggest hypocrite.'

'I didn't mean ...'

'But it is different. You must see that. My father's never played a part in my life. He's just some man who looks like me. Your father was everything to you. Your whole world. Isn't that worth fighting for?'

The lump was back. Bigger this time. 'I'm no good at fighting,' she whispered. 'When I fight I just make things worse.'

'That's because you were fighting alone. You don't have to now. I'll help. You know I will.'

She shook her head.

'Why not?'

She didn't answer.

'Why not?'

'Because I'm scared.'

'You think I don't know that?'

Tears came into her eyes. She wiped them away. 'I didn't mean to upset you,' he said gently. 'I just want you to think about it. And to know that I'm here if you need me.'

She managed a smile. 'I do know that.'

Again they drifted into silence. Comfortable, as before. He continued to dig at the ground. She sat and watched him. His presence made her feel safe. She didn't know what she would do without him in her life.

I hope Becky lets me keep him.

She looked up at the sky. It was a perfect blue. But in her mind she saw clouds.

He made a joke. Smiling, she kept her fears to herself.

*

197

At twenty past eight that evening, Rebecca let herself into the flat.

It had been a long day. Business in the shop had been brisk, she'd had to cover for someone who was off sick, and she had just spent nearly an hour sitting on a crowded, sweltering tube train that had broken down. She was feeling tired and irritable as she shut the door behind her.

Music was playing in the living room. 'Mike?'

He called out a greeting from the bedroom. She poured herself a glass of water and went to drink it on the balcony. The evening air was humid and still. In one of the gardens below, two small boys ran after a football. She envied them their energy.

Michael appeared, wearing her favourite blue T-shirt. The sight of him made her feel better.

'This is a surprise,' he said. 'Thought you were seeing your friend Jenny tonight.'

'Cancelled. She had to work late.'

'Is that why you look stroppy?'

'No. London Transport takes full credit for that.'

He laughed, putting an arm round her shoulder. She began to describe her homeward journey. In the background, the two boys shouted with excitement at their game.

'Robert phoned today,' she told him.

'Why?'

'Does there have to be a reason?'

'You wouldn't mention it if he'd just called for a chat.'

That was true. 'He's having a barbecue on Sunday.'

'And you want us to go?'

She nodded, bracing herself for the protests.

'OK.'

She masked her surprise. 'We'll just make an appearance. There's no need to stay all day.'

'We can if you want. As long as you're enjoying it, I don't mind.'

She was touched. 'Thanks.'

He stroked her hair. She smiled up at him. 'But that's days away. This evening you have me all to yourself.'

He began to look uncomfortable. 'That's the thing. I'm having a drink with Max.'

Her good mood evaporated. 'Since when?'

'This afternoon. He phoned me at work.'

'I see.'

'It's not a problem, is it?'

'No.'

'You did say you were going to be out.'

'I know.'

'So what's the face for?'

'What face?'

He raised an eyebrow.

'It's just—' She struggled for appropriate words.

'Just what?'

'We spent all weekend with him.'

'So?'

'So we don't want to see him all the time.'

'We don't see him all the time.'

'It feels like it,' she said before she could stop herself.

He frowned. 'Not to me. Anyway, you don't have to see him. I'm the one he's expecting.'

'So I'm not invited? Charming.'

'I didn't mean that. Your name didn't come up. Why would it? You'd made plans.'

'Which have now fallen through, freeing me to enjoy a boring evening alone.' She paused. 'Unless I come too.'

Momentarily his eyes widened. 'Well, sure. If you want.'

She didn't know why she'd said that. The last thing she

wanted was an evening of small talk, easy charm and the need to feel grateful. No, she definitely didn't want that.

Not when Mike doesn't want me there.

She looked down at the stone floor of the balcony. It was so small. No room for a barbecue, if ever they decided to hold one. Not that it mattered. She was sure Max would allow them to use his garden. All they had to do was ask.

She raised her head. Michael was staring at her, expectantly. 'Is that what you want?' he asked again.

'No. I don't feel like going out.'

'Fair enough.' He showed no relief. But she was sure he felt it.

'You could stay in with me.'

He looked at his watch. 'I can't cancel now. I'm late as it is.'

'Better run along then.' She paused, then added snidely, 'Be sure to have a wonderful time.'

'Why are you being like this?'

Because you're mine. You belong to me and no one else.

'I'm not being like anything.'

He sighed. 'It's just a drink, that's all.'

'And a conversation.'

'I suppose so.'

'Are you going to talk about me?'

'No.'

'So what will you talk about?'

'I don't know.'

'You must have some idea. You've got to talk about something.'

'It's not like that,' he said suddenly. 'We don't have conversations. It's not so two-way as that. I seem to do all the talking when I'm with him. I don't intend to, but it's just the way it works out. I talk, he listens. He's a good listener.'

His words stung. 'And I'm not?'

'I didn't mean that.'

'But you can't talk to me the way you can talk to him?'

'I didn't mean that either. You know I can talk to you. It's just different with him. Like when you talk to your mother. You talk. She listens.' He smiled encouragingly. 'It's no big deal.'

She didn't want to act like this. Not over a couple of hours in a pub. He was right. It was no big deal.

Not yet.

He took a deep breath. 'Max usually carries a mobile. If you want I'll phone and cancel. Say that something's come up. He'll understand.'

For a moment she was tempted. But she knew she would hate herself if she agreed.

'No. You should go.'

'I won't be late, OK?'

'OK.'

He left. She remained on the balcony. The air was cooler now. The two boys had left the garden, and everywhere was still and peaceful. Amazingly so for central London. It was a lovely place. They were lucky to live here. Even if it was starting to feel like a prison.

It was wrong to feel like this. Something good had happened to Michael. She loved him and wanted to be pleased. Not jealous and resentful, like a spoiled child forced to share a favourite toy.

She told herself not to be silly. But the feelings refused to go away.

Nine o'clock. Michael, now half an hour late, rushed along the Old Brompton Road.

The pub was in a side street facing a row of terraced houses. Max sat at a wooden table outside reading the *Evening*

Standard, a Scotch cradled in his hand and a cigar smouldering in the ashtray. A pint of lager stood invitingly in front of an empty seat.

He sat down. 'Is this for me?'

Max smiled in welcome. 'It is.'

He felt sticky with the heat and took a deep draught. 'Sorry I'm so late.'

'Don't worry. Becky explained that you'd been held up.'

'You spoke to Beck?'

'Yes. I've just phoned the flat.'

'What did she say?'

'Simply that you'd been delayed but were on your way.'

'Oh. OK.' Relieved, he downed more lager. 'I needed this. Thanks.'

The dark eyes studied him curiously. 'What else should she have said?'

'Nothing.'

Max took a drag on his cigar. 'You seem anxious. Is something wrong?'

He shook his head.

'Are you sure?'

'Yes.'

'I thought Becky had plans tonight.'

'They fell through.'

Max sipped his Scotch. 'But she didn't want to join us.'

He made up an excuse. 'She didn't feel too well.'

Max looked thoughtful. Michael wished he hadn't phoned the flat. At the next table a group of young men boasted loudly about how much they'd drunk at some party.

'Does she mind you being here?'

'No. She was the one who insisted I came.' He stopped, but then added, 'Not that I didn't want to.'

'Even if it meant leaving her when she was ill?'

202

He regretted his earlier choice of words. 'She's not ill as such. Just a headache.'

Max nodded. 'That explains it.'

'Explains what?'

'Why she sounded tense.'

'Why? What did she say?'

'Only what I told you. Don't you believe me?'

'Yes, of course.' He wished he'd kept his mouth shut. Anxiously he studied Max's face, looking for signs of suspicion.

But there was none. The eyes were benign. Max nodded towards the next table where the boasting grew ever more extreme. 'Incredible, isn't it, how two pints of shandy and a Babycham can be made to sound like enough alcohol to give the five thousand a hangover from hell.'

Michael laughed. The lager was doing its work, and he began to relax. His glass was almost empty. So was Max's. 'Do you want another?' he asked.

'In a minute.' Max breathed a smoke ring into the air and smiled contentedly. 'It was a good weekend, wasn't it?'

'Fantastic.'

'We'll do it again soon. Just the four of us this time.'

Michael wasn't sure how keen Rebecca would be on the idea, but looked enthusiastic anyway.

'Caroline really liked Becky,' Max told him.

'Beck liked her too.' He wasn't sure about that either, but had no intention of rocking the boat. 'And she's really excited about the exhibition. She says it's like a dream come true.'

'It's no more than she deserves. I'm just glad I could help. I'm very fond of her, you know.'

'And she is of you.' He downed the rest of his glass.

'Even if she does consider me a threat.'

The lager turned sour in his throat before settling in his stomach like a lead weight. 'Why do you say that?'

203

'Because it's true.'

'No, it's not. She really likes you.'

Max was still smiling. The eyes were warm, but they were also shrewd. Eyes that could not be deceived. Michael's heart started to race.

'I'm not a fool, Mike.'

'I know that. But you're wrong about this.'

'Don't misunderstand me. I understand her feelings. I only met you a few weeks ago, and already the two of us have become extremely close. It's only natural she should view me with some suspicion.'

'She doesn't.'

'I didn't mean to cause trouble between you.'

'You haven't. I told you, she really likes you.'

'And I told you that I'm not a fool.'

The eyes continued to study him. Two dark orbs that held him like magnets. He felt trapped and suddenly angry to have been put in this position by two people who were supposed to care about him.

This caused him to speak without thinking.

'Look, she doesn't feel threatened. Why should she? There's no way you could ever be a threat. She's going to be my wife, for God's sake, and nothing could be more important than that. I'd never put you before her. You'd have to be mad to think otherwise.'

His heart was still pounding. He exhaled slowly.

And realised what he'd said.

The smile remained in place. The eyes, warm and unblinking, continued to study him.

He swallowed. 'I'm sorry. It wasn't supposed to come out like that.'

He wiped his mouth, staring down at the table. Drops of lager had spilled on to its surface. He traced them with his

204

finger, wishing more than anything that he had stayed at home that evening.

'You don't have to explain anything,' Max told him. 'I understand.'

'You are important to me. You must know that.'

'But not as important as Becky.'

'It was a stupid thing to say. I didn't mean—'

'It wasn't stupid,' said Max gently. 'That's how it should be. She's your future. I'm just—' he sighed '—a stage in your life that you'll pass through and leave behind. Like you did your foster parents.'

The words stung. He was sure they weren't meant to, but they did. Just as his must have done.

Poetic justice.

'It's nothing like that,' he said.

He continued to stare at the table, watching his fingers make shapes with drops of golden liquid.

'I told you, didn't I, that I had no illusions when they took me in. I told you that I knew exactly what was going on.'

'You did.'

'Well, that was a lie. I did have illusions. Great big shining ones. I was so sure this was going to be it. A family. People who would care about me and to whom I could belong. Everything I'd ever dreamed of. But I was wrong. When they looked at me they didn't see a person. Just a social statement.

'No one has ever treated me the way you have. When I'm with you I feel like I have a father. I don't think Becky understands just what that means to me. How can she? Her family has always been there for her and she just takes them for granted.'

He stopped, hoping for a response. But there was none. Just an expectant silence.

'What I'm trying to say is that our relationship isn't just a stage. Not to me. It's much more than that, and I don't want to lose it.'

'You won't,' Max told him. 'I promise you that. You're the closest thing I've ever had to a son, and I don't want to lose that either.'

Michael found himself remembering another evening in a London pub. An evening spent with a man who had looked exactly like him. A man who would have felt nothing if he'd dropped dead of a heart attack there as they drank together.

He looked into the eyes of his companion, saw the wealth of affection contained there, and offered up a silent prayer of thanks for its existence.

'You don't have to worry, Mike. Everything will work out for the best. That's a promise too.'

He nodded.

For a moment Max's expression was serious. Then it relaxed. 'Enough of this. Didn't you say something about another drink? Well, make mine a double and be quick about it.'

Laughing, Michael rose to his feet.

'One thing,' said Max suddenly.

'What?'

'Don't tell Becky we've had this conversation. She'd only feel awkward with me, and that's the last thing I'd want. It'll be our secret, OK?'

'OK.'

'Good.'

Feeling much happier, Michael made his way to the bar.

Max watched him go. Slowly the smile faded from his face. His eyes became thoughtful and sad.

He took another drag on his cigar. It was almost finished. He stubbed it out and prepared to light another.

FOUR

Wednesday lunchtime. Rebecca sat in a crowded bistro near Holborn, eating her salad and listening to her school friend Lorna complain about her new boss. The third place at the table remained empty.

She sipped her mineral water. 'I wonder what's happened to Em.'

'Got lost, hopefully.' Lorna rolled her eyes. She was a petite redhead with a strident voice, impish face and wicked sense of humour. 'Why did you have to invite her?'

'She's my friend.'

'God knows why. If she was any lamer she'd be in a wheel-chair. You should have dropped her in kindergarten. Obviously you're a closet masochist, but I'm not, so next time make sure it's just the two of us.' Lorna swallowed a mouthful of paella and looked around her. 'This place is a dump. Mind you, it's better than the dive Phil dragged me to last night. As much cur-ried dog as you can eat for a fiver, with salmonella thrown in free.' She laughed raucously. Rebecca watched people walk past the window, squinting into the sun. Still no sign of Emily.

'It's great news about the exhibition,' Lorna told her.

She nodded.

'You don't seem very excited. You've been banging on about that elusive lucky break for years. Now it's happened, you should be spinning cartwheels.'

'Not while I'm eating. It could be rather messy. I'll do a backflip when I've finished.'

'I should think so. You're really lucky. A fabulous flat and the landlord from heaven.'

Rebecca speared a piece of limp lettuce with her fork. 'The landlord from heaven,' she said with sudden bitterness. 'Aren't I the lucky one?'

'Do I detect trouble in paradise?'

She felt embarrassed. 'Everything's fine.'

'Don't go coy on me. If there's a problem, I want to know.'

'There's no problem.' Emily was approaching. She waved, grateful for the distraction.

Emily sat down, smiling at Lorna, who responded half-heartedly. A waitress appeared with another menu.

'Sorry I'm late,' said Emily after ordering.

'You haven't missed much,' Lorna told her. 'Just Beck bitching about her benefactor.'

'I wasn't!'

'Yeah, right.'

'I wasn't. I like him. He's a really nice man.' As she spoke she listened to her voice and realised how unconvincing she sounded.

'But?' prompted Lorna.

'I don't know.'

'Sure you do.' Lorna looked at her watch. 'I don't have to go for a few minutes. Tell us, Beck. We're your friends.' She turned to Emily. 'Aren't we, Emolina?'

Emily flushed. She hated being called that. 'Of course,' she said quietly.

'So let's hear it.'

'This is between us, OK?'

'No, we're undercover journalists! Of course it's between us. Now spill the beans.'

Rebecca pushed her plate to one side. 'I liked him at first,' she began. 'And I've tried to keep liking him since, I really have. There's no reason not to like him. But we've known him only a few weeks and suddenly it's like we're his best friends. He invites us to places. He suggests we do things together, and I have to say yes all the time because I don't want to risk offending him. He's very generous, and I am grateful, but sometimes it feels like he's buying his way into our lives and it really bothers me. I just wish he'd go away.'

The waitress arrived with Emily's quiche. Lorna lit a cigarette.

'You're right about not wanting to piss him off,' she told Rebecca. 'Not yet, anyway. So why not make the most of his generosity? Get him to take you to the expensive places you've always wanted to go to. Then, when the exhibition's over, you can start declining his invitations and eventually he'll get the hint.'

'It's not that simple.'

'Yes, it is. Unless you want to stay in the flat, but I thought you were planning to buy somewhere.'

'We are.'

'So what's the problem?'

'Mike thinks he's wonderful. If ever I say anything critical he looks at me like I'm a complete cow.'

As she spoke, Rebecca felt Emily's eyes on her and found herself wondering whether Emily thought her a cow too.

'And I'm not,' she added quickly.

'Course you're not,' agreed Lorna.

'The two of them have become really close. I think Mike views him as a surrogate father.'

Lorna snorted.

'Well, you may think it's stupid, but that's the situation. Mike won't agree to our dumping him like that.'

'Then you'll have to make him.'

'How?'

'By laying down the law. You want this man out of your life. Mike will just have to accept it. Which he should. After all, if he loves you he should want you to be happy.'

'And what about Mike's happiness,' said Emily suddenly. 'Or doesn't that count for anything?'

Lorna frowned. She did not like being interrupted, especially by someone she despised. 'We're not talking about Mike,' she said dismissively.

'And what if he doesn't accept it?' asked Rebecca.

'Then give him an ultimatum. Either he ends the friendship or you break off the engagement. That should bring him to heel pretty quick.'

Rebecca was shocked. 'I couldn't do that!'

'Of course you could. Phil had this nerdy cousin who was always hanging round. I couldn't stand him so I forced Phil to choose between us. Trust me, Beck, it works.'

Rebecca shook her head, while noticing that Emily's colour was rising.

'Why not?' Lorna blew a cloud of smoke into the air and stared at her mischievously. 'Are you frightened he'll choose the landlord over you?'

'No! Of course not!'

'Then do it. Mike will survive without his surrogate daddy. After all, he's twenty-four. It's high time the big baby was weaned.'

Emily started to laugh. The sound was harsh, angry and completely out of character.

'It's so easy for you, isn't it?' she said to Lorna. 'You with the banker father and stay-at-home mother and the big house and the holidays and presents. Nothing has ever gone wrong in your life, has it? Nothing has ever been taken away from you. You don't know anything about suffering or loss. Your life has been as perfect as it's possible to be, and still you want to take from other people.'

Rebecca felt a chill run through her. Though Emily's words were directed at Lorna, she wondered if, at some deeper level, they were also aimed at herself.

'Em . . .' she began.

Emily ignored her. 'You make me sick. You think you're so worldly, but you don't know the first thing about real life. You're the most complacent, self-satisfied person I've ever met, and I pity Phil. I really do. Just like I'd pity anyone who was stupid enough to waste their life on someone as shallow as you.'

Lorna paled. Clearly the words had struck a nerve. Emily's back was ramrod straight, her gaze bold and scornful. There was no trace of the timid girl Rebecca had known all her life. She had been replaced by someone who was more than a match for Lorna.

Momentarily at least.

Then, slowly, Lorna began to smile.

'You don't want to feel bad about Phil, Emolina. I may be complacent and I may be shallow, but at least I'm not a frigid basket case who reaches for the sick bag whenever a man is desperate or drunk enough to try and touch me.'

Emily's composure collapsed. She seemed to wither in her seat, as if her body were a balloon that had sprung a leak.

Rebecca was appalled. 'Lorna!'

Lorna's smile remained. 'Don't lecture me. If she can't stand the heat she should stay out of the kitchen. Or indeed the bed-room. Isn't that right, Emolina?'

Emily turned towards Rebecca, her eyes wide with betrayal. Rebecca was too ashamed to meet her gaze. 'You didn't have to say that,' she told Lorna.

'But I did, so big deal. I have to go. Next time I see you, make sure it's just us.' Lorna threw some money down on the table and made for the door.

'Why?' demanded Emily.

'Look, Em—'

'How could you have told her about that?'

'I'm sorry.'

'Sorry! You think that makes it all right? You know what she thinks about me. That all I'm good for is to be laughed at.'

'She doesn't think that.'

'Of course she does! She always has. Any excuse to make me feel bad and she jumps at it.'

'That's why I told her. I just thought—' She stopped, wishing she'd said nothing.

'You thought she'd feel sorry for me. That she'd pity me. Well, I don't want her pity. I don't want anyone's pity!'

Rebecca stared down at the table. The cloth was faded and stained. It looked dirty, just like she felt.

'It was stupid, I know. But I didn't mean to hurt you. You're my best friend.'

Silence.

'I'm sorry, Em. I really am.'

She waited for a response, but none was offered.

'I don't know what else to say.'

'It doesn't matter. Forget it.'

'I shouldn't have told her. It was stupid.'

'But you meant well.'

She sighed. 'Yeah, I meant well.'

Another silence.

'I don't care,' said Emily eventually. 'Who cares what she

thinks? The only time she's happy is when she's trashing other people.'

Rebecca risked a joke. 'She probably thinks the Pope's a transvestite.'

For a time, Emily's expression remained solemn. Then, slowly, she began to smile. Rebecca smiled too. The tension began to ease.

They ordered coffees. Rebecca stirred hers slowly. Emily did likewise. 'You're not going to lose Mike,' she told Rebecca. 'That's what this business with Max is really about, isn't it?'

Rebecca nodded. 'I feel threatened. It's ridiculous, but I do.'

'Mike adores you. You're the most important person in his life. Max's arrival on the scene isn't going to change that.'

'I must seem like the most selfish person in the world. And I'm not. I'm happy for Mike. I really am.'

She stopped. Emily was staring at her.

'Well, I want to be.' She exhaled. 'It's just all happened so fast. I haven't got used to it yet.'

'But you will.'

'I hope so.'

Her eyes wandered over the bistro. She and Mike had had lunch here a couple of months ago. Before they had moved into the flat and allowed Max into their lives.

'And what if I don't?' she said suddenly. 'What if I carry on feeling like this?'

'You won't.'

'But what if I do? What if it gets worse and worse? It'll just cause trouble between us.'

'Not if you don't let it.'

'I wish we'd never taken the flat. I wish we hadn't met him.'

'But you did, and you have. You can't rewrite history, Becky. All you can do is make the best of it.'

'Or give Mike an ultimatum.'

Emily shook her head.

'Why not?'

'Because you might lose him.'

'You think he'll put Max before me?'

'No, he'll choose you. You know he will. But he'll hate you for it. So much so that it could end up driving him away.'

Rebecca swallowed.

'Don't do it to him. It's not fair. Whatever you think about Max, he means an awful lot to Mike. He hasn't exactly been swamped with parental love, has he? Don't try to take it from him now.'

Rebecca was stung. 'I don't need you to tell me about Mike.'

'Don't you?'

The two of them stared at each other.

'You can't make him choose,' said Emily softly. 'It's the worst thing you can do to someone. No one should be forced to give up someone they care about. Not ever.'

Rebecca had a sudden image of Emily's mother. A gentle woman with the same chestnut hair, dark shadowed eyes and hesitant smile as her daughter.

And, as always with the image, came the guilt.

She was tired of the guilt. She wanted to escape from it.

Just as sometimes she wished she could escape from Emily.

But she couldn't. They were best friends. The bond between them could not be broken. They were bound together for ever.

'You don't have to worry. I won't do that. If he's happy, then I'm happy too.'

A waitress was hovering. She signalled for the bill, then made her way to the lavatory.

Emily remained where she was.

She stared at the wall but did not see it. She was thinking of a winter's evening when she was seven years old. The evening her mother had died.

Hazy memories. Youth, and the trauma of the occasion, had smashed them into fragments: a collection of images that fell far short of a complete whole. The dazed expression on her father's face. The anxious smiles of people she barely knew and wished would go away. The gale that had been blowing all day. And the dreadful realisation that the secure world she had taken for granted was now crumbling beneath her feet.

And mixed up among them was the image of another girl. Seven years old, like herself. An exceptionally pretty girl with blonde hair and green eyes who expressed her sympathy in the robotic manner of one who had learned her lines by heart.

The girl she should have been.

There were times when she wanted to scream at the injustice of it all. But it would do no good. Fate, like history, was not concerned with fairness. Its cards fell randomly and the choice was simple. Play the hand dealt or remove yourself from the game.

The waitress approached with the bill. Emily pushed her memories to one side and reached for her purse.

Four p.m. Michael, who had been in a meeting, returned to his office to find Stuart reassuring a distressed-looking Julia.

' … then he got really stroppy and accused me of being lazy. And I'm not!'

'Don't take any notice,' said Stuart soothingly. 'Everyone knows how hard you work.'

Michael sat down. 'Is Graham giving you a hard time?'

'Not Graham,' Stuart told him. 'Jonathan Upham. He's being a right prick.'

This seemed out of character. 'How come?'

'Some new deal's just come in from one of Jack Bennett's

215

clients. The best one we've had for months, apparently. Jack told Belinda Hopkins that she could do the next one, but she's on holiday this week, and Jack's away until Friday, so Jonathan's doing groundwork in the hope that Jack will let him handle it instead. Rumour has it that only one person in our department will be offered partnership next year, and another big deal under Jonathan's belt can only help his chances.'

'So now,' continued Julia, 'he's told me to do loads of research and wants the results this evening. I told him I had urgent stuff for Graham, but he didn't want to know.'

'What's the research about?' asked Michael.

She told him and he smiled. 'Then stop panicking. I did a note on that last year.' He looked through one of his files, found the note in question and gave her the document number. 'It all turned on one case, which I'm sure hasn't been over-ruled, but you'd better check with the library. Assuming it hasn't, just print off a copy and give it to Jonathan. It's got everything he wants to know.'

Her relief was beautiful to behold. 'Thanks. I don't know what I'd do without you two.' She rushed off towards the library.

Stuart rolled his eyes. 'Business as usual.'

Laughing, Michael began to check his e-mails.

'Nick phoned,' Stuart told him. 'Wondered if we wanted a quick drink this evening. Are you up for it?'

He wondered what Rebecca would say if he accepted. Then decided that he didn't care. 'Sure.'

'Corney & Barrow at six. OK?'

He nodded, concentrating on his computer screen. In the distance he heard the sound of footsteps approaching. Quick, determined footsteps. Kate Kennedy strode into the room.

She stood in the doorway, all hairspray and gold buttons, almost blinding them with the rictus grin so beloved by those who are about to deliver bad news.

'The department precedents need updating. Someone must review them all, check which provisions are antiquated, and do the necessary redrafting.'

This was dreadful news indeed. People had been known to throw themselves off buildings rather than update the precedents. The job would take weeks, and as the work could not be charged to a client the unfortunate victim's billing figures would nose-dive, resulting in major grief from Graham and an adverse effect on the end-of-year bonus.

And it was only a few days ago that Kate had stopped Michael by the coffee point and said, with a meaningful smile, that his drafting was first class.

His heart sank. He needed this like he needed a hole in the head.

'So,' continued Kate, 'can you come and see me tomorrow morning, Stuart? We'll decide how you should go about it.'

Stuart?

Stuart's nod looked more like a shudder.

He expected Kate to leave, but she didn't. 'How are things going, Michael?' Her smile was as bright as ever. So she was going to dump something on him after all. He prayed that it wasn't another lunchtime lecture.

'Um ... fine. Incredibly busy.'

'That's what I like to hear. And well done again on Digitron. An excellent job.'

He was taken aback. Kate dished out compliments with the same regularity that a miser gave to charity.

'Thanks.' He masked his surprise.

'And what about you, Stuart? All well?'

Stuart, too depressed to speak, gave another nod.

'Good.' She made a rare joke. 'So we're all happy campers, then.'

'You can say that again,' said Stuart archly.

Kate left the room.

'Oh, fuck!' Stuart buried his head in his hands.

Michael, feeling an uncomfortable mixture of relief and guilt, tried to offer words of comfort.

Ten past six. Michael sat with Nick Randall at a window table at the Corney & Barrow wine bar in Broadgate Circle. The bar was packed with young professionals, and the air was thick with the sound of raucous laughter and bellowed orders for drinks.

Nick was a blond, delicate-looking young man in his mid-twenties, whose rather effeminate manner had not stopped him cutting a sexual swath through the female employees of Cox Stephens. He had started articles on the same day as Michael and Stuart; the three of them then progressed through the departments together, becoming friends in the process.

Nick lit a cigarette and breathed smoke through his nose. 'What's the gossip, then?'

'You tell me. You're the one who never does any work.'

Nick smiled. He worked in the commercial property department, and as Cox Stephens' reputation in this area was weak, his workload was rarely taxing. 'Not true. I'm busy at the moment. I actually did nine chargeable hours yesterday.'

'And you're still standing?'

'Barely. I had to go and lie down afterwards. But for a brief moment I knew how it felt to be a real man.'

They both laughed. Stuart, still looking fed up, arrived with a bottle of Beaujolais and three glasses. 'Nick claims he's busy,' Michael told him.

'Pigs claim they can fly.'

'It's true,' Nick insisted. 'And I have your department to thank.'

'Naturally.' Stuart began to pour the wine. 'We're not known as the engine of the firm for nothing.'

'Which one of our colleagues has rocked your world?' asked Michael.

Nick crossed himself.

'Yeah, hail Mary and all that. Now answer the question.'

'I did.'

Stuart and Michael exchanged glances.

'The man who walks with God and dates archangels.'

'Who?'

'Cox Stephens' very own Messiah. Jack Bennett.'

'Oh, right.' Michael sipped his wine. 'Very funny.'

'Who's joking?'

'He may have brought in some new clients, but that hardly makes him a Messiah.'

'It does. You owe your job to him.'

'What are you talking about?'

Nick looked about him. The bar was popular with people from the office. Once he was sure that no fellow employees were in earshot, he began to speak.

'You know about last year's accounts?'

'I know they were disappointing.'

'That was the official story. Last week I had lunch with Sarah Hill, secretary to the managing partner, and she gave me the real one.'

He waited expectantly.

'The figures weren't so much disappointing as absolutely disastrous. The rent on the new premises is crippling, the Hong Kong office is heavily in the red, and the loss of the Quickshop account is hurting much more than expected. Partnerial salaries took a major nosedive. Things were so bad that we

219

were looking at widespread redundancies in property and litigation, and there was talk of redundancies in your department too. Some of the partners on the management committee didn't even think that would be enough and were considering trying to get the firm absorbed by one of the giants.'

Stuart whistled.

'Then Jack Bennett arrives with his magic client list and suddenly things start picking up. Many of his clients had been relying on in-house lawyers to do all their legal work, but they'd expanded so fast that they couldn't cope, resulting in a vast backlog which has all come our way. You may not have noticed it so much in your department. After all, we've always been reasonably strong in mergers and acquisitions. But the workload in property is really taking off. It's the same in litigation, and in IP, and suddenly everything in the financial garden is starting to look rosy.' Nick raised his glass. 'So, three cheers for Jack.'

'Three cheers,' echoed Stuart.

'Yeah, three bloody cheers.'

Nick frowned. 'Don't you like him?'

Michael shrugged.

'He seems a nice bloke. Everyone in our group thinks so. What's the problem?'

'The man's a saint. What problem could there be?'

'Well, be careful one doesn't develop.' Nick took another drag on his cigarette. 'You should watch out. You know how confrontational you can be. The partnership will do anything to keep Jack happy. They might show you the door if Jack decides he doesn't like you.'

'He's decided that already.'

Nick looked surprised. As did Stuart. 'Jack doesn't dislike you, Mike. What makes you think he does?'

Another shrug. 'Stuff.'

'That business with Dial-a-Car? But Jack told me that you'd done a fantastic job.'

'Not that.'

'What, then?'

For a moment Michael considered telling them, then decided that it would be better not to bring his private life into the office. 'Nothing. Don't pay any attention to me.'

Nick smiled. 'We never do.'

'And just be grateful,' added Stuart, 'that you weren't the one who got lumbered with the precedents.'

That was right. He hadn't been the one.

An idea had come to him. One that seemed ridiculous but which he did not feel able to ignore.

Nick and Stuart were staring at him. 'Are you all right?' asked Nick.

'Fine.' He downed his wine and poured himself a refill.

Thursday. Noon. Rebecca stood with Clare behind the counter at Chatterton's.

The lunchtime rush was starting. Increasing numbers of people made their way to the non-fiction section. Rebecca entered an old woman's credit card through the system and waited for the printout.

'Four,' whispered Clare.

She looked up. Clare's romance with the sales rep had not worked out, but she was still eager to meet Mr Right and had started giving all men marks out of ten as they made their way down the stairs. The current target was a slim, intense-looking young man with glasses and a rucksack. He was actually rather good-looking, but Clare liked her men rugged.

The machine printed off the receipt. Rebecca gave the old woman a pen to sign with and put her cookery book into a bag.

'Ten,' hissed Clare.

'Shush.'

'Look!'

She did. A Will Carling clone in a Savile Row suit was making his way to the entertainment section.

'Don't you agree?'

'Stop it!'

The old woman was replaced by a teenage boy with lank blond hair and a Kurt Cobain T-shirt, clutching the Robert Massie biography of Nicholas and Alexandra. 'I've read this,' she told him. 'It's fantastic!'

He beamed, blissfully unaware that a few minutes earlier he had scored a meagre three. 'It's for my course,' he told her.

She entered the barcode into the system and took his money. 'Are you at UCL?'

He nodded. An elderly man with a bad leg and bottle-rim glasses made his way down the stairs. 'Zero,' whispered Clare.

She bit her lip, trying not to laugh. The boy stared at her curiously. Giving him his change she said, 'I hope you enjoy it.' Keith from the fiction section arrived to cover while she took her lunch break. She served her final customer: a rather anxious-looking young woman who was buying a book on interior design.

'Eight,' whispered Clare.

She didn't dare look up. She would only burst out laughing if she did.

'No, nine.'

Curious, she raised her head.

And saw Max.

He was standing at the bottom of the stairs, dressed in a sports jacket and linen trousers. The casually smart style that suited him so well. He saw her and began to make his way over. She watched him approach, feeling suddenly cornered.

'I was passing,' he said, 'and hoped you might join me for lunch.'

She considered making an excuse but was worried he would know she was lying.

'Certainly.' Her tone was as enthusiastic as she could make it.

'Wonderful. Is now a good time?'

She nodded. The queue of customers had eased temporarily, and she could sense Clare staring curiously at them. 'This is Max Somerton,' she explained. 'He's our landlord.' A pause. 'And friend. This is Clare. She was the one who introduced us to your last tenants.'

Max smiled at Clare. 'So it's you I have to thank for providing me with such excellent replacements.' He spoke slowly and easily, his voice as smooth as velvet. Rebecca found herself hearing it as if for the first time and realised just how seductive an instrument it could be.

And it was working on Clare. She blushed, then said flirtatiously, 'My pleasure.'

Max turned back to Rebecca. 'There's a good French restaurant in Chancery Lane. I thought we might go there.'

This didn't seem like a good idea. The last thing she wanted was a long-drawn-out meal. And this time she had a valid excuse. 'I only have an hour. It might be a bit rushed.'

'Perhaps somewhere nearer then?'

She felt relieved.

And then Clare said, 'Don't worry about time, Beck. Take as long as you want.'

'What about your break?'

'I'll grab a sandwich later. Forget about me. Have a nice time.'

'You're very kind,' Max told her, still smiling.

Again Clare blushed.

223

There was nothing for it. Rebecca fetched her bag and followed Max up the stairs.

Half an hour later they were sitting together at a table in Chez Gerard waiting for their starters.

The restaurant was crowded. Men and women in business suits occupied the tables around them. Max produced his silver cigar case. 'Do you mind?' he asked.

She shook her head.

'Are you sure? I can survive without them.'

'No, please go ahead.'

He lit one. She looked about her, watching the other diners. He followed her eyes. 'Trying to spot a captain of industry?'

'Checking whether I knew anyone. There's a law firm across the road called Denton Hall. One of Mike's college friends works there.'

'I didn't know that.'

'No reason why you should.'

'I suppose not.'

She hoped her words hadn't sounded bitchy. They weren't meant to.

Well, not really.

She found herself thinking about Mike. He had seemed pre-occupied the previous evening, but when she had questioned him he had insisted that nothing was wrong.

Out of the corner of her eye she saw a waiter approaching with a tray. She hoped he was bringing their starters, but he stopped at a nearby table. Not that it mattered. She was under no time constraints. Clare had seen to that.

Her wine glass was nearly empty. She rarely drank at lunchtime, but today she had wanted something to help her relax.

224

Max buttered a piece of bread. 'I wonder,' he said, 'if I could ask your advice about something?'

'About what?'

'Mike.'

She felt herself tense.

'His birthday is next Thursday, and I'd like to buy him a present of some sort. Nothing lavish, you understand. Just a token. I thought perhaps one of those pocket electronic organisers. What do you think?'

There was no need to think. She knew he'd hate it. He was always joking that people who used such things were so anally retentive that they couldn't even take a piss unless a specific toilet break was logged into their day planner. She would remind him that her brother Robert swore by his organiser, and then he would give her a meaningful look.

She was surprised Max would suggest such an inappropriate present. Pleased too. For a moment she was tempted to say that it was a great idea. But that would have been too obvious.

'To be honest, I don't think that would be a success.'

He looked disappointed. 'Oh, well, back to the drawing board.' He took a drag on his cigar then looked at her hesitantly. 'Do you have any suggestions?'

She nodded.

'Forgive my asking. It's just that you know him so much better than anyone.'

'Yes, I suppose I do.'

And don't you forget it.

'Well, he's just finished reading *I, Claudius* and really enjoyed it. There was a BBC series with Derek Jacobi. I'd thought about buying him the videos. Perhaps you could instead.'

'You think he'd like that?'

'I'm sure he would.'

'Then videos it will be. Thank you, Becky.'

'Pleased to help.'

They smiled at each other.

'What are you giving him?' he asked.

'A new jacket.'

'What colour?'

'Dark blue. He'll look really good in it.'

'You enjoy buying him clothes, don't you?'

'Did Mike say that?'

'Yes.'

'Well, someone's got to. If it was up to Mike, he'd spend his whole life in jeans and T-shirts.'

'He didn't mean it as a criticism,' said Max quickly. 'In fact, he said that it was wonderful how you always knew both what would suit him and what would make him feel comfortable.'

She felt embarrassed. 'I just like him to look nice.'

Again he smiled. 'It's a little more than that though, isn't it?'

'What do you mean?'

'That it's more than just being able to choose the right clothes.'

'Is it?'

'It is to Mike.'

His directness confused her. She lowered her eyes.

'It's having someone who can read him like a book. Someone who knows him better than he knows himself. Someone he can trust to get things absolutely right.'

His words struck a chord deep within her, echoing things that Michael had said himself. Things that she had always laughed off, fearful that they were uttered simply to make her feel good.

Now she knew they weren't.

She felt a warmth in the pit of her stomach. Her defensiveness faded, replaced by intense pleasure.

'That's what I want,' she said awkwardly.

She looked up. The smile remained, but a sadness had crept into the dark eyes. He took another drag on his cigar and breathed smoke into the air. 'Do you remember the suit I wore at the party you came to?'

She nodded.

'Lavinia bought it for me. She enjoyed buying me clothes.'

Rebecca remembered the glamorous creature she had met so briefly. 'I'm sure her taste was much better than mine.'

She expected him to make light of her remark, but he didn't. The sadness remained. 'Oh, it was good. Every single thing she chose suited me perfectly. But not one felt comfortable.' A sigh. 'Understandable, really. What we had was all appearances. All surfaces with no depth. There wasn't a fraction of the understanding you share with Mike.'

She was surprised at his honesty. Surprised and flattered. Unexpectedly she found herself feeling sorry for him. 'But now there's Caroline,' she said tentatively. 'Things could be different with her.'

'I hope so,' he said quietly.

The waiter arrived with their starters. Max extinguished his cigar. She tasted her soup, added a pinch of salt, then tried again. Perfect.

He was watching her closely, clearly anxious that she enjoy her food. His eyes were a mixture of warmth, concern and sadness. She realised that she had been a fool to feel threatened. Mike was hers and always would be. They belonged to each other. Only a fool would think otherwise.

As if reading her mind, he said, 'There's something very special between the two of you. Something that very few people are lucky enough to find.'

'I think so.'

'So does Mike. A light comes into his eyes when he talks about you. I've seen it in other people when they speak about

227

the person they love, but never as brightly as it shines in his. His whole world revolves around you. If you were to leave him, it would fall to pieces.'

She smiled. 'I'm not going anywhere.'

'I'm glad he's found you. He deserves something magical after all he's been through. Losing his mother. The foster parents. The Children's Home.' Another sigh. 'That terrible business with the Harringtons.'

Her smile began to crumble.

'Poor boy. How traumatic that must have been for him. Though you hardly need me to tell you that.'

Who are the Harringtons? What is he talking about?

'No one should have to go through something like that. It isn't right. But at least it's in the past now. You have each other, and that's all that matters.' He speared a snail, its surface shiny with garlic butter. Then he frowned. 'But you're not touching your soup. Is it not good?'

She didn't answer.

'Please say if there is something wrong with it. I can send it back.'

She shook her head.

'It's no problem. It's not as if we're under time constraints. We can take as long as we want.'

And that was right. They could sit there all afternoon, making meaningless small talk while she tortured herself with thoughts of what other aspects of his past Michael had chosen to share with someone other than herself.

'It's fine.' She took another mouthful. The salt granules scraped her throat like sandpaper.

'Well, now, let's talk of happier things. Richard Markham wants to meet you. He's out of the country this week, but we can set something up on his return. Would that be acceptable?'

She nodded.

228

'Good.'

He refilled her glass. She continued with her soup but had lost her appetite, and the bowl the waiter collected was nearly as full as the one he had brought.

Half past eight in the evening. Rebecca heard Michael letting himself into the flat.

She stood in the living room. The bolognese she had planned for supper remained in the fridge. There were things that needed to be discussed before they ate.

The evening air was sticky. He stood in the hall, his tie slack around his neck, wiping sweat from his forehead.

'Who were the Harringtons?' she asked.

'Who?'

'Don't play dumb with me. I want to know who they were.'

He put down his briefcase and walked into the room. 'What's going on? Why are you so uptight?'

'Max took me out to lunch today. We were discussing your childhood. He started talking about these people called the Harringtons, going on about what a terrible business it was and how traumatic it must have been for you, assuming, quite naturally, that I'd know exactly what he was talking about. The only problem was that I didn't have the first clue, and that's why I want to know who they were!'

Her voice was becoming shrill. She took a deep breath, trying to calm herself.

He began to look uncomfortable. 'It's no big deal ...'

'Who were they, Mike?'

'Just some people.'

'What people?'

'Foster parents. I was placed with them when I was about six.'

'And what was so terrible about that? Were they abusive?'

His eyes widened. 'No, not at all.'

'So why the big trauma?'

He didn't answer.

'Well?'

'They were the reason I ended up in the Home.'

'Why? What happened?'

He rubbed the back of his neck with his hand. 'I'd already been with half a dozen foster families by the time I was placed with them. I was a disruptive kid, so I never lasted anywhere for long. In each place there'd always been loads of other children all fighting for attention. The Harringtons didn't have any children of their own, and I was the first one they'd ever fostered. They made a fuss of me, made me feel special and wanted.

'After I'd been with them a couple of months they fostered another boy. I think his name was Nigel. He was about my age, but much quieter and far better behaved. They made a huge fuss of him, too, and I was jealous. I used to fight with him all the time. I didn't want to share them with anyone.

'Then one day a social worker came to see me. She said that the Harringtons wanted to adopt Nigel, but they didn't want to adopt me because they didn't think they could cope with my behaviour. So, instead, I was being moved on to yet another foster family.' He sighed. 'It was ironic, really. I'd been disruptive before, but that was nothing compared with how I became after that. I was so angry all the time that it made me unmanageable. In the end no foster parents would touch me, so they dumped me in the Home.'

He paused. Exhaled. 'So, now you know about the Harringtons.'

His smile was appeasing. She wanted to respond. She could only guess at how painful such a rejection must have been.

But all she could think of was how he had chosen to share his pain with someone else.

'So why did I have to find out about them from Max?'

His smile faded. 'Oh, for God's sake!'

'Why?'

'It was nearly twenty years ago. There's been a lot of water under the bridge since then. I haven't even thought about them for ages.'

'It's hardly been ages. Max has only been on the scene a matter of weeks, and already he could go on *Mastermind* and pick them as his special subject.'

'I didn't set out to tell him.'

'So how did he find out, then? ESP?'

'No. I just meant that it wasn't a conscious decision. We were just talking one time—'

'Having one of those wonderful conversations where he never actually says anything.'

He looked exasperated. 'If you must know, he was asking me how much of my life I could remember before the Home. I'd been talking for ages and suddenly it all came back. What had happened. How it had felt. I suppose I'd buried it before. The way you do with memories that are painful.'

She gave a harsh laugh. 'How fortunate Saint Max was on hand to bless the exhumation.'

'Well, at least it wasn't you!'

She felt as if she had been slapped.

His face was black with fury. 'You're unbelievable! I tell you about something that hurt me more than you can imagine, and all you can do is have a tantrum because you weren't the first to know!'

'I'm not having a tantrum!'

'Just listen to yourself! Me! Me! Me! Fuck everyone else's feelings! The only thing that matters is that the spotlight remains totally focused on you!'

'That's not true!'

'Like hell it's not!'

She swallowed. Her throat felt raw. Too much salt at lunchtime, perhaps.

Silence hung over them, like a storm cloud waiting to explode.

'I didn't mean that,' he said eventually.

He sounded sincere. She wanted to believe him, even though she knew it had been deserved.

She felt dirty with shame.

'I'm sorry, Mike. I shouldn't have acted the way I did. I'm not surprised you'd want to forget an experience like that. I'm only sorry you had to go through it at all.'

He shrugged. 'Like I said, it was nearly twenty years ago.'

'It must still hurt, though.'

'No.'

'I *do* care. You must know that.'

A nod.

'I wish I could take the pain away. I'd give anything to be able to make it all disappear.'

She stopped. In her head the words had sounded strong, but now they were spoken she could see them for the platitudes they were.

She waited for a response, but none was offered.

'I'm sorry, Mike. Really I am.'

'It's not a competition, Beck,' he said suddenly. 'You'll always come first. You know that, don't you?'

'Yes.'

She risked a smile. Slowly he responded: a half-hearted gesture that didn't quite reach his eyes. But at least it showed willing.

'Why don't you go and get changed? I'll make supper.'

'OK.'

He left the room. She remained where she was, wishing that she could wipe the conversation away.

But she couldn't. And she only had herself to blame.
I am not selfish. I am a good person. I am. I am.
I know I am.
She went to make the supper that neither of them wanted.

FIVE

Friday morning. Half past ten. Michael sat at his desk, staring into space.

A distribution agreement lay before him. He was supposed to be reviewing it for a client but was unable to concentrate. All he could think about was his argument with Rebecca.

He wished he hadn't lost his temper. He knew his words had hurt her, and the knowledge made him feel ashamed. She was the last person in the world he wanted to hurt.

And yet another part of him was glad that he had done so. A darker part that resented her self-absorption and had relished the chance to dent her complacency.

It was an unpleasant mix, and one that did not make for a productive state of mind.

His telephone rang. Letting the call go through to Kim, he looked down at the agreement, seeing nothing but rows of black lines. Eventually his eyes stopped focusing, the lines merging into each other like a dark stain spreading across the white of the page.

'Mike.'

He looked up. Kim stood in the doorway.

'That was Sonia on the phone.'

His mind was still elsewhere. 'Who?'

'Sonia. Jack Bennett's secretary. Jack wants to see you right now.'

His thoughts of Rebecca faded, replaced by disquiet. 'Why?'

'Don't know. She just said you should haul your arse into his room pronto.'

He made his way towards Jack's office. Jack, talking on the telephone, gestured to a chair in front of his desk. He sat down and looked about him. The office was incredibly tidy. He knew that Jack had a virtual phobia about mess: that he found it impossible to work unless everything around him was in a state of perfect order.

Kim had told him that. She had heard it from Sonia.

But then it was hardly classified information.

Jack put the phone down. 'Thanks for coming so quickly.'

'Sonia said it was urgent.'

'Not really.' Jack looked concerned. 'Were you in the middle of something?'

'Nothing important.'

'Good.' Jack smiled. Michael did likewise. In the corridor outside, Graham Fletcher bellowed for his secretary.

He looked at a framed photograph on Jack's desk. A pretty, blonde woman sat on a garden swing with two small boys who looked just like her. Jack's wife Liz and their sons Ben and Sam.

Sam was virtually deaf in one ear. Jack had had a brief affair during the pregnancy, and though not a religious man had always felt that Sam's condition was some sort of punishment for his infidelity.

Liz had taken Jack's betrayal very hard. Jack adored his wife and was terrified of losing her, but he had a high sex drive, and their love life had been sporadic since Sam's birth. Jack's constant dread was that sheer frustration might force him to stray again and so risk losing Liz for good.

Max had told him that.

And he had told him some other stuff.

His knowledge made him feel guilty. As if he were a voyeur of someone else's inner life.

'A new deal's just come in,' Jack told him. 'Another software company buying up a rival. Jonathan Upham's done some background research.'

Michael nodded. Clearly he was going to be asked to help with the donkey-work. He hoped Jack gave the deal to Jonathan, as he couldn't stand Belinda Hopkins.

'I need someone good to run with it, and you're the man.'

'Me?'

'Yes. If you want to, that is.'

Momentarily he was lost for words.

'Do you?'

'What about Belinda? I thought she was getting your next deal.'

Jack waved a hand dismissively. 'Don't worry about her. There'll be other deals. But this is a good one, which will help you build on the knowledge of the industry you gained on Digitron.'

Michael nodded.

'You need to develop your experience of the computer industry. It's the future, for this firm certainly. And as one of our rising stars, it's where your practice should be focused.'

'A rising star?'

Jack nodded. 'That's how we see you. There's a great future here for you, Michael.' He stopped. Then added, deliberately, 'But I'm sure you know that already.'

Michael felt embarrassed. He lowered his eyes.

And found himself remembering the idea that had come to him over drinks with Nick and Stuart. The idea that had seemed ridiculous, but which he had not felt able to dismiss.

Because it had been true.

'Yes, this deal will be excellent experience,' continued Jack. 'And it should be fun too. Which is good. After all, we want you to be happy in your work.'

It was true. He was sure of it. But there was one way to be certain.

He looked up. 'I am happy in my work,' he said politely.

Jack beamed. 'Glad to hear it.'

'Except for one thing.'

The eyes widened slightly. 'And what's that?'

'I do a lot of work for Vadex. They're one of Jeff Speakman's clients. It's really tedious stuff, just revamping agreements and doing company admin. I think it's time somebody else got lumbered.' He paused. 'Don't you?'

Jack hesitated. But only for a moment.

'That sounds fair enough. Leave it with me.'

And that was when he knew for sure.

He stared at Jack. The Messiah. The saviour of the firm. The man with the magic list of clients.

Most of whom had been given to him by Max.

And what could be given could also be taken away.

It all made sense now. Why Kate Kennedy hadn't lumbered him with the precedents. Why Graham Fletcher hadn't forced him to go to Hull. Why some of the other partners seemed just a little bit friendlier than they had been before.

Because they wanted to keep him happy. For if he wasn't, he might just start whispering grievances into the ear of someone who had the power to do the firm an immeasurable amount of harm should the inclination arise.

He felt disturbed that others would think him capable of

such behaviour. He would never try to make trouble in that way.

And even if he did, Max wouldn't act on his complaints. *Would he?*

He took a deep breath then let the air out slowly.

'Look, Jack, I'm really pleased you've asked me, but I think Belinda should do this deal.'

'Why? Do you feel out of your depth?'

'No.'

'Good, because you're more than capable. Anyway, I'd be supervising, and you could come to me with the slightest problem.'

He shook his head. 'If I do this deal it might cause bad feeling, and I wouldn't want that. There'll be other deals, as you said. Perhaps I could do one of those.'

'Is that what you'd prefer?'

He nodded.

'Very well, then.'

'Thanks, Jack.'

'No problem.'

Again he found himself looking at the photograph of Jack's family. Just an ordinary family with its chest full of skeletons.

He sensed Jack's eyes on him and smiled awkwardly. Jack did the same.

He's wondering what Max has told me. He's wondering how much I know.

'Thanks,' he said again.

'I should probably be thanking you. Belinda on the warpath is a frightening prospect.'

'But nothing a stake and a clove of garlic couldn't solve.'

They both laughed. To an outside observer they were just two colleagues sharing a joke. A month ago they would have been. But things were different now.

'And forget what I said about Vadex. I wouldn't want to lumber someone else.'

'OK.'

He rose to his feet and made for the door.

'Michael.'

He turned.

'Are you seeing Max soon?'

'Yes.'

'Give him my best, won't you?'

'Of course.'

Kate Kennedy stood in the corridor, talking to one of the partners from litigation. She gave him a friendly smile. Kate, who never bothered to acknowledge anyone unless she needed them to do something.

He went to the coffee point to get some water. Julia stood there, gossiping with another of the trainees. She smiled in welcome. Gratefully he joined in their conversation.

On Sunday Rebecca's brother Robert held his barbecue.

Robert lived in a terraced house on a street facing Clapham Common. Michael and Rebecca left the tube at Clapham South and walked the final part of their journey.

It was a still, oppressive summer afternoon. There hadn't been a drop of rain for days, and the city lay buried under a blanket of heat. The common was full of people exercising their dogs, chasing frisbees or lying on the grass reading Sunday papers and soaking up the sun.

They moved slowly through the humid air. There was little conversation. The tension from their row on Thursday night had yet to disappear. Rebecca looked up at the sky and said that she thought the weather would break that evening. Michael nodded half-heartedly. His thoughts lay elsewhere.

He was troubled by the situation at work and wished there

was someone with whom he could share his concerns. Rebecca would have been the obvious choice, but Max was so sensitive a subject that he had not felt able to say anything. This had made him feel angry, which had done little to ease the friction between them.

The other choice was Max himself. The two of them were meeting the following evening for a swim at a private club in Mayfair, followed by dinner. Rebecca had raised no objection to the arrangement, but he knew she wasn't happy about it and this made him angry too.

They reached Robert's house. Rebecca rang the bell. Robert answered the door, wearing baggy shorts, a Hawaiian shirt and wrap-around shades. The very sight of him made Michael feel sick. He wished he hadn't agreed to come, but it was too late to escape now.

Rebecca kissed her brother's cheek and handed him the bottle of wine she was carrying. 'How's it going?' she asked.

'Fine. Mostly work people at the moment, but more college friends should be arriving soon.'

'Thanks for the invitation,' said Michael politely.

Robert smiled maliciously. 'Well, I did hesitate at first. After all, who could ever forget the last family party you attended? But Becky assures me that you're no longer the social liability you once were.'

'Robert!' exclaimed Rebecca.

'I'm only joking. You know I'm only joking, don't you, Mikey?'

Normally Michael would have let it go. That was what Rebecca would want him to do. But this was not a normal day.

'Sure I do,' he said affably. 'And even if I do revert to type and kick someone's arse, it's comforting to know that you'll be on hand to lick it better.'

Rebecca looked horrified. He smiled at her. 'Relax. We're

just joking with each other. We both love a good joke. Isn't that right, Rob Rob?'

Robert's own smile vanished. Clearly he had not expected retaliation and had no more prepared put-downs. 'Absolutely,' he said sullenly.

There were footsteps behind them. More guests arriving. 'Why don't we just go through?' suggested Rebecca.

Robert nodded. And then said: 'One thing, Beck. Emily's here. Mum called last night and insisted I invite her.'

Rebecca looked anxious. 'Is David coming?'

'No. He's away this weekend.'

'Well, we'll keep an eye on her.'

'Yeah, we'll make sure she feels welcome,' added Michael meaningfully.

'What's got into you?' demanded Rebecca as they made their way through the house.

'You need to ask?'

She frowned. 'I don't understand you sometimes.'

'That's obvious.'

She looked hurt. He felt ashamed. But not enough to apologise.

They followed the smell of smoke and barbecue sauce out into the tiny garden. About a dozen people in their twenties and thirties stood in small groups, each holding beer bottles or wine glasses. The sound of Oasis echoed from a portable stereo balanced on a chair.

Once they had food, they went to join some colleagues of Robert's whom Rebecca knew. Michael spotted Emily, wearing a pale blue, long-sleeved summer dress that would have looked old-fashioned on someone else but which perfectly suited her Pre-Raphaelite elegance. She was sipping wine and listening to a solemn-looking woman talk about the state of the London property market. Emily nodded attentively, but he could tell she was bored. Their eyes met. She looked pleased to see him. He was pleased to see her too.

Time passed. The sun continued its journey across the sky. Shadows started to creep across the grass, and, as more guests arrived, the party expanded into the house. Michael, still in the garden, saw Emily standing alone at the drinks table. 'I'll go,' he told Rebecca, then made his way over.

'Enjoying yourself?' he asked.

'Not terribly.'

'Shame on you. I'm having a wonderful time.'

'Really?'

'Of course. The sun is warm, so is the alcohol, and so is our host. What more could I want?'

She laughed softly. It was an attractive sound, and one that he heard too rarely. 'Let me pour you some warm wine,' he said, filling both their glasses.

'I called you on Friday,' she told him.

'Sorry I didn't call you back. Bad day.'

She didn't ask questions, just looked at him with a mixture of sympathy and concern. Briefly he considered telling her what had happened. But Rebecca was only feet away, and he felt inhibited.

'Nothing I couldn't handle, though,' he added.

He sipped his wine. It tasted of apples. 'So why did you call? Did you have some news?'

She looked uncomfortable. 'What news should I have?'

'You know what news.'

'I haven't phoned him yet. But I will. Tonight, maybe.'

'Do it. Call me tomorrow and let me know what happened. Call me, even if he's not there.'

'It may be another bad day.'

'Doesn't matter if it is. I'm sorry about Friday, Em. Things just got a bit weird. It wasn't that I didn't care.'

242

Slowly a smile crept across her face, like sunshine after rain. He felt a sudden wave of affection for her. She, more than anyone else, brought out the best in him.

Her gaze drifted over his shoulder. Suddenly her eyes widened.

He turned. Two men in their mid-twenties had just entered the garden from the kitchen. Both were tall. One was blond, slight and wearing a baseball cap; the other was dark and powerfully built, with heavy features, small eyes and a bad-tempered mouth.

'The dark one's David,' whispered Emily.

David was a friend of Robert who worked in an insurance company. At the start of the year he had taken Emily out a couple of times, insisting on paying for everything. After their second outing he had taken her home where, the worse for drink, he had made it clear that he wanted to stay the night. When Emily tried to turn him down he had become belliger-ent, reminding her of all the money he had spent on her. When this approach didn't work either he had announced that he would leave only after a goodnight kiss and promptly grabbed her. At this point, a frightened Emily had scratched his face, then become hysterical, and it had taken all of David's powers of persuasion to stop her calling the police. The two of them had not seen each other since that evening.

Some people, most notably Robert, felt that Emily had over-reacted. But Michael was not one of them, and as he watched David share a joke with his companion he felt his hackles rise.

Rebecca appeared beside him. 'I'm sorry,' she told Emily. 'He's not supposed to be here. Do you want to go inside?'

'I'm fine here, really.'

'That's right,' agreed Michael. 'Don't let that creep spoil your afternoon.'

Rebecca began to ask Emily about work. Michael watched

243

David whisper something to his companion, who began to stare at Emily. They moved through the other guests, making their way towards the bar. Both moved unsteadily. Clearly they had already had a bit to drink.

He felt Rebecca's eyes on him. *Don't start anything*, they said. *Just let it go*.

David and his friend reached the bar. David whispered something else and the friend began to snigger. Michael saw Emily flinch and told himself to keep calm. In the background, Peter Gabriel played over the buzz of half a dozen conversations and the distant sound of traffic.

David opened a bottle of beer. The friend whispered something. David nudged him and the friend stumbled, bumping into Michael. 'Sorry,' he blurted out, then sniggered again.

Rebecca watched him apprehensively. He gave her a reassuring smile, not wanting trouble any more than she did.

'Doesn't matter,' he replied.

'So kind,' said the friend. His tone was provocative. Michael chose to ignore it. Beside him Emily was telling Rebecca about a new author the agency had just signed up. There was a tremor in her voice. He tried to ignore that too.

And then David said, 'Careful, Al. Get within five feet and she'll scream rape.'

Michael's good intentions vanished. He put down his drink. 'Are you trying to be funny?'

'Mike!' hissed Rebecca.

'What's it to you?' David asked him, his expression an aggressive sneer.

'Yeah, what's it to you?' echoed Al.

'Keep out of this,' Michael told him.

'Hey, what a tough guy.' Al began to prod Michael's chest with his finger.

Michael laughed. Al looked confused. Michael reached

244

down, grabbed Al's balls and gave them a hard squeeze. Al squealed, his legs collapsing beneath him. Michael shoved him out of the way and faced up to David.

'Well? Are you trying to be funny? Because you're not. The only thing funny about you is how laughably inadequate you are.'

'Mike!' Rebecca again. He ignored her, the blood pounding in his head. Slowly he breathed through his nose, trying to calm himself.

David's piggy eyes blazed with menace. 'You shouldn't have said that.' He was two stone heavier than Michael, but his power was dulled by alcohol. Michael spread his feet wide in readiness for the impending physical confrontation.

'Really? What are you going to do about it? Slap me around, the way you did Emily? Don't I need to be a girl for you to do that?'

David threw a punch at Michael's head. Michael, his balance secure, dodged it, then slammed his fist twice into David's kidneys. David roared, then doubled over in pain. Michael pulled his arm back, ready to strike again.

'Mike! Stop it now!'

Rebecca grabbed his arm, her face a study in mortification. Everyone else was staring at him, including Robert, who stood in the doorway of the kitchen, leaning against the frame, his arms folded.

And a huge smile on his face.

'We're leaving,' Rebecca told Michael. Still holding his arm, she propelled him towards the door. Emily followed them.

Robert led them through the house into an empty room then shut the door behind him.

'I'm so sorry, Em,' he said. 'I didn't invite David. I don't know what he's doing here.'

'Liar!' shouted Michael. 'You planned this all along!'

'That's not true.' Robert turned to Emily. 'You don't believe that, surely?'

For a moment Emily just stared at Robert with eyes that gave nothing away.

Then slowly she shook her head.

Robert turned back to Michael. 'You should stop throwing accusations about. It just makes you look stupid.'

Michael's blood was still up. 'Why don't you make me?'

'Mike, stop it, please!' Rebecca sounded desperate.

'Yes, do,' agreed Robert. 'Haven't you upset Emily enough?'

'*I* haven't upset her.'

'You've just broadcast her private business to the whole party. I'd be pretty upset if I were her.'

His fury began to dissipate, replaced by shame. 'I'm sorry, Em,' he said awkwardly.

'There's no need,' she told him.

'I just hope it won't spoil the rest of the party for you,' said Robert.

'I think it would be best if I left.'

'Well, I don't blame you after the exploits of Rambo here. I'll see you to the door.'

Emily moved past Michael. 'I'm sorry, Em,' he said again. She didn't reply.

But as she reached the door she turned, fleetingly, mouthed the word 'thanks', and gave him a grateful smile.

'Why did you have to get violent?' demanded Rebecca once they were alone.

'He provoked me.'

'You shouldn't have let him. Violence achieves nothing except to make you look a complete thug.'

'David's the thug. At least I don't get my thrills from intimidating women.'

She looked despairing.

Robert re-entered the room. 'Poor Emily. She really didn't need that.'

'That's enough, Robert,' said Rebecca forcefully. 'All this phoney concern. You don't fool me.'

Robert adopted a hurt expression. 'What a thing to say. And you my own dear sister.'

'You invited him on purpose. It was a vicious thing to do! How do you think Emily felt?'

'Who cares how she felt?'

'You should.'

'Well, I don't.' He paused. 'And neither do you.'

'That's not true!'

'Cut the crap, Beck. This is me, remember? If anyone's being phoney here it's you. Have you forgotten what it was like when we were kids, with little Miss Ghost of Christmas Past hanging around like a bad smell? The only reason we ever tolerated her was to keep Mum off our backs.'

'She's my friend!'

'You only see her out of guilt. What sort of friendship is that?'

'I don't feel guilty!'

'Yes, you do, and it's stupid. I don't, so why should you?' Robert snorted. 'Sometimes I think you must get off on playing the martyr.'

'Maybe she does,' Michael told him. 'But it's better than getting off through causing pain.'

'I think we should go,' said Rebecca quickly.

He nodded.

'That temper's a real worry, isn't it?' said Robert slyly.

'You don't need to worry about my temper.'

'Oh, but I do. After all, there's my sister's safety to consider.'

'I'm not in any danger,' said Rebecca.

'Aren't you? Have you forgotten what happened at Dad's

party? Imagine if you'd been on the receiving end of that.'

'She never would be,' insisted Michael.

'And anyway,' added Rebecca, 'you engineered that. Just like you engineered things today.'

A mischievous light came into Robert's eyes. 'You really must learn to keep it under wraps,' he told Michael. 'To get anywhere in business you need a cool head.'

Michael smiled. 'Thanks, but I'm not so desperate that I need career advice from you.'

The light remained. 'Oh, but it's not from me. It's from Max. He told me that over lunch, and if anyone should know about what it takes to succeed in business, then he should.'

Michael's smile faded. He couldn't believe what he had just heard.

'You had lunch?'

Robert nodded. 'On Friday. He phoned me in the morning, then took me to some fancy Thai restaurant. Very near your office, actually. We were there for hours and had a great time. He wanted to know all about my partnership chances and said he'd try to push some clients my way. We're having lunch again next week to talk about it some more.'

The sense of betrayal was like a kick in the groin. Max knew how much he hated Robert.

He stared at the ground, not trusting himself to speak.

'We're leaving right now,' announced Rebecca. Her voice was harsh and demanding.

He followed her out of the room.

Twenty minutes later they sat side by side in a crowded tube compartment, the air stale and thick with heat. Michael was dripping with perspiration, his clothes sticking to his skin. Normally he hated to feel so uncomfortable, but this time he didn't care. His head was too full of Robert's revelation.

'Why did they have lunch together?' he asked for the third time.

Rebecca said nothing.

'It doesn't make sense. They don't know each other.'

'They do now,' said Rebecca. Her voice was cold.

They stopped at a station. Two more passengers boarded, and the train began to move again. The whirring, clunking sound of the engine filled the compartment.

'But they didn't know each other before. Why would Max phone him up like that?'

'How would I know?'

'It can't have been much fun. Robert may have said it was, but I don't believe him. They don't have anything in common. Robert just isn't the sort of person Max would like.'

Rebecca exhaled.

The train stopped in a tunnel. Now their voices were the only sound.

'What do you think? Can you see Robert getting on with Max?'

'Will you shut up!'

Michael jumped. As did the other passengers.

Rebecca's face was crimson.

'Max! Max! Max! He's all you talk about these days. You may think the sun shines out of his backside, but I don't and I'm sick of hearing his name. I know he's been good to us, and I know I should be grateful, but I can't stand the way he keeps forcing himself into our lives! I wish he'd bugger off back to Budapest and leave us alone!'

All the other passengers stared hard at their books, their shoes or the advertisements on the wall. One teenage boy was trying not to giggle. Flushing, Rebecca lowered her head.

Michael sat and watched her. She seemed like a stranger suddenly; someone he was seeing for the first time.

A single thought came into his head. A dark, disturbing thought.

How well do I really know this person?

They made the rest of their journey in silence.

Nine o'clock that evening. The traffic, so loud on Streatham High Road, was little more than a whisper by the time it reached the house where Emily sat alone.

It was an Edwardian semi-detached in a quiet side road. Once it had housed a single family; now it was divided into six flats, one of which belonged to Emily.

The flat had no hall. The front door opened on to a living room, off from which lay a small kitchen, bathroom and bedroom.

Emily sat on a sofa in the living room, the telephone clasped in her hand. It was growing dark now, but she had not put on a light. She stared out of the open window, over the backs of the neighbouring houses, watching the night descend.

Slowly she dialled the number and put the phone to her ear, her finger hovering over the disconnect button in case anyone should answer. It rang six times, then stopped. Her finger tensed, but she heard nothing except the comforting hiss of the answering machine, followed by a short message spoken in a man's voice. A soft, gentle voice that cut at her heart like a razor. A reminder of what her life had once been, what it was now, and of everything she had lost on the way.

She put down the receiver and ran a hand through her hair. Long, thick and luxuriant. Her mother's hair. She was her mother's daughter. People had been telling her that all her life, offering it as if it were a source of consolation rather than a reminder that this was a woman whom she would only ever see clearly in her dreams.

Her eyes wandered over the room. It was simply furnished:

cheap furniture, dull grey carpet, white walls. It was sparse, but it was hers. A place to which only she had the key. A place where her secrets could remain hidden. A place where she need not live in constant fear of discovery, derision and scorn. She had dreamed of such a place since childhood, and after all she had lived through it was comforting to know that some dreams could still come true.

But now she had realised that it was not what she had wanted after all. For though the flat was tiny, there were times when she would sit here alone and feel as if she were in a great cathedral. Somewhere that was all space and shadow, in need of another human presence in order to be filled.

Thoreau had written that many men lived lives of quiet desperation. To her it felt more like a dull resignation. She had been alone since she was seven years old. She was used to being alone, or at least that was what she told herself. But sometimes the sense of emptiness was like a cancer inside her, consuming her spirit, devouring her will to live.

She heard noise overhead. Her upstairs neighbours were entertaining. She stared up into the darkness and felt ill with the need for contact. Someone who belonged to her and to whom she could belong. *You are mine and I am yours. Our bond is as old as time and can never be broken.*

Again she dialled the number. Again the message played. She listened to it over and over, while watching the last drops of colour drip out of the sky.

SIX

Monday morning. Quarter to twelve. Rebecca, who was working a late shift, walked along the Strand towards Chatterton's bookshop.

She had come from West Hampstead. Susie, a school friend who worked in a merchant bank, had just been sent to Madrid for a couple of months and had asked Rebecca to keep an eye on her flat while she was away.

It was a beautiful July day. People moved slowly, enjoying the sun. Rebecca was not one of them. She had other things on her mind.

Like Robert's lunch with Max.

She had been able to think of nothing else since the barbecue. She couldn't stand the idea of Max befriending her brother. It was bad enough that he had intruded into her relationship with Michael. Was he going to intrude into her relationship with her family too?

She didn't want to feel like this. Career success meant a great deal to Robert, and because she loved him she wanted him to achieve his goals. Max was in a position to help him do so. She should have felt gratitude rather than this unsettling mixture of jealousy, resentment and suspicion.

Entering the shop, she made her way downstairs, heading towards the cloakroom at the back of the store.

'Becky!'

Clare was hurrying towards her, a huge smile spread across her face.

'What is it?'

'Come and see.'

She followed Clare into the office. It was piled high with boxes of new stock that had yet to be unpacked and dozens of advance readers left by enthusiastic sales reps. In the corner was a table. On it stood a computer.

And beside it lay an enormous bouquet of white lilies.

Lilies were her favourite flowers. Once, after she and Michael had had a particularly heated argument, he had sent her a similar bouquet, with a note that said how sorry he was and how much he loved her.

That had been four months ago. There had been no real arguments since then. Until now.

She felt a warmth in the pit of her stomach. 'They're beautiful.'

'And must have cost a fortune,' Clare observed.

'He shouldn't have been so extravagant.'

'You don't seem surprised.'

She felt herself blushing. 'I am a little.'

'Well, not as much as me. God, I couldn't believe it.' Clare blushed too. 'You don't think he fancies me, do you?'

'Who?'

'Mr Somerton. The note just said "With thanks again for my new tenants", but it's such a lavish bouquet that I couldn't help wondering.'

'Max sent these to you?'

Clare nodded. 'I'm sure he doesn't. Probably way out of my league, anyway. But his card was attached to the note, so it's not impossible. Should I phone him?'

Rebecca shook her head. Her head began to pound.

'I think I should. Just to thank him.'

'Don't.'

'But he must want me to. Why else would he attach the card?' Clare giggled like a schoolgirl in the throes of a first crush. 'He may be older than me but he's got the sexiest voice I've ever heard.'

The pounding was intensifying. She felt pressure building behind her eyes.

'I thought about him all afternoon when he took you out and kept wishing it was me.' Another giggle. 'I *am* going to call. You never know, one day it might be.'

'I said don't!'

Clare jumped.

'They're just flowers. They don't mean anything. Trust me, you're not his type at all, and if you phone him you're just going to look stupid.'

Clare paled, her former brightness now blanketed by hurt. 'I see.'

Rebecca felt ashamed. Clare was a good friend, and did not deserve to be spoken to like that.

Even if she had been the one who had found them the flat.

'I'm sorry. I didn't mean that the way it sounded. But he's already got a girlfriend, and I don't want you getting your hopes up.'

Clare nodded. The look of hurt remained. 'Well, it was an enjoyable daydream while it lasted,' she said with quiet dignity. 'I'd better get back before Keith's swamped.' She left the office.

Rebecca stared at the floor, hating herself.

And hating Max even more.

But though she hated him, she could not escape him. Not when he found it so easy to infiltrate every aspect of her life.

She looked at the flowers. Though still in their wrapping, their scent permeated the office, filling her nostrils, making her feel that she would choke.

The Apennine Club was situated in a tall, grey building in Berkeley Square.

It was a private members' club with bedrooms, a restaurant and a bar. The staff, all of whom seemed older than God, carried out their duties lethargically but with exquisite good manners. Most of its members were foreign businessmen who preferred its old-world charm to the impersonal efficiency of a hotel. Max had joined twenty years ago, simply to have access to a swimming pool near his office. Though he had long since abandoned any ties to the area, he had developed an affection for the club, and so kept up his membership.

The swimming pool was in the basement: all stone and marble, like a room in a Roman villa. At the bottom of the pool a mosaic showed dolphins leaping through waves. Michael, sitting at its edge, tried to count them, but the motion of other swimmers distorted the image.

Max continued to plough through the water, his stroke easy and powerful. Michael felt lazy and unfit, the way he always did when he came swimming. He would start with so much enthusiasm, shooting past everyone, burning up his energy so that he was forced to stop and watch older men outdistance him, just as Max was doing now.

He shivered. There was little heating in the basement, and drops of water cooled against his skin. Max reached the side and stared up at him. 'Why aren't you swimming?'

'Had enough.'

'Get back in. I'll race you over two lengths.'

He shook his head.

'Not in the mood?'

'No.'

'Hardly surprising.'

'What's that supposed to mean?'

'You've been in a foul temper since we got here. What's up with you?'

It would have been easy to explain, but he wanted an unsolicited admission of wrongdoing. It was childish, but it was how he felt.

He shrugged.

'Come on. Just two lengths. Then we can talk about what's on your mind.'

Reluctantly he slipped back into the cold water, stubbing his toe as he did so. Wincing, he cursed under his breath.

'Ready?' Max asked.

'Yes.'

'Is ten seconds enough?'

'For what?'

'Your head start.'

'I don't need a head start.'

Max smiled provocatively. 'Think you can beat me without one?'

'Easily.'

'We'll go on three, then. You count.'

He looked down at the far end of the pool and felt a sudden need to win. Taking a deep breath he steeled himself. 'One. Two. Three!'

He kicked off hard, swimming a few yards underwater before surfacing and launching into a crawl. Quickly he found his rhythm, breathing on every fourth stroke, moving fast, leaving Max behind.

On finishing the first length, he turned in a somersault. He moved too quickly, the blood rushing to his head so that he ended up dizzy and disorientated. Again he tried to find his rhythm, but he had swallowed a mouthful of water and felt sick. He floundered, losing speed, watching Max cruise towards the finish line while drifting in behind, feeling angry and humiliated.

'You should have taken that head start,' observed Max, who was barely out of breath.

'I made a mess of the turn.'

The same provocative smile. 'That really stung, didn't it? You shouldn't rise, Mike. It's just gamesmanship. If you rise you lose your focus, and that makes you vulnerable.' Max gave him an affectionate smile. 'What am I going to do with you, eh? You get provoked too easily. But you know that already.'

He did. Robert had proved it the day before.

'I don't need a bloody lecture, OK?'

Max whistled softly. 'OK. I'm off to get changed. Stay here if you want.'

It was tempting, but he still wanted that apology. He climbed out of the pool.

The changing rooms were nearly empty. Just a couple of elderly men, stowing their clothes in lockers before heading for the pool. Michael sat, surrounded by the smell of sweat and dirty towels, trying to fasten his cufflinks.

'You should do more exercise,' said Max, who was already dressed and ready to leave.

'Is that a fact?'

'You're rising again. Relax. It's not a criticism.'

'You know the hours I work.'

'You should still find the time. It's true what they say. A healthy body really does make a healthy mind.'

'Is that another gem you shared with Robert?'

'So that's the reason for your mood.'

He shrugged. The cufflink refused to go through the hole.

'Should I have discussed it with you first?'

'I don't care. It's your life.'

Max sighed. 'Oh Michael ...'

'Oh Michael, nothing! How do you think I felt when I found out?' As he spoke he was startled by the petulance in his voice. The same petulance he sometimes heard in Rebecca when she argued with her parents, prompted by frustration that though she was an adult they could still make her feel like a child. He had never thought to hear it in himself.

'Why don't you tell me?' asked Max, sitting down on a bench opposite.

'Can't you guess?'

'Would I ask if I did?'

He fastened the first cufflink and turned his attention to the second. 'You know how much I hate him.'

'I also know that he's Becky's brother. I'm very fond of her. When I took her out for lunch she told me about Robert's progress. I have contacts and saw a way to help him.'

'She didn't ask you to.'

'Not directly.'

'Not indirectly either.'

'But I'm helping him anyway. Is that a crime?'

He didn't answer.

'Is she displeased?'

That was an understatement. He opened his mouth to say so then shut it again. Diplomacy called for silence. He shook his head.

'Good. It was the right thing to do, then.'

He breathed deeply, the rank air sticking in his throat. 'You should have told me. Robert sprung the news at the barbecue, and I didn't know what to think.'

'Well, now you do.'

'Yeah, now I do.'

He stared down at the floor, wanting reassurance but not sure how to ask for it. He decided to try a humorous approach. 'And I think it was very noble of you. There can't be many worse things than two hours of Robert blowing his own trumpet.'

'You shouldn't be so hard on him. He's not that bad. A little too pleased with himself, perhaps, but good company none the less.'

The words stung. 'Better than me?'

'In your present mood.'

'You don't know him like I do.'

'Perhaps, after Wednesday, I'll know him better.'

'Wednesday?'

'We're having lunch again.' A pause. 'Unless you object, of course.'

Again he didn't answer.

'I'll take silence as consent.'

'He uses people.'

'We all use people, Mike. Haven't you worked that out yet?'

The words made him feel unworldly and naïve. Like a child in need of protection from the outside world. He thought to himself: *This isn't me; I'm stronger than this.*

His toe still hurt. He rubbed it with his hand.

'You should put something on that,' Max told him. His tone was gentle.

'I will.'

'Do it tonight, OK? Don't let it get infected.'

Nodding, he struggled with the second cufflink. He felt tired, though he had little reason to do so. His day in the office had not been taxing, its highlight being another SOS from Alan Harris at the law centre. Another property issue that he had referred on to Nick Randall. But Nick had been busy and suggested passing it on to a senior assistant called Catherine Chester. 'We can trust her, Mike,' Nick had assured him. 'She won't let the cat out of the bag.'

He hoped that was right, but it seemed unlikely that Cox Stephens would make any objections, even if Nick was wrong.

'Jack's been strange with me lately,' he said.

'In what way?'

'He seems wary. Like he's worried that if he pisses me off I might complain to you, and that you might make him sorry. How stupid can you get?'

Max didn't react.

'It is stupid, isn't it?'

'Very.'

It wasn't the answer he had wanted. He swallowed down his disappointment. 'Thought so.'

Silence.

'Look,' said Max eventually, 'something's come up this evening. Do you mind if we skip dinner?'

He did, but was too proud to show it. 'No, I don't mind.'

'We'll go out another night.'

'Sure.'

They made their way out of the changing room.

As he crossed Berkeley Square, Michael watched a red sports car approach.

Mr Harrington had had a sports car. He could remember sitting in the front, with the roof down and a bag of sweets on his lap, shouting with excitement as the wind buffeted his face, while Mr Harrington, a tall, balding man with a kind face, smiled indulgently at him from the driver's seat.

For years his memories of the Harringtons had lain dormant. Now he thought about them every day, remembering the affection and security they had given him, and how another boy called Nigel had come along and stolen it all away.

Just as Robert might steal Max.

He stood and watched the car until it was out of sight.

Tuesday. Rebecca walked out of Chatterton's at the start of her lunch hour.

She was alone. All her lunch hours had been kept free that week for last-minute shopping for Michael's birthday. As it was, everything was already prepared.

The big day was Thursday, and she had planned a quiet, intimate evening for the two of them. She was taking the afternoon off and would spend it making a Thai curry. The recipe involved so much chilli that her insides churned at the prospect, but as Michael's stomach seemed to be lined with concrete she was sure it would be a success. After the meal, and the opening of presents, they would round off the evening watching a film. She had spent the whole of last Saturday marching round the shops hunting for a video of von Stroheim's *The Merry Widow* starring the ill-fated Mae Murray. At five o'clock she had been about to give up when finally she had found a copy in a tiny shop off Tottenham Court Road. If Michael's delight was half her own, it was sure to be a popular gift.

She was looking forward to Thursday. Her only worry was that Max might try to intrude on the action. But last night her fears had eased slightly. Michael had returned home earlier than expected in a mood that suggested his evening with Max had not gone well. She had made no comment, but the thought had pleased her immensely.

Emily had phoned last night, wanting to take the two of them out for a drink on Wednesday as a pre-birthday celebration. She had agreed readily enough, still feeling bad about what had happened to Emily at the barbecue. Perhaps they would ask Michael's friend George along too. Though she had been too preoccupied recently to think of organising a dinner party, she still wanted to introduce him to Emily and this could be the perfect opportunity.

She passed through Trafalgar Square and on towards Piccadilly Circus. The weather was cooler than it had been, and it was pleasant to walk through the streets in no particular direction. But as she made her way along Piccadilly, then turned right into Burlington Arcade, she realised that she knew exactly where she was going.

Leaving the arcade, she entered Cork Street. The Hampton Connaught gallery was showing an exhibition by a Polish artist whose name was familiar but whose work was not. For a moment she hesitated, then made her way inside.

It was virtually empty. The only other people there were a well-dressed, middle-aged couple and an attractive Asian girl of about her own age who was standing behind the counter. She began to examine the work that hung on the walls: dark, acrylic images on canvas. Close up they seemed nothing more than random shapes, but as she stepped back they gained definition and transformed into visions of startling beauty. She felt unnerved by the artist's talent and wondered how her own, less innovative works would look when hung on these walls.

'Do I know you from somewhere?'

The girl at the counter was staring at her. There was no sign of the couple.

'I don't think so,' she replied, then realised that she had seen this girl somewhere before. But where?

By way of answer the girl said, 'Were you at St Martin's?'

'Yes.'

'I thought I recognised you. You were on the fine art course. So was I, but you were a couple of years below me.'

She smiled. 'Small world.'

'How have you fared since graduation?'

'OK.' She felt self-conscious about mentioning the exhibition. 'What about you?'

'I don't paint any more. One thing college taught me was that I was never going to be outstanding enough to make a name for myself.'

She felt awkward. 'I'm sorry.'

'Don't be. I wasn't that dedicated anyway.' The girl smiled too. 'My name's Indira, by the way.'

'Rebecca.'

'Not Rebecca Blake?'

Rebecca opened her mouth to say yes.

And then, overcome by embarrassment, said, 'No.'

'Do you know her?'

'I did, but only slightly. Why?'

'She's taking part in a show we're doing in October.'

'Right.' Rebecca paused. 'She's done very well.'

Indira laughed. 'That's one way of putting it.'

'What do you mean?'

There were footsteps outside the gallery. Two elderly women stood by the door, looking at the promotional posters. For a moment they seemed on the point of entering but then moved away.

'What do you mean?' she asked again.

'The show's for half a dozen new artists. We'd lined up five of them from end-of-year shows last summer but were still looking for a sixth.

'A couple of months ago we received some interesting slides from a girl who's studying at the Slade. I went to see her work, and it was fantastic. William Blake on acid, if you can imagine that. Anyway, I managed to persuade Richard, the gallery owner, to go and see, and he was as bowled over as I was, so

263

we asked this girl if she wanted to be in the exhibition and naturally she jumped at it.

'Then, a few weeks ago, a friend of Richard's brought her new boyfriend to see him. It turns out that this boyfriend is some relative of Rebecca Blake. Her father-in-law, I think. Anyway, he wanted us to include her in the show. We had a look at her stuff, which was technically good but completely lacking in flair. So we said we'd already got enough people for the show.

'Then the boyfriend opened his wallet and offered us a bankers' draft, payable the day after the exhibition opens, in return for her inclusion. He also guaranteed that all the paintings we exhibited would be bought, no matter what the price tag. The end result was that the William Blake girl got dumped, and Rebecca Blake took her place.'

Rebecca's throat was dry. 'How much was the draft for?'

'A lot.'

She plucked a figure from the air. 'Five hundred pounds?'

Indira laughed. 'Add a couple of zeros.'

'You're joking!'

'Hardly. It's stupid to get annoyed about it. These things do happen. But I felt like I'd discovered the William Blake girl, and she thought this was her lucky break. She was devastated when it all fell through.'

'I bet she was.' It came out as a virtual whisper.

'Oh, well. She'll make it some day. People that good usually do. It just makes me sick when mediocrities use their bank balances to jump the queue. But we're all in it to make money, and, as Richard says, you don't kick a gift horse in the mouth.'

Rebecca nodded.

'Are you all right? You look a bit pale.'

'I have to go. Sorry for taking up your time.'

'You haven't been. Stay and have a coffee.'

Rebecca ignored her. Fighting to keep her composure, she left the gallery.

As Rebecca was speaking to Indira, Michael was sitting at his desk, willing his telephone to ring.

He had phoned Max that morning. Mr László had answered, informing him that Max was out, but expected back shortly. 'I will have him call you the moment he returns,' Mr László had promised. But that had been hours ago.

He made his way towards the coffee point. As he waited for the kettle to boil he heard Jack Bennett call his name.

'Mike, I've got a franchise agreement here from a client in Bristol. Do you have time to look at it for me?'

'Sure.'

'Good.' Jack handed it over. 'Sonia's opened a new file, so get the details from her.'

'OK.'

Jack turned to go. Surprised at the abruptness of their conversation, Michael felt a sudden need to prolong it.

'I saw Max yesterday.'

'Really?'

'Yes. I passed on your regards, as you asked.'

'Thanks.'

'He sends his.'

A nod.

'He was on great form.'

'Good.'

'We went to the Apennine Club. It's an amazing place, like something out of Dickens.' As he spoke he studied Jack, trying to gauge his reaction. Last time they'd spoken, Jack had been eager to please. There wasn't as much eagerness now. Or was he just being paranoid?

'We had a great time.'

Jack looked at his watch. The gesture felt like a slap in the face. But if he was losing Max's favour, then Jack could afford to bestow a few slaps.

'Have you been there? It's just off—'

'Look, Mike, I'm sorry, but I've got a conference call with Chicago starting any second. I'm glad you had a good time. Could you report on the agreement by Thursday?'

'Certainly.'

Jack rushed off.

A conference call. So that explained it. Everything was as it should be.

Then why hasn't Max phoned me back?

Because he had been held up. He would call soon. Nothing had changed. Nothing at all.

But his anxiety remained.

Six o'clock. Rebecca let herself into the flat.

As she closed the door behind her she took a deep breath, filtering the air through her nostrils, searching for the smell of tobacco smoke.

She did this now every time she entered the flat. Checking for some trace of his presence. The man who had shown her nothing but kindness. The man who had paid a fortune to help her realise her ambitions. The man who had dazzled Michael and was now starting on her family and friends. The man whom she had come to hate more than she had ever hated anyone in her life.

This couldn't go on. She had to do something. But what?

SEVEN

Wednesday evening, quarter past seven. Rebecca made her way along the Strand, towards the pub where she was meeting Michael and Emily.

She walked quickly, eager to arrive on time. Michael was going to be late, and that would give her the chance to tell Emily about her discovery in the art gallery.

She was desperate to tell someone. Her parents would have been the preferred option but they were away on holiday. Robert would have been her next port of call, but she was upset at his sudden friendship with Max and knew that any discussion on the subject would just lead to an argument. Then came Emily, then Lorna, but neither had been available when she'd phoned.

And that left Michael.

Normally he would have been her first choice. But not now. The situation between them was too delicate. She was planning to use his birthday as a chance to repair the cracks that were appearing in their relationship and didn't want to jeopardise that by telling him something he would just take as further evidence of Max's benevolence.

Assuming, of course, that he didn't know already.

So she would unburden herself to Emily. Part of her hated the thought of telling. She had been so proud that her work was considered strong enough for inclusion in a prestigious show. Now she would have to admit that all the muscle was in Max's wallet.

But she was also frightened and needed to share her fears.

She entered the pub. It was a huge Gothic structure with a high vaulted ceiling and dark, sombre decor in keeping with its previous incarnation as a bank. Young professionals swarmed about the bar like ants, all boasting about the triumphs of the day. She spotted Emily, then saw that Michael had already arrived.

'Em's bought champagne,' he said, handing her a glass.

She thanked Emily. 'I thought you were going to be late,' she told Michael.

'My meeting was cancelled.' He downed his glass and poured himself another. 'Did you speak to Robert this afternoon?'

'Should I have done?'

'No. Just wondered.'

'Well, I didn't.'

He looked disappointed. Robert had been scheduled to have lunch with Max that day, and she knew the idea troubled him. It troubled her too.

'It's crowded in here,' Emily observed.

Rebecca watched Michael down another glass. It was unusual for him to drink so fast.

'Noisy as well,' continued Emily.

'We could go somewhere else,' Rebecca suggested.

'I told the barman this was a birthday drink, and he said there was a private room we could go and sit in. Shall we have a look?'

'OK.'

They made their way to the rear of the pub and a door in a small alcove. Rebecca followed Emily inside, only to find that the room was in darkness. 'Em, are you sure this is the room he meant?'

'Surprise!'

The lights went on.

She looked around her, not believing what she was seeing.

The room, though dominated by a huge dining table, was packed with people. In the mass of faces she spotted Clare, Lorna and boyfriend Phil, her college friend Liz and boyfriend John, Michael's school friend George, college friend Tim, workmate Stuart and his girlfriend Helen.

And at their centre stood Max.

He stepped out of the crowd, a smile of welcome spreading across his face. Rebecca, convinced that he was going to hug her, fought an impulse to back away. Instead he kissed Emily on the cheek. 'Thanks for all your help. I couldn't have done this without you.'

'You knew about this?' Rebecca sounded shrill and hastily modified her tone. 'I mean, you might have said something.'

Emily looked uncomfortable. 'That would have ruined the surprise.'

'Indeed it would,' agreed Max, turning his smile towards her. 'I wanted to do something for Mike's birthday but remembered him saying that the two of you had yet to have an engagement party. So I thought to make this a double celebration and surprise you both. I hope you don't mind.'

Suddenly Rebecca felt like laughing. Of course there had been no engagement party. Michael loathed parties. He would hate all this even more than she did. She turned towards him, offering up a silent prayer of thanks that Max had, at last, overplayed his hand.

Then her heart sank.

Michael's look of happiness was almost pitiful. Like a child on Christmas Eve who has dreamed himself forgotten before awakening to find a full stocking at the end of the bed. He didn't care that this was a party. All that mattered was the identity of the host.

'I don't know what to say,' he said sheepishly.

'No need to say anything,' Max told him kindly. 'Just do me a favour and enjoy your evening.'

'And do the rest of us a favour,' added George, 'by not talking about silent films.'

People began to laugh.

'Or the Companies Act,' added Stuart.

'Oh, fuck off!' said Michael. He was laughing too.

They were all laughing now. The sound hurt Rebecca's ears. She stood next to Michael, surrounded by their friends, feeling like a martyr being fed to the lions. She wanted to leave, but that was out of the question. Not when she was one of the guests of honour.

They made their way to the table. Embossed name cards stood on each plate. She found herself between Stuart and Lorna's boyfriend Phil. Next to Phil was Lorna, then Max, then Clare. Michael was at the other end, flanked by Emily and Max's girlfriend Caroline.

Emily sat next to George. Rebecca had never dreamed that the two of them would meet in circumstances such as these.

There was no sign of Robert. Perhaps he had not been invited. Perhaps he had eaten too much at lunch.

Uniformed staff appeared with their starters. The pub, like so many others in the City, served food that was as good as that found in many an expensive restaurant. She picked at her

270

smoked salmon, trying to remember to smile, knowing that she was expected to be happy. The alcohol flowed: champagne, fine wines, and spirits for those who wanted something stronger. She watched George share a joke with Emily, then with Michael and Caroline. Michael looked as relaxed and happy as she had ever seen him. She hated him for that.

Caroline was studying her. The eyes were both curious and sympathetic. Perhaps Caroline sensed how much she was hating this. Perhaps Caroline was hating it too.

The starters were cleared away. As they waited for the main course, Max lit a cigar. Thick, dark smoke drifted into the air. Instinctively she held her breath, trying to block out the smell.

But she could not block out the sound of his voice. It crept towards her through the laughter, clear and melodious as the chiming of church bells, dripping into her ears like drops of venom.

He was a marvellous host: the complete master at working a room, exchanging a few words with everyone, delivered with a smile so benevolent that each recipient felt singled out and special and stared at him admiringly long after he had turned his attention to someone else. He asked Lorna and Phil about their career aspirations, listened attentively, offered encouragement and advice interspersed with jokes, charming them both. Lorna, who had once advised her to expel Max from her life, was now eating out of his hand like a tame bird. Then he turned his attention to Clare, provoking the same infatuated giggles that his flowers had done.

The main course arrived. Duck in a rich sauce. She tried to eat, but the smell of cigar smoke was in her mouth. Her food tasted of ash and she felt sick. It was only quarter to nine. This could go on for hours yet. She didn't know if she would last.

The plates were cleared. She covered hers with a napkin to

271

conceal how little she had eaten. Her stomach was churning. Downing a glass of mineral water, she breathed deeply, trying to steady herself. Though the windows were open the air seemed still and oppressive. She was on the point of making an escape to the cloakroom when Max rose to his feet and the table fell silent.

He cleared his throat. 'Before we have dessert I'd just like to say a few words.' He smiled. 'And I do mean a few, so there's really no need to reach for the razor blades.'

Laughter echoed round the table.

'I haven't had the pleasure of knowing Becky and Mike for very long, but as I'm sure you'll agree it doesn't take long to realise what a very special couple they are.'

'Hear! Hear!' cried George. Good-natured applause rang out.

'In the course of our brief acquaintance, both have come to mean a great deal to me, and as a token of our friendship I have a small present for them.' He reached inside his jacket pocket and removed a thin white envelope.

'It's a subscription to *Corporate Lawyer Weekly*,' called out Stuart.

More laughter, the sound made raucous by alcohol. Rebecca stared down at the table, dreading what was to come.

'Becky,' continued Max, 'I think this should be opened by you.'

The hair rose on the back of her neck. Slowly she raised her head. Max was offering the envelope, giving her the same easy smile she remembered from their first meeting. She forced her features into a suitable expression of gratitude. Hatred burned inside her like fire.

Taking the envelope she tore it open. Inside was a single sheet of paper, some sort of printed receipt.

'What is it, Beck?' asked Michael.

All eyes were on her and she could take nothing in. She registered the word 'destination'.

'Yeah, what is it?' said someone else.

'I'm not sure.'

'Then let me explain,' said Max. 'It's a booking for a three-week holiday in the Fijian islands. Open-ended, so you can go whenever the fancy takes you. I know how much you want to see that part of the world. I only hope the reality is as wonderful as you would wish.'

For a moment there was silence. Then, yet again, people began to applaud. 'Fantastic!' cried someone.

And it was. The perfect present. She couldn't have asked for anything better.

Except to have her life back.

She looked at Michael, hoping for some sign of indignation. Praying for it.

But there was none. He gazed at Max, his expression one of dazed gratitude.

'You're pleased?' Max asked him.

Oh Michael, say something. Tell him to get out of our lives.

Michael nodded.

Max turned towards her. 'And you?'

She stared at the receipt, the type blurring before her eyes. A simple 'thank you' would suffice, but she could not bring herself to utter the words.

Lorna reached across the table, prodded her in the ribs, and said, 'What do you say, you lucky cow?' Lorna, who had been her friend since early childhood. Lorna, who had claimed to understand her feelings about Max.

Lorna, whom Max had won over with a smile and a few well-chosen words.

Just as he had won over Michael, Robert and Emily.

Just as he could win over anybody.

She cracked.

'You can't do this!'

She rose to her feet, tearing the receipt into pieces.

'You can't buy your way into our lives like this! Who the hell do you think you are?'

A collective gasp rose up around her. Max's smile faded. 'I'm very sorry—' he began.

'We don't want your apologies! We don't want your presents! All we want is you out of our lives!'

'We?' Max turned towards Michael. 'Is that what you want, Mike?'

Michael stared down at the table, his face as white as chalk.

'If it is, all you have to do is say.'

'Tell him, Mike!'

Michael raised his head. His eyes locked with hers.

Then he shook his head.

His eyes were full of reproach. As, it seemed, were everyone else's. All of them, wide with shock at such rudeness in the face of marvellous generosity.

Unable to bear their condemnation, she ran from the room.

She let herself into the flat and sat down on the sofa bed. Breathing slowly, she fought for composure. But it was no good. The tears came in a flood.

Time passed. Eventually she heard a key in the lock. Michael stood before her, his expression as reproachful as it had been in the restaurant.

'Go away,' she told him. 'Get back to your party. That's where you want to be.'

'It was our party, not just mine, and your outburst ended it. What possessed you to act like that?'

'You're the one who's been possessed.'

'What are you talking about?'

274

'Max. He's got you wrapped round his little finger. You're so dazzled by him that you can't see what he's really about.'

'He's not about anything. He's our friend.'

She rose to her feet. 'Oh Mike, why can't you see it? Max doesn't care about you. He just sees you as a puppet. Someone whose strings he enjoys pulling.'

'That's not true!'

'Yes, it is! This man is on some sort of sick power trip. He uses his money and charm to buy into people's lives, then he starts playing games with them.'

'Crap!'

'It's happening already. He's turning us against each other. Now he's trying to turn me against Robert. God knows what he'll do next.'

'He hasn't bought me!'

'Don't kid yourself, Mike. As far as he's concerned, we're all for sale. At least I was expensive. Fifty thousand pounds. That's what my exhibition will cost.' She saw his eyes widen. 'You didn't know that, did you? Well, it's true. Ask the gallery if you don't believe me. Robert will be expensive too. The introductions will need to be good if he's to get partnership. Clare was cheap. Just a big bunch of flowers. But he really hit the bargain basement with you, didn't he? No need to spend a penny. All you cost was a pat on the head and permission to call him Daddy!'

His cheeks coloured as if he'd been struck.

Shame swept over her. Two months ago she would never have been capable of such viciousness. But a lot had changed since then.

He turned and walked out of the room.

She ran after him. 'Mike, wait.'

He ignored her.

'I'm sorry.'

'Sorry?' He turned back. 'You think that makes it all right?'

'I'm frightened about what he's doing to us.'

'He's not doing anything!'

'Yes, he is! Look at us. Always at each other's throats. We were never like this before we met him.'

'And whose fault is that? Whose jealousy is to blame?'

'What are you saying? This isn't about me, it's about him.'

'Is it?'

She swallowed.

'You're such a hypocrite. You've always had people to love you. Your parents, brother, grandparents, aunts. The list just goes on and on. The only person I have is you. Until I met you there was no one. You used to tell me how you wished there was someone else who cared about me too. Well, now someone else has come along and you really hate it, don't you?'

She shook her head.

'This man treats me like a son. Don't you understand what that's like for me? Can't you imagine how that makes me feel?'

'Of course I can!'

'So why can't you be pleased for me? Why do you have to try to destroy it?'

'Because that someone else is Max! All right, I admit I was jealous at first. If you want to despise me for that, then go ahead because I deserve it. But it's not about jealousy now. You say that Max is our friend, but you're wrong. He isn't interested in friendship, he's interested in control.'

'That's not true.'

'We have to break from him, Mike. Before we get in too deep.'

'No way.'

'We have to.' She ran a hand through her hair. 'I know how you feel about him, and I don't want to hurt you, but we don't

276

have any choice. This man is dangerous, and I want him out of our lives.'

He shook his head. 'You've got it wrong. You're completely paranoid.'

His eyes were cold. She knew that there was no hope of reasoning with him. No hope at all.

But there was another way.

For a moment she hesitated. If she crossed this bridge there was no going back. But it was the only hand she had left.

'Perhaps I am paranoid,' she said slowly. 'But the fact remains that I want us to finish with him. If you don't agree, then I'll finish with you.'

'What are you saying?'

'Him or me. That's your choice, Mike. You can't have both.'

His face grew pale. 'I don't believe you.'

'Stay here if you want. Carry on letting Max get his claws into you. But I'm packing my stuff and leaving this flat tonight, and if you don't come with me then it's over between us for good.'

'You don't mean that.'

'Watch me.'

She walked away, her heart pounding. In her head she heard Emily's warning that this course of action would be her ruin.

'Becky!'

She entered the bedroom and took out a suitcase from the wardrobe.

He followed her into the room. 'What are you doing?'

'What does it look like?' Opening a drawer she took out a pile of jumpers.

'Stop. This isn't funny.'

She began to pile the jumpers into the case. 'I'll stay at Susie's until I find somewhere else. I'll give you the address so you can forward any mail.'

'You can't do this to me!'

'But I am. I don't see why you should be upset. You've got Max now, and clearly he's a far better, nobler person than I could ever be. I'm sure he'll be very good to you until he gets bored, dumps you and finds someone else whose life he can turn upside down.'

He grabbed her arm. 'Becky, please don't do this. We can work it out. I'll talk to him, ask him to back off and not crowd you so much. He'll understand, I know he will.'

'It's too late for that, Mike. Come with me. I love you, and I want us to be together, but we're not going to last with this man in our life. We have to break from him. It's the only way.'

He stared at the floor.

'Phone him now, Mike. Tell him what we've decided. Then we can leave.'

At first he did nothing. She watched him, fighting an urge to scream.

Then, slowly, he shook his head.

'Very well, then.' She took off her engagement ring and handed it to him. 'You'd better have this.'

'OK! You win. I'll do it. I'll phone him.'

There were tears in his eyes. She put her hand on his arm. 'It's the right thing, Mike. You'll see.'

'Don't,' he told her. 'Just don't. Not now.'

He walked out of the room. She heard him pick up the phone and dial a number. Remaining where she was, she put the engagement ring back on her finger. She had gambled and she had won. He had chosen her over Max.

But he'll hate you for it. So much so that it could end up driving him away.

That wouldn't happen. She wouldn't let that happen. They were strong, and they would survive this.

Wouldn't they?

It was warm in the room, but suddenly a shiver ran through her.

Pushing her fears to one side, she began to pack for both of them.

EIGHT

A slow Monday morning, twelve days after the ill-fated party. Michael, who had been at an internal meeting, returned to his desk.

There were three messages on his voicemail, two from clients, the third from Rebecca. She hoped his day was going well and promised to make a chicken casserole for dinner. It was a dish she hated but was one of his favourites. The latest peace offering. She spoke quickly, in that excessively bright tone that denoted nerves, asking him to phone if he had a free minute. He had one now but made no attempt to call.

Kate Kennedy appeared, wanting to know how Stuart was faring with the precedents. She stopped to chat with Michael, her behaviour as warm as it had been two weeks ago. He felt like telling her that she didn't have to bother any more because he was no longer the person of influence that he had once, briefly, been.

All the partners continued to handle him carefully. That was the strange thing. Jack Bennett had called him into his office at the end of last week, a benevolent smile on his face, and announced that a new deal had come in on which he could assist. 'It'll be excellent experience,' Jack had told him, 'and will really raise your profile.' He had sat there, trying to manifest all the symptoms of enthusiasm, while wondering how much Jack knew.

Perhaps he knew nothing. Perhaps Max had kept what had happened to himself.

He thought back to their phone conversation on that terrible evening: how he had tried to explain the situation, struggled to find the right words, only to discover that he didn't need to say anything. Max had guessed what was coming and wanted to make it easy for him, accepting the situation with quiet dignity, apologising that things had worked out so badly, and wishing him success in the future.

'You mustn't feel bad about this, Mike,' he had said in conclusion. 'I always knew our friendship was just a stage. Now it's time for you to move on.' Perhaps he was right.

But it didn't feel that way.

Kate left. Stuart, the only other person from the office to have attended the party, stared at him anxiously. He was about to suggest lunch when Kim came to tell him that Peter Brown was waiting in reception.

'Who?'

'Peter Brown.'

He checked his diary but nothing was marked. 'Are you sure it's me he wants?'

'He seemed to think you're expecting him.'

'Who does he work for?'

'Don't know. He said it was personal, not business.'

The reception was packed with people in business suits, all reading newspapers or talking into mobiles. He asked the receptionist for Peter Brown and she indicated a young man

281

of about twenty-five in an expensive three-piece suit sitting reading a paperback. Michael approached him. 'I'm Michael Turner.'

Peter rose to his feet, smiled and offered his hand. 'Pleased to meet you.' He was tall and blond. Handsome, too, in a *GQ* sort of way. 'These are great offices.'

'Yeah, they're OK. Look, I'm sorry but—'

'You don't have much time,' said Peter, trying to finish the sentence for him. 'Well, here it is, then.' He handed Michael the paperback he had been reading: a collection of M.R. James's ghost stories. 'I like this stuff too. Have you tried Sheridan Le Fanu?'

'Why are you giving this to me?'

'You left it behind when you moved out.'

He was confused. 'You're living in Camberwell?'

'Pelham Gardens. Max Somerton's flat.'

'He's got new tenants already?' There were no grounds for it, but still he felt betrayed.

Peter nodded. 'We moved in on Saturday.'

'We?'

'Jenny and me. Jenny's my fiancée. Didn't Max tell you about us?'

'No.'

'That explains it.' Peter smiled apologetically. 'Sorry, I thought you knew who I was. We found the book behind the sofa, and Max said it must be yours. I work at an investment bank down the road, so he suggested I drop it in and say hello. I thought he'd told you to expect me, but I probably got the wrong end of the stick.'

Michael nodded. 'How did you find out about the flat?'

'From my boss. He owned the flat we were renting in Fulham but needed it back. Fortunately he's a friend of Max and knew that your flat was available, so we got that instead.'

'Have you met Max?'

Peter beamed. 'Isn't he a great bloke?'

'You think so?' He tried to sound nonchalant.

'Definitely. He's been very generous to us.'

'How?'

Peter shrugged. 'He just has.'

'Why? What has he done?'

'Well, he came round with champagne the evening we moved in, and then took us out for dinner.'

'One meal and a bottle of champagne? It's hardly the height of generosity.' He knew he was being vindictive and hated himself for it. But he could not stop.

Peter looked surprised. 'It's not just that,' he said defensively. 'Jenny studied piano at college and wants to be a concert pianist, but at the moment she's just waitressing and giving the occasional lesson. Max told me that he knows some people who might be able to help her. We're having lunch this week to talk about it some more.'

He felt a lurch in the pit of his stomach. 'I see.'

'I'd better go. It was nice to meet you.'

He walked Peter to the door. They shook hands again. 'One thing,' he said. 'Where did Max take you for dinner?'

'The Savoy Grill. Have you been there?'

He swallowed. 'Just once.'

He made his way back to his office. It was empty now. Stuart had left a note to say that he'd gone for lunch with Nick Randall and asking him to join them if he had time.

A red light was flashing on his telephone. Another voice message from Rebecca, still sounding too cheerful and still asking him to call. He picked up the receiver, then put it down again. Safer to wait. At this moment in time he would only say something he'd regret.

The paperback was still in his hand. It didn't look familiar.

283

Perhaps it had belonged to the previous tenants, Alison and Neil.

He went to join Stuart and Nick. They had ordered chicken casserole. He did likewise.

Wednesday lunchtime. Rebecca was halfway down Fleet Street when she heard someone call her name. She turned to see Emily hurrying towards her.

'Beck, I've been calling and calling. Why haven't you phoned me?'

'Why do you think?'

Emily paled. Rebecca felt the familiar stirrings of guilt and pushed them to one side. 'I'm in a rush,' she said curtly.

'I know you feel angry.'

'That's one way of putting it. Betrayed would be another.' She laughed. 'You know the ironic thing? That evening I was going to tell you how I felt and ask your advice about what to do. God, what a fool I was.'

'You could tell me now.'

'I wouldn't waste my breath.'

They stood facing each other with people pushing past them. Emily looked hurt. Rebecca tried to maintain her animosity but found herself remembering a frightened girl of seven who had just lost her mother.

A girl who could, so easily, have been herself.

Then the guilt was back, together with the sense of obligation. An emotional ball and chain that she could never escape, no matter how hard she tried.

She felt drops of water on her face. The start of a summer shower. 'Look, this is stupid. If we're going to argue then let's do it somewhere dry.'

Five minutes later they sat together in a crowded coffee bar.

'Max phoned me at work,' Emily explained. 'He said he

wanted to throw a surprise party for you and Mike but didn't know who to invite. He asked me to contact your friends on his behalf.'

'Why did you agree? You knew how I felt about Max.'

'Because I knew how Mike felt about him, too, and how much the party would mean to him. I never dreamed you'd react the way you did. The last time we talked you said you were going to make the best of the situation for Mike's sake. That if he was happy, then you were happy too.'

Rebecca watched the steam rise from her coffee. 'I tried, but I just couldn't.' She sighed. 'So I made him choose and now things between us are worse than ever. I'm doing everything I can to make it up to him, but nothing seems to work. I don't know how to make things right.'

'You could change your mind,' said Emily gently.

She shook her head.

'But if things are so bad ...'

'I never want to see that man again.'

'Mike does, though.'

'It's too late now, anyway. Max has moved another couple into the flat. They've only been there five minutes and already he's wining and dining them. The girl wants to be a concert pianist and he's promising her the world. The poor cow probably thinks he's the best thing since sliced bread. She has no idea how much damage he's going to wreak in her life.'

'You don't know that.'

'That's what Mike said.'

'What else did he say?'

'Nothing. He didn't have to.'

'He's bound to feel resentful, Beck. I tried to warn you.'

'It's a pity you didn't warn me about Robert. Another consequence of all this is that Max has decided not to get involved in his career. He told Robert that it was out of consideration

285

for my feelings, which is a joke. Of course Robert's furious, and we had a huge row on the phone. I was really upset when I came off the line, and Mike just stood there and looked at me like I deserved it.'

She sipped her coffee. It was cooler now. Emily stared at her expectantly.

'Now Mum and Dad are getting involved too. They're driving up tomorrow so we can all sit down and resolve this. I've tried to stop them, but they've insisted. They think they can make it all better, but they're just going to make things worse.'

Tears came into her eyes. She wiped them away. 'You did warn me and I knew it would be difficult, but I just didn't expect it to be like this. Mike refuses to discuss it. I've tried to get him to talk, but he just says that it's done now and we have to make the best of it.' She swallowed. 'Sometimes it's like living with a stranger.'

'You have to give him time to work it out.'

'How much time? I can't go on like this for much longer.'

'Well, you'll just have to.' Emily's voice was firm. 'I know it's hard for you but, believe me, it's much harder for Mike. You know how much his relationship with Max meant to him, and yet you forced him to end it. Of course he feels angry, and after this business with the new tenants he feels rejected too.'

Rebecca stirred her coffee, watching the dark liquid churn in the centre of the cup.

And then something struck her.

'How do you know what he feels about the new tenants?'

Emily began to look uncomfortable.

'He's talked to you about this already, hasn't he?'

No answer.

'Hasn't he?'

A nod.

'When?'

'We've spoken on the phone.' A pause. 'And we've had lunch a couple of times.'

She felt betrayed. 'And no doubt he spends the whole time telling you what a complete bitch I am.'

'No.'

'Oh, sure!'

'He just wanted someone to talk to.'

'He could talk to me.'

'Not the way he feels at the moment. I'm trying to bring him round, but it's going to take time.'

'Bring him round! What is this? Who asked you to act as peacemaker?'

'No one, but you two are my closest friends and—'

'This is our relationship! Mike's and mine! It's got nothing to do with you, so stop interfering!'

'I'm not interfering! I'm trying to help!'

The coffee bar fell silent as people began to listen to their argument. Rebecca was too angry to care. 'Help? That's a joke! Every relationship you've ever had has been a complete fiasco!'

Emily flushed. 'That's not true!'

'Yes, it is! You're the last person in the world who should be giving us advice, and if you don't want our friendship to end then you'd better stop having cosy discussions with Mike about our problems right now!'

Suddenly Emily leaned across the table.

'Fine, if that's what you want. After all, whatever Becky wants, Becky gets. But you'd better make sure that Mike understands the situation too. Why not tell him you'll end the engagement if he ever talks to me again? It's worked before, and I'm sure it'll work again.'

Emily's eyes were cold and judgemental. Like those of a stranger. Just as Michael's so often were now.

She felt ashamed. In the background other conversations

started up again. The show was over. Life returned to normal.

'Do you think I'm proud of hurting Mike? There isn't a second when I don't hate myself for it, but I didn't have any choice. If things had stayed as they were, Max would have destroyed our relationship, and I couldn't let him do that.'

She waited, hoping for agreement, but there was none. Not when there was something else she had to say.

'But I'd never drop you, Em. I'm sorry I shouted. I only did it because I'm scared.'

'You don't need to be scared. Everything will work out fine.'

'Do you think so?'

'Of course.' A pause. 'After all, this is your life we're talking about.'

More guilt. She couldn't face it now. Not with things the way they were.

'I'm late,' she said quickly. 'I have to go.'

She rose to her feet. For a moment Emily remained where she was, her eyes still cold.

Then her face became a mask. As smooth and serene as a classical sculpture.

They left the coffee bar together.

The following afternoon, Michael, sat at his desk trying to concentrate on amendments to a share purchase agreement.

There was a knock on his office door. A harassed-looking Jeff Speakman appeared, holding a document.

'Bruce Hammond's in a meeting with clients in Con Seven. He needs this urgently, and all the trainees are still in one of those bloody lunchtime talks. Do me a favour and take it down?'

The conference rooms were on the ground floor. He took the lift and stepped out into the lobby. It was empty, save for

Jack Bennett who was handing over some papers to a couple of clients. He moved towards the corridor that led to the conference rooms.

One of the clients laughed. It was an attractive sound. Deep, rich and melodious. Like velvet.

He turned.

Max stood in the doorway, smiling as he checked and signed the papers Jack had given him. Beside him stood Peter Brown, wearing the mellow expression of someone who had drunk rather too much wine at lunch and would suffer for it during the afternoon.

Forgetting about Bruce Hammond, Michael stood and watched them.

Jack asked Peter a question. As Peter replied, Max nodded encouragingly, then gave him an avuncular pat on the shoulder. Jack noticed Michael. He raised a hand in greeting. Automatically Michael did the same.

Peter and Max looked over. Peter beamed affably and mouthed the word 'hi'. Max stared at him with uninterested eyes, then turned his attention back to his papers.

Michael made his way up the corridor, towards Con Seven, knocked on the door and entered.

Bruce Hammond, a notoriously difficult partner from the litigation department, sat at a table with three other men. The table was covered in opened files and the remains of a tray of sandwiches. The window was closed and the air was thick with cigarette smoke.

'You took your time,' Bruce told him.

He handed the document over. Bruce exhaled irritably. 'We need four copies.'

He shrugged.

'Well, don't just stand there. Go and find a photocopier.'

'Do I look like a bloody secretary?'

Bruce jumped, as did the clients. Michael was in real trouble now. Such behaviour was a sackable offence.

He walked out of the room and back to the lift. The lobby was empty. Just the security man, sitting at his desk, watching the world go by.

Kim had left a message on his chair telling him that Rebecca had called. He stared at the message for some time, then picked up a Biro and began to draw circles round her name. The motion of his hand grew faster and faster until he had ripped the paper to shreds.

Eight o'clock in the evening. Michael walked out of West Hampstead tube towards his new home.

He was unsteady on his feet. An after-work glass of wine with Stuart had turned into a full bottle and a couple of Scotches. Rebecca hated to see him drunk, and he sensed a confrontation looming. The prospect filled him with a dark excitement.

The afternoon had been uneventful. No comeback yet for his rudeness to Bruce Hammond. Perhaps Bruce was still tied up in his meeting and unable to register a complaint. But one would be made, and then it would be all over for him at Cox Stephens. He should have been worried, but his head was too full of other things for him to care.

Susie's flat was the bottom half of a terraced house in Ash Lane, a quiet side street off the Finchley Road. Susie would be back in a month, and then they would have to move again. Rebecca kept showing him details of possible rentals, and he would nod and try to muster some enthusiasm while wanting to scream that they had already walked out on a perfectly good flat. One that was now lost to them for ever.

And it wasn't the only thing that was lost, either.

Mr Blake's blue Saab was parked outside the flat, its surface gleaming in the late-evening sunshine. Mr Blake had it polished twice a month. Michael watched a bird fly overhead and willed it to deposit on the bonnet, but it didn't, so he spat on the shining surface himself.

He stood in the hallway. Rebecca appeared from the living room, her smile unable to conceal tiredness and anxiety. 'I'm sorry,' she whispered. 'I tried to stop them coming. Don't worry about saying hello. I'll get rid of them, then make supper.'

'I'm not hungry.'

Her smile wavered, but only for a moment. 'I'll make it anyway in case you change your mind.'

'That's up to you.' He walked into the kitchen and poured himself some water.

It was a good-sized kitchen. The sort where half a dozen people could sit together and not feel crowded. The one in Pelham Gardens had been so small that he and Rebecca had found it difficult to cook there together.

He wondered if Peter and Jenny were finding that now.

Voices reached him from the living room. Robert's was accusing, Rebecca's defensive, their mother's placating, and their father silent save for the occasional snort. A game of happy families in which he had no part to play.

He stared up at the ceiling. There was a small crack in the plaster, just as there had been at Pelham Gardens. Max had pointed it out to him once, joking that it only went to show that there really wasn't room to swing a cat. He had laughed at that.

Perhaps Peter had laughed too.

The glass was still full. He let it drop into the sink, where it shattered into pieces. The voices fell silent. Then Rebecca called his name.

They were waiting for him in the living room. Rebecca sat

291

with her mother on the sofa, wearing the worried expression she always did when he and her family came together. Mr Blake and Robert stood by the window. Both glared at him. He gave Mrs Blake his most dazzling smile. 'What do you think of our new home?'

'It's very nice.'

'Charming, isn't it? We're so happy here we could just shit.'

Mrs Blake flinched.

'Mike!' exclaimed Rebecca.

He laughed. 'Relax. We both know your parents think the world of me. The odd obscenity isn't going to change that.'

'You're drunk,' proclaimed Mr Blake.

'I am, and when you snort you look like a walrus, so I guess it's right when they say that no one's perfect.'

Mr Blake's jaw dropped. As did Robert's. Michael felt excited. 'You look fat, Rob Rob. Must be all those expensive lunches. Shame they had to end, but we all know who's to blame for that.'

Robert flushed angrily. Rebecca hung her head.

'I think that was uncalled for,' said Mrs Blake.

'Anyway,' added Robert, 'it's nothing to do with you.'

'Oh, but you're wrong. It has everything to do with me.' He perched himself on the edge of the sofa and smiled at Rebecca. 'Wouldn't you agree?'

'We're trying to have a family discussion,' Mr Blake told him.

'Don't let me stop you. After all, I'm family too. That's right, isn't it, Beck? Or is there anyone else I have to drop before we tie the knot?'

'That's enough, Michael,' said Mrs Blake.

He rose to his feet. 'What about George? After all, he's Jewish, and we can't have him spoiling the wedding photos because of it.'

'You should leave,' announced Robert.

He stared at Rebecca. 'Or how about Stuart? Nice guy, but a Scouse accent. Maybe I should dump him too. Tell you what. Why don't I make a list of all the people in the world who matter to me and then you can order me to dump the lot of them.'

She looked up, on the verge of tears. 'Mike, please. I understand how you must feel but—'

He laughed harshly. 'How could you possibly understand? You've never lost anything in your perfect little life, so don't sit there and tell me that you understand.'

'Max is right about you,' said Robert suddenly.

Startled, he turned. 'What do you mean?'

Robert began to smile. 'You should hear what Max says about you.'

'What does he say?'

'Robert,' cried Mrs Blake. 'This isn't going to help anything.'

'So what? He should hear.' Robert took a step towards Michael, then lowered his voice, trying to mimic Max. 'Ah, yes, Michael. Nice enough chap, but a whiner. You can never have a decent conversation with him. All he does is bleat on and on about his childhood.'

'That's not true!'

'Oh, but it is. Want to hear more?' Robert's eyes were shining. 'Max said that listening to you was like listening to a maudlin record with a big scratch down the middle. He said that you're weak. No backbone. You try to act the big man but really you're just an overgrown kid crying out to be understood. He said he was fond of you in the way he'd be fond of a stray puppy.'

'You're a fucking liar!' A red mist was forming before his eyes.

'He thinks you're a kid. An emotional cripple. Someone

293

who'll never amount to anything when he's still trying to blame his druggie mother and petty crook father for everything that's ever gone wrong in his life.'

The mist took over. He head-butted Robert. Anaesthetised by rage, he felt no pain himself. Just a mild thud, accompanied by the sound of breaking bone.

Then Robert was falling backwards, screaming, his hand covering his nose.

They were all screaming. Robert. Rebecca. Her mother. Her father, too, for all he knew. His forehead felt wet. He wiped it with his hand and found blood on his fingers.

His rage vanished, replaced by shock and disbelief. He ran from the room.

Half an hour later he stood in the drawing room of Max's house where Mr László had asked him to wait, his arms wrapped round himself as if for protection.

Max entered, his eyes widening as he took in Michael's appearance. 'God almighty!'

'Why did you say those things about me?'

'What things?'

'You know what things!'

'Look at you, you're shaking.' Max strode across the room and put a restraining hand on his shoulder.

Michael looked into his eyes, searching for signs of scorn but finding only warmth and concern. Pain sliced through him like a knife. He didn't dare trust Max now. 'This was a mistake. I shouldn't have come here.'

'Of course you should. But you need to calm down and tell me what's happened.'

'And what will you do then? Sneer about me to Robert, or Jack, or Caroline? Is that all I ever was to you? Someone to laugh at and pity?'

'Christ, no!' Max looked appalled. 'Who's put this garbage in your head?'

'It's not garbage!'

'It was Robert, wasn't it? This is the sort of petty spiteful-ness I'd expect of him.'

'I trusted you! I told you things I've never told anyone else! Well, Becky was right after all! You can't be trusted, and the fact that I did just shows what a complete fool I am!'

Both hands were now on his shoulders. He tried to pull away and the grip tightened. Max leaned closer so their heads were almost touching.

'Michael, listen to me, because I'm only going to say this once. I have never said a harsh word about you to a living soul. Moreover, if someone was foolish enough to bad-mouth you in my presence then I'd make them regret it if it took me the rest of my life. That is the truth, for you to accept or reject as you see fit. But if you reject it, then you leave this house right now and we never see each other again.'

A lump came into Michael's throat. He attempted to swal-low it down. 'They're just words, that's all.'

'So you'd trust Robert over me? Someone you've always hated as much as he's hated you? If that's the case, then you really are a complete fool.'

'That's no answer. You're just twisting things.' Again he tried to free himself.

But the grip was powerful. 'Of course it's an answer. Robert's seen a chance to cause you pain and he's taken it.' A pause. 'And it's worked, hasn't it?'

Michael, close to tears, didn't trust himself to speak.

'Hasn't it?'

A nod.

'Do you really think that little of me?'

'I want to believe you.'

'Then do. You know you can. You mean the world to me, Mike. Distrust other people if you want to, but you never need doubt me.'

The voice wrapped itself around him like silk, slowly dispersing his anger and soothing his disquiet.

'So, what's your answer? Do you believe me?'

'Yes.'

'Good.'

They stared at each other. In the background a phone began to ring. Michael heard footsteps, the sound of Mr László talking into the receiver, then a soft knock on the door.

'Not now,' called out Max.

'It might be important.'

'You're important.'

'More than Peter and Jenny?'

Sighing, Max touched Michael's forehead. 'That's some bruise forming. Did Robert give it to you?'

'In a manner of speaking.' He thought of what he'd done and felt ashamed. 'I've behaved like an idiot.'

'You don't have to justify yourself to me. I'm on your side, and I always will be.'

Michael explained what had taken place. Max said nothing, just listened, nodding occasionally.

'What should I do?' he asked when he had finished.

'What do you think you should do?'

'Go back, I suppose. Try to sort it out.'

'I think that would be a mistake. Best if you stay here, just for a few days until things cool down.'

'That isn't going to happen. This is the opportunity Becky's parents have been waiting for. They've probably already reported me to the police for GBH.'

'I doubt it. And even if they have, the police will only view it as a family row that became a little overheated.'

'I'm not family.' He paused. 'Anyway, it's more complicated than that.'

Max waited expectantly.

'Becky's last boyfriend was called Eric. He'd been at school with Robert and the two of them were friends. He was like most of Robert's friends: unimaginative and not too bright. The sort of person that Robert can dominate, and beside whom he can shine.

'Becky's parents loved him. He adored Becky, always laughed at Mr Blake's jokes, and, best of all, still lived in Winchester. I think they secretly hoped that Becky would marry him, move back home and give them half a dozen grandchildren they could see every day. Maybe she would have done if I hadn't come along and ruined it.

'Becky introduced me to Robert first. The three of us went out for dinner and it was a disaster. I tried to be friendly but he spent the whole evening trying to wind me up, talking about "Eric this" and "Eric that". I think he wanted me to be dazzled by him, and when he saw that I wasn't he resented me for it.

'A few weeks later Becky took me to Winchester to meet her parents. They were quite cool towards me. Robert had already started putting the knife in, and they were gearing up to dislike me as much as he did.

'During our visit there was a big party to celebrate Mr Blake's birthday. Robert invited Eric and spent the whole evening plying him with drink and making up stories about the terrible things I was supposed to have said about him. Eric got completely worked up and at the end of the evening he made a lunge for me. He was a big guy. I had to defend myself, and in the scuffle I ended up knocking out one of his teeth. Of course Becky's parents saw the whole thing as my fault and decided that their darling daughter was throwing her life away on a delinquent thug. What happened this evening will just confirm their prejudice, and there's no way they'll let it drop.'

'Oh, I think they will,' Max told him.

The certainty in the voice took him by surprise. 'You don't know that.'

'Don't I?'

'What do you mean?'

Max shook his head dismissively. 'Nothing. Forget I said it. I just don't like seeing you so worried. Tell me, did you bring anything with you when you left the flat?'

He shook his head.

'Well, let's go round there and pick up enough to see you through the next few days.'

He was confused. 'I thought you said I shouldn't go back.'

'If Robert's nose is broken then he and his family will be drinking foul-tasting coffee in Casualty as we speak. That means the coast will be clear.'

'Look, I'm not sure—'

'Well, I am. You're not alone, Mike. You've got me, and I promise you that everything is going to work out OK.'

Max steered his car into a parking space opposite the flat. Michael, sitting in the passenger seat, realised that earlier that evening the same space had been occupied by Mr Blake's Saab.

Leaving Max to light a cigar, he walked towards the flat, noticing that someone had left the living room light on. He let himself in.

And was confronted by Mr Blake, his fleshy face crimson with rage.

'Thought you could skulk back unnoticed, did you? Well, no such luck! I knew you'd try something like this, and I'm here to tell you that you're going to be very sorry for what you've done to my son!'

Michael felt his stomach lurch. 'Look, Mr Blake ...' he began.

'Don't you bloody Mr Blake me, you little thug!' The sunken eyes seemed on the point of bursting out of their sockets. The mouth was just opening to unleash a fresh barrage of bile when Max walked in and said, in his most charming voice, 'Mr Blake, what a pleasure to see you again. I hope you enjoyed the rest of your birthday.'

Mr Blake, thrown completely, made a monumental effort to compose himself.

Max gave Michael a reassuring smile. 'Why not go and get your things together?' he suggested before turning back to Mr Blake. 'Perhaps the two of us could have a quick word somewhere with an ashtray.' He gestured towards the living room. 'In there, perhaps?'

Mr Blake took a deep breath. 'Do you know what he's done?'

'I do. That's a splendid tan, by the way. You went to Barcelona, I understand, which is one of my favourite cities. Tell me, where did you stay?' As Max spoke, he manoeuvred Mr Blake into the living room and closed the door behind them.

Michael, left alone in the corridor, wanted to eavesdrop on their conversation but felt suddenly afraid at what he might hear. Instead he made his way to the bedroom, where he collected his work suit and packed a bag with a few clothes and toiletries before warily making his way back to the hall.

The door of the living room opened. Max and Mr Blake stepped out. Max was still smiling. And so was Mr Blake. A furtive, guilty smile that sat uneasily on his heavy features.

Max saw him. 'Why don't you give me the bag?' Michael, too busy staring at Mr Blake, hardly noticed him take it. Mr Blake returned his gaze. The familiar dislike was in his eyes but the smile remained.

Max offered Mr Blake his hand. 'Please give my regards to your lovely wife.'

'I will,' Mr Blake assured him.

Michael opened his mouth to speak. Max shook his head, put a hand on his shoulder and guided him out of the door.

'All this excitement has given me an appetite,' said Max as he started the engine. 'What do you fancy? Indian? Thai?'

'I'm not hungry.'

'You need to eat. If you don't want to go out then I'll have Mrs László cook something.' Max guided the car down the street. 'That might be best. After all, you've got a busy day in the office tomorrow.'

'No, I haven't.'

'Really? Then you're to phone in sick and I'm taking you to Suffolk for a long weekend. Just the two of us.'

'I can't do that. I need to see Becky.'

'And you will, but now is not the time. Trust me. She'll be feeling as raw as you are, and the most probable outcome of a face-to-face meeting right now is a permanent split. Is that what you want?'

'Of course not.' He hesitated. 'I mean—'

'You don't know what you want, Mike. How can you? This is all too immediate. You have to give yourself some distance and work out how you feel. A change of scene will help you do that.'

The car stopped at traffic lights. Max smiled encouragingly. 'We'll drive up there tomorrow morning, play some golf, have some good meals, walk on the beach and talk it all through. Figure out what you really want and how to achieve it. What do you say?'

'You really think that's best?'

'I do. And if you want to talk to Becky then there's always

the telephone.' Max continued to smile. 'Now stop worrying.'

The traffic lights turned to green. The car moved forward, leaving the quiet residential streets behind, making for the noise and lights of central London. Max put on a CD of Barber's *Adagio for Strings*. It was one of Michael's favourite pieces. He wanted to sit and listen, but there was something he had to know first.

'What did you say to Mr Blake?'

'Put him a proposal he couldn't refuse.'

'What proposal?'

'That if he made sure that no assault charges were brought against you, I'd make sure that Robert acquired a list of new clients sufficiently impressive to guarantee him a partnership before the end of the year.'

'And he agreed?'

'Of course. I told you once that everyone has their weak spot. Mr Blake's weakness is his love for his children.'

The choice of words troubled him. 'Love shouldn't be a weakness.'

'Oh, but it is. The greatest weakness known to man. It can sap the strength faster than any disease, and there is no known cure.'

As he spoke, Max's eyes remained fixed on the road ahead. Michael sensed that though the words were meant for him, Max was in fact talking to himself.

He trusted Max but still felt uneasy. Sitting back, he tried to concentrate on the music.

NINE

Sunday evening. Michael, just returned from Suffolk, stood in the hallway of Max's house. Max followed him in, carrying a weekend bag.

Mrs László, a small, plump woman with a kind face, appeared from the back of the house to say that supper would be ready in fifteen minutes. 'But Mrs László,' said Max gently, 'I told your husband we'd be having dinner on the way back.'

'Fifteen minutes,' repeated Mrs László before heading back to the kitchen.

Max groaned.

'Maybe she didn't get the message.'

'Don't you believe it. That woman lives to cook. In her book anyone under twenty stone is chronically undernourished.'

Michael smiled.

'You were very quiet on the journey.'

'I'm OK.'

The dark eyes were full of concern. 'You can tell me, you know.'

'You've listened to enough of my grief over the last three days.'

'That's what I'm here for. Are you wishing you'd phoned Becky?'

He nodded.

'You could phone her now.' A pause. 'If you know what you want to say.'

But that was the problem. After three days of talking he still didn't.

As early as Friday lunchtime he had wanted to call her, full of remorse and fearful that he had lost her for ever. And Max, who had good reason to think ill of her, instead acted as her champion, agreeing that a call was a good idea and reminding him in that beautiful, restful voice how special she was, how lucky he was to have found her and how terrible it would be if the two of them were to part.

'Of course,' Max concluded, 'if you do make up then it may be hard for the two of us to see each other. But I accept that. Becky's wishes are the most important thing.'

And as he listened, the doubts began to whisper inside his head. Why were her feelings so important? What about his own? If they were always to take second place, then was she really so great a loss?

Remorse faded, replaced by anger and resentment, which had lasted until early evening when he started to long for the sound of her voice. Max, sympathetic as before, had again urged him to call, reminding him of just how important her feelings were. This in turn rekindled his anger, so throughout the weekend his emotions had swung from one extreme to another like a pendulum, leaving him confused as to just what he really did want to achieve from a phone call.

'Do you know what you want to say?' asked Max.

He shook his head.

'Then leave it. Call her at work tomorrow when you don't run the risk of speaking to one of her family.' Max smiled reassuringly. 'Things often seem clearer after a good night's sleep.'

Perhaps they did, but he wouldn't bet on it.

He took his bag upstairs. His room was on the second floor, at the front of the house and directly above Max's. Putting the bag on the bed, he opened the window and stared down at the street below. An expensively dressed middle-aged couple climbed out of a Mercedes, arguing loudly in what sounded like Russian. He had read somewhere that many newly rich Russians had bought houses in central London, offering briefcases of money to bewildered estate agents. It would take many briefcases to buy a house like this.

He went to open his bag. What he saw above the bed stopped him in his tracks.

The painting that had hung there was gone. In its place was his framed *Napoléon* film poster.

His other film posters covered the walls, while his CD player, discs and videos sat on the desk below a row of shelves full of his books.

He opened the wardrobe. His suits, shirts and trousers hung on a rail. His other clothes were folded in drawers, and his shoes lay in pairs on the floor.

There were footsteps in the corridor. Max stood in the doorway.

'What's all my stuff doing here?'

Max looked apologetic. 'I phoned Mr László yesterday. As it seemed likely you'd be staying here a little longer, I asked him to pick up some of your work shirts. He took it upon himself to bring everything else too.'

Again he looked round the room. How long had it taken Mr László to collect all this stuff? How had his doing so looked to Becky? Had she helped him pack?

304

And had she been glad to do so?

'I'm sorry, Mike. He didn't want you to find yourself short of anything.'

'No risk of that now.'

'Try not to be angry. He meant well.'

'Did he see Becky? What did she say?'

'We didn't talk about that. When he realised he'd blundered, he became upset, and I didn't have the heart to start interrogating him.' Max sighed. 'Anyway, if someone's to blame, then it's me. My instructions should have been clearer.'

Michael felt embarrassed. 'I don't blame you. You've been fantastic about all this. I don't blame Mr László either. It was kind of him to go to so much trouble.'

'Are you sure?'

'Yes.'

'Good. Come and have something to eat.'

'Must I? I'm not hungry.'

'But Mrs László's made a seafood risotto. She knows it's one of your favourites. Just a few bites. It would make her so happy.'

Michael managed a smile. 'OK.'

Together they made their way downstairs.

Half past eight the following morning. Michael, dressed in his suit, prepared to leave for work.

He felt exhausted. His sleep had been disturbed by dreams of running through the corridors of the Home in Bow, following the sound of Rebecca's voice but never able to find her. He had spent much of the night lying awake, staring up into the darkness, waiting for the morning and the chance to start putting things right between them.

Max appeared from the dining room. 'Sure you're up to a day in the office? Why not stay here and take it easy?'

'I should go in. There are things I need to do.'

'Will you phone Becky?'

'Yes.'

'Do you know what you want to say?'

'Not really.'

'You want her back, Mike. I can see it even if you can't. That's what you must say.'

'But if I do get back together with her, then where does that leave us?'

'Don't worry about that. I'm not going anywhere. But now it's time for you to sort this mess out. Call her at work, where she won't have her family around to cause trouble.'

He nodded.

'No Robert to try and put the knife in.'

He smiled. 'Amen to that.'

'Absolutely.'

Something in Max's tone caught his attention. 'What do you mean?'

Max began to look uncomfortable.

'You meant something, didn't you?'

'No.'

'Yes, you did. What are you keeping from me?'

'Nothing.'

'You're lying. You told me to trust you, so why are you lying to me?'

'Because it's something you don't need to know.'

His heart began to race. 'Something about Becky?'

No answer.

'What did Robert say?'

'It doesn't matter. The whole thing was absurd. Anyone can see how much she loves you.'

At first he was confused. 'Of course she does. I know she does.'

Then came understanding.

'Is she cheating on me? Is that what he said?'

'What does it matter? The whole thing was a pack of lies.'

His legs felt weak beneath him. He put his hand on the telephone table to steady himself. 'I want to know what he said.'

'Something about an ex-boyfriend. It wasn't an affair, just a single night. But you mustn't—'

'Which ex-boyfriend? Eric?'

'Mike!' Max looked angry. 'It isn't true, and I want you to drop it right now.'

'How can you be sure?'

'Do you really think I'd have got where I am without being able to tell when someone is lying to me?' Max's expression softened. 'You have to trust me on this. There is absolutely no truth in it. None at all.'

Michael stared down at the white carpet, breathing deeply, trying to steady himself. 'OK. I'm sorry. It's just that the idea really freaked me out.'

'You don't have to explain.' The tone was soothing. 'I understand.'

'I can't believe Robert would say that to you. What a bastard!'

Max shook his head. 'Try not to hate him. Underneath the swagger he's really just a lonely individual who'd give anything to have someone care about him the way Becky cares about you.'

Michael shook his head. 'That's no excuse.'

'Well, maybe you're right. You know, he even tried to suggest that this boyfriend had given Becky a disease. I was about to order him out of the restaurant when I realised that he only meant the flu.'

Becky had had flu. After her last weekend in Winchester. The home of her parents.

And Eric.

Max began to look worried. 'Mike, it's nothing. You have to put this out of your head.'

Michael turned and made for the door.

Noon. He sat at his desk, the telephone in his hand, preparing to dial the number of Chatterton's bookshop.

He had already tried to phone Emily to find out what she knew. She might have been Rebecca's best friend but she was his friend too. He was sure she would tell him if she knew something.

But she was not available. Away in York, helping out at some literary festival.

That left Rebecca herself.

He dialled the number. It rang four times, then someone answered. He recognised her voice, opened his mouth to speak, then hung up. This couldn't be done on the telephone. He needed to see her face when she answered the questions he would put to her.

Half an hour later he strode along the Strand, perspiring in the muggy midday heat so that his shirt stuck to his skin like fly-paper.

As he approached the shop Rebecca emerged with Clare. He called her name and she turned. Momentarily her face lit up. In spite of his anger he still felt his heart lift.

Then her expression became a frown. 'What do you want?'

'What do you think?'

Clare whispered something. 'There's no need,' Rebecca told her.

'I think there is,' Clare replied, giving Michael an encouraging smile before slipping back into the shop.

They faced each other on the pavement while the lunchtime

crowds jostled around them. 'I suppose you want to talk,' she said.

'No, I want to go ballroom dancing.'

'Don't raise your voice to me, Michael. Not after what you've done.'

He started to laugh. 'After what I've done? You're funny, Beck. Ever thought about trying stand-up?'

'If that's your attitude, then forget it. I've got better things to do with my lunch hour.'

'I can imagine.'

Her eyes narrowed. 'What's that supposed to mean?'

'You work it out.'

'I'm not in the mood for games.' She made as if to go.

'Don't walk away from me!'

Passers-by were staring at them. Two teenage girls began to giggle. He didn't care, and neither did she. Her eyes began to flash. 'Why not? Does it hurt your feelings? Well, why should I care? You've made it perfectly clear that you don't give a damn about mine!'

'That's not true.'

'The Michael Turner I knew had courage. If he was going to break up with me he would have told me to my face rather than hiding in Suffolk and sending one of Max's flunkies to collect his stuff.'

His anger receded, as unexpectedly he found himself on the defensive. 'I didn't send him. Max did.'

'That figures.'

'You don't understand. He was only supposed to get a couple of shirts. I was horrified when I found out what he'd done. I knew how much it would upset you.'

'As if you care.'

'I do!'

'It's been four days, Mike. You haven't phoned once. Not to

ask how Robert's doing. Broken nose, but he'll recover – thanks for asking. Not to ask how I'm doing. Terrible, if you really want to know. Four days and not a single call.'

The heat was overpowering. He wiped sweat from his forehead. 'I wanted to call.'

'But Max wouldn't let you, I suppose.'

'No. He thought I should.'

'But in spite of all his encouragement you didn't get around to picking up the receiver. Which was just what he wanted.'

'Crap!'

'Face it, Mike. He's turned you into his puppet. He pulls the strings and you jump.'

'I'm not a puppet!'

'I defended you! You put my brother in Casualty, but I kept defending you. Mum and Dad were screaming at me to finish with you, but I wouldn't. I told them that Robert had provoked you, that it wasn't your fault and that I wouldn't hear a word against you. Mum won't even talk to me now! She said she was ashamed I was her daughter.'

Tears came into her eyes. 'And what do you do? Nothing! You don't call me. You send someone else to pack up your stuff. Can you imagine how that made me feel?'

Shame swept over him. He didn't answer. In the distance Nelson's Column stood proud against the perfect blue sky.

'I deserved better than that. You hurt me so badly. I couldn't live with myself if I'd hurt you like that.'

Unable to face her gaze, he hung his head. Then, staring down at his dusty shoes, he remembered why he was here.

'So how do you live with the fact that you spent the night with Eric?'

He looked up, staring into her eyes, searching for signs of indignation or confusion. But finding only alarm.

He forced out a laugh. 'Good was it? Can't see it somehow.

310

You told me once that he wasn't much cop in the sack, but perhaps he's improved.'

She swallowed. 'It's not what you think.'

'You spent the night with your ex-boyfriend! What am I supposed to think?'

'You could think about trusting me, rather than jumping to stupid conclusions.'

'So I'm stupid, am I?'

'I didn't mean that.'

'I want to know everything. Was Winchester the first time? Have you met him since? How long has it been going on?'

'Nothing's going on! You've got this all wrong.'

'So what happened?'

She held up her hands in a gesture of placation 'OK, I'll tell you. I went out on the Friday night with a girlfriend from school and we bumped into Eric in a pub. He'd been seeing some girl, but she'd just broken up with him, and he was drunk and in a terrible state. I had Mum's car, so I gave him a lift home, made him some coffee and we sat and talked. That's all.'

'Oh, sure!'

'It's true! I felt sorry for him. I've known him most of my life, and I hated to see him unhappy. He just needed someone to talk to.'

'So why did you stay the night?'

'Because it was the early hours of the morning and I was too tired to drive. He made up the spare bed for me. That's the truth. It was completely innocent.'

'So why didn't you tell me?'

'Because I knew how you'd react. I thought it better if you didn't know.'

'Well, too late now.'

'Who told you? Robert?'

'It doesn't matter who told me.'

'It was Max, wasn't it?'

'What if it was?'

It was her turn to laugh.

'What's so funny?'

'You are. Someone who had a mind of his own before he was lobotomised by Max Somerton.'

'This is nothing to do with Max. This is about you and Eric.'

Again she laughed. 'Forgive me. What was I thinking of? Max is perfect. He could never be at fault.'

'You're the one who's at fault.'

'Of course. Max said so, and he's never wrong.'

'At least I know he'd never lie to me.'

In spite of the heat she grew pale. 'Oh Mike,' she said softly. 'Is that really how it is now? You can trust him but you can't trust me?'

'Looks that way, doesn't it?'

'Then he's won.'

'What do you mean?'

'That it's over between us.'

'Haven't we been down this road before? Aren't you supposed to order me to stop seeing him? Isn't that part of the script?'

'Not any more.'

He felt a sudden lurch in the pit of his stomach.

'When we first got together, I thought you were the most exciting person I'd ever met. You'd had a difficult life, but you'd risen above it. You had this strength inside you, this drive to succeed, and it made me feel alive just being with you. But all that's gone now. Max has destroyed it, and in the process he's destroyed us too.'

She took off her engagement ring and offered it to him.

'It won't work, Beck. Not this time.'

'It's not a ploy, Mike. This is real. This is the end.'

He shook his head. 'I don't want this.'

'But I do.'

He looked into her eyes. He knew she meant it.

She continued to hold out the ring. This time he took it.

They stared at each other. This time he was the one whose eyes were watering. Angrily he shook his head. 'If you walk away from me then it really is over. I'll never have you back, no matter what you do.'

'I know,' she said and turned to leave.

'Becky!'

She turned back.

'Don't do this.'

She took his face in her hands and stared into his eyes. 'I believe in you,' she whispered. 'I always have and I always will. Never forget that. You can do anything you want with your life. Don't let someone else control it for you.'

She kissed his cheek, then moved away. This time he didn't call out but stood and watched her walk out of his life, while people pushed past him, all wrapped up in their own emotions, oblivious to his pain.

TEN

Thursday lunchtime. Three days later. Michael, returning to his desk from the library, saw a phone message on his computer screen. Just a financial adviser, trying to sell him a pension.

Rebecca had used to phone a dozen times a day, wanting to tell him things or just to hear the sound of his voice. Sometimes, when busy, he had found the constant calls annoying, but now they had stopped he would have given anything to have that annoyance back in his life.

Kim had left a fax on his chair: twenty pages long and marked 'urgent'. Unable to concentrate, he pushed it to one side. Stuart's chair was empty. He was in one of the downstairs conference rooms, trapped in an endless client meeting.

Jack Bennett appeared in the doorway. 'Am I disturbing you?'

'No.'

'There's a conference call this afternoon on the Chassock deal at half past four.'

He nodded.

'It's not an important call. Don't worry if you're too busy.'

'I'll be there.'

Jack remained where he was, shuffling awkwardly. Michael realised that to an outsider it might seem he was the partner and Jack the assistant.

'Not too overworked, then?' Jack asked.

'No.'

'Well, be sure to say if you are.' A pause. 'How's Max?'

'Fine.'

'Good. Please—'

'I'll give him your regards.'

Jack left. Michael stared at his desk, depressed at the thought of the conference call. The client was a windbag, and it was bound to run on for hours. But he didn't have to take part if he didn't want to. Jack had said so, but it was Max he had to thank.

It was a week since his run-in with Bruce Hammond, and he had yet to be called to account. The previous afternoon he had bumped into Bruce in the staff canteen, and Bruce had smiled affably as if nothing had happened. He probably had Max to thank for that too.

The realisation troubled him. He knew he was talented and had the potential to succeed. But he wanted that success to be based on the strength of his own abilities rather than on the power and influence of another.

There were times when he hated this situation. But the feeling unsettled him because it was almost akin to hating Max, and he could never do that.

Over the last three evenings he had spent hours sitting in Max's study, pouring out his heart, often in tears, while Max had listened in silence, smiling sympathetically in a way that was more soothing than a thousand words of comfort.

No, he could never hate Max.

The phone rang and he recognised Max's mobile number on the display. It came as a surprise, as Max was supposed to be having lunch with some Dutch businessmen who wanted to buy one of his shareholdings. He picked up the receiver. 'Hi. Was the meal cancelled?'

'Sadly not. I've left my companions to stuff themselves with tiramisu and come up with a better offer while I give you a call. You seemed so down last night. I've been worrying about you.'

He was touched. 'There's no need.'

'Do you mind me calling? I don't want you to feel smothered.' The voice was warm and soothing.

'I'm glad you have.'

'Do you have plans tonight?'

'No.'

'I'm having dinner with Caroline. A Thai place just off Bond Street.'

'Oh, right.'

'Why don't you come? She'd like to see you.'

He hesitated. 'Are you sure? The two of you haven't seen each other for a while.'

'Of course. Don't you feel up to it?'

'Not really.'

'You have to start living again, Mike. I know it's hard, but it is the best thing.'

'OK, then.'

'Good.' Max gave him details of the restaurant. 'We're meeting for drinks at half past seven, so it may be easier for you to come straight from the office. Take it easy in the meantime and don't let Jack bully you.'

No chance of that.

He put the phone down. The urgent fax lay on his desk like a reproach. He went to the coffee point instead.

On the way back he saw Julia looking downcast. Kim had told him that Graham was in a foul mood, and he suspected that Julia was bearing the brunt of it. 'What's up?' he asked. 'Is Graham giving you a hard time?'

She nodded.

He tried to think of something encouraging to say. 'Still, not long before you escape to the commercial property department. Apparently Catherine Chester's a great person to sit with. It must be your reward for putting up with Graham.'

For a moment she smiled.

Then a strange expression came into her face. 'Graham's not that bad,' she said suddenly. 'If he gives me a hard time it's only because I deserve it.'

She headed off towards the lift. Surprised, he stood and watched her go.

Quarter to eight. He arrived at the restaurant.

A waitress in the costume of old Siam directed him to a small bar to the left of the main dining area. It was empty save for Max and Caroline, who sat, waiting, while oriental music played softly in the background. He saw them before they saw him. Though speaking in low voices, he could tell by their expressions that the conversation was a tense one.

They realised he was there. Caroline smiled, a strained gesture that just missed her eyes. A barman came, and he ordered lager. 'We were worried you'd got lost,' Max told him.

'Sorry. A conference call ran on.'

'Don't apologise. The others won't be here until eight, anyway.'

'Others?'

Max lit a cigar. 'Clients of Caroline's.'

'Prospective clients,' explained Caroline. 'That's what tonight is all about.' Her tone was crisp.

He felt uncomfortable. 'I don't want to be in the way.'

Instantly her expression softened. 'You won't. It's lovely to see you.' She rubbed his arm. 'I'm so sorry about Becky.'

'Thanks.'

Another couple entered the bar. He wondered if they might be the prospective clients, but they ordered drinks and went to sit by themselves.

'Is there no chance of patching things up?' Caroline asked him.

'I don't think so.'

'Would you like to?'

His drink arrived. 'Yes,' he said quietly. The main restaurant was filling now, and the hiss of conversation drifted towards them, mixed with the scent of spicy food. The barman left a bowl of crackers on their table. He ate one, only to realise that he had little appetite.

'Well, then, there's a chance,' Caroline said. Again she smiled. A proper one this time. 'Hang on to that, Mike. You two were good together.'

'He hardly needs reminding of that,' said Max sharply.

Her smile faded. 'I only meant that these things often have a way of working themselves out.'

'Not in my experience,' Max told her. 'A split this serious can never be rectified.'

The words stung. He sensed that Max was right, but still they stung. A lump formed in his throat. He swallowed half his drink, as if trying to wash it away.

'That's not true, Max,' said Caroline. 'There's always hope.'

A snort.

'There is!'

Max stubbed out his cigar. 'Why are you doing this?'

'Doing what?'

'Trying to raise his expectations. Can you imagine how

318

upsetting this has been for him? The last thing he needs is a hope-springs-eternal speech.' Max put a hand on Michael's shoulder. 'Are you OK?'

'I'm fine.' He took another gulp of his lager, giving them both his best smile.

But Max's eyes held him. Full of sympathy and under-standing. They were comforting, but they were also weakening.

'You're not, are you?'

The lump was back. He didn't trust himself to speak. A waiter came and led the other couple into the restaurant.

'I'm sorry, Mike,' Max continued. 'You're not ready for this yet. Why don't you head home?'

Gratefully, he rose to his feet.

'I didn't mean to upset you,' Caroline told him. She looked upset herself.

'You haven't, honestly.' He looked at his watch. Five to eight. 'I hope it goes well with the clients.'

Max downed the rest of his drink and stood up. 'Let's go, then.'

'You're coming too?'

'I'm not leaving you on your own in this state. What do you take me for?'

Caroline's eyes widened. 'You can't go! This is a huge account for me. I need your support.'

'Mike needs me too. Or doesn't that matter?'

'Of course it does, but—'

'But what?'

Michael felt uncomfortable. 'Look, I'll be all right on my own.'

'But what?' repeated Max. 'Michael's life has just fallen apart. Do you really think some contract is more important than that?'

'I didn't mean that. I just—'

'Yes, you did.' He stared at her with eyes as cold as granite. 'I thought you valued the feelings of others, but clearly I was mistaken. Well, I'm sorry, but I don't want to waste any more time or emotion on someone whose priorities are so distorted. Goodbye.'

The blood drained out of Caroline's face.

Max turned. Caroline grabbed hold of his arm. 'Max! Please! You can't do this!'

He shrugged her off. 'Your guests will be here in a minute,' he told her. 'Don't let them see you in this state.'

Then he marched a bewildered Michael out of the restaurant.

Outside, they stood together on the pavement waiting for a taxi.

'You can't just break up like that.'

Max breathed smoke into the warm evening air. 'Why not?' he asked. 'It wasn't working out between us anyway.' His tone was so nonchalant that he might have been talking about the weather.

A taxi was approaching. Max flagged it down. 'Are you hungry? We could stop for a bite to eat on the way home.' His eyes were as warm as always. Michael remembered the coldness they had shown to Caroline and prayed that they would never show such coldness to him.

Because he needed Max, shameful though it was to admit. In the last year he had grown used to having people love him and had come to depend on those who did. Rebecca had loved him, but now she was gone and Max was all he had left.

The taxi arrived. Max opened the door and he climbed inside.

*

Friday morning. Emily, who had been at a meeting, returned to her desk to find two phone messages waiting on her chair. One was from a French publisher, enquiring about a new novelist the agency was representing; the other was from her father, asking her to call.

She began to tremble, a disturbing mixture of excitement and dread. Picking up the receiver she dialled the number, her hand shaking so hard that three times her finger slipped and she had to start again.

It rang and then was answered. A gentle voice said, 'Hello.'

'It's me.'

She heard him exhale. Fighting his emotions perhaps. Just as she was.

'How are you?' he asked.

She could have told the truth but knew that it was not what he needed to hear. 'I'm well. And you?'

'Fine.'

'Good.' She knew that another question was hoped for but could not bring herself to ask it. Eventually he supplied the answer.

'Sheila's well too.'

Silence. He coughed. The way he always did when he was nervous. She waited.

'The thing is, we've decided to get rid of the armoire. It takes up too much space.'

'I see.' She tried not to sound indignant. It would only embarrass him.

'Sheila thought we should offer it to you. Do you want it?'

'Yes.'

'Then it's yours.' A pause. 'Do you think six hundred pounds is unreasonable?'

Her composure collapsed. 'It belonged to Mum! How can you ask me for money?'

She heard him sigh. 'It belongs to me now.'

'No, it belongs to her. Just like every other thing Mum ever valued.' She laughed harshly. 'All except one.'

Another silence.

'Please don't be like this,' he said weakly.

'Why not? Does it disturb your peace of mind? God forbid that I should ever do that.'

He gasped. She knew her anger frightened him, that it could only serve to widen the distance between them, but still she could not contain it.

'Because it's not your fault, is it? Nothing ever is. Fault requires action, not inertia.'

'Emmie—'

She flinched. 'I'm not Emmie. Not to you. You lost the right to call me that a long time ago.'

'Why must you be like this?'

'Do you really need me to tell you?'

He started to answer. More protests and denials that she didn't want to hear. She shut her eyes, as if that would block out the sound of his voice.

And in her self-imposed darkness she remembered the stillness. The beautiful, peaceful stillness that had come to a girl of eighteen, on the verge of making the biggest mistake of her life.

It hadn't frightened her then, but it did now.

She retreated behind a shield of formality. 'You'd better sell the armoire. I don't have anywhere to keep it.'

'Are you sure?'

'Yes. I must go.'

'Goodbye, then.'

She braced herself to put down the phone but couldn't do it.

'Dad!' The word felt foreign to her. She spoke it so rarely now.

'What?'

'I love you.'

'And you're still my Emmie.' His voice trembled. 'You always will be.'

The line went dead.

She put down the receiver. There were tears in her eyes, but she refused to let them fall. Tears would not resolve the situation. The past was set in stone, and what had been done could never be undone.

She tried to compose herself. The French publishers were waiting to hear from her. But an hour passed and she had still to make the call.

Twenty to one. Michael sat at a window table of a wine bar in the shadow of St Paul's waiting for Emily.

She was late. He checked his mobile was switched on while praying that she wouldn't call and cancel. There were so many questions he wanted to ask. How was Rebecca doing? Did she ever talk about him? Was there anything to suggest there might still be a chance for them?

It was raining. A summer shower that would be gone as quickly as it had come. People ran for cover in the street outside. Emily entered the bar and made her way to the table. Drops of rain shone in her hair like diamonds. A waiter took her drinks order and left two menus. She pushed hers to one side. 'I'm not hungry.'

Alarm bells started ringing. He tried not to show concern. 'Are you sure?'

She nodded.

'Well, I'm starving,' he lied. 'I'll order a big pizza and you can have a slice.'

Her hair hung over her face. As she brushed it back he saw that her eyes were red. 'Em, what is it?'

She told him about her conversation with her father. 'Didn't handle it very well, did I?'

'You were upset. It'll be better next time.'

'Assuming there is one. I keep telling myself that he's worth fighting for, but I don't think I believe it any more. I can't forget what happened. I can't forgive it either.'

'It wasn't easy for him, Em. You have to remember that.'

Her face darkened. 'And just how easy do you think it was for me?'

Her bitterness disturbed him. Gently he covered her hand with his own. 'I'm on your side. I'm sorry if I said the wrong thing. I just don't like seeing you upset, that's all.'

Slowly she smiled. It made her face beautiful. A classic Pre-Raphaelite oval, just as Rebecca had always said.

He felt an ache in his heart.

'You're thinking about her, aren't you?'

He nodded.

'I'm sorry, Mike. I shouldn't have dumped my problems on you.'

A waiter arrived to take their food order, making a joke about the weather as he did so. Michael feigned amusement while watching a group of young professionals sit down at the next table.

'Have you seen her?' he asked when the waiter had gone.

'Yes.'

'How is she?'

'OK.' A pause. 'She talked about you.'

'What did she say?'

'That she was worried about you. That she hoped you weren't too upset.'

He held his breath, waiting for her to say more. But nothing came.

'Is she missing me?'

Still nothing. She lowered her eyes while water from her hair dripped down on to her blouse.

'I need to know, Em. Is there a chance?'

'There's no chance. It really is over as far as she's concerned. Nothing you could do would make her change her mind. The best thing is to try to forget her.'

Suddenly he was eight years old again, listening to a social worker telling him that his mother was dead. The social worker had been an earnest man with John Lennon glasses and a huge birthmark spread across his cheek. He had stared at the mark, focusing all his attention on it, trying to ignore the fact that he felt as empty as if someone had scooped his insides out with a knife. Just as he felt now.

'I'm sorry,' she told him.

'It's not your fault. Thanks for being honest.'

'I'd never lie to you.'

'I know that.'

'You're not alone, Mike. You have me.'

The people at the next table were discussing office politics. He recognised one of the men as someone who had been at his college at Oxford.

'I'm here for you,' Emily told him. 'I always will be.'

'I know that too. I'm lucky to have a friend like you.'

She shook her head. 'I'm the lucky one.'

He managed a smile. She lifted his hand and held it against her cheek. Then she kissed his palm, a tiny gesture full of tenderness.

And desire.

'I love you, Mike. We're the same, you and I. We know what it's like to be alone in the world. We know about the fear and the pain. Together we could make it all go away.'

He felt dizzy. Instinctively he tried to pull his hand away.

325

But she clung to him. 'I understand you better than Becky ever did. I wouldn't have made you give up Max. I'd never make you give up anything you cared about.'

'Em …'

'She doesn't want you any more. She's discarded you like trash, but I would never do that. You could be happy with me. You could love me far more than you ever loved her.'

'No!'

He pulled his hand away. The wine bar fell silent as everyone turned to look, including the man from his old college who sat at the next table. Clive Southgate: an English student who had wanted to become an actor. Now he was probably slogging his way up the career ladder at a merchant bank. It was strange the way life worked out.

'You're wrong, Em,' he said. 'I love you, but as a friend. I need you to be my friend.'

A look of desperation came into her face. 'And what about what I need? Don't you care about that? Doesn't anybody care about that?'

'I care. Of course I do.'

'Why must it be her? All our lives it's been her. Just for once, why can't it be me?'

He didn't answer. There was nothing he could say. She stared at him, as conversations resumed around them. Her eyes were huge saucers full of pain. He wished he could make the pain go away, but he couldn't. Not in the way she wanted.

'I'm sorry,' he told her, hating the weakness of his words but knowing that there was nothing else he could say.

She took a deep breath, struggling for composure. 'You don't have to apologise. I'll be your friend. Your confidante. Whatever you want me to be.'

The waiter arrived with the pizza he'd hoped they would

share. But when they left the restaurant it remained untouched on the table.

'Are you sure you don't have it in stock?'

A nod.

'Absolutely sure?'

'Yes.'

It was Monday morning. Rebecca stood with Clare behind the counter at Chatterton's, forcing herself to smile while the old woman scowled at her. 'I expected it to be in this week.'

'Well, I'm afraid it's not.'

'Check your computer.'

'I've done that twice already.'

'Well, do it again!'

'There's no point.'

'I don't like your attitude, young woman. You should learn some manners.'

'For God's sake! We don't have the bloody book, so stop going on about it!'

The old woman's jaw dropped.

Clare took charge. 'I'm so sorry, madam,' she said sweetly. 'My assistant Keith will take your details so we can send you a free copy when it arrives. In the meantime—' she took Rebecca's arm '—perhaps we could have a word?'

'I don't need a lecture,' Rebecca said once the two of them were in the office.

Clare looked furious. 'How dare you talk to a customer like that!'

'She deserved it.'

'I don't care. You're paid to rise above it, and if you don't you could find yourself out of a job.'

'Big deal.'

'Oh, I forgot. This job's only a stopgap before you take the art world by storm. Well, try to remember that it's not like that for everyone. I'm manageress of this shop. I've worked damn hard to get here, and if that woman makes a complaint it's not just you who could be facing the sack.'

Rebecca felt ashamed. 'They wouldn't fire you,' she said quickly. 'You're the reason this shop is doing so well. I'll tell them that it's all my fault and that they'd be mad to let you go.'

Clare's expression softened. 'Let's forget it then. I do understand how hard things are for you right now but just be careful, OK?'

'Do you think she will complain?'

'Probably. Cranks usually do. We're talking about a woman who bought a Delia Smith cookbook and then returned to the shop carrying a cake she'd made, demanding a refund because it didn't look as good as the one in Delia's photograph.'

Rebecca nodded.

'That's your cue to laugh.'

She tried, but it was a poor effort.

'You could call him, you know.'

'And say what?'

'That you're not eating or sleeping. That you look a wreck.' A pause. An affectionate smile. 'And that I hate seeing you like this.'

'I'll be all right.'

'At least think about it. One phone call and you could be back together.'

She shook her head. On the table, behind Clare, was a tray of cream cakes. Whenever a member of staff had a birthday, they always bought cakes for the others. It was a tradition. She always saved hers for Michael. That was a tradition too.

'It's what you want, Becky. I'll bet my life it's what he wants too.'

'But it's not what Max wants.'

A Danish slice sat in the centre of the tray. Michael's favourite. But not this time.

She swallowed. 'We'd better get back. I'm sorry about before, Clare. I promise it won't happen again.'

Together they made their way back to the desk.

Wednesday afternoon. Five o'clock. Michael walked from the library to his office.

He was thinking about Emily. She had left numerous phone messages, and he had yet to call back. He had tried to convince himself that it was because he was too busy, but the truth was that he didn't know what to say to her.

She had asked that her outburst remain their secret, which was fine. And that they continue their friendship as before, which was not so easy. A declaration of that nature could never be forgotten.

He kept asking himself if he was to blame. Had he led her on in some way? Could his behaviour have tricked her into believing that something more than friendship was on offer?

But he had to call her soon. It wasn't fair to keep putting it off. If she wanted to pretend that nothing had happened, then that was what he must do.

As he approached his office he heard laughter. Julia and another trainee called Paul were standing in front of Stuart's desk, the three of them sharing a joke. He smiled as he entered. 'What's so funny, then?'

The laughter stopped, replaced by a nervous silence. He felt uncomfortable, as if he were an intruder in his own room.

'It's nothing,' Julia told him. Both she and Paul began to look guilty.

An unpleasant suspicion came to him. 'It must have been something.'

'I had to do a company search,' explained Paul. 'For Kate Kennedy. I got the pages in the wrong order.'

'What's funny about that?'

Paul shrugged. 'Well, you know …'

'No, I don't, but you were laughing your heads off when I walked in. So what's the joke?'

'It's no big deal, Mike,' said Stuart reassuringly.

'Well?'

Paul stared at the ground.

'You were laughing at me, weren't you?'

'No!' Julia's eyes widened with horror.

And fear.

Suddenly he knew exactly what was going on.

'You'd better go,' he said brusquely. 'I've got work to do.'

'They weren't laughing at you,' said Stuart once Julia and Paul had left.

Michael's eyes scanned his desk, searching for a draft agreement. He found one and threw it on to Stuart's lap. 'I want two copies of that now.'

'What?'

'Don't argue with me. Just do it.'

Stuart looked bewildered. 'Why are you acting like this?'

'Because I can. After all, I'm not like you any more. I'm special. I'm the partners' golden boy, and if I ever catch you gossiping about them I might decide to report it and screw your career.' He sat down at his desk and ran a hand through his hair. 'God, Stuart,' he said slowly, 'is that what you think?'

'Of course not. I know you better than that.'

'But it's what the others think, isn't it? If I hadn't been so preoccupied with Becky I would have noticed the signs earlier. Julia's been odd with me for a while now. Some of the other trainees have, too, and yesterday Nigel Wilson phoned me with a trivial company law question and was grovellingly apologetic

330

for wasting my time. Nigel and I started here on the same day. We've always helped each other out. How could he think that about me?'

They stared at each other while in the corridor outside one of the secretaries cursed the fax machine. 'Do you remember Susan Cobham?' Stuart asked him.

'No.'

'She was a summer student while I was a trainee in commercial property. All the trainees in the department liked her, and whenever we went for a drink and a bitching session we'd ask her along. Then someone found out that her uncle was the chairman of SaverCo, our biggest client at the time. Immediately the invitations stopped, in case anything she heard got repeated into the wrong ear. I'm sure she wouldn't have compromised any of us like that, but no one wanted to take the risk.'

Michael exhaled slowly. 'Just as they don't want to risk it with me.'

'Try to see it from where they're standing. You used to be the rebellious, outspoken one in the department. You were the one power junkies like Graham Fletcher and Kate Kennedy disapproved of, but suddenly they're bending over backwards to be nice to you. Rumours are spreading about your high-powered connections, and people wonder if they can still trust you.'

'Of course they can. Anyway, I don't have connections.'

'And I don't have a brain.'

'I didn't ask for this. It wasn't something I sought out.'

'Don't beat yourself up about it, Mike. Nothing's changed as far as I'm concerned. We're still friends, and I trust you absolutely. Others will too. Just give them time to realise you're still the same old revolutionary you always were.' Stuart looked at his watch. 'It's nearly half past five. Let's have a drink at Corney & Barrow and talk about it.'

'Sure.' He laughed sadly. 'It's not like anyone will reprimand us for leaving early.'

In spite of the early hour, Corney & Barrow was already packed. Stuart went to buy drinks while Michael, unable to find a table, stood watching people mill around him.

A plump, scruffy girl of about twenty, carrying a rucksack, entered the bar. She cried out 'Sean!' and began to make her way towards a young couple in their early twenties dressed in suits. The woman was Asian, the man Caucasian. Both were tall and attractive, with elegant features. The woman's eyes were dark and lively. The man's were blue and serene, devoid of any trace of the fear they had contained when last he'd seen them.

Which had been on a cold October afternoon fifteen years ago, standing on a street corner in Bow, watching a frightened nine-year-old called Sean being driven away to a new life in Canterbury.

The bar seemed to fade. For a moment he was overwhelmed with memories: the smell of the Home – a mixture of polish, burned food and dirty clothes – his constant longing for peace and privacy, and the sense of total abandonment as he watched that car drive away.

His stomach tied itself into knots. He couldn't deal with these feelings. Not now. He turned quickly, trying to escape, bumping into a man nearby and causing him to spill half his drink. The man swore, and a few people glanced over to see what was happening.

Sean was one of them. His eyes were full of the friendly disinterest of one who has never seen the object of sympathy before and does not expect to again.

Then they widened.

At first they just stared at each other. Slowly, Sean began to smile.

Apologising to the man, he watched Sean talking excitedly to his companions. Then they made their way over.

'I don't believe it,' said Sean slowly. 'I never thought I'd see you again.' The Home Counties accent disorientated Michael. The Sean he remembered had had a different accent. But then, fifteen years ago so had he.

'Looks like you were wrong.'

'Yes, it does.' Sean continued to smile. 'This,' he said, gesturing to the Asian woman, 'is my girlfriend Maya. And this—' he turned to the girl with the rucksack '—is my sister Cathy.'

'You don't have a sister.'

'He does now,' said Cathy brightly.

'Mum and Dad adopted Cathy a year after they adopted me,' Sean explained.

'Pity me,' laughed Cathy, 'getting stuck with him.'

Old feelings of protectiveness rose up in Michael. 'There's nothing wrong with him.'

She looked embarrassed. 'I was only joking.'

A group of women had moved into the space behind him. One of them was wearing Calvin Klein's Obsession: Rebecca's favourite scent.

'Sean used to talk about you all the time,' Cathy told him. 'It drove us all mad.'

'Sorry.'

Again she looked embarrassed. 'It didn't really. We liked hearing about you.'

He nodded. The woman behind him was laughing: a light, airy sound that reminded him of Rebecca too. He had lost her now, just as he had once lost Sean, only to be reunited with a professional man who bore no trace of the frightened boy who had once been the most important person in his life. That boy no longer existed, just as fifteen years from now the girl he loved would have metamorphosed into a happy housewife with a husband and children and only the faintest memories of a man called Michael Turner.

'Mum and Dad,' he said softly. 'Things have changed for you since Bow.'

'We're meeting them for dinner tonight. Why don't you come? They'd love to meet you.'

'There's no point. I'm not the person you told them about. Not any more.'

Again they stared at each other. Both bewildered at the transformation in the other.

Maya put her hand on Cathy's arm. 'Come on,' she said softly. 'Let's leave them to talk.' The two of them slipped away.

'Please come, Mike,' said Sean. 'It would mean a lot to all of us.'

'I'd rather not. Don't think I'm not pleased to see you. It's just that this is a difficult time for me.'

Sean looked concerned. 'Can I help?'

He smiled ruefully. 'Last time we were together you were the one who needed help.'

'Maybe it's time for me to repay the favour.'

'You don't owe me anything.'

'Yes, I do. I would never have survived in that place if it hadn't been for you.'

'Forget it. Sharing a room with you was the happiest time of my childhood. I'm glad things worked out for you. You deserved it.'

Silence. While around them the air was full of the laughter of others. So many times Rebecca had urged him to trace Sean. Whenever he had imagined their reunion, she had always been standing at his side.

A terrible sense of emptiness swept over him. 'Well,' he said as cheerfully as he could manage, 'it's been good to see you. Take care of yourself.'

Sean looked hurt. 'Couldn't we meet for a drink sometime? I mean, just to catch up.'

He shook his head. 'Like I said, I'm a different person now.'

'You're not so different.'

'But you are.'

Sean sighed. 'Can I tell you something?'

'If you want.'

'Do you remember the photograph you sent me? The one of me and my mother in a garden that I thought I'd lost.'

He nodded.

'I had it framed and kept it on my bedside table. Even though I have a new family, I've never forgotten her. That picture helped keep my memories alive, and I'll never be able to thank you enough for sending it back to me.' An awkward pause. 'I just wanted you to know that.'

'Thanks, Sean. That means a lot to me.'

'So you take care of yourself, too, OK?'

'OK.'

Sean walked away, back to Maya and Cathy, who were waiting at the other end of the bar. Michael watched him go. The girl behind him kept laughing – the same, throaty laugh that was so like Becky's.

Stuart appeared, carrying drinks. 'Bloody bar staff are on a go-slow. Who were you talking to?'

'Just someone I used to know.'

He sipped his drink, but his mouth was full of the scent of Rebecca's perfume and the stale stench of the Home. 'I'm sorry, Stu, but I can't stay here. I'll explain tomorrow.'

He pushed his way through the crowds towards the door.

Half an hour later he was walking along Arundel Crescent.

As he approached Max's house he saw a tall, slender girl with short blonde hair standing outside.

'Becky!'

He ran along the pavement towards her. She had her back to him and seemed lost in thought, so that when he put his hand on her shoulder she let out a cry of alarm, whirled round to face him and he saw that it wasn't her at all.

'I'm sorry. I thought you were someone else.'

She nodded, looking flustered. Again he apologised, then slipped past her, up the stairs towards Max's front door. There was no need to ring the bell for admission. Max had given him his own set of keys.

He closed the door behind him. Two letters lay on the hall table, both addressed to him. Peter must have brought them round from the flat.

Max appeared from the living room, followed by the sound of the television news. 'Did you see your mail?'

He nodded.

'I'll speak to the post office. Have your stuff redirected here.'

'Is that necessary? I probably won't be here that long.'

'I'll do it anyway. It saves messing about.' Max smiled. 'I called you at the office but was told you'd left early. Where did you go?'

'For a drink with Stuart.'

'Must have been a quick one.'

'Wasn't really in the mood.' There was a glass panel by the door. Through it he could see the girl with blonde hair still standing on the pavement.

The dark eyes studied him. 'What is it?'

'There was a girl outside the house. She looked like Becky, and I thought, just for a moment ...'

'We've talked about this,' said Max gently. 'It's over, Mike. You have to let go.'

'It's not that easy.'

'I know that. It's the hardest thing in the world. But we'll get through it together, I promise we will.'

'We?'

'Of course. Your problems are my problems now, and we fight them together.'

The words made him feel dependent. Like a child. He tried to push the feeling away. 'I don't need someone to fight beside me.'

'We all need someone. The worst thing in this world is to be alone. But you're not alone now. You'll never be alone as long as I'm alive.'

Something stirred in his memory. Something dark and unsettling. 'That's what your uncle said when your father was dying. He swore that you'd never be alone as long as he was alive.'

A pained look came into Max's eyes. 'That's true,' he said. 'And then, a few weeks later, he abandoned me. Are you afraid I'm going to do that to you?'

He shook his head.

'Maybe just a little afraid?'

Silence. The television news ended and was replaced by the weather. More sunshine was forecast. Another glorious summer day.

'I traced my uncle,' Max told him. 'Did I ever tell you that? Just like you once traced your father. He'd ended up in Manchester running a taxi company. Did quite well for a few years, until rivals moved in and put him out of business. Then he discovered he had cancer. He had no family or close friends and spent the last months of his life alone in hospital, dying a year before I started searching.' A sad smile. 'Ironic, really.'

'I'm sorry. I didn't mean . . .'

'I'm not my uncle, Mike, and you're not your father. They made their choices, just as now we make ours. Let's not make their mistakes.'

He nodded.

'Let's go out tonight. See a show or something. It'll help take your mind off things.'

'I thought you were busy. Aren't the Dutch back in town?'

'Indeed they are. Still panting to buy my shares. Well, I think they can wait a little longer.'

'They might lose interest.'

'What if they do? It's only money.'

He stared into the dark eyes and for a moment everything in his life was uncomplicated and clear. Just for a moment.

'I've got a paper in the other room,' Max told him. 'Let's decide what to see.'

Again he looked through the glass panel by the door. There were people on the pavement, but of the girl with blonde hair there was no trace.

ELEVEN

Wednesday morning. Two weeks later.

Michael lay in his bed at Arundel Crescent. Though it was not yet seven, sunshine already streamed under the curtains and across the room.

He stared at his *Ten Commandments* film poster hanging on the far wall. At first it had seemed out of place in these surroundings, but with time came familiarity, and now there were moments when he could not imagine it hanging anywhere else.

Rising from the bed, he looked out of the window at the perfect blue sky. Down below a man appeared from a nearby house, climbed into a car and drove away. David Bishop, chairman of a leading merchant bank. David always left his house at seven. You could set your watch by him.

He entered the en suite bathroom and stepped into the shower. A sophisticated heating appliance hung on the wall. It had taken some time to master, but now he adjusted the controls with the skill of an old pro. Water blasted his face like a hammer, driving away the last vestiges of sleep.

Back in the bedroom he opened the wardrobe. His suits

hung ready, together with an array of shirts, all ironed by Mrs László. He had told her that it wasn't necessary and she had smiled, nodded and ignored him completely. Not that it mattered. He wouldn't be staying much longer.

Would he?

He knew he should leave. Max had said as much. 'You'll be wanting your own place, Mike. The last thing you need is me around all the time, cramping your style. I'll miss you, of course, but I know it's for the best.' The words were meant to encourage him, but instead had acted as a reminder of just how much he had grown to need Max's emotional support, and although he had contacted several letting agencies he had yet to view the properties they offered.

Not that he had had much opportunity to do so. His leisure time seemed to be taken up with dinners, plays, trips to Suffolk and other outings Max had arranged in order to keep his mind off things, and which he felt he could not refuse for fear of offending one to whom he owed such gratitude. So days turned into weeks, and slowly he began to think of this house as home.

He fastened the buttons on his shirt, then picked out an Italian suit he had bought last year from Moss Bros. Rebecca had thought it a good fit. Max had suggested otherwise. 'You're going places, Mike, and you need to dress the part. So no more off-the-peg stuff. Let me take you to my tailor for a fitting.' He had protested at the expense, but his objections had been brushed aside. 'Forget the cost. Let's just call it a late birthday present.'

There had been a number of those. His battered old CD player had been relegated to a cupboard, replaced by a top-of-the-range music system. It sat on the desk in his room, next to a new laptop computer, while new designer casuals hung in his wardrobe and a new Rolex hung from his wrist. In recent weeks he had learned not to look in shop windows for fear that Max would think he craved what was displayed there and rush to buy it for him.

He fixed his cufflinks then sat on the bed, skimming through a brochure from a luxury car dealership. The previous evening, on the way to a restaurant, Max had dragged him into the showroom and urged him to take his pick. Once again his protestations had fallen on deaf ears. 'I think of you as a son. If you'd grown up with me I would have bought you a car years ago, so all I'm really doing is making up for lost time.' The words had been accompanied by a smile that contained just a trace of hurt, so that he had felt churlish and obliged to accept the offer.

Putting down the brochure he stared at the *Ten Commandments* poster. Rebecca had bought it for him. Three months ago his greatest fear had been losing her and finding himself alone again. Now that fear had been realised, but he was not alone. He had Max, a man who had unexpectedly entered his life and given him a love that was unconditional. Uncritical. Unrelenting.

He made his way to the dining room. Max already sat at the table, wearing his dressing gown, eating toast and reading the *Financial Times*. He frowned as Michael sat down. 'That suit won't do, Mike. I'll make an appointment with the tailor for the end of the week.'

Michael poured himself some orange juice while Mrs László appeared with a pot of coffee. 'A cooked breakfast for you?' she asked.

'I'll just have toast.'

'A cooked breakfast for you,' said Mrs László cheerfully, before disappearing back to the kitchen.

'Oh God.'

Max laughed. 'Don't try to argue with her. It's a waste of energy.'

'Ain't that the truth.'

'Are you doing anything tomorrow night?'

'Why?'

'Sam Provsky's in town for a couple of days. A Canadian acquaintance of mine who owns a restaurant chain and is just starting up operations in this country. He's been using a West End firm for his legal work but isn't that impressed with them, so I want you to persuade him over dinner to instruct Cox Stephens instead.'

'Me? But I'm only a junior assistant.'

'Don't worry. All you have to do is sit there, smile and leave the serious talking to me. Trust me, Mike, Sam and I have history, and I know exactly what buttons to press. Having a client like that will look wonderful on your CV when you move to pastures new.'

'He wouldn't be my client, though. He'd be the firm's.'

'We'll let Jack believe that. But we'll know different.'

'I may decide not to move.'

Max smiled. 'Oh, I think you will.'

He knew better than to argue. Mrs László appeared with a plate of bacon, eggs, mushrooms and sausages. He took a few bites, then moved the food about the plate, trying to give the impression that he had eaten more than he had.

'You look run down,' Max observed. 'What you need is a proper holiday. Friends of mine have a house in Nassau. A beautiful place with a pool, right by the beach. The nightlife's good too. We could get flights this weekend. How does a couple of weeks sound?'

'Things are busy at work. We're signing a deal soon, and I can't just take time off.'

'Sure you can. They'll manage without you for a fortnight.'

Perhaps they could. And even if they couldn't, no one was going to raise objections.

He pushed the food around his plate.

'You don't have to finish that,' Max told him. 'It's enough that you've shown willing.'

He rose to his feet.

'Hey. Wait a minute.' Max walked over to him. 'You seem upset. Have I said the wrong thing?'

'No.'

'Yes, I have. Throwing my weight around, telling you what to do. I must seem like a bully sometimes, but it's only because I want the best for you.'

He managed a smile. 'Like tailored suits.'

Max smiled too. 'Especially tailored suits.'

'It just feels wrong sometimes.'

'What does?'

'You buying me all these things.'

'They're only objects, Mike. Buying you things makes me happy. Is that so terrible?'

'You've done so much for me already.'

'Not compared with what I'm going to do.' Max looked into his eyes. 'We're so alike, you and me. We both know what it is to be alone in this world. I was sixteen when I left Bow, with nothing but a few pounds and a determination to make something of my life. There was no one to help me. I had to do it all on my own, and it was a long, hard fight. Well, I want better for you. For you everything will be easy. I'll make sure of it.'

Michael nodded, uncertain what to say.

Suddenly Max hugged him, crushing him against his chest. Startled by this outpouring of emotion, he stood quite still, allowing himself to be held, telling himself that he was lucky to have someone who cared about him so much.

Eventually Max released him. They stared at each other. Max's eyes were full of unconditional love. He was fortunate

343

to have that love. Even if sometimes it felt as if he was being suffocated.

He went to get ready for work.

Two o'clock. Michael, who had been out to buy a sandwich, made his way across Broadgate Circus back to the office.

He was deep in thought. Emily had phoned that morning. Since her declaration in the wine bar, the two of them had twice had lunch together. Each time the atmosphere had been strained as both tried to pretend that nothing had changed between them. The situation upset him. He wanted to keep her friendship, to be there for her when she needed him, but wasn't sure how to do so.

So preoccupied was he that it took him a while to realise that someone was calling his name.

He turned to see Peter Brown approaching. Though not in the mood for a conversation, he managed a smile. 'Hello. How's things in the flat?'

'Fine. We're very happy there.' As he spoke, Peter shuffled awkwardly, as if wanting to say something but uncertain how to proceed.

'Is something the matter?' prompted Michael.

'Can I ask you something?'

'Yes.'

'You know Max pretty well, don't you?'

'Suppose so.'

'Have Jenny and I offended him in some way?'

'Why do you ask?'

Peter looked uncomfortable. 'It doesn't matter. Forget it.'

Michael's curiosity was roused. 'Tell me. Maybe I can help.'

'During our first week in the flat we saw a lot of Max. I told you how he bought us champagne and took us for dinner, and he also took me out to lunch. At the end of the week we decided to take him out as our guest as a way of saying thank you. But when I phoned to suggest it he said no.'

Michael thought of all the dinners and theatre trips. 'Well, he has been quite busy recently.'

'But it was his manner. He was really cold, as if I was bothering him. Which was odd because we'd only had lunch a couple of days earlier and he couldn't have been nicer. I've phoned a couple of times since—'

As he listened, Michael noticed Peter's tie.

'—and his reaction was just the same—'

It was blue with red stripes. Peter had worn it the last time they'd seen each other, in the foyer at Cox Stephens.

'—so I was a bit confused—'

Peter had had lunch with Max that day. The two of them had stood together in the foyer, Max smiling benevolently at Peter. The jealousy and resentment he had felt had been so powerful that he had ended by breaking both Robert's nose and his relationship with Rebecca.

'—and I wondered if you knew—'

He remembered a paperback book that lay in his desk at work. A collection of stories by M.R. James. He was sure it had never belonged to Rebecca or himself. It must have been left by the last tenants.

But that wasn't possible either. The book had been found behind the sofa. They had moved the sofa when they moved in themselves, and there had been no trace of it then.

He had only met Peter because of the book. Max had urged Peter to bring it round in person. Peter had been full of Max's warmth and generosity, and he had felt jealous then too. But there was no need to be jealous now. Not when that generosity had stopped a few days later. Just as he broke up with Rebecca.

He felt a queasiness in his stomach.

'You haven't offended Max,' he said suddenly. 'Don't think that.' A pause. 'I'm sure he feels the same about you as he always did.'

He sat at his desk, thinking about what Peter had told him.

'Can you do me a favour?' asked Stuart, who was about to disappear for a client meeting. 'I'm supposed to phone the New York office. They've sent me financial information on a US company and the figures don't add up. I'll be tied up all afternoon, so can you do it for me?'

'Sure.'

Stuart handed him the papers. 'You need to speak to Alan Bradley. He's the new corporate guy they've just recruited.'

He dialled the number, grateful to have something else to think about.

Alan was an affable-sounding Englishman who quickly cleared up the ambiguities. 'How's life in the Big Apple?' Michael asked him.

'Wonderful. Mind you, I've only been here a week, so things are bound to change.'

'Were you working in London before?'

'Yes, with Carter Curzon. I'd been with them since I qualified.'

'When did you qualify? Ninety-five? Ninety-six?'

'Last September.'

Last September?

'That means you qualified the same time as me.'

'Really?' Alan sounded interested. 'Where were you at uni?'

'Oxford.'

'My friend Brian Scott went there. Did you know him?'

'No. Alan, I have to go. It was nice talking to you.'

After putting down the phone he ran a hand through his hair. An ache had started in his head. He stared at the wall, waiting for it to clear.

'Mike.'

Kim stood in the doorway. 'Jack Bennett needs to see you urgently. Something about the Chassock deal.'

He made his way to Jack's office. Jack sat at his desk, looking stressed. 'Chassock's MD just phoned. He's got an internal meeting and needs us to fax him the accounts for all the target companies. I know you had copies made last week. Where are they?'

'In that file.' Michael gestured to a blue ringbinder on Jack's shelf. 'I got one of the trainees to do it. Sorry, it should have been labelled.'

'Could you organise the fax? I've got a crisis building on something else.'

He nodded. Jack began to look through the file and suddenly his eyes widened. 'How many subsidiaries are there?'

The ache in his head was intensifying. He tried to focus. 'About twenty-five.'

'But there's only a dozen sets of accounts here.' Jack continued to flick through the pages. 'And some of them are nearly three years old. There must be more recent sets than that. Which trainee did you use?'

Last September. Alan qualified last September.

'Which trainee?'

'John Marshall.'

'Did you check his work?'

'No.'

'But you know how slapdash he is. You should have checked.'

'I'll check now.'

'But we don't have time! They're expecting the fax any minute.' Jack exhaled. 'You really should have stayed on top of this, Mike. Now we're going to look completely incompetent.'

He didn't react, his head too full of other things.

'And you couldn't care less, could you?' Jack rose to his feet, his face crimson. 'Look at you. Standing there like none of this matters. It probably doesn't to you now you've got well-connected friends watching your back the whole time. Well, try to remember that the rest of us don't have that luxury. This job is our livelihood and not just some well-paid way of passing the time between one expensive dinner and the next!'

The words felt like a physical blow. Turning abruptly, Michael walked out of the room and back to his office, where he shut the door behind him and stood in the centre of his room, breathing deeply, trying to calm himself.

There was a knock on the door. Jack stepped inside. The anger was gone now, replaced by apprehension.

'I'm sorry, Mike. I had no right to talk to you like that. I hope you'll put it down to pressures of work and not hold it against me.' A pause. 'I hope you don't feel the need to—'

'Tell anyone?'

Jack's eyes were fearful. They made him feel dirty as well as upset that someone would consider him capable of such vindictiveness. 'You don't have to worry,' he said quickly. 'I deserved it anyway. I give you my word that I won't tell anyone.'

Jack visibly relaxed.

'Provided you tell me what happened with the New York job.'

'New York?'

'You know what I'm talking about. One morning Jeff Speakman asks me if I want to be seconded, and then, that afternoon, he tells me that I'm too junior to go. But I wasn't too junior. That wasn't the reason, was it?'

At first Jack didn't react. Then, slowly, he shook his head.

'How did Max find out?'

'I told him. The two of us had lunch the day Jeff spoke to

348

you. We talked about your progress. As I remember, it was the only thing we did talk about. I mentioned the possibility of the New York secondment because I thought he'd be pleased. Well, more fool me. The last thing he'd want would be for you to leave the country.'

Suddenly Michael was very tired. His limbs felt as if they were turning to lead, so heavy that he would be able to move them only with the help of another.

'You must despise me,' Jack told him. 'I must seem weak to you.'

He shook his head.

'You don't have to pretend. It's written all over your face.' Jack smiled sadly. 'Do you know the tragic thing? You assistants still think that to achieve partnership is to achieve a position of power. But you're wrong. All I am is a well-paid employee with no real power at all. My clients are the powerful ones. They give me my reputation, and if I were to start losing them then everything I've worked so hard to achieve would start to crumble. So try not to think too badly of me. I'm not proud of what I did, but I had no choice.'

Michael found himself remembering Jack's first day at the firm. Jack had gone round the whole department, exchanging a smile and a friendly word with everyone. A warm, affable man, keen to be accepted and refusing to stand on ceremony. He had admired Jack for that.

That evening he had told Rebecca of his admiration. The two of them had sat together on the sagging sofa in their flat in Camberwell, sharing wine and a Chinese takeaway and watching a Hammer Horror film. At one point he had gone to the kitchen, then crept back into the room, putting his hand on Rebecca's shoulder and letting out a low moan. She had screamed and jumped out of her seat, sending food and wine spraying everywhere, so they had spent the rest of the evening cleaning the walls and trying to wash the stains out of the carpet.

He stared at Jack, a small, stocky man with a kind face whose future he could damage immeasurably should he so wish. He had that power now.

But he didn't want it. There was only one thing he really wanted.

'Forget about the accounts,' Jack told him. 'I'll get someone else to check them.'

'There's something I have to do. Do you mind if I leave early?'

Jack shook his head. What else could he do?

He entered the non-fiction section of Chatterton's bookshop. It was empty save for an elderly man browsing through the history section.

Rebecca stood at the till with Clare. When she saw him she grew pale. His own face felt cool. Perhaps he was pale too.

'I need to talk to you.'

She shook her head.

'Just five minutes, please. After that I'll never bother you again.'

'Go on, Becky,' said Clare softly. 'I'll cover. It's not like we're rushed off our feet.'

Rebecca reached for her bag. 'Come on, then,' she said before starting up the stairs.

He sat beside her on a bench in Trafalgar Square, staring at the ground, struggling to find the right words.

'I can't stay long,' she said. 'It's not fair to impose on Clare.'

He watched a lone pigeon hovering by his feet and wished he had some food to give it.

'No, you wouldn't,' she told him.

'Wouldn't what?'

'Give it part of a sandwich if you had one. Wasn't that what you were thinking?'

'Yes.'

'Whenever we came here you'd eat your lunch in two minutes, then nick half of mine and insist I feed the rest to our feathered friends. I used to go back to the shop hungrier than when I'd left.'

'And spend all afternoon eating chocolate and phoning me to say that I was ruining your figure.' He smiled. 'Stuart used to say it was a miracle I got any work done.'

'How is Stuart?'

'Good. Helen's just got a promotion. It's all he talks about.'

'Will you congratulate her for me?'

'Sure.'

Silence. The pigeon wrote him off as a dead loss and hopped away. A group of Japanese tourists photographed themselves at the foot of Nelson's Column, laughing as they squinted into the summer sunshine.

'So why am I here, Mike?'

'Do you want to leave?'

'I'm still here, aren't I?'

Another silence. She was the one to break it. 'Look, maybe this isn't—'

'I wanted you to know that you were right.'

'About what?'

He sighed. 'About me being Max's puppet.'

He waited for her to gloat. To say I told you so. But when she turned towards him her eyes were sympathetic.

'Aren't you pleased?' he asked.

'Not when it upsets you this much.'

He stared up at the sky. Still a perfect blue. It seemed as if the summer was never going to end. 'I'm not upset.'

She didn't answer, but he knew she wasn't fooled.

351

'You don't need to stay here any more. I just wanted to tell you.' He exhaled. 'And to say that I was sorry. I know it's too late to make a difference, but I do mean it.'

His hands rested on his knees. She covered one with her own. 'Tell me what's happened, Mike. You need to tell someone, and who better than me?'

So he did. Described the events of the day and the conclusions he was starting to draw. He spoke slowly, worried that he might leave something out.

'How do you feel?' she asked when he'd finished.

'Confused. Afraid.'

'You shouldn't be afraid. Max would never hurt you. I know I said he was just using you, but that was only because I was angry. Whatever he's done has been because he cares.'

'Doesn't make it right, though, does it?'

'That depends.'

'On what?'

'On you. You've always wanted to be successful and achieve something with your life. Max wants that for you too. With him behind you the sky's the limit. You could fly all the way to the moon.'

'But he'd be the one at the controls.'

'It could still be an amazing ride.'

'But it wouldn't be my life. You warned me once never to let Max control it. At the moment that's exactly what's happening.'

'So what do you want?' she asked. 'What do you really want?'

'Do you remember that day we went to Hampton Court?'

'Yes.'

'We looked for ghosts in the palace.'

'Unsuccessfully.'

'We spent hours in the maze.'

'You got us lost.'

'We ate ice-creams by the river.'

'You ate half of mine, then made me feed the rest to the ducks.'

'And at the end of the day, as we waited for the train, you told me that you loved me.'

He heard her sigh.

'I couldn't remember anyone ever saying that to me before. Not even my mother. At that moment all the crap in the past no longer mattered. The only thing that mattered was being with you. Having you in my life. The two of us against the world.'

He stopped speaking. And waited.

'You haven't answered my question,' she told him.

'Yes, I have.'

His eyes had remained fixed on the sky. Now he turned and saw that she was crying. He started crying too. She put her arms round him and they hugged each other, their bodies locking together, while round their feet pigeons continued to prowl for scraps of food.

Half past seven. Michael sat on his bed at Max's house, his possessions assembled in bags at his feet. He was ready to go now. There was only one more thing he had to do.

Tell Max.

He had returned to the house two hours ago to discover that Max was out and not expected back before seven. So he had told Mr László that he would be in his room and asked to be informed when Max returned.

He heard footsteps in the corridor, then a knock on the door. 'Come in,' he said.

Max's expression was one of concern. 'Aren't you feeling well?'

Then he saw the bags.

Michael rose to his feet, his throat dry. 'I went to see Becky today,' he said. 'We talked for ages and—'

'You're giving it another try.'

'Yes.'

Max exhaled slowly. He stood quite still, waiting. The wall behind Max's shoulder was bare. Ready for the return of the landscapes that had always looked better here than his film posters had done.

'You're making a mistake, Mike.'

'I don't think so.'

'It's over. You said so yourself.' The voice was calm and very soothing. It began to wrap itself round him, dulling his senses, hindering his ability to think.

Angrily he shook his head. 'You were the one who said that. Not me.'

'You're setting yourself up for more heartache. Think of what's gone on between you. All the things you've said and done to hurt each other.' Max put a hand on his shoulder. 'Do you really want to go through that again?'

He threw off the hand. 'This isn't fair.'

'Don't push me away, Mike. All I want to do is protect you from pain.'

He looked down at the floor and the bags that surrounded his feet. 'But I don't want you to. This is my life. You can't live it for me.'

'I'm not trying to do that.'

'Aren't you?'

Silence. Save for the beating of his heart. Max was wearing expensive Italian shoes. He had been bought several pairs himself, but they were not his style.

'Very well,' said Max eventually. 'Start seeing her again if that's what you want. But take it slowly. Don't rush back into a relationship. And stay here in the meantime.' The voice was

354

so restful. No trace of anger whatsoever. It would have been easier if there had been anger.

'I can't do that,' he said.

'There's no need for you to leave.'

'Yes, there is.'

He looked up again. Though Max's voice was steady his face was a mask of pain. Michael hated himself for what he was doing but knew that he had no choice.

'I'd give anything for things to be different. You and Becky mean more to me than any two people ever have. But my life doesn't work with both of you in it, so I have to choose.'

Max took a deep breath. 'Michael, listen to me. For your own sake, please don't do this. You're making a mistake that you're going to regret for the rest of your life. But it's not too late to change your mind.'

'I'm sorry. You don't know how much. You've treated me like a son, and I will always be grateful—'

'Enough.' Max held up his hand for silence. 'Go, if that's what you want,' he said calmly, before gesturing to the desk where the computer and music system remained. 'You haven't packed everything.'

'I'm only taking what I came with.'

'I bought them for you. Take them or leave them as you want. I'll order you a taxi.'

'Max.'

'What?'

He swallowed. 'Try not to hate me for this. I have no right to ask that, but please try.'

The eyes didn't blink. And the voice, when it came, was as beautiful as ever.

'I will never hate you, Michael. That's the one thing I will never do.'

*

355

Rebecca heard the doorbell ring in Ash Lane.

Relief surged through her. She had been so afraid that Max would talk Michael into staying. Joyfully she threw open the door and found Emily standing there, holding a bottle of wine.

'What are you doing here?'

'You invited me. We arranged it last week.'

It was true. She had forgotten in the excitement of the day. Emily stepped into the hallway and handed her the bottle. 'What's going on?'

'Mike and I have made up. We're going to try again.'

'I don't believe it.'

'Neither do I.' She shut the door. 'It's all happened so fast. He came to see me this afternoon and—'

'You can't get back together! You can't!'

Emily's face was a study in anguish. Rebecca felt a chill run through her as what had only ever been a suspicion now took on the substance of truth.

They stood in the hallway while a Cranberries CD played in the living room.

'Em, listen—'

'You don't care about him. You never have.'

'That's not true.' She tried to keep her voice steady.

'Yes, it is. To you he's just an ornament. Something to display as yet another symbol of your perfect life.'

She felt her face growing hot. 'I think you'd better leave.'

'Why? The truth hurts, does it?' Emily took a step towards her. 'And it is the truth. You don't know the first thing about caring. You forced him to give up someone who really mattered to him. What sort of person does that?'

Rebecca's composure snapped. She took a step forward too. 'And you do care, I suppose? That's why you fed him those lies about my saying that I'd never have him back under any circumstances. I never said that. You know I didn't!'

'Well, it doesn't matter now, does it?' Emily's eyes were flashing. 'Because in the end you're the one who wins. Just as you always do. Don't you ever get tired of taking from me?'

'I've never taken from you!'

'What about my mother?'

She couldn't believe what she was hearing. Emily had never come out and said it before.

'You may have forgotten about her, but I haven't! You took her from me. Then my father, and now the only guy I've ever cared about. When is it going to end?'

She slapped Emily's face.

Gasping, Emily put a hand to her reddening cheek. Rebecca, her palm stinging, stood and faced her.

'Don't you dare throw your mother at me! Not ever! I'm sorry she's dead, I really am, but it wasn't my fault. You've been making me feel guilty since we were children, and I'm sick to death of it. I can't even look at you now without feeling guilty, and it's got to stop. You are not my responsibility, and if things are bad in your life then for once try doing something about it rather than just whining and trying to blame everything on me!'

Emily turned and walked out of the door.

Rebecca remained where she was. She had said what needed to be said.

Then remorse swept over her. Putting down the wine bottle, she rushed outside. 'Em, I'm sorry. Please come back. We can talk about this, can't we?'

She stood on the doorstep, calling, but to no avail.

*

Michael sat in a taxi as it drove towards West Hampstead.

A cricket match was being broadcast on the radio. The taxi driver, who was clearly a sports fanatic, kept giving him a running commentary. Though he made appropriate noises of interest, his attention was far away.

He kept thinking of the look of anguish on Max's face. He knew that he had been manipulated. That Max had wanted to control him. But still he felt ashamed.

The taxi turned into Ash Lane. Rebecca was standing outside the flat. She looked upset, but when she saw the taxi approach a smile began to spread across her face, like the appearance of spring after a long, cold winter. Suddenly all the doubts and fears were gone.

They stood together on the pavement. Her eyes were red. 'You've been crying,' he said. 'Were you worried I wouldn't come?'

'Perhaps. Just a little.'

'I had to see him. Try to explain.'

'Did he understand?'

He sighed. 'I don't think so.'

'Do you think you've made the wrong choice?'

'No. It feels like I've spent the last few months sleepwalking. Going through the motions while someone else pulled the strings. But that's all over now.' He touched her cheek. 'I'm awake again, and this is real.'

They hugged each other, then, together, began to carry his possessions into the flat.

Ten o'clock. Emily sat on a bench at Blackfriars Station. She had been there for over an hour, watching three trains for Streatham come and go.

She walked to the end of the platform and the start of Blackfriars Bridge. The Thames rolled away before her, its surface shining with light reflected from nearby buildings. In the distance she could see the dome of St Paul's, illuminated for the evening, a shining beacon of London's majesty and power.

The City had been her home for two years now. Eight million people were her neighbours. Each day she walked among them, silent and unseen, feeling herself become transparent. Terrified that one day she would vanish altogether, dissolving into mist to be scattered by the wind.

Michael was the only person who had ever understood that. She had reached out for him, wanting him to save her, but he had chosen Rebecca and left her to save herself.

She touched the skin on her arm: so pale that it seemed she could look through it and see the ground beneath.

It's happening already. I have no substance. I am ceasing to exist.

A train pulled into the station. She entered the compartment. A group of young men stood by the door, drinking beer and sharing jokes. By accident she nudged the arm of one of them. Softly she apologised. He carried on laughing, so oblivious to her presence that she might have been a ghost.

Half past ten. Mrs László, carrying sandwiches and coffee, knocked on the door of Max's study.

He was sitting in his comfortable chair, a cigar between his fingers. She placed the tray on the desk beside him. He watched her, the ghost of a smile on his face. He had not asked for anything, but she knew he would not rebuke her. In the six years she had worked for him he had never once spoken harshly to her husband or herself.

She felt a twinge of rheumatism in her fingers. A sign that she was getting old. Soon the house would be too much for her, and they would have to leave his employment. The prospect filled her with sadness, but not dread. Though they had little in the way of savings, she was sure he would never let them starve.

'You should eat something. Just a little. It will do you good.'

She spoke in Hungarian. He had told her once that his parents had come from Budapest, and though he didn't understand the language she knew it pleased him to hear it spoken. He nodded now, as if her words made perfect sense.

'I'm sorry he has gone. I know how much you will miss him.'

She waited, hoping for an answer, but he said nothing. Silently she crept from the room, closing the door behind her.

Midnight. Max still sat in his study, the sandwiches and coffee untouched by his side. A cigar smouldered in the ashtray beside the stubs of all the others he had consumed.

He stared at the fireplace in front of him, but in his mind he was far away, remembering a cold February evening in 1957 when he had sat on a bench in a draughty room, his few possessions clutched in a bag on his knee. Adults had fired questions at him in a flat, alien tongue, while children gathered behind them, all with lean faces and hungry eyes that shone at the prospect of the sport this bewildered newcomer would surely provide.

He had tried to tell them who he was. To explain that he did not belong here. That he had an uncle who loved him and would be coming for him soon. But the adults just talked over him, and in the end he had sought refuge inside himself, staring placidly up at them while behind his eyes thoughts of fear and fury blazed like fire.

His cigar had burned itself out. He lit another, inhaling slowly and breathing smoke across the room.

And now, as then, his thoughts were his own.

PART THREE

POSSESSION

ONE

Monday morning. Five days later.

Michael stood in Jack Bennett's office, the door closed behind him. Through the window, above the neighbouring office blocks, he could see the dull, grey September sky. The heatwave that had enveloped London for months was now over. There was a briskness to the air, a reminder that winter was on its way.

'I'm resigning.'

Jack didn't look surprised. Proof that good news travelled fast.

'I thought you should be the first to know.'

'Thank you.' A pause. 'Though I'm sorry to hear it.'

Like hell.

'Obviously I'll work my three-month notice period.'

'Where are you going?'

'I don't know yet.'

Jack nodded.

'Well, I'd better start spreading the word.' He turned to leave.

'One thing.'

'What?'

Jack rose to his feet. 'Are you sure you're making the right decision?'

'I can't stay here. Not after what's happened.'

'I'm not talking about this place.'

'What, then?'

'Come on, Michael. You're not a fool.'

He hadn't expected this level of directness. 'I'll be OK,' he said quickly.

'Max isn't someone you cross.'

'I haven't crossed him.'

'Are you sure he sees it like that?'

'That's between him and me. It doesn't affect your client list.'

Jack looked uncomfortable, and he felt ashamed. 'Sorry. That was unnecessary.'

'But deserved.'

It was time to go. But there was something he needed to say.

'I never meant to make things difficult for you. For what it's worth, I liked you from the moment you arrived here, and I'm sorry Max got in the way of that.'

'So am I.' Jack smiled ruefully. 'Had circumstances been different, you and I could have made a really good working team. If you need a reference I'll be happy to provide one. You have my word that it will be absolutely first class.'

They shook hands.

'Good luck, Mike.'

'Thanks, Jack.'

As he headed down the corridor he passed Graham Fletcher's office. Julia had now escaped to commercial property, and a new male trainee sat in her desk, receiving a lecture from Graham on punctuality.

Graham noticed him pass. Two weeks ago he would have received a strained smile, but now it was the old glare. The sight cheered him. A reminder that slowly his life was reverting to normal.

He made his way back to his desk, while all around him the air was full of telephones and fingers on keyboards as the office went about its daily business.

'Wow!'

Clare removed the CDs from their wrapping paper, her face shining. Rebecca watched her, feeling pleased. The two of them sat together in the office at Chatterton's, drinking coffee from chipped mugs.

'We didn't miss one, did we? Mike was convinced we had.'

'No, this is the complete set.' Clare studied the cover of Seven and the Ragged Tiger. 'I can't believe I once considered John Taylor the sexiest man on the planet. Now I'd score him at three and a half, but I still love Duran Duran. You shouldn't have been so extravagant.'

'Yes, I should. Now you've finally bought a CD machine you need something to play on it. Anyway, it's the least I can do to say thanks for putting up with me.'

'I haven't had to put up with anything.'

'Yes, you have. You've been a brilliant friend, Clare, and I'm really grateful.'

Clare looked embarrassed. 'Well, don't flatter yourself that it was all down to the goodness of my heart. Truth is, it wouldn't be any fun round here without you.' She looked at her watch. 'Now drink up so we can go and relieve Keith.'

Rebecca finished her coffee. Clare smiled at her. 'Are you happy?'

She nodded. She was.

Well, most of the time.

She couldn't stop thinking about Emily, try as she might. Force of habit, perhaps.

Their friendship was over. She was sure of that. Resentments that had festered since childhood had been allowed to surface, and the resulting damage could not be repaired. A clean break was the only option now. The best thing.

Back at the counter they dealt with the early-lunchtime rush. A gaunt, prematurely balding man made his way down the stairs. 'Two,' whispered Clare.

She choked back laughter. Clare looked pleased. 'Let's grab a pizza after the rush and have a proper talk. I'll get Susan to cover for me.'

The prospect pleased her. Lunches with Clare were fun. Free of the tensions she had so often felt with Emily.

She wondered what Emily was doing for lunch. Was she meeting someone? Would she eat alone? Would she eat at all?

A handsome man of about forty made his way to the counter. 'Nine,' hissed Clare.

She entered a customer's credit card details into the machine, gave her a pen to sign the slip and bagged her book. A biography of George Eliot. The sort of thing Emily would enjoy.

Handing the woman her book she tried to concentrate on the game.

As Rebecca was serving behind the counter, Emily was sitting at her desk in the Baker Connolly Literary Agency.

A manuscript lay open in front of her. An Arthurian epic, written by a tax inspector. 'Could you skim through it,' Kevin had asked, 'and let me know what you think?' She was halfway through now but could remember little of what she'd read, a fact that reflected more on her state of mind than on the state of the prose.

She gazed out of the window. It had been raining heavily for about an hour, but at last the skies were clearing. Her office felt stuffy, and she needed a change of scene. Picking up her purse, she made her way outside, on to streets that were slippery from the downpour. Office workers swarmed round her, clutching bags of sandwiches. She knew she should eat but had no appetite, and instead made her way up the stone steps of St Paul's Cathedral.

The air inside was cool and still. Though dozens of people were there, the interior was so vast that it still appeared empty. And beautifully peaceful. The main altar lay in front of her, so far away that it seemed she could walk for hours and never reach it. The dome rose above her, high enough to touch the sky.

She searched for a quiet place to sit. There was a particular row she favoured towards the front on the left. As she made her way towards it, she looked at the others who had also sought out the peace of the cathedral: a young couple with rucksacks reading a guidebook, an elderly woman who knelt in silent prayer, and a contained-looking middle-aged man in a business suit, holding a raincoat, staring into space.

Max.

She whispered his name, but he didn't hear. Nervously, she tried again.

He heard this time. His eyes had the glazed quality of one lost in thought, and at first he didn't seem to know her. Then, slowly, he smiled in recognition and gestured to the seat beside him.

'I didn't mean to disturb you,' she said as she sat down.

'You haven't. Please don't think that.' His voice was welcoming but subdued. 'I didn't know you were religious,' he said.

'I'm not. My offices are across the road, and I often come at lunchtime. I find it restful.'

He nodded, his hands kneading the raincoat. It was the first time she had seen him without a cigar. Behind her, someone whispered a private prayer.

'Are you religious?'

'If so I've come to the wrong place. I was baptised a Catholic.'

She remembered that he was Hungarian. Michael had told her.

'I haven't been here for years,' he continued. 'I had a meeting in the area, got caught in the rain and needed a refuge. I'd forgotten just what a magnificent place it is. The exterior doesn't begin to do it justice.'

As he spoke his eyes studied her. She sensed there was something he wanted to ask and guessed the question before it was spoken.

'Have you seen Michael recently?'

She shook her head.

'He's back with Becky now. Did you know that?'

'Yes.'

He stared down at the floor. 'I tried to talk him out of it. That's a shameful thing to admit, but it's true. I felt sure he was making a mistake.'

'Perhaps he was.' A young couple moved into the row in front and began to discuss the architecture.

He shook his head. 'I was the one who was mistaken. I couldn't see it then, but I do now. They belong together. Only a fool would think otherwise.'

She felt an ache in her heart. 'So all's well that ends well.'

'Indeed.'

She looked at the space about her. So enormous it seemed that all the people in the world would never fill it. There were times when her flat seemed just as vast, and just as empty.

'I wish I didn't miss him so much.'

She couldn't deal with someone else's pain. Not when her own was so raw. 'I have to go. I'm sorry.' She made her way to the end of the row and hurried up the aisle.

But before leaving the cathedral she turned back. He was still in his seat, staring into space, so wrapped up in his thoughts that it was as if they had never spoken.

Later that afternoon she returned to her desk and found a message on her chair.

Jude Hale phoned. Will call back in ten minutes.

Her heart sank. Jude was a young, humourless, self-obsessed novelist whose work dealt exclusively with inner-city drug users, all of whom ended up dying of overdoses or becoming priests. Kevin had signed Jude three years ago, hoping to catch a ride on the *Trainspotting* wave, but found him so objectionable that day-to-day management had been delegated to Emily instead. Jude was scheduled to do a reading next week in a small bookshop off Charing Cross Road and would be calling to complain about the lack of publicity.

The phone rang. Bracing herself, she picked up the receiver. 'Hello.'

'Emily? Is that you?'

It wasn't Jude. The voice was beautiful. Deep and smooth. Just as it had been in the cathedral.

She confirmed her identity 'Is this a bad time?' he asked.

'No.'

'I wanted to apologise for lunchtime. I upset you.'

She felt flustered. 'You didn't. Not at all.'

She heard him sigh. 'Oh, I think I did. You caught me at a particularly low moment, though that's no excuse.'

'Yes, it is,' she insisted, then realised that her words sounded like an implied criticism. 'Not that there's anything to excuse. I was the rude one, rushing off like that.'

369

'You're very kind. I haven't forgotten how you helped organise Michael's birthday party, even though you must have known it would cause friction between Rebecca and yourself. Please believe me – I didn't mean any offence.'

'None was taken.'

'Thank you.'

She waited for him to say goodbye but heard nothing but his breathing. In the silence her eyes roamed over her desk. An Empire State Building paperweight sat at the centre. She had never liked it much, but it had been a present from Rebecca so she had felt obliged to display it prominently. The obligation was gone now, but old habits died hard.

'Did you stay much longer?' she asked finally. 'In the cathedral, I mean?'

'About an hour. It is restful, as you said. I felt better when I left.'

'I'm glad.'

'And now I'd like to make amends. Are you free for dinner this evening?'

'You don't need to do that.'

'But I'd like to. Though perhaps you have plans.'

'No, but the thing is . . .'

'I understand. You've had a busy day and are probably longing for an evening at home with your feet up rather than a few hours listening to my clumsy attempts at small talk.'

She thought of her flat. Another evening spent there, with no company save the dark hiss of her own thoughts.

'I'd love to come.'

'Good.' He sounded delighted. 'Let me book somewhere, then phone you with the details. Would that be acceptable?'

'Yes.'

As she put down the phone there was a tapping sound on the window. The rain had started again. She sat and watched it, feeling slightly detached from reality, so that when Jude phoned and began complaining she barely noticed.

Half past eight. She sat with Max at a table by the window in a Chinese restaurant on Gerrard Street, sipping wine, waiting for her main course and watching the crowds making their way to the theatres on Shaftesbury Avenue.

Max was having Peking duck as a starter. In place of the business suit, he wore a comfortable sports jacket and good linen shirt. She was still in the dress she'd had on all day. Pale green, with a high collar and long sleeves. Work had been so busy she had not had time to go home and change. The petite blonde woman at the next table was wearing a little black number. She felt frumpy in comparison.

'That type of dress really suits you,' he said, as if reading her mind.

'It's rather old-fashioned.'

'That's what I meant.' He nodded towards the next table. 'Anyone can show off skin. It takes real elegance to show off clothes.'

Michael had said the same thing once. Perhaps, like Max, he had just meant to be kind.

'Do you like the restaurant?' he asked.

'Very much. It's not too smart.'

'Would you have preferred somewhere grander?'

She felt embarrassed. 'Not at all. I only meant that I've never really felt comfortable in expensive restaurants.'

He smiled. 'Neither do I. For the first half of my life dinner out was a bag of fish and chips washed down with a can of lager, and even now there's something in me that objects to paying hundreds of pounds for a meal. Sadly, when you're rich, that's what people expect.'

'I don't.'

'That's very refreshing.'

A waiter lit the candle on their table. She sipped her wine and watched a well-dressed couple enter a restaurant on the other side of the street. The Oriental Pearl.

'That's where Mike and Becky go,' she told him.

'Where?'

'The Oriental Pearl. It's Mr and Mrs Blake's favourite restaurant. They always eat there when in London.'

He nodded. The remnants of Peking duck lay on the table between them. Mr and Mrs Blake's favourite dish.

It's true what the song says. Always something there to remind me.

'I'm sorry,' she said awkwardly.

'You can talk about him.'

His eyes were warm and somehow sympathetic. She wondered how much he guessed.

Moistening a finger, he began to move it back and forth through the flame of the candle. She remembered her father doing the same thing in a Winchester restaurant while her mother had told him to be careful and she had sat between them, eating strawberry ice-cream. A small Italian place – her mother's favourite. They had stopped going there after she died.

'Do you mind if I smoke?'

'No.'

He lit a cigar and breathed smoke into the air. The rich smell mingled with the scent of spices that reached them from the other tables. People nearby were complaining loudly about their jobs.

'Have you been to the Whispering Gallery?' she asked.

'Once. Years ago now.'

'My parents took me when I was six. Mum explained how the acoustics worked, then Dad and I whispered messages to

372

each other. Some of them were quite rude, and two old ladies sat down between us and overheard them. Mum pretended to be shocked, but actually she thought it very funny.'

'You look like her, don't you? Mike told me.'

She shook her head.

'Isn't it true?'

'Superficially. She was far more attractive.'

'That doesn't surprise me.'

She was startled. 'That my mother was prettier than me?'

'That you'd think she was.'

She blushed. A waiter arrived with their main courses. Chicken with cashew nuts for her, king prawns in spicy sauce for him. He extinguished his cigar while she served herself some rice then took a bite. Though coated with sauce, the chicken still tasted dry.

'Which parent do you look like?' she asked.

'My father, I think. They died when I was five and I have no photographs. Just memories.'

'It must have been terrible. Losing them both when you were so young.'

A nod.

'Do you have any other family? I mean, back in Hungary?'

'Some distant cousins. I've never tried to find them, though. Blood alone can't make a bond, much as we might wish that it could.'

That was true enough. Michael had found that out when he had traced his father. He had told her all about it. And she had told him things too.

Again she felt an ache in her heart. 'So we're both alone, then.'

He looked surprised. 'Isn't your father still alive?'

'We rarely see each other.'

She waited for him to question her, to tell her what a shame

373

it was that the two of them were not in regular contact. But he didn't. She was grateful for that.

He speared a prawn and put it in his mouth, chewing purposefully. She liked the way he ate. A drop of dark sauce fell on to his shirt, spreading slowly across the white material. He carried on regardless.

'Your shirt.' She pointed to the stain.

He dabbed at it with a napkin, managing only to make it worse. 'I'm sorry, you can't take me anywhere.' He laughed sheepishly. It was an attractive sound. She remembered how apprehensive she had been about coming. But there had been no need.

'You must feel so proud,' she said suddenly. 'Of everything you've achieved.'

'It's not that impressive.'

'I think it is. Mike does too. He admires you more than anyone. He told me that if he achieved only half your success it would still be twice as much as he deserved.'

'Thank you, Emily. I appreciate that.'

'Call me Em if you like. Emily's so formal.'

'Em, then. I'd return the favour, but my name doesn't really allow for abbreviation. M, perhaps. What do you think?'

They both laughed. He gestured to her food. 'May I try?'

She nodded. He took a mouthful, chewed thoughtfully, then frowned. 'A little bland.' Spearing another prawn he held out his fork towards her. 'Taste this. It's good.'

She shook her head.

'Please, you'd be doing me a favour. I have a bottomless pit as a stomach, and with my central European heritage I put on weight faster than a method actor preparing for the role of Fatty Arbuckle.'

Again she laughed. The fork remained in front of her face. She took the prawn, chewing slowly, savouring the flavour.

Strong and rich. She liked it. He smiled at her, a trace of sauce at the side of his mouth. She liked that too.

'Delicious,' she announced.

He held out a second mouthful. This time she took it without protest. Then another. Until eventually the plate was empty.

The waiter cleared the table. Her hand rested on the table-cloth. Suddenly he covered it with his own. 'I'm so glad you came. I was feeling very low this morning. You can't imagine how much you've cheered me up.'

Again she blushed. 'You've cheered me up too.'

He gave her hand a squeeze, then released it. The waiter offered them dessert menus. 'I'm having one,' he told her. 'Will you join me?'

She rarely ate sweet things. But this time she nodded.

They placed their orders, then he lit another cigar. His hands were large and powerful, but he moved them with remarkable grace. Like eagles circling the flame of the candle while never allowing their wings to be scorched.

Her father had strong hands. Their strength was deceptive, giving no indication of the weakness of the man to whom they belonged. She loved her father more than anyone in the world, but he could never have achieved one fraction of what Max had.

The desserts arrived. She ate hers slowly.

Half past ten. She stood on Shaftesbury Avenue, feeling over-whelmed by the bright lights and the noise, waiting for Max to flag down a taxi.

At last one arrived. 'Streatham,' he told the driver before pressing two twenty-pound notes into her hand. 'For the fare.' Her protestations fell on deaf ears. 'I insist.'

'Thank you.'

He kissed her cheek. His skin felt rough but warm. 'I meant what I said,' he told her. 'You really have lifted my spirits. Have a safe journey.'

'You too.'

The cab drove off towards Cambridge Circus. He remained on the street, his hand raised, watching until she was out of sight.

There had been an accident up ahead. The traffic, already slow, now came to a virtual halt. The driver began to mutter. Her journey would be a long one, but it didn't matter. She had more than enough money for the fare.

She looked about her at the hundreds of people going about their lives. None of them knew her. If she had been the one in the accident they would not have cared.

But the evening had left a warm glow in the pit of her stomach. And for that brief period of time she didn't feel so alone.

TWO

Friday evening. Half past seven. Michael left West Hampstead tube and made his way towards Ash Lane.

It had been a busy day. After resigning, he had expected his workload to dry up. The good stuff largely had, but there was still a vast array of dross that people were now all too eager to dump on him, accompanied, in the case of Graham Fletcher, by disparaging remarks about his competence. Once, such remarks would have made his blood boil; now they were just water off a duck's back.

Part of him regretted his impending departure. Though people such as Stuart would remain friends, he would miss seeing them on a daily basis. But there would be other friends in the next job. One chapter ends and another begins. It was the way of life.

The evening was cool and still. He walked along West End Lane, past the pubs and restaurants, stopping at a newsagent to buy a giant Toblerone. A video of the 1922 version of *Nosferatu* waited on the kitchen table, a bottle of wine cooled in the fridge, and Rebecca would be in the kitchen, preparing something special to eat. Just another Friday night at home. His heart soared at the prospect.

On entering the flat, he made his way into the living room. The Pet Shop Boys were playing on the stereo and Rebecca was arguing with someone on the telephone. Judging by her tone, the caller was her mother. He could guess what the row was about and felt guilty.

Her face, tense from the conversation, lit up when she saw him. 'I have to go now, Mum. Mike's here.' A bellow issued from the handset, and the row continued.

He looked about the room. A mass of bright colours, all frills and pastels, with china figurines on every available surface. Laura Ashley meets My Little Pony. There was little space for their own possessions, most of which were in boxes in the spare room. It wasn't to his taste, or Becky's, but Susie would now be in Madrid until Christmas and had asked them to stay on as tenants. And they did need somewhere to live.

Rebecca put down the receiver and they sat together on the sofa. He wanted to put his feet on the coffee table, but half a dozen china pigs had got there first.

'How was she?'

'Need you ask?'

'This will cheer you up.' He showed her the Toblerone.

It did. They each ate a triangle, then another. 'Now put it out of reach,' she told him.

'Not on the table. The pigs will eat it.'

'They won't. They're too cute.'

'They're hideous. And the pink one with the bow round its snout has doubled in size since we moved in. Why can't we have mice, like normal people?'

She laughed. He put his arm round her, pulling her close. 'I'm sorry things are difficult.'

'There's nothing for you to be sorry about.'

'Isn't there?'

'If they won't accept us being together, then it's their loss.'

'They're your parents, Beck. You can't cut them out of your life.' Six months earlier he would have sold his soul for her to do just that. But a lot had changed since then.

'They'll accept it eventually. After all, I'm the only daughter they've got. But if they don't, then so be it. You're the most important person in my life. I didn't appreciate that before, but I do now.'

It was growing dark and shadows began to creep across the room. He lifted her on to his knee, the two of them cuddling together in the twilight, while the pigs observed them placidly and the Pet Shop Boys sang about the virtues of West End girls.

'You look tired,' he said.

'Just one of those days. Do you mind if we get a takeaway?'

'Let's call that pizza place on the corner. They deliver.'

'Good. That way you stay here.' She tightened her hold round his waist. 'There's chocolate on your teeth.'

'And on yours.' He attempted to lick them clean. She tried to squirm free of his grasp, inadvertently knocking one of the pigs on to the carpet. 'God, have I broken it?'

'No. Shall I have a go?' He raised his foot.

Again she laughed. 'I really, really hate those pigs,' he told her. 'Can we find a drawer to put them in?'

'OK.'

'I like this sofa, though.'

'So do I. Much more comfortable than the last one.'

He nodded.

'Do you miss the old flat?'

'No.'

'No.' She stroked his hair. 'You miss him, though, don't you?'

He shook his head.

'It's all right, Mike.'

He sighed. 'I do sometimes. But I'll get over it.'

'Do you know who I miss?'

He did.

'There were so many times I wanted to be rid of her. I didn't want the constant sense of guilt. But now she's gone I can't stop worrying. I never could have guessed I'd feel this way.'

'I never guessed the way she felt about me. Perhaps I should have done.'

She rubbed the back of his neck. 'You didn't ask her to feel like that.'

'Maybe not. But I still feel responsible.'

'Me, too, Mike. Me, too.'

Tuesday morning. Half past eleven. Returning to the office after a meeting, Emily stopped at a coffee bar on Great Portland Street.

It was virtually empty. A young couple sprawled on a sofa at the back, and two middle-aged women sat at a table by the counter. She ordered a mineral water then perched on a stool by the window, reached into her bag and pulled out the Arthurian epic she had tried to start last week.

Much to her surprise, it was proving thoroughly enjoyable. The dreadful quality of the writing only added to its considerable charm. Lancelot looked and sounded like an LA surfer dude, and Guinevere – the perfect Merchant-Ivory heroine save for a complete inability to keep her clothes on – was always swooning in his well-muscled arms. As for Arthur – a Yorkshire farmer, judging by the accent – he, too, was now showing a decided preference for surfers, and she kept expecting Merlin – spaced-out hippie, still tripping from Woodstock – to summon all three for a spot of marriage guidance.

She turned the pages, sipping her water and trying not to laugh too loudly.

'Em.'

Max stood before her, looking apologetic. 'Sorry. Got caught in the traffic. Have you been here long?'

'I've only just arrived.'

Moving to the counter, he ordered a cappuccino, sharing a friendly word with the youth who was serving. He pointed at a tray of pastries and raised a quizzical eyebrow. She shook her head. Smiling, he ordered one anyway.

She watched him, marvelling over how this friendship had come to pass.

The morning after their dinner she had sent him a short thank-you note. An automatic gesture of politeness, not intended to elicit a response. But he had phoned her the day he received it, and in the course of their conversation had mentioned that he would be in the area around lunchtime and suggested they meet for a coffee if she was free. She was, so they had.

And then again at the end of the week.

And now today.

He perched on a seat beside her, placing between them a plate with a cream slice and two forks. 'Go on,' he said encouragingly.

'I'm not very hungry.'

'Please. You have to help. I'm looking more and more like Chubby Checker every day.'

Laughing, she cut herself a piece and chewed slowly.

'Good?'

'Very.'

He sipped his cappuccino. 'How was your meeting?' she asked.

'Agreeable.'

'Are shareholder meetings generally agreeable?'

'They are when you vote yourself a sizeable dividend. How was yours?'

'Fine.'

'Are meetings with publishers generally fine?'

She nodded. They were.

Just not today.

There had been no meeting. She had told the office that she was at the dentist. Any excuse to escape for a couple of hours.

'These meetings mean a lot to me,' he had told her. 'You're the one person I can talk to about what's happened, and it's a great comfort.' She hoped that was true.

But it seemed that most of the talking was done by her. It was largely superficial. Things that had happened at work. Problems with public transport. The minutiae of day-to-day life in the metropolis. But occasionally, without meaning to, she would touch on other themes. Her childhood. Parents. Hopes and fears. She would speak for a matter of seconds, then realise what she was doing and retreat back to neutral ground. And he would study her with those dark eyes, never asking difficult questions, making her feel that if she did choose to expose herself she would not be judged harshly.

'Mike phoned me yesterday,' she told him.

'How was he?'

'He just left a message. There hasn't been a chance to call back.'

'Will you?'

'Why shouldn't I?'

'Because it hurts too much.'

She felt a tightness in her stomach.

'Did you think I hadn't guessed?'

She didn't answer. He continued to study her. There was a small line of froth on his upper lip.

Suddenly she felt an urge to stretch out her hand and gently wipe it away.

Confused, she retreated to the sanctuary of daily life. 'One of our authors is giving a reading tomorrow night. Someone called Jude Hale. I have to go and give moral support.'

'I've never been to a reading.'

'This one will be awful. I'm sure of it.'

He nodded.

'The author's no good. The agency are planning to drop him.'

Silence. Save for the beating of her heart.

'Would you like to come?'

'Yes.'

There was movement to her right. The young couple were leaving. The man's hair was as dark and luxuriant as Michael's.

She tried to picture Michael with a few grey hairs; wondered if they would suit him. The way they suited Max.

He had finished his drink. 'Will your colleagues be expecting you back?'

She shook her head. They all knew how long things could take at the dentist.

'Then let's have another. A hot chocolate for you, I think. It's time you started living dangerously.'

Again she laughed. Wiping the froth from his lip, he made his way to the counter.

Noon. Michael sat in the offices of recruitment consultants Carter Clark.

It was a basement room with no windows, bare walls and an overhead light too powerful for the limited space. It felt like an interrogation room, which, in a way, it was.

Brian Price, the consultant, recently out of university and

bursting with enthusiasm, studied his CV. 'This is impressive. For someone only a year qualified you've done an awful lot of deals.'

'Thanks.' He sipped his industrial-strength coffee.

'Are you looking for an in-house job or do you want to stay in private practice?'

'Private practice.'

'That's probably sensible. Two years post-qualification is usually the best time to think about going in-house.' Brian cleared his throat. 'Why do you want to leave Cox Stephens?'

He gave the answer he had prepared in his head. 'Our corporate group are focusing more and more on the computer sector, and I don't want to become sector-specific. I'd rather do a broader range of work across different types of industries.'

'Well, you're in luck. Now's a good time for people looking to move jobs. I can think of some City firms who'd be interested in your CV, and many of the new American operations are in need of good corporate people. Let me show you what vacancies we've got …'

Twenty minutes later Michael stood on Blackfriars Bridge, watching boatloads of tourists cruise up and down the Thames, waving cheerfully in spite of the dreary weather.

He phoned Rebecca on his mobile, but she was tied up in a management meeting so he called Stuart instead.

'How did you get on?' Stuart asked.

'Not bad. Various possibilities were mooted.'

'Such as?'

'Saunders Bishop. Randall Watts Hooper.'

'You don't want to go there. I did a deal with them once. Their corporate partners are wankers.'

'It's a job. Beggars can't be choosers.'

'Did you tell him you'd already resigned?'

'I thought it safer to keep that quiet. Otherwise he'd only start asking difficult questions. Fortunately at least two of the firms he mentioned want someone to start as soon as possible, so hopefully it won't be a problem. How are things back at the ranch?'

'Bloody awful. Graham's dumping crap left, right and centre. He's leaving the office at half past one so don't come back until after then.'

'OK. Thanks, Stu.' He was on the point of hanging up when he thought of something. 'By the way, can you and Helen make dinner on Saturday? Becky wants to see you both.'

'I'll check with Hel, but I'm sure the answer will be yes. See you later, mate.'

After buying sandwiches from a street café he walked down on to the Embankment and found an empty bench. A breeze blew off the water. He sat gazing across the grey water at the South Bank.

The Oxo Tower stood like an Art Deco finger jabbing at the sky. He remembered Max pointing it out to him as the two of them sat on a bench just like this one after their showdown in the lavatory at Cadogan's. Back then he had felt happy that something wonderful had happened in his life, with no notion of how wrong it was going to go.

He wondered what Max was doing now. Was he busy? Had he made up with Caroline? Had he met someone else?

Is he missing me?

He hoped not. More than anything he wanted Max to forget all about him.

But perhaps that wasn't true. People only ever missed those they cared about. And he wanted to be missed.

He took his mobile from his pocket. One call wouldn't hurt, would it? Just to say hello. To try and apologise once more. To show that, in spite of the choice he'd made, he did still care.

Slowly his fingers tapped out Max's number. The phone began to ring. But as he waited he thought of the lies and the manipulation and felt suddenly afraid. Before the call was answered he pressed the disconnect button.

He wanted to be missed. But not to be controlled.

He dialled Chatterton's instead.

Rebecca, out of her meeting now, was delighted to hear from him. 'I've been thinking about you all morning. How did you get on?' The sound of her voice was like a tonic. As they spoke he walked away from the river, up towards Fleet Street and a part of town that he did not associate with Max.

The reading was not going well.

Jude Hale stood in the fiction section of an independent bookshop off Charing Cross Road reading an extract from his latest novel, *Death Junkies*. Forty chairs were set out in rows before him. Seven were occupied: three by bookshop staff, two by members of the public and two by Max and Emily.

Emily keep looking at her watch. Jude had been reading for half an hour, and she could feel her eyes glazing over. She wondered if Max felt the same.

She wished she hadn't asked him to come. This was even worse than she'd feared. Jude had once worked in this shop and had persuaded the manager to suggest the reading to his publishers. The publishers had thought it a bad idea and tried to talk Jude out of it, but to no avail. A woman from their publicity department had promised to come, before phoning at the last minute to say that she had sprained her ankle. Emily envied her her clumsiness.

Nervously she looked at Max. He gave her a conspiratorial smile, his expression one of wry amusement. She returned the gesture and felt herself relax.

Jude finished. After a smattering of applause, he asked for questions and was greeted by silence before the embarrassed shop manager raised two points about characterisation. A scowling Jude gave curt answers to both, after which they began to move towards a makeshift bar at the back of the store where wine and crisps were waiting.

'Please don't feel you have to stay,' whispered Emily. 'I do, but you don't.'

'Of course I'll stay. My car's parked outside. I'll give you a lift home afterwards.'

'There's no need.'

'Need has nothing to do with it. Let's get a drink.'

They stood together in the corner sipping Lambrusco. 'The booze at these events is never very good,' she told him.

The look of amusement remained. 'Will you stop apologising for everything?' He lit a cigar, then went to find an ashtray.

She sipped her drink, willing the two members of the public to shower Jude with praise. Sadly both were far more interested in the free alcohol, and once again it was left to the shop manager to boost the artistic ego. Suddenly Jude excused himself and began to make his way over. She retreated into an alcove, not wanting anyone else to hear the abuse she was about to receive.

'It was a very good reading,' she said with as much conviction as she could manage.

Jude glared at her. A tall, intense man who looked as if he could be Kevin Spacey's anaemic younger brother. 'It was a shambles.'

'I don't think that's true.'

'It's like a bloody morgue! I told you we needed publicity, but you didn't listen.'

'But Jude, that's for the shop and publishers to do.'

He snorted.

'And there was publicity. An ad in the paper. A plug on local radio.'

'Well, it wasn't enough. I don't know what I pay you people

for. You get your commission and what do you do for it? Bugger all!'

She flinched. Desperately she tried to think of some pacifying words.

And then heard Max say, in his most charming tone, 'I don't think that's quite fair.'

She had not heard him approach. Startled, she turned towards him. As did Jude.

'And who are you?' he demanded.

'Someone who doesn't appreciate the way you're talking to Emily.'

'I pay her wages. I can talk to her any way I want.'

Max smiled. 'I suppose that's one way of looking at the situation. The other is to say that Emily's agency has done you a huge favour in agreeing to represent, judging by this evening's reading, quite awesomely mediocre work, and that consequently a little more politeness is called for.'

Jude's eyes widened.

'Max ... ' began Emily.

He made a soothing noise. 'And now,' he told Jude, his tone as charming as ever, 'I think it's time for an apology.

'Fuck you!'

Still smiling, Max extinguished his cigar. Then he slammed his fist into Jude's stomach.

Jude doubled over in pain. Max took him by the hair, yanked his head up and stared into his eyes.

'You will apologise to Emily right now,' he said softly, 'and tomorrow morning you will phone her boss to tell him that you are delighted with the work she's done on your behalf and that he's a lucky man to have so capable an employee. Failure to do either will displease me immensely, and I am not, if you'll forgive my use of your charming analogy, someone you fuck with. Do I make myself quite clear?'

A frightened nod.

'Good. If you apologise now, Emily and I can go and have dinner, and you can return to your adoring public. What do you say?'

Swallowing, Jude turned to Emily. 'I'm sorry I was rude. I'm grateful for all you've done.'

She stared at him. All the arrogance was gone. He looked cowed and humiliated.

And she was glad.

'That's all right,' she told him.

Max released Jude and took her arm. 'Shall we go?'

Together they made for the door.

Quarter past eleven. Max stopped the car in the street outside her house.

She unfastened her seatbelt. The evening was over and it was time to say goodnight. She waited for him to do so, but he remained silent.

'It was a lovely dinner,' she said eventually.

'The restaurant wasn't too smart, then?'

'Definitely not. Just right.'

'I'm glad.'

'Would you like to come inside?'

Silence. She fiddled with a lock of her hair, wishing she had said nothing.

'Sorry. Stupid idea. It's so late that you'll want to get back.'

'It's not so late.'

They walked into the house, across the hallway and up the first flight of stairs. The carpet was drab and the paintwork shabby. A far cry from Kensington and the world he inhabited.

She led him into the flat and turned on the light. He stood in the centre of the room, looking about him. She searched his face for signs of dismay but found none.

Leaving him to inspect her books, she went to make coffee. Her kitchen was tiny but cheerful. All greens and blues. She had decorated it herself. Postcards covered the fridge door, most written by Rebecca and Michael.

She took the coffee into the other room. They sat together on a small sofa by the window, while the dull thud of rock music echoed from the flat above. 'I'm sorry about the noise,' she said.

'Did I tell you about the first flat I ever owned?'

'No.'

'It was over a fish shop in Lewisham. Only two rooms, and the walls were so damp that stains kept appearing through the paint. The man who ran the shop adored Herman's Hermits and played their records constantly. Every morning I would wake to the smell of mackerel and the wail of "Mrs Brown, You've Got a Lovely Daughter". I've yet to find an alarm clock half as effective.'

She smiled. He picked up a framed photograph from the coffee table. 'Is this your mother?'

'Yes.'

'Then I was right.'

'Right?'

'That you judge yourself too harshly.'

'You didn't know her. She was a very special person. Kind, gentle and with the most beautiful smile you've ever seen. That's the thing I remember best. Her smile.'

She stopped, fearful that she was embarrassing him. But he continued to stare at the photograph with eyes that were full of nostalgia and regret.

'My mother had the loveliest voice,' he said softly. 'My father used to play folk tunes on a violin and she would sing. Her voice was very low and very sweet. I can barely remember her face, but I can still hear her voice as clear as a bell.'

'I still miss her,' she told him. 'Even now, after all this time. It's stupid, but I can't help it. There's never a day when I don't think about her and wish she was still here.'

He turned towards her. His eyes were gentle.

'Why do you hate yourself so much?'

A lump came into her throat. 'Don't—'

'When I look at you I see someone who is intelligent, compassionate, generous and loyal. Someone who is elegant and has a face like a painting. Someone who is beautiful both inside and out.'

'Beautiful?' She spoke the word slowly and deliberately, as if learning a foreign language.

He nodded.

She pulled up the sleeves on her dress, revealing the jagged, self-inflicted scars that covered the skin on her arms. 'Is this beautiful?'

He stared at them, unblinking. Then, putting down her mother's picture, began to trace them with his fingers. 'Oh Emmie,' he said, calling her by the name that was only ever used by her father. His voice was soft and very tender. It made her feel vulnerable. She took refuge behind scorn.

'I'm not beautiful, generous or compassionate. You don't know me at all, Max. You shouldn't presume that you do.'

'But you presume to know me. You have done since the day we met in the cathedral.'

His words threw her completely. She shook her head.

'When you're with me you never stop apologising for the fact of our being together. You believe that someone with money could never genuinely enjoy the company of someone who has none. When you look at me you see my wealth, and you judge me for it.'

'That's not true.'

He smiled sadly. 'Everyone does it. That's the thing that no

391

one ever tells you about wealth. That it ends up defining you. Relationships become like business transactions, with people offering themselves in trade for some small part of your status and power. That was the wonderful thing about Michael. He cared about the person behind the big houses and expensive cars, and that's why I miss him so much.'

His words stung. 'I care about that person too.'

'Then allow me to care about the person behind the scars.'

'She isn't worth it.'

'Let me be the judge of that.'

She stared down at her arms. The scars were like tiny snakes living in her flesh. Gently he pulled down the sleeves of her dress. 'Perhaps I should go. I'm sorry if I've upset you, Emmie. Please believe that your friendship means the world to me, and I would never willingly do anything to hurt you.'

She looked into his eyes. Her father's were the same colour. But they had never made her feel this safe.

She touched his cheek, feeling the warmth of his skin. He took her hand and kissed the palm. Every nerve in her body exploded. She felt weak with desire.

'Please don't go,' she whispered.

'Are you sure?'

'Yes.'

'Even though I'm so much older than you?'

'I don't see the years. Or the cars or the houses. I care about the person behind them all.'

'And you are beautiful,' he said, drawing her to him.

Emily woke in the darkness of her bedroom. She lay on her side, enveloped by his arms and the warmth of his body, his breath soft against her neck as he nuzzled at her ear. Sighing contentedly, she wallowed in the feeling of togetherness. The clock by her bed showed 6.47.

'I have to go,' he whispered.

'Go?'

'Breakfast meeting. I did tell you.'

Perhaps he had. But she didn't remember.

She felt sick.

'Don't get up,' he told her. 'Stay where it's warm.'

As he climbed out of the bed she turned on the bedside light, then sat, watching him dress. His torso and limbs were powerful, but to her he had been wonderfully tender.

He was her second lover. The first had been a boyfriend at college, someone who had had little idea of how to make the act of love enjoyable for a woman. She had always viewed sex as something coarse, but Max had shown her that it could be beautiful.

For her at least.

In her euphoria she had not stopped to think what it might have been like for him.

'Will I see you again?' She struggled to keep the tremble out of her voice.

'Of course.' He fastened his tie. 'I'll call you.'

Probably he would. He was a kind man, but he was also worldly. Too worldly for someone like her.

She swallowed. The taste of his skin was in her mouth. 'You don't have to. Not if you don't want.'

Putting on his jacket he came and sat beside her. 'It's early yet. Go back to sleep.'

He kissed her forehead. Quickly. Chastely. The way one kissed a friend. She would settle for friendship if that was all he wanted to offer.

But could their friendship survive this?

He left the room. She heard the front door closing behind him. Then, much fainter, the sound of a car driving away.

393

She remained sitting up in bed, her hair falling around her shoulders, watching the cold, hard light of morning creep into the room.

Half past eleven. Emily sat at her desk, skimming through piles of submission chapters from aspiring authors. Her head ached, but still she was grateful for the work. It helped take her mind off other things.

Footsteps approached. Kevin, a cheerful thirty-something, who was already completely bald, stood holding an A4 envelope. 'The most enormous bouquet of flowers has been delivered.'

Her heart lifted.

'For Janet. A thank-you from that new author she just sold to Transworld. Why can't all clients be like that?'

She swallowed down her disappointment. 'Why, indeed?'

He nodded at the chapters. 'Any I should look at?'

'A historical thriller about the Hellfire Club. The author's a PhD, so it's strong on atmosphere and period detail.'

'Great. Give it to me now and I'll have a look.'

It was buried somewhere on her desk. As she searched, he held up the envelope. 'A courier's just dropped this off for you. It'll be the revamped Paul Baxter cover, which we must pray is better than the last one. Shall I open it?'

'Sure.' She located the chapters but not the covering letter, and began to plough through another pile of papers.

'Oh, I'm sorry. I had no idea it was personal.'

She looked up. Kevin handed her the contents of the envelope. Two first-class Eurostar return tickets to Paris, together with a hotel reservation slip.

And wrapped around them was a short note, written in a strong, confident hand.

Emmie,

Le Tremoille is in a side street off the Champs-Elysées.

It may not be the most famous hotel in Paris, but it is, in my opinion, the most beautiful. This weekend you and a guest of your choice can decide for yourselves.

Love

Max

P.S. Not that I'm trying to influence your decision, but I thought you should know that I'm not doing anything this weekend.

The joy was overwhelming. She burst into tears.

Kevin looked horrified. Desperately she tried to contain her emotions. 'It's something good,' she told him. 'Something wonderful.'

'Well, God help us if you ever get bad news.'

She started to laugh. His expression relaxed into one of amusement. 'I'm glad it's something good. Shall I make myself scarce for a bit?'

'Thank you.'

He left the room. Breathing deeply, she struggled for composure. She could not afford to get hysterical. Not when there was an invitation to be made.

A glass of water stood on her desk. She sipped it slowly, waiting for her heart to slow.

Then, wiping her eyes, she reached for the telephone.

THREE

Saturday evening. Michael, clutching a bottle of white wine, strode down West End Lane.

It was just after seven, and Stuart and Helen were due for dinner at half past. Leaving Rebecca to watch over the spaghetti carbonara, he had popped out to stretch his legs and return last night's video. Two bottles of wine and six cans of lager were already chilling in the fridge, but as Stuart could drink for England he had also made a further stop at the off-licence just in case.

As he approached the flat he saw that the parking space opposite, empty five minutes ago, was now occupied by a silver Vauxhall Astra. There were no other spaces, so Helen would have to park in another street. He decided not to tell Rebecca, who had become increasingly tense as the evening approached and didn't need something else to worry about.

He let himself into the flat. Voices echoed from the living room. Hopefully their early arrival hadn't thrown Rebecca too much. He walked through the half-open door. 'Hi. Did you have trouble parking?'

Rebecca was standing by the window holding a box of Godiva chocolates. Next to her stood Sean, together with his girlfriend Maya.

'Surprise,' said Rebecca, rather hesitantly.

He didn't answer. Just stared.

'I'm sorry we didn't bring wine,' said Sean. 'Becky said not to bother.'

He found his voice. 'We've enough already.'

'We didn't mean to be so early,' Maya told him. 'The traffic was better than expected.'

'Good.'

'We passed a pub on the way here called the General's Arms,' added Sean. 'A friend of mine used to live around here and that was his local. He said it was a nice place.'

'It is.'

Silence. Tension hung in the air like static.

'Maybe,' Michael continued, 'we could have a drink there after the meal.'

The relief was palpable. All three started smiling. As did he.

'Have a seat while I open some wine. And if you break any china pigs then the first round at the General's is on me.'

He walked into the kitchen, put the new bottle in the fridge and took out a cold one. Rebecca followed him in. 'Stuart and Helen aren't coming,' she said. 'Stuart spoke to Sean after you left the wine bar and found out who he was. He knew I'd been pushing you to trace Sean, so when we got back together he phoned and told me what had happened. I know I should have told you, but I was worried you'd say no and—'

He covered her mouth with his hand. 'I love you,' he whispered. 'You don't know how much.'

Tears came into her eyes. They hugged each other.

397

Then, pushing him away, she turned her attention to the food. Carrying the wine, he went to entertain their guests.

Eight o'clock. Emily, wearing a pale blue dress that she had bought especially for her trip, sat at a dressing table in Le Tremoille Hotel. Paris was still basking in the last remnants of summer, and through the open window she could hear laughter as people wove their way through hooting cars on to the outdoor cafés and restaurants that lined the Champs-Elysées, all eager to make the most of what could be the last balmy evening of the year.

Slowly she ran a comb through her hair. It hung below her shoulders, framing her pale, oval face and shadowed eyes. Her best feature, so she had always been told, just as it had been her mother's. She was sure her mother had worn it with more elegance, but never in a setting as beautiful as this.

Though a hotel, Le Tremoille had only eight rooms, and with its staff in uniforms of grey and gold the place seemed more like the private house of a wealthy aristocrat. Their suite had all the formal elegance of pre-revolutionary France, with gilt mirrors, pale wallpaper, antique furniture and subdued lighting.

Her feet ached from the exertions of the day. That morning they had visited the Louvre, where the *Mona Lisa* and *Venus de Milo* had moved her less than Géricault's eerie *Raft of the Medusa*. In the afternoon they had walked through the Tuileries to Ile de la Cité, where she had gazed up at the Gothic edifice of Notre-Dame and imagined Quasimodo staring down at them. Max had wanted to take her shopping, but instead they had ended the day strolling along the banks of the Seine. 'Are you sure you wouldn't prefer the boutiques?' he had asked at one point. 'Quite sure,' she had replied, and in spite of the sigh and shake of the head, his smile told her that he was pleased.

That evening they were eating dinner in the tiny hotel

restaurant. He had proposed taking her to the most expensive place in the city, but she loved the peace of Le Tremoille and wanted to enjoy its atmosphere while she could. This had prompted more sighs and shakes of the head, but again she sensed that he was pleased with her choice.

The suite door opened and footsteps crossed the salon. He had been out to buy cigars. 'Did you find your brand?' she asked as he entered the room.

'Eventually. At a little Algerian tobacconist on the corner.' He sat down on the bed, an ornate four-poster that had once, according to the manager, belonged to a cousin of Louis xvi. 'You look lovely,' he told her. 'Have you thought about how you'd like to spend tomorrow?'

'I'd like to go to Versailles. I know it's sad and touristy, but it's something I'd enjoy.'

'Haven't you been there before? You mentioned a school trip.'

She nodded. Then, blushing, said, 'But I'd like to see it with you.'

'Then you shall.' He walked over to the dressing table, put his arms around her and kissed her cheek. He smelled of cologne and tobacco. 'This is your weekend, Emmie, and I want it to be as perfect as possible.'

That was true. It was her weekend.

And it was perfect.

She hoped there would be more times like this. That this could be the start of something magical between them. But if this was all she ever had with him, then it was still more than enough. She would treasure the memory of this weekend until the day she died.

He kissed her again. 'Shall we go and eat?'

'Yes.'

Taking her hand, he led her towards the door.

*

Quarter to ten. Michael, his hair damp from the rain, stood at the bar in the General's Arms.

It was a vibrant place, all greens and reds, with a karaoke machine in the far corner and a snooker table at its centre. He paid his money, then carried two pints of lager through the smoky air towards the table by the door where Sean waited. Rebecca and Maya were drinking coffee back at the flat.

He swallowed a mouthful of lager. In the background a tone-deaf woman savaged 'Bridge over Troubled Water'. 'I hope no one sings "My Way",' he told Sean.

'Or "I Will Survive". God, I hate that song.'

'But the all-time worst is "Seasons in the Sun".'

Sean shook his head. '"Fame". Nothing so grisly.'

'We used to watch that show every week.'

'Sitting on those dilapidated armchairs in the television room.'

'You were a complete junkie for that show. Had to have your weekly fix. Once I got into a fight with a skinhead who wanted to watch snooker because I was frightened you'd go into convulsions if we switched channels.'

'I remember that. Was his name Terry?'

'No. Terry was the fat kid with ginger hair who loved the show almost as much as you did. Don't you remember? He idolised Leroy the rebellious dancer and used to mimic his New York slang. He even tried the pimp walk, which got him some very iffy looks on Mile End Road.'

They both laughed, while the tone-deaf woman launched a full-scale assault on 'The Power of Love', teenagers argued over snooker scores and the people on the next table complained about the health service. Outside, the rain was coming down in sheets.

'I hope they're having better weather in Norfolk,' observed Sean. 'My sister Cathy is hiking with friends, and I have visions of her eating cold baked beans in a leaking tent.'

'You two are really close, aren't you?'

'Yes, though she gets on my nerves. She's very assertive, and because I'm not she tries to fight my battles for me. It makes me feel ineffectual sometimes, but I don't really mind.'

'Did I ever make you feel like that?'

'All the time.' Sean smiled. 'But I didn't mind that either.'

'You must have been jealous when your parents adopted her.'

'Not really. Mum and Dad handled it really well. They made it seem that I was the one taking her in and giving her a home, and that made me feel protective.'

'Was it difficult? Learning to call them Mum and Dad?'

'With Mum, especially. I still missed my real mother, and it seemed disloyal to replace her with someone else. But they handled that well too. They never pushed anything, and let me call them Sue and Tony. One day I realised that I really did love them, and that they were exactly the people my mother would have chosen to take her place. From then on they were Mum and Dad.'

Michael smiled. 'I'm glad.'

'You'd like them, Mike. They're good people. They've given Cathy and me their name and their love, but they've never tried to make us forget who we are. They've always told Cathy that they'll support her completely if she wants to trace her real parents. They've said the same about my real father, but I've never tried to find him. Tony's my father now, and I don't want another one.'

Michael nodded. Someone on the next table was smoking a cigar.

'I traced my real father when I was eighteen,' he said. 'My foster father had just died, and my foster mother had moved to the Bahamas. They'd never allowed me to be close to them,

401

but I still felt abandoned. I'd been left some money in the will, so I hired a private detective to trace my father for me.

'My father's name was John Matthews. Another glorious product of the British care system who'd done time for theft and drug offences. When I found him he was on the dole, living in a council flat in Catford. I phoned, told him who I was and suggested a meeting, expecting him to tell me to bugger off. Instead he seemed delighted at the prospect.

'We met in a pub. He looked exactly like me. It was like staring into one of those fairy-tale mirrors and seeing yourself twenty years older. It gave me this really warm feeling inside.

'But it didn't last. He didn't care that I was his son. Within fifteen minutes he was dropping hints about how broke he was, and I realised that the only reason he'd agreed to meet me was that he'd heard my accent and assumed I had money. In the end I wrote him a cheque for half what my foster father had left me and told him that I didn't want to see him again. He seemed quite happy with that. He didn't even bother to say goodbye.'

Sean whistled. 'That must have hurt.'

Michael picked at his beer mat. The smell of cigar smoke hung in the air around him. 'You know what hurts the most? The feeling that people only want you for what you have or represent, rather than for who you are. To my foster parents I was a status symbol; to my father, a private goldmine. Only one person has made me feel like a son. Sadly, that didn't work out either.'

Sean looked surprised. 'I thought you didn't remember your mother.'

'I'm not talking about her.'

'Who, then?'

'Long story.'

'I'm a good listener.'

'Let's leave it for another evening.'

Sean smiled. 'Will there be one?'

'I hope so.'

'So do I. Fifteen years is a long time. Let's not lose each other again.'

Michael raised his glass. 'I'll drink to that.'

They toasted each other, while drunken singers continued to massacre classic songs and rain pounded the window.

Max's voice woke Emily. Morning had come already, though she felt as if she'd had no rest at all.

But their bedroom was in darkness, illuminated only by those streetlights bright enough to penetrate the curtains. And his conversation was not directed at her.

He lay on his back, shifting restlessly, crying out in a guttural tongue she did not understand while his arms pummelled the sheets as if fighting an invisible opponent. It was dangerous to wake a dreamer, but such was his distress that she felt she had no choice. She put her hand on his forehead and found his skin sticky with sweat. Softly she spoke his name.

He woke with a start, his eyes circling wildly as he tried to determine his surroundings. 'It's all right,' she said gently. 'You're in the hotel. There's no one else here. Just me.' Again she reached out to touch him.

Roughly he pushed her away, sitting upright in the bed, throwing sheets and pillows on to the floor. He rested his back against the headboard, running a hand through his hair, sighing over and over as though in pain. She watched him nervously. 'Shall I get you some water?' she whispered. 'Would you like me to do that?'

He didn't answer. Just sat there, breathing heavily, like a wounded animal. Fearful, she began to edge away, only for him suddenly to grab her and press her against his chest. 'Don't

403

go,' he begged, crushing her in his arms so she felt she couldn't breathe. 'Stay here with me.'

They remained like that for some time. The night was perfectly still, and the only sound was that of his heart pounding in his chest like a steam engine. At last it began to slow.

'What did you dream?' she asked him. 'Was it about your parents?'

'No.'

He had told her something of his early life. 'Was it the uprising? The refugee camp?'

'Worse than that. The worst dream there can be. The dream of being powerless.'

'How were you powerless? What was happening?'

He shook his head. 'It's over now. It was just a dream.' His hold loosened. Gently he stroked her hair. 'You're shaking. I'm sorry I frightened you.'

She kissed his cheek, wiping perspiration from his brow. 'It doesn't matter.'

'I'll make it up to you tomorrow. We'll go to Versailles. We'll do whatever you want to do.'

'We don't have to do anything.'

A look of great sadness came into his face. 'Oh Emmie,' he whispered. 'What are you doing here with me? You deserve better than this.'

'I don't think so.'

He continued to stroke her hair. 'You're a child. You don't understand.'

'Understand what?'

'That I don't love like other people. The fact of love is never enough. When I love someone I want to control them. Make them a prisoner who can never escape.'

Again she wiped his brow. His breath was warm against her face. 'If they loved you they'd never want to escape.'

404

'I wish I could believe that. Michael loved me. That should have been sufficient, but it wasn't. I tried to bind him to me and ended up driving him away. My love is bad, Emmie. All it does it suffocate.'

'But at least it's strong. The object of love knows that they're needed and that your world would collapse if they weren't a part of it. My father loves me more than anyone, but he doesn't need me. If I were to die tomorrow, his life would go on just as it has for years.'

He shook his head.

'It's true. He doesn't need love. He's a weak man and his needs are very different.'

'You think I'm strong? After tonight?'

'Yes.'

'I'm frightened of being abandoned. Where's the strength in that?'

'In being able to admit it.'

They sat together in the darkness, both of them naked. Her hands massaged his scalp, while he caressed the small of her back. She had never been so exposed with another human being, and never felt so safe.

'I remember a day,' she said softly, 'when I was at college. I had flu and spent the day in bed, listening to a discussion programme about how strange and illogical love can be. A woman had written in anonymously. She wrote that she was happily married and had four daughters. She loved all her children equally, except for the second. This girl was no more beautiful or talented than her sisters, but her mother loved her to distraction. She was ashamed of this preference and kept it hidden, but she knew that if ever she had to choose between keeping this child or the rest of the family she would sacrifice the others every time.

'That's what I want. To be loved the way that woman loved

405

her daughter. It wouldn't matter that I was being controlled or possessed. I just want to be the centre of someone's universe. To know that they couldn't go on living if I was taken from them. Before I die I want to know what it is to be loved like that.'

'You will be,' he whispered. 'I promise you that.'

They kissed each other, slowly and tenderly. 'Are you tired?' she asked him. 'Do you want to sleep?'

'Will you watch over me if I do?'

'There'll be no more nightmares. I'll keep them all away.'

'I know you will. But I don't want to sleep.'

'Neither do I.'

They made love, there in the darkness of the room, in a night so still that it seemed they were the only two people in the world.

It was five in the morning. Michael, his eyes red from crying, sat on the sofa listening to the sounds of Rebecca moving about the kitchen. The overhead light was off, and the only illumination came from a tiny lamp in the corner of the room.

She reappeared, carrying a glass of water. He drank it gratefully, his throat sore after hours of talking. She drew the curtains then sat close beside him. The box of Godiva chocolates stood unopened on the table in front of them.

'So much for pigging out,' she said.

'Put it in the drawer. Give the china porkers a treat.' Gently he touched her ear. 'Poor Beck. It's a miracle I haven't bent this off completely.'

Sean and Maya had left at midnight. Once they'd gone, Michael and Rebecca had sat together, watching a late-night film, while he described childhood memories of Sean and his joy at their reunion. As he spoke, other, more distant memories had begun to surface. Memories of being taken from his mother and of all the trauma and heartache the separation had caused. Memories he had never allowed himself to remember fully because the pain was too great.

'It's done now,' he said softly. 'Finished. Tonight has been like saying a proper goodbye to her. Making my peace and finally letting go.'

She didn't answer. Just moved closer still.

'And I want to promise you something.'

'What?'

'That if we ever have a child, I'll do everything in my power to give it the happiest possible life. Every day I'll fight to protect it from pain, loneliness and fear. I promise that when the time comes I'll be the most perfect father I can be.'

She picked up his hand and kissed it.

Then she placed it on her stomach.

'That time has come,' she whispered. 'I would have told you before, but I wanted to find the perfect moment. This is it.'

He stared at her. Completely lost for words.

Her eyes were anxious. 'Say something. Anything. Please.'

He tried to speak, but emotion overwhelmed him. His tears came, just as they had earlier that evening. Her face relaxed. Smiling, she began to cry too. 'Thank you,' she said. 'That was what I needed to hear.'

They remained on the sofa, his hand resting on her stomach, watching the old day die and the new one begin.

Sunday evening. Emily stood in the kitchen of her flat.

Max had dropped her there an hour ago. He hadn't come in this time. Just walked her to the door. No further meetings had been arranged between them, but she knew she would see him again.

Half past eleven. Though normally asleep at this hour, she made no move for bed.

Two new postcards brightened her fridge door, both bought that morning. The Galerie des Glaces and the Petit Trianon. The good weather had lasted throughout the weekend, allowing them to explore Versailles outside as well as in. There had been far less conversation than on the previous day. After the night they had spent, proximity had been more important than talk.

The telephone rang. She knew who it was and what was coming before she picked up the receiver. Though trembling, she felt completely calm.

'I've lived in this house for ten years,' he said. 'I love it more than any home I've ever had. But I can't live here now. Not without you.'

'You don't have to.' It came out as a sigh.

'I'll come and fetch you. I'll be there within an hour.'

'I'll get a cab. That will be quicker.'

'Don't bring anything. Just yourself. I'll give you everything else you need.'

She pressed the disconnect button, then phoned a local taxi company. While waiting for the car she packed a small bag. Just enough to last a few days. The rest would be provided.

Her driver was a stout, middle-aged Russian woman who swore like a trooper at any motorist who crossed her path. 'These drivers. All are idiots. Bloody hell!' The car's heater wasn't working but she didn't care. Anticipation kept her warm.

'Where you going?' the driver asked.

'To see a friend.'

A wry smile. 'Your man?'

'My man.' The words felt good on her lips.

'Posh part of town. He rich, yes?' A blue Audi cut in front of them, prompting a bleep of the horn and a waved fist. 'Idiots. All these people. Bloody hell! How old you are?'

'Twenty-four.'

'Same age as Magda. She my daughter. Still in Russia.' A loving smile. 'My little baby. You pretty, like her.'

They drove into Arundel Crescent. He was waiting on the steps outside his house. The driver peered at him. 'That your man?'

'Yes.'

'Older than you.'

'I don't care.'

'No. You love him, so you not care.' A squint. 'He looks good man. Kind.'

She paid the fare. The woman smiled at her. 'You be happy, little baby.'

'Thank you.'

She climbed out of the car. He stood there, perfectly still, waiting for her.

She stared up at him, and suddenly happiness made her feel faint.

He opened his arms and she went to him.

FOUR

Monday morning. Quarter to nine. Emily lay alone in Max's bed, the sheets wrapped around her, the curtains still drawn.

The room was simply furnished. White walls, brown carpet, sober antique furniture. She had imagined something far more lavish. Not that she minded. The simplicity was somehow reassuring, convincing her that she was not totally out of place.

Footsteps echoed in the corridor. Max entered, wearing a red silk dressing gown decorated with Chinese dragons. He carried a tray, bringing with him the smell of coffee and burned bread.

He drew the curtains, flooding the room with grey autumn light, then placed the tray on the bed and returned to the warm space he had vacated. She stroked his gown. 'You look very handsome in that.'

He smiled.

'Where did you get it?'

'Lavinia bought it for me.'

'Becky told me about her.' A pause. 'She was very beautiful.'

'Absolutely exquisite.'

Again she looked about the room. She wondered if Lavinia had liked its simplicity too.

He put his arm around her, kissing her forehead. 'And that was her curse. Her whole life was about being beautiful. She could never forget it. When we had sex it was as if I was a support player while she posed for an imaginary camera.'

His words made her happy. She stroked his chin, the roughness of early-morning stubble scratching her skin. No doubt Lavinia would have hated that. But she didn't.

Scars still adorned her arms. Once they had been a source of shame. But he never seemed to notice them, and was teaching her not to either.

She looked at the tray. A pot of coffee. Grapefruit juice. Charred croissants and a bunch of grapes. 'Mrs László wanted to cook for us,' he told her, 'but I wouldn't let her. I did all this myself.'

She poured the coffee. Thick enough to bend a spoon. 'So I see.'

'Very Hungarian. You'll learn to love it.'

'I'm going to be so late.'

He shook his head.

'I'm due at work in ten minutes.'

'You're not going to work.'

'But Max—'

'No arguments.' His arm tightened around her. 'You're staying here with me.'

'There are things I have to do.'

'The only thing you have to do is keep me warm. Now eat something or I'll think you don't like my cooking.' He covered a piece of croissant with butter and jam, then offered it to her. As she ate, he stared at her, his eyes suddenly troubled. 'It's starting already,' he said softly.

'What is?'

'My trying to control you.'

She didn't reply.

'You're not afraid?'

'No.'

And she wasn't. She had no fear of control. Not if it meant being wanted.

Would he want me if he knew about the stillness?

The thought came unbidden, momentarily disturbing her peace of mind. Quickly she pushed it away. He never would know. She would not tell him, and there was no one else in his life to do so.

The smile had returned to his face. She sipped her coffee. Too strong, but it was how he liked it. She would learn to like it too.

Noon. Michael put down the telephone.

'Well?' demanded Stuart, taking a break from the precedents.

'Two interviews at the start of next week. Saunders Bishop and some American place. Randall Watts Hooper are making positive noises too.'

'Brilliant! At this rate we'll be celebrating your new job on my stag weekend.'

Stuart and Helen, after ten years of cohabitation, were marrying in a month's time. Michael, to his delight, was going to be an usher. 'Have you decided where we're going yet?' he asked.

'Cardiff.'

'Cardiff?'

'The whole point of the weekend is to get completely hammered. As I've never been to Cardiff before, and am unlikely to go again, it doesn't matter if I'm barred from every pub in the city.'

Michael's phone went, but he let it ring through to Kim. 'It also means that no one will recognise you when you're chained to a lamppost wearing nothing but suspenders and a bra.'

Stuart's eyes narrowed. 'That's not happening.'

'Want to bet?'

They laughed. He longed to tell Stuart about the baby, but Rebecca had wanted to keep it their secret for just a little longer.

Kim popped her head round the door. 'Mike, Becky's holding.'

He picked up the receiver. 'You're cosmopolitan. What do you know about Cardiff?'

'I've just tried to phone Em at work. We have to meet right now.'

Half an hour later they sat together in a crowded sandwich bar near Liverpool Street.

'I don't believe it,' he said.

'They were seen together at a book reading. The description fits perfectly. It's Max.'

He drummed his fingers on the plastic table surface. 'That doesn't mean they're having a relationship.'

'He took her to Paris for a weekend. How romantic can you get? And apparently Em's been completely dreamy for days. Sue, the receptionist, kept trying to quiz me about him. As Em's supposed best friend, she assumed I knew everything.'

He shook his head, trying to take it in.

'She's off sick today. I tried her at the flat but there was no answer, which means that she's with him. God, Mike, what are we going to do?'

'Do?'

'We have to do something. This is Max we're talking about.' Rebecca's face was flushed and she was breathing hard. He rubbed her arm.

'Hey, calm down. You're pregnant, remember.'

She exhaled slowly. 'OK. I'm sorry. I just can't stand the thought of Em getting close to Max. You know how vulnerable she is.'

He nodded. The thought made him anxious too.

And jealous.

He stared down at the table.

She sighed. 'I have to go. Clare will be expecting me back.'

They left the bar. Crowds jostled around them on the street, all eager to make the most of their lunch hour. He waved to a secretary he recognised from the office, while in the background a street vendor sold an *Evening Standard* to a man who resembled the social worker who had told him his mother was dead. The day's headline was something about education cuts. The sky was clouding over, promising more rain that afternoon.

He gave her a hug. 'We'll talk about this properly tonight. Decide what needs to be done. In the meantime, promise me you won't do anything.'

'If you promise too.'

'Of course.'

As he watched her walk away he uncrossed his fingers. He knew what needed to be done, and it did not involve Rebecca.

At seven o'clock the following evening he sat with Max in the same private drinking club in Soho they had visited on the evening of Mr Blake's birthday. A glass of wine stood, untouched, on the table in front of him. Tension was already giving him a headache.

Max sipped his cognac. 'Where did you tell Becky you'd be this evening?'

'At a work do.'

'I see.'

414

'What did you tell Emily?'

'I take it she's the reason for our meeting?' The voice was cool and formal.

'What else?'

Max lit a cigar, using the candle at the centre of the table as his lighter. 'I didn't tell her anything. She had plans herself. Birthday celebration for a colleague.'

'You let her go to work, then.'

Max looked at his watch. 'She'll be home by eight, and I want to be there when she returns, so let's drop the insinuations and cut to the chase.'

He stared down at the pitted surface of the wooden table. The same one they had sat at before. He traced the carved letter 'R' with his fingers. In the background a group of businessmen laughed raucously at a shared joke.

'I'm waiting,' Max told him.

'You know what her life has been like.'

A nod.

'Things haven't been easy for her.'

'I am aware of that.'

'So don't hurt her to get back at me.'

He looked up. Max stared levelly at him, the dark smoke from his cigar mingling with that of the candle like two ghosts dancing in the air. 'Is that what you think I'm doing?'

'You tell me.'

'Have you never considered that Emily might matter to me? Or do you think me incapable of caring for another human being?'

He didn't answer. The flickering of the candle was hurting his eyes.

'I cared about you. Or have you forgotten that?'

'No.'

'Perhaps you're just concerned for my welfare. Emily wasn't

415

good enough for you, so why should she be good enough for me?'

The words stung. 'I never thought she wasn't good enough. She's a wonderful person. Whoever ends up with her will be very lucky.'

'Which is what I consider myself.' Max smiled. 'At last we appear to agree on something.'

Michael tried to contain his frustration at the way the conversation was going.

'Most of the women I've been involved with were shallow and mercenary. To find someone who is neither, and who cares for me as much as Emily appears to do, is wonderful indeed.' A pause. 'And if you think I'm going to break off a relationship that is making me so happy, just because you ask me to, then you're mistaken.'

The eyes continued to study him, making him self-conscious. 'I'm not asking you to break it off.'

'Do you want me to be happy?'

'Of course.'

'I'm happy now, and so is Emily. So let me make a suggestion. Get on with your own life and leave me to get on with mine. What do you say?'

He felt boxed into a corner. There was nothing to do but nod.

'And now I must go.' Max downed the rest of his cognac and rose to his feet.

'Becky's pregnant.'

The words came unbidden. Spoken to stop the conversation from ending before he felt ready to say goodbye.

Slowly Max sat down again. 'How long has she known?'

'A few weeks. She's only just told me.'

'And how do you feel?'

'Thrilled.' A pause. 'Scared.'

416

'Why are you scared?' Suddenly the voice was infused with its old warmth. 'Do you think you might make the mistakes your parents did?'

At first he didn't respond. Then, slowly, nodded.

'You mustn't be afraid. I told you once that you weren't your father, just as I wasn't my uncle. We make our own choices in this life, and I know you'll make a superb father when the time comes.'

'Thanks.'

They smiled at each other. For a moment everything was comfortable and easy.

'You shouldn't have resigned, though.'

His smile faded. 'How did you know about that?'

Max breathed smoke into the air. 'I've been talking to Jack on a regular basis since you were in short trousers. That won't change because of what's happened between us.'

'It's my choice.'

'Of course.' Again Max rose to his feet. 'Now I really have to go. We'll keep this conversation secret. Not a word to either Emily or Becky, agreed?'

'Agreed.'

'Stay and finish your drink if you want. Take care of yourself, Mike. Becky, too.'

He remained at the table, staring at the flickering flame, surrounded by the sound of laughter and the smell of alcohol and cigar smoke, frustrated at the way things had gone.

Thursday morning. Rebecca walked into Baker Connolly's reception. Sue, the youthful receptionist, resplendent in black eyeliner and crucifix earrings, sat surrounded by piles of manuscripts and the morning's mail. She smiled at Rebecca. 'Didn't know you were coming in,' she said.

Michael didn't know either. His view was that they should

leave the situation well alone. But what he didn't know couldn't hurt him.

'Just happened to be in the area. Is Em around?'

Sue checked the switchboard. 'She's on the phone, but I'm sure she won't mind you going through.'

Rebecca, far less confident, made her way down the corridor to the tiny corner office. As she approached, she heard Emily talking softly.

Then she giggled. A light, warm, flirtatious sound.

Rebecca stood in the shadow of the doorway, not wanting to reveal her presence. Emily sat in her chair beneath the window and its view of St Paul's. Her legs were tucked under her, the receiver pressed between ear and shoulder. A delicate pink illuminated her normally pale face.

Another giggle. 'No!'

A hiss echoed from the receiver.

'There are things I have to finish. One o'clock.'

More protests.

'Quarter to, then. But no earlier.' The giggling started again. 'You first.' She waited, then blew two kisses. After putting down the receiver, she remained curled up in her chair, a dreamy smile on her face.

'Em.'

The smile faded. 'What are you doing here?'

Rebecca closed the door and sat down in the spare chair. 'I wanted to see you.'

'So you thought you'd turn up unannounced.'

'You didn't leave me any choice. If you won't return my calls then what else am I supposed to do?'

A cup of coffee stood steaming on the cluttered desk. Emily traced the rim, then licked drops from her finger. The darkness of the liquid surprised Rebecca. Emily had always drunk her coffee white.

'It doesn't matter. I knew you'd show up once the news filtered through.'

'What news?'

'Come on, Becky. I may have been a burden, but I was never a stupid one.'

They stared at each other. Rebecca had been prepared for anger. But Emily's breathing was slow and easy, and her eyes were as calm as pools of water on a windless day.

'Does it upset you so much to see me happy?'

Rebecca shook her head.

'Then what? He's evil? He's going to hurt me? I happen to think otherwise. And even if I'm wrong it's no longer your concern.' A leisurely sigh. 'So thank you for coming, but please don't do it again. We have nothing to say to each other.'

'Em . . .'

'Goodbye, Becky.'

The eyes remained calm. And completely distant. There was none of the old vulnerability and need. The realisation made Rebecca feel oddly bereft.

She tried to prolong the conversation. An Empire State Building paperweight stood on a pile of letters on the cluttered desk. 'I gave you that. Do you remember?'

Emily picked it up, turning it over in her hand. 'It's pretty.'

'I thought so.'

Casually Emily lobbed it into the air. It sailed over Rebecca's head, smashing on the ground behind her chair.

There were voices in the corridor. 'It's all right,' Emily called out. 'I dropped a mug.' Her eyes remained fixed on Rebecca, while her long, elegant fingers rubbed at the sleeve of her dress.

Then, slowly, she pulled it back and began to caress the scarred skin beneath.

'Em!'

'Frightened someone will find out I used to cut myself?' A

419

shrug. 'What if I did? I was angry. I had a lot to be angry about, don't you think?'

'I know that. I'm not saying—'

'But you still want me to be ashamed. That way I remain your little doormat, just like I've always been.'

Rebecca began to tremble. 'You've never been that!'

'I'm not ashamed any more. That's something he's taught me. Now I think you should leave. I have a lunch date in half an hour, and there are things I need to do before then.'

There was nothing for it. She made her way out of the room, her feet slipping over fragments of the shattered paper-weight.

Friday evening. Emily stood in the kitchen in Arundel Crescent stirring sauce in a pan while chicken pieces warmed in the oven and vegetables stood waiting on a chopping board. A huge cheesecake chilled in the fridge, and a video of *Shakespeare in Love* waited in her bag.

The kitchen was like a unit in a luxury display room. Mrs László kept it spotless, but that evening the Lászlós were absent and it was her domain. She kept wiping the surfaces around her, terrified of leaving a single stain.

Much of the room was in shadow. She worked by the light over the cooker, enjoying the sense of intimacy it gave. It was at least six times the size of her tiny box in Streatham, but when she tried to compare the two she kept seeing the kitchen in her father's house in Winchester with the pale blue walls and the battered wooden table around which she, her father and stepmother had eaten dinner, night after night.

But she didn't want to think about that.

Max had wanted to drive up to Suffolk that night, but she had persuaded him to wait until the next morning. Michael and Rebecca had their Friday night rituals. Just for once she wanted a Friday night of her own.

Beethoven's *Eroica Symphony* played on the portable CD machine. Classical music had never really been her thing, but Beethoven was one of Max's favourites and for his sake she wanted to like it too.

The steam from the pans was making her hot. She turned on the overhead fan, brushing a lock of hair from her face.

'Don't you dare.'

He leaned against the doorframe, wreathed in the light from the hall, wearing battered cords and a short-sleeved shirt, his arms folded in front of him.

She covered the sauce. 'Don't what?'

'Cut your hair. That's what you're thinking, isn't it?'

It wasn't, but she nodded anyway.

'I love your hair. Cut a single lock and it's over between us.'

She smiled. 'I wouldn't dare.'

'Good.'

The water for the potatoes started to boil. 'Aren't you supposed to be reading the paper?' she asked.

'Thought I'd come and watch.'

'Well, you can't. I'll call when it's ready.'

He didn't budge. Just kept watching. The scrutiny made her self-conscious, and she dropped half a potato on the floor. 'Look what you made me do.'

He laughed. A warm, comfortable sound. 'Then let me help.'

She washed the retrieved potato under the sink. Not that it was necessary. Mrs László kept the floor so clean they could have eaten their meal off it.

'I could lay the table.'

'It's done.'

He looked confused.

'The dining room.'

'I see.' A pause. 'Isn't that a bit formal?'

'Perhaps.' She hesitated. 'I don't really like eating in kitchens. I promise I'll tidy up afterwards. There won't be any extra work for Mrs László and—'

Making soothing noises, he crossed the room and wrapped himself around her. She stroked the silky hairs on his forearms while he nibbled her ear. She giggled. 'Stop it.'

'I'm hungry.'

'Be patient. There's cheesecake for pudding.'

A groan. 'You know about me, Emmie. Why do you want to make me so fat?'

'I don't care if you're fat. You can be the fattest person in the world.'

He sighed contentedly, his breath warm against the back of her neck. 'Well, maybe this once. After all, the way to a man's heart is through his stomach.'

'My father used to say that.'

Silence. His hold remained firm, but she could tell he was no longer smiling. The food steamed away oblivious.

'You hate it when I talk about him.'

He didn't answer.

'Don't you?'

'I hate it when you even think about him.'

'He's my father,' she said gently.

'And what sort of father was he? Hardly one to be proud of or waste sentiment on.'

'Max!'

He turned her roughly towards him, his fingers digging into the flesh on her arms so that she winced in pain. His face was dark with anger. 'Stop wasting affection on him. I don't want to share you, not even in thought.'

She stared into his eyes. Saw the reds and greens of the

greedy love that burned there. Others might have been frightened by its hunger. But not her.

'You don't have to share me,' she told him. 'I belong to you entirely.'

He hugged her. Behind him the kitchen table lay wreathed in shadows, conjuring ghosts of evenings she longed to forget.

But she was not afraid.

FIVE

Monday lunchtime. Michael sat in an interview room at the offices of Saunders Bishop.

The offices occupied the top half of a high-rise near the Barbican and had glorious views across the City and the Thames. 'We're very proud of our views,' the receptionist had told him. 'As our assistants spend most of their lives at work, we believe in giving them something attractive to look at.' Michael, unsure whether this was meant as a joke, had laughed politely.

It was a two-person interview team. Peter Hislop and Wendy Scott, both forty-something partners in the corporate department. Peter was smooth and debonair, with public-school good looks and carefully dyed hair. Wendy was plump and homely, with an easy smile and a Midlands accent. He tried to guess who would be 'bad cop', but both were so welcoming that it was impossible to tell.

He sipped his Evian while Peter described the firm's history, its current position in the market and the benefits and opportunities available to its employees. 'We've doubled in size in the last decade, and at our current growth rate we should become the most profitable firm in the City within the next three years.' It was all very interesting, but he didn't need a PR spiel and wished they would focus on his CV instead.

At last they did. Wendy lit a cigarette. A clear sign of evil, which she then negated by saying, 'You should be very proud of this.'

'Very proud,' echoed Peter.

He felt embarrassed. 'I've been lucky.'

'I'm sure luck had nothing to do with it,' Wendy told him.

Unsure how best to answer, he remained silent. She scanned his work experience. Above her head hung an abstract painting of the Tower of London. He wondered why so many law firms had hideous art in their conference rooms. When she'd finished she exchanged glances with Peter. 'Now we'd like to ask you some questions, if we may.'

It was time to check his technical knowledge. 'Of course,' he replied, praying that they didn't focus on buy-back provisions in shareholder agreements.

'What is Max Somerton like as a client?' she asked.

He stared at her.

Instantly she looked uncomfortable. 'I'm sorry. That wasn't meant the way it sounded. We just wondered whether he has any particular requirements as to the way his work is carried out.'

'It doesn't matter what they are,' added Peter. 'Our view at Saunders Bishop is that a client can be as demanding as he likes provided that bills are paid on time.' A nervous laugh. 'Though we're sure that won't be a problem with Mr Somerton.'

A pounding started in his brain. He blinked, trying to steady himself.

'Does he,' continued Peter, 'have any specific billing requirements?'

He found his voice. 'He's moving his business to you?'

Wendy nodded. 'That's what he's led us to believe, confidentially of course. He's also intimated that other Cox Stephens clients may follow.' She smiled. 'But then, you know this already.'

'You're lucky,' Peter told him, also smiling. 'You have a good friend there. With him behind you, you could go a very long way.'

Wendy sipped her coffee. 'He made it clear that you should be the one to do all his work, and as the volume is going to increase so much it's likely to take up most of your time.'

The walls seemed to be closing in on him. He felt as if he were suffocating.

Peter stared at him. 'Is something the matter? Are you not feeling well?'

'I won't work here if Max Somerton is your client.'

Wendy frowned. 'What are you talking about?'

'You heard me. I won't work for him.'

'But why ever not?' asked Peter.

'What the hell does it have to do with you? I won't work here if he's your client! That's all there is to it!'

Peter jumped. As did Wendy. Michael ran a hand through his hair, trying in vain to keep his emotions in check.

Silence.

Eventually Peter spoke. 'Well, thank you for clarifying that for us.'

His throat felt dry. Quickly he downed the rest of his Evian while Wendy studied his CV for the second time. 'This is very impressive.'

And it was. He knew it was.

But it didn't matter. Not when it was Max they wanted.

426

Wendy asked a question about a deal he'd done. Peter followed with one of his own, before inviting him to raise any issues he might have. Explaining that everything had already been covered, he waited to be shown the door.

As Michael was being interviewed by Saunders Bishop, Emily stood in a shop in Jermyn Street trying to choose a pair of cufflinks. A middle-aged shop assistant hovered attentively by her side.

'Are there any you think the gentleman would like?' he asked.

She pointed to a pair of dark blue ovals surrounded by a silver band. 'I'll take those, please.'

As he boxed and wrapped them, she studied her surroundings. An old-fashioned gentleman's outfitters bereft of a single item to catch the female eye. Whenever she was out with Max he would always try to buy her things. She was learning not to look too closely at objects in shop windows in case he sensed desire and rushed to acquire them for her. But there was nothing to tempt her here. The irony made her smile.

The assistant ran her credit card through the machine then gave her the voucher. 'I'm sure the gentleman will be delighted,' he told her. She hoped he was right.

She signed her name with a Mont Blanc fountain pen engraved *To my darling Emmie*. A present from Max. No one had ever called her Emmie except her father until Max had come into her life and made the name his own.

Once her father had been constantly in her thoughts, but now she hardly thought of him. Occasionally she would try, but her brain seemed reluctant to accept the instruction. Not when it meant doing something that would displease Max.

The assistant helped her on with her coat. She felt the soft sting of the bruises on her upper arms, left by Max's hands the previous Friday night. Her skin was delicate and bruised easily. It would take another week for them to fade. Not that it mattered. She wore them with pride.

The assistant faced her, his expression sober and respectful. She longed to show her bruises to him. Just to be able to share them with someone. But his reaction would have been shock, and that was not what she sought. Instead she thanked him for his assistance and made her way out into the street.

She walked up Piccadilly, towards Leicester Square, moving slowly through the lunchtime crowds. The wind was up, and she wrapped her arms around herself for warmth.

She approached the HMV store. A young professional couple stood hand in hand studying a display in its window. The woman was a diminutive blonde with demanding eyes; the man was dark and powerfully built, with heavy features and a bad-tempered mouth.

David. The man who had once tried to force himself on her and then made light of it at the barbecue.

Once she had found his proximity threatening. Now she saw him as nothing but a second-rate bully. A type Max could eat by the dozen without spoiling his appetite.

'Hey! Tough guy! Remember me?'

They turned towards her. His eyes widened in recognition.

'Course you remember. I'm the one who turned you down, and you were such a gentleman that you responded by telling everyone I was frigid.'

Passers-by began to slow down and stare. The realisation made her feel powerful.

'What's your problem?' demanded the girl.

'He is. Your scumbag boyfriend. Has he tried to force you yet? He will soon. It's the only way he knows how to feel like a man.'

'I think you should stop,' David told her. His face was red.

'Don't hit me, David. It won't make your penis any bigger.'
She turned to a middle-aged woman festooned with shopping
bags. 'He can probably only find it with a microscope and
tweezers. Next to him you'd think a shrimp was well hung.'

The woman moved away, but not before a faint smile had
spread across her lips. Others were smiling too. David's blush
darkened. His girlfriend grabbed his arm. 'Ignore her. She's a
freak. Let's go.'

'Goodbye, tiddler,' she called after them. 'So long, shrimp
boy.'

Smiling, she walked on towards Leicester Square.

As Emily was denigrating David's manhood, Michael was following Mr László into the drawing room at Arundel Crescent.

Max sat on a sofa reading the *Financial Times* and listening
to Prokofiev. He nodded to Mr László, who slipped quietly
away, closing the door behind him.

'Won't you sit down?'

Michael shook his head.

'How about a drink?' Max rose to his feet and made his
way to the drinks cabinet. 'What can I get you? Scotch?
Brandy?'

'Just cut it out!'

He was shaking. He breathed deeply, trying to calm himself.

'Why are you doing this to me?'

Max poured himself a whisky. 'Doing what?'

'I've just had an interview with Saunders Bishop, who are
convinced that you're about to move all your legal business to
them.'

Max looked surprised. 'That's a little optimistic of them.'

'Oh, really.'

'They're on my shortlist, certainly, but then again so are
Randall Watts Hooper and an American firm whose name I

can never remember.' Max thought for a moment. 'Steinman Barth something. Do you know who I mean?'

He did. Steinman Barth McAllister. They were interviewing him the following Monday just before his Randall Watts Hooper interview.

The air seemed to drain out of the room. Again he felt as if he couldn't breathe.

'Why?' he asked.

'Why what?'

'Becky's pregnant, I need a job and you're destroying my chances of finding one.'

'Helping them, I would have thought.' Max downed his whisky, then poured another. 'This is good stuff. Sure I can't tempt you?'

'I don't want a drink!'

A surprised smile. 'Why are you being so hostile? We're not enemies, are we?'

'You tell me.'

'I hope you weren't this spiky with Saunders Bishop.'

He didn't answer.

Max looked amused. 'You didn't cause a scene, did you?'

'Well, how did you think I was going to react?'

Suddenly Max began to laugh. He leaned back against the drinks cabinet, his head bowed, his body shaking with mirth.

Michael stood and watched him. A single thought came into his head.

Does he really hate me this much?

'I can just see you launching into a tirade in the interview room.' Another wave of laughter. 'Poor interviewers. They probably didn't know what had hit them. Well, I guess you can kiss your chances of employment there goodbye. Yet another casualty in the never-ending saga of your impulsiveness.' A sigh. 'Oh Michael, what in the world am I going to do with you?'

'Do with me?'

Max raised his head. He was smiling, his eyes shining with indulgent affection. They frightened him more than fury would have done.

He fought an urge to back away.

'Look, Max, I don't want to anger you. All I want is to make a good future for Becky and our child.'

No reaction. The eyes didn't even blink.

'I know I walked away from you, and you've got every reason to hate me for that. But you've got Emily now. Doesn't that count for anything?'

The smile faded. The expression became troubled.

'You said she made you happy.'

Silence.

'Was that just a lie?'

'She does make me happy. Happier than I could ever have imagined.'

'That's what I want. Happiness for both of you. You could have a good future together, so I'm begging you, please don't try and damage mine.'

Max downed his drink. 'You shouldn't have come here. I want you to leave.'

'Max, please ...'

'If you don't want my help then I won't give it. You're on your own.'

He swallowed. 'I wish things didn't have to be this way.'

'Just go.'

Nine o'clock that evening. Emily sat with Max in that same drawing room. They had finished their evening meal and now drank coffee while watching the evening news.

She leaned against him, feeling the warmth of his body. His arm was draped around her, a dark blue oval adorning his cuff.

431

She traced its surface with her finger. 'Do you really like them?'

A nod. His eyes remained focused on the screen, where a reporter described the latest shift in government policy.

She sipped her coffee. Still too strong, but the taste would grow on her. There were drops of dark liquid on his lips which she wiped away with her hand. Normally he would have tried to bite her finger, but this time his only reaction was a half-hearted peck on her palm. 'Are you cross with me?' she whispered.

'No.'

'Honestly?'

'Honestly.' His arm tightened around her. 'I could never be cross with you, Emmie. Not ever.'

'What is it, then?'

'I want to ask you something.'

She waited expectantly.

'You enjoyed last weekend, didn't you?'

'Yes.'

'You liked Suffolk? You liked the house?'

'Of course.'

He turned towards her. 'What if we made Suffolk our permanent home?'

She tried to take in the idea. 'Is that what you want?'

He nodded.

'Why?'

'Because you make me happy.'

Confused, she stared at him.

'All I've done in this city is strive after money and power. I always believed they were the only things in this world that really mattered, and that any behaviour was acceptable in their pursuit. You've changed all that. I never knew what real happiness was until I met you, and now I've found it I want to enjoy it in a place where I don't feel soiled by my past.'

432

She felt a warmth spread through her.

'Then let's go,' she told him.

'Don't you want to think about it?'

'What's there to think about? I want what you want.'

A sadness came into his eyes. 'Oh Emmie,' he said softly. 'It makes me sad when you talk like that. You're just a child. You know nothing of life, or what you really want from it.'

'Don't I?'

He touched her face. 'You think I'm so strong, don't you? So sure of everything. But you're wrong. All I am is a middle-aged man with a dirty past, stealing your youth to give myself a cleaner future.'

'You think my past is so clean?'

'I know it could never compare with mine.'

She thought of the stillness. For a moment she could almost hear it.

But it *was* in the past. That was where it would stay.

'You say I know nothing of life. Perhaps that's true. But one thing I do know is that I've never wanted anything as much as I want to be with you.'

He took her hand and held it against his cheek. The sound of the television seemed to fade. Lost in the intensity of the moment.

'It'll be a very different life,' he told her. 'Very isolated.'

'We're isolated now. We rarely go out. We don't see other people.' She smiled. 'And I wouldn't have it any other way.'

'Neither would I.'

He switched off the television and pulled her on to his lap. Together they began to plan.

Wednesday morning. Rebecca stood with Clare behind the counter at Chatterton's. Her thought were of Michael. For the last few days he had seemed troubled, but when she had tried to talk to him about it he had insisted that nothing was wrong.

She suspected he was anxious about finding another job but didn't want to burden her with his fears because of the pregnancy. Though touched by his concern, she wished he would open up.

Clare nudged her arm and pointed towards the history section. 'Isn't that Max's girlfriend?'

Rebecca turned, expecting to see Emily. But it was Caroline, dressed in an elegant Armani suit, who browsed through the new titles.

She nodded, then added: 'Ex-girlfriend.'

They watched her move between the shelves. It was a slow morning, and there were only a couple of customers in the shop. At first Rebecca was inclined to keep her distance but then decided that she should say hello. Excusing herself, she made her way over.

'Caroline.'

A smile of recognition. 'I remember you saying that you worked in this area. How are you?' The voice was as low and throaty as Rebecca remembered. In her hand was a biography of Nelson.

'Fine. And you?'

'Fine.' A slight hesitation. 'Michael?'

'We're back together again.'

'I'm so pleased. I always thought you two were good together.' In the distance a middle-aged couple made their way to the cookery section.

'Thank you.' A pause. 'I'm sorry about you and Max.'

Caroline turned the book over in her hands. 'These things happen,' she said nonchalantly. 'I'm seeing someone else now. This is for him, actually.' Again she smiled, a relaxed gesture to show that the earlier comment had not caused embarrassment or offence. Just the behaviour Rebecca would have expected from a sophisticated woman of the world.

Someone who was worlds apart from Emily.

'Max is seeing one of my friends.'

She hoped for a reaction but none came.

So she began to prod.

'She's only my age.'

A nod.

'She doesn't have much experience with men.'

Another nod. The eyes gave nothing away.

'I think he really cares about her.'

A laugh. Small and bitter.

'You don't agree?'

Caroline shrugged. 'What business is it of mine?'

'None, I suppose. But I'd like to know what you think.'

Caroline considered this. 'Very well,' she said eventually. 'I think Max has more emotional defences than anyone I've ever seen. No one is allowed to get close to him. The only person he's capable of loving is himself.'

Rebecca shook her head. 'That's not true. I know he loved Michael.'

'Of course. That's the point. When he looks at Michael he sees himself.' Caroline handed Rebecca the book. 'This isn't what I wanted after all.' She turned and made for the stairs.

Rebecca watched her go, a single thought buzzing in her brain like a wasp trapped in a closed room.

So what does he see when he looks at Emily?

An hour later she sat in the office staring at the telephone.

She knew she shouldn't do it. At their last meeting Emily had made it perfectly clear how things stood between them. A lifetime's friendship smashed to smithereens, just like the paperweight. The sensible thing would be to leave well alone.

435

But she couldn't. She had to try to do something.

She traced the surface of the receiver with her finger, bracing herself to make the call.

Suddenly it rang.

Frustrated, she snatched it up. 'Hello.'

'Becky?'

'Em? Is that you?' She couldn't believe it.

'Are you surprised?'

'Yes.'

'I can't blame you. Last time I hardly rolled out the welcome wagon.' The voice was soft and strangely detached.

'It doesn't matter.' Her own tone was neutral. She didn't want to risk Emily's hanging up.

'But things have changed since then. Max and I are leaving London. We're going to live in Suffolk.'

'Suffolk? But what about your job?'

'Max will provide for me.'

'And your friends?'

A soft laugh. 'What friends? No one here is going to miss me.'

'I will.'

Silence.

'I will, Em. You know that, don't you?'

'Yes, I think you probably will. We've known each other all our lives, haven't we? No one, not even my father, has been so permanent a fixture. But now I'm starting a new life, and before I do I think we should meet, just once, and make peace with each other before we go our separate ways.'

She struggled to contain her excitement. A meeting was better than a telephone call. Far more chance of making Emily listen to what she had to say.

'I'll meet whenever you want,' she said encouragingly.

'Saturday evening. I'm spending it at my flat, deciding what I want to take. You could come and help me choose.'

'Of course.' On Saturday Michael would be in Cardiff on Stuart's stag weekend, so she would have no distractions. 'What time?'

'Eight o'clock?'

'Perfect.'

'See you then.'

'Em?'

'What?'

'I'm glad you called.'

Something of the old warmth crept into the voice. 'So am I.'

She put down the receiver. For a moment she felt intensely happy.

Then she remembered her objectives for Saturday night, and the unease returned.

Friday evening. Michael and Stuart made their way along Fleet Street, pushing through crowds of people who wore the happy, excited faces of those about to start the weekend. Even the air seemed charged with a sense of anticipation.

They were going to meet Richard, a barrister friend of Stuart's who worked in the Temple and who was driving them down to Cardiff for the stag weekend. Stuart was talking excitedly about the celebrations to come. Michael tried to sound equally enthusiastic, but his mind was on other things.

Max was always in his thoughts. Like a giant shadow he could not outrun, however hard he tried.

Brian Price, the recruitment consultant, had been indignant at the suggestion that details of his job applications had not been kept completely confidential. 'We at Carter Clark treat client confidentiality as of paramount importance. Our clients can trust us absolutely.' He sensed that Brian was telling him the truth. But somehow Max had known.

Max had said that he would no longer interfere. 'You're on

your own.' Those had been his words. For what they were worth.

And even if they were true, and he did go and work at another firm, there was nothing to stop Max from moving his business there at a later date.

An in-house job might be a safer option. But even that had its dangers. 'That's the thing about Max,' Jonathan Upham had once told him. 'He knows everyone. People with money usually do.' Company chairmen. Directors. Executives. None of whom would be averse to a wealthy patron offering financial input in return for just a little say in how things were done.

He couldn't be sure of escaping Max's influence, whatever he did.

They approached Chancery Lane. Rebecca stood on the corner, holding his wallet, forgotten that morning in the rush to pack his weekend bag. Fortunately she had realised and brought it in herself.

He kissed her cheek. On the other side of the road a taxi driver cursed a stalled camper van. 'Any news?' she asked him.

'None,' he lied, not wanting to spoil her weekend with the news that he had just been rejected by Saunders Bishop.

She smiled. 'Doesn't matter. Something good will happen soon.'

He didn't share her optimism but nodded anyway.

Stuart punched his arm. 'We'd better go.' The taxi driver continued to swear.

'Have a fantastic time,' Rebecca told Stuart, 'and don't get too drunk.'

There was a swerving of brakes, a cry and then a thudding sound. The taxi driver had pulled out recklessly from behind the van and hit a cyclist, a young man barely out of his teens, who now lay motionless in the road.

Rebecca gasped. Stuart whistled between his teeth. The traffic came to a standstill, as did the flow of pedestrians. Everyone just stood and stared.

A police car arrived with two officers. The older one squatted beside the stricken cyclist, while the younger questioned the taxi driver, who stood by his cab, his face as white as chalk. In the distance an ambulance made its way towards the scene, its siren wailing, while other cars parted before it like the Red Sea before Moses.

'He's younger than us,' whispered Rebecca. She was on the verge of tears. 'Think of his parents. Oh God, please don't let him be dead.' Michael, knowing the associations such an accident had for her, held her close.

The ambulance arrived, and the paramedics tended to the cyclist. The older officer began to talk to a woman bystander. Next to her stood a middle-aged man smoking a cigarette. A nondescript man with John Lennon glasses whom Michael would never have noticed but for a striking resemblance to the social worker who had told him his mother was dead.

Stuart sighed. 'Look, Mike, we're going to have to leave.'

The same man he had seen buying an *Evening Standard* outside the café where Rebecca had told him of Max's involvement with Emily.

Is Max having me followed?

'Mike?'

He told himself that the idea was ridiculous. The café was only a couple of miles away. No distance at all, really. It must be a coincidence.

But the fear remained.

'Richard will be waiting.'

He shook his head. 'I'm not leaving Becky.'

'Yes, you are.' She gave him a gentle push. 'I'll be OK. I'm leaving too. I can't watch this any more.'

He felt a sudden urge to hug her, but Richard was waiting and there was no time.

As he followed Stuart into the Temple he turned and watched her walk away. A slender, beautiful girl with short blonde hair, heading off in the direction of the Strand. The stricken cyclist lay between them, tended to by the paramedics, while the middle-aged man finished his cigarette and crushed the stub beneath his heel.

SIX

Saturday. Just before dawn. Emily woke to find herself alone in the bed with only a warm indentation where Max's body had been. She whispered his name.

'I'm here, Emmie.'

His voice crept towards her through the stillness of the room. He stood by the window, wearing his dressing gown, gazing out at the sleeping city.

'What are you doing?'

'Waiting for the day to begin.'

She sat up, wiping sleep from her eyes. 'Did you dream? You should have woken me.'

'You looked so peaceful. I didn't want to disturb you.'

'You wouldn't have been.'

'No, I suppose not.' A car drove by in the street below, the light from its headlamps momentarily banishing the shadows from his face. His eyes were troubled. 'Poor Emmie,' he said softly. 'You're the most selfless person I've ever met. Life should have been kinder to you.'

'No, it couldn't. Not now I have you.'

'I wish you could have found someone better than me.'

'There's no one better. I wouldn't want them, even if there was.' Putting on her own dressing gown she went to join him. He wrapped himself around her like a blanket. Outside, the darkness was starting to lift. 'The wait is over,' she told him.

He nodded. 'It's here.' There was something like awe in his voice.

Together they watched the new day spread across the sky.

Quarter to nine. Rebecca sat on the tube as it made its way towards the West End.

She was due at work in fifteen minutes. Normally she hated working on Saturday and losing a day with Michael. But he was away in Cardiff, so she didn't mind this time.

The compartment was half-empty. A refreshing change from the congestion of a weekday commute. A book lay open on her lap, but she didn't read it. She kept thinking about the courier from the previous afternoon, hoping that he wasn't dead and that any injuries were merely superficial. It never ceased to frighten her how quickly a human life could be snuffed out. She raised a silent prayer for God to watch over those she cared about.

One of her hands rested lightly on her stomach. It was too early for any movement, but still she kept hoping.

The previous night she had bitten the bullet and phoned her parents with the news. She had been prepared for anger or dismay, but after the initial shock both had been delighted. Her mother had wept, and her father had begged her to come home for a celebratory weekend as soon as possible. 'And bring Michael too. He and I are never going to be close, but for the sake of my grandchild I'm willing to try again.' She had shed tears herself at that point, knowing that Michael would try,

442

too, and daring to hope that this could be a new beginning for all of them.

Just as Suffolk would be a new beginning for Emily.

She thought of the evening that lay ahead, and, not for the first time, wondered if she was doing the right thing. Emily was an adult after all, and as such was responsible for her own actions. Who was she to interfere?

The tube arrived at her station. She made her way towards the door.

Half past eleven. Michael sat with Stuart and the rest of the stag party, eating a late breakfast in a small café opposite Cardiff Castle. The air was thick with the smell of fried food.

Though there were eight at the table, conversation was muted. Most were walking wounded from the night before and preferred to sit in a haze of their own wretchedness. Someone called out for more coffee while Michael cut into his Welsh rarebit. 'That looks disgusting,' Stuart told him.

'Tastes good, though.'

'If you say so.' Stuart, who was immune to hangovers, swallowed his last piece of bacon and rubbed his hands together. 'Eat up, everyone. Castle tour starts in fifteen minutes.'

Groans echoed round the table.

'You disgust me,' he told them, 'in your indifference to our national heritage.'

'Bugger off, you fascist,' muttered Richard, who sat in front of an untouched breakfast, looking particularly rough.

Stuart scooped egg and beans on to a fork and held it out to him. 'Here comes the magic train with a special delivery.'

Richard turned an even whiter shade of pale and rushed for the lavatory. Laughter echoed round the table.

Michael sipped his coffee, staring out of the window, watching the Saturday morning shoppers parade past. From what he had seen, Cardiff seemed an attractive and friendly city. A good place to live. Far away from London.

But was it far enough away from Max?

Buried among the crowds, a nondescript middle-aged man stood on the other side of the street, smoking a cigarette. He felt the first chill of recognition.

Then the man was hailed by a woman and two teenage girls, all weighed down with shopping bags. Together they crossed the road and entered the café, laughing over some shared joke like any other family. They sat at a nearby table. The man ordered rarebit, just as he had.

'Mike?'

Stuart was staring at him. 'You were miles away.'

'Just thinking.'

Richard, still white as a sheet, returned to the table.

'About where you'd rather be?'

The comment took him by surprise. 'What do you mean?'

'You've seemed out of sorts since we got here. I was worried you might be wishing yourself somewhere else.'

He felt ashamed. 'Of course not,' he said quickly, while Brian, one of Stuart's friends from Liverpool, regaled the rest of the table with a description of his worst-ever hangover.

'Are you sure? After all, you and Becky have only just got back together. Perhaps you'd rather spend the rest of the weekend with her. I'd understand if you did.'

He shook his head. 'I wouldn't miss this weekend for anything. If I seem distant it's only because I keep thinking about the accident. It freaked me out.'

Stuart smiled sympathetically. 'Me too.'

'So what about the castle tour? I'm ready if you are.'

'Just let me finish my coffee.'

He tried to concentrate on Brian's story, but his eyes kept drifting back to the crowds who filled the street outside.

One o'clock. Emily ate lunch in the dining room at Arundel Crescent.

She was alone. Max was out but expected back soon. She had told Mrs László she wasn't hungry, but her words had fallen on deaf ears.

After swallowing a final mouthful of steak and potato, she pushed away a plate that was still half-full. Though she had not asked for food, still she felt guilty. A hangover from childhood when money had been tight and waste frowned on.

From the kitchen came the sound of activity. She prayed no pudding was being prepared. Had she eaten there, as Mrs László had suggested, she would have known for sure. But to do so would only have stirred memories she would rather forget. Mrs László had raised no objection, though perhaps she had been secretly put out. Not that it mattered. Max would have understood.

She looked about her. It was a beautiful room. Deep-red carpet, pale white walls adorned with paintings, and a mahogany dining table. The only disappointment was the view of the walled garden at the back of the house. In Suffolk, the previous weekend, she had been able to eat her meals while gazing out at the sea. Soon she would be able to do that every day. When she began her new life.

Max worried that he was forcing the move on her. She wished she could reassure him, but it was not possible to tell him the real reasons for her desire to leave all traces of her past behind. To wipe a soiled slate clean and start all over again.

Mrs László appeared in the doorway. 'You have finished?'

'It was delicious. I just wasn't terribly hungry.' She waited for a look of disapproval but none came.

'Pudding is nearly ready,' Mrs László announced as she cleared the plates away. 'Only ten minutes.'

'You're very kind.'

Smiling, Mrs László left the room. A tiny, wizened woman, wrinkled as a prune. A mere fifty-six, according to Max. Only four years older than her mother would have been had she lived.

She reached for her wine glass, studying her hands as she did so. Her fingers were long and elegant. A pianist's fingers, just as her mother's had been. She could still remember sitting beside her at their battered old piano tapping out Beatles songs. 'You must have proper lessons,' her mother had said, and she had nodded eagerly while wondering if Rebecca, who had no interest in music, would be forced to take lessons too.

Even then, each had been a constant presence in the life of the other. Their mothers, best friends since school, had wanted to create the same bond between their daughters, while never stopping to consider what common ground could exist between a lively, extrovert child who drew people to her like moths to a light, and one who was quiet and introspective, happiest when playing imaginative games alone. From earliest childhood they had shared outings and parties, each tolerating the other while dreaming of the day when they would be allowed to go their separate ways.

That day would have come, too, had fate not decided otherwise.

It had been a windy Thursday, when she was seven years old. The day of their shared dance class at a leisure centre in the middle of Winchester. Dance was Rebecca's passion, and though it had little appeal for Emily their mothers insisted that the activity be shared. It was Mrs Blake's turn to take and collect them, but Rebecca, who had been promised a chocolate cake for tea, threw a tantrum when told there would not be time to make one. So Emily's mother had agreed to escort them instead.

She had walked them to the centre then gone to run some errands. When the class was over, the two of them had stood on the steps outside, surrounded by the other budding ballerinas, waiting for her to return. They waited and waited, Rebecca complaining about a favourite television programme she was missing.

Eventually, to their surprise, they saw Mrs Blake hurrying towards them. Her eyes red from crying, she told them that Emily's mother had been knocked down by a car while crossing a road.

In the weeks that followed, people kept telling Emily that her mother hadn't suffered. That death had been instantaneous. They kept on and on, as if the knowledge would make bereavement easier to bear. But it didn't. With the loss of her mother the whole fabric of her life began to collapse.

Her father was an administrative officer with the local council. A quiet, passive man who had looked to his wife to provide the energy and drive so lacking in his own personality. Now she was gone, what little spirit he possessed seemed to disappear, and he surrendered himself to abject grief with no thought for his daughter. In the months that followed, Emily came to believe that his loss was greater than her own, and that to trouble him with her problems would place too heavy a burden on his already overtaxed emotions. Slowly she learned to bury her feelings of anger and loss behind a facade of calm resignation.

Not that she was always with her father. Mrs Blake, racked with guilt, had insisted that she spend as much time as possible with them. 'You're to think of this house as a second home,' she had been told. 'After all, you are Becky's best friend.' Rebecca, plagued by her own sense of responsibility, did her best to promote this illusion, so that in time their relationship became a Gordian knot that neither could break.

In those early years her time at the Blake house had been like visits to another world. A place of happiness and laughter where she longed to belong but more often felt like a spectre at the feast. Though Mrs Blake was always kind to her, Robert made little attempt to mask his dislike, and sometimes she overheard Mr Blake complaining at her constant presence in their family life.

Then she would return to a home that was as silent as a tomb. She would tiptoe round her father, trying her best to make him happy and not disturb his peace of mind, while thinking of Rebecca safe in the bosom of her family and wanting to scream at the injustice of it all.

When she was eleven, another momentous change took place in her life. Her father remarried. Her stepmother, Sheila, was a secretary at his office: a tall, angular, hard-faced woman who, in their first meetings, displayed nothing but warmth towards her future stepdaughter. 'I'm sure you and I will be tremendous friends,' she had announced, and Emily, seeing her father happy for the first time in years, had nodded politely while trying to quell her instinctive mistrust.

It was on their return from honeymoon that she learned how things would be. Having spent the time at the Blake house, she arrived home to find her father waiting for her in the hallway. 'Your stepmother's having a lie-down,' he had told her. 'Why not take her a cup of tea?' Making her way upstairs, she had heard movement coming from the storage room where her mother's possessions were kept. Standing in the doorway, she had watched Sheila rummage through boxes of clothes, examining each item before throwing it on to a pile in the middle of the room. Nervously she cleared her throat, and Sheila turned towards her. There was no warmth in the eyes now. They were cold and completely territorial.

'What are you doing?' she had asked.

'Sorting through trash.'

'Those were my mother's things.'

'Not any more. Everything in this house belongs to me now.'

There were times, in the years after she left home, when she would wonder at the demons that had driven Sheila to behave the way she had. Self-hatred perhaps, or a feeling of worthlessness so intense that it could only be exorcised through destroying the spirit of another. But these were only guesses. Sheila had no family and never talked about her past. Only two things could be said about her with any degree of certainty. She had an infinitely stronger personality than her husband, and she was an extremely destructive woman.

Within weeks of the marriage her will was law. Emily's father, a ship without a rudder since the death of his first wife, was happy to let his second take control of his life. He ate the food she wanted him to eat. Wore the clothes she wanted him to wear. Saw the friends she wanted him to see.

And, when it came to his daughter, developed the views that she wanted him to share.

Sheila's campaign built slowly. A never-ending flow of criticisms, delivered in a friendly voice to conceal the venom beneath. One day it was Emily's ungainly appearance. The next, her supposed inability to make proper friendships. 'People don't really like you, Emily. They just see you as someone they can use. I hate telling you these things, but who else cares enough to do so?' Bit by bit, Sheila chipped away at her already limited self-esteem, so that she came to believe herself ugly, stupid and worthless. And her father came to believe it too.

After the first year, the war intensified. The kitchen table became a gladiatorial arena, where, night after night, she was forced to confront the endless list of her failings. For hours at a time, Sheila would recite examples of her flaws, all in the same tone of frustrated bewilderment. 'I don't know what's to become of you, Emily. I really don't. God knows what you'll ever amount to. I sometimes think it would be easier to give up on you, but for your father's sake I won't throw the towel in yet.'

Sometimes, when it all became too much, she would seek refuge in tears. But no shelter was given. The denigration just continued: a persistent battering from Sheila's harsh voice and the look of quiet disappointment in her father's eyes.

Until it ended the way it always did. An order to go to bed, and the same, bittersweet words. 'You think I'm hard on you,' Sheila would say, 'but one day you will thank me for this.'

And all the while, her visits to the Blakes continued. A silent presence in their home, she endured Robert's scorn and Mr Blake's uninterest while watching Rebecca grow more beautiful and accomplished every day, secure in non-judgemental love. Someone who would never know what it was to hate herself. A golden representation of everything she ached to be.

When she was eighteen she gained a place at York University to read English. No one, herself least of all, had expected she would gain the necessary grades. Her father had felt pride at her achievement until Sheila set about destroying it. 'Many girls in her class are going to Oxford and Cambridge. But that's the story of her life, isn't it? Always settling for second best.' She had spent the rest of the afternoon crying alone in her bedroom, feeling more inadequate than ever.

But worse was to come.

The day before her departure was spent in Winchester, doing last-minute shopping. Sheila, who had been visiting friends, gave her a lift home. As the car headed homewards she dropped the bombshell.

'Your father and I have come to a decision about your future. We both feel that you're too dependent on us. You're a young woman now and must learn to stand on your own two feet. So we think it would be best if you stayed in York for your college holidays.'

She couldn't believe what she was hearing. 'You mean I can't come home?'

'It won't be practical anyway. Your father and I are planning to move to a smaller house. We've seen a place that would be perfect. But sadly there won't be room for you.'

She found her voice. 'This isn't what Dad wants.'

A sigh. 'Oh, but it is.'

'And that's because you've told him, isn't it?' Her voice became shrill. 'He's my father. He's all I've got. You can't do this to me!'

They slowed for traffic lights. Sheila turned towards her, a smile of triumph spreading across her face. 'But I am. I know you think I'm hard on you.' A pause. 'But one day you will thank me for this.'

At that moment all noise simply died away. Sheila's voice. The roar of the traffic. The howling in her brain. A stillness came upon her. She heard nothing but the steady beating of her own heart.

They reached the house. Sheila made her way towards the kitchen. Emily remained in the hallway, revelling in the peace and the absolute clarity that came with it. At last she knew what had to be done.

She walked into the kitchen. Sheila stood at the sink, rinsing through a coffee cup. Opening the cutlery drawer, Emily pulled out the sharpest knife.

Sheila turned. Her eyes, always cold and contemptuous, now filled with terror. She had never seen Sheila frightened before. The sight was like a religious experience. She lunged forward.

A cry pushed its way into her consciousness. Hands grabbed

her from behind before she could strike. In the tunnel vision of her murderous purpose she had not seen her father sitting at the kitchen table.

The knife fell from her hands. The stillness began to recede. Sheila backed away, screaming. She realised she was screaming too, primitive howls of frustration and rage.

Sheila had become hysterical, demanding that the police be called. 'Go ahead,' Emily had cried, pulling up her sleeves and showing her scars. 'Because I'll tell them that you did this to me, and worse too. You can't imagine what I'm going to tell them, you twisted bitch! And they'll believe me!'

Then her father had started to cry, burying his head in his hands and wailing like a traumatised child. She had stood and watched him. A man she had once believed strong but now knew to be as weak as water. A man she had thought would always love and protect her, but who had abandoned her the moment her mother died. A man she would always love but had come to despise.

'You win,' she told Sheila. 'He's yours. I won't fight for him any more.'

She had left the house that night and had never returned. In the years that had followed she had often felt frightened and lonely and ached to have him back in her life.

But not now. Max had banished those feelings for ever.

Perhaps, one day, she would tell him about the stillness. She sensed he would not judge her too harshly. That he would find it in his heart to understand.

Mrs László re-entered the room carrying a chocolate mousse. She accepted a serving and began to eat. Mrs László watched, smiling. A tiny woman of fifty-six. She wondered what her mother would have looked like at that age, and if she would have been happy at the way her daughter's life had finally worked out.

She hoped so.

Eating her mousse, she waited for Max to return.

Half past one. Rebecca, who had just had lunch with Sean's girlfriend Maya, hurried past the National Gallery trying to keep ahead of the rain clouds.

She was feeling happy. It had been an enjoyable meal, and one that had left her with the sense of having found a good new friend. Almost the first thing Maya had done was invite her and Michael for dinner the following Saturday night. She had accepted gladly, sure that Michael would be as delighted at the prospect as she was.

As she entered the Strand she saw a man hailing a taxi. A tall, heavy-set, middle-aged man with light brown hair that was turning grey.

Max.

In one hand he held a small, blue Tiffany bag. Emily had always loved Tiffany jewellery. Once she had bought her a small necklace as a birthday present.

In the other was a large bouquet of red roses. Emily's favourite flower.

He saw her. His eyes widened.

They stood, staring at each other, while people milled around them and the first drops of rain began to fall. He smiled, a small, hesitant gesture.

Instinctively she did the same.

Then the taxi arrived and he climbed inside.

She watched it drive away towards Trafalgar Square, where Michael had suggested they eat lunch the following week. No doubt he would insist she share hers with the pigeons.

But it didn't matter. Not when she had him back again.

Just as Max had Emily.

She thought back to her conversation with Caroline.

Remembered the way Caroline had denigrated Max's ability to love.

But he had loved Michael. A greedy, possessive love that was doomed to failure. Michael was too strong a person to allow himself to be controlled. As was Caroline.

But not Emily. Lonely and self-hating as she was, to be smothered by the all-consuming love of another would be her ultimate fairy tale.

Was Caroline jealous? Jealous that Emily could bond with Max in a way she never could?

Was she jealous herself? Jealous of no longer being needed? Jealous of finding that she was not indispensable?

She made her way back to Chatterton's. In her preoccupation she failed to notice a middle-aged man with John Lennon glasses who stood by the entrance. He watched her enter the shop then took a mobile phone from his pocket and began to dial.

Half past five. An agitated Emily paced up and down the drawing room.

Max should have been back hours ago. He always phoned if he was going to be delayed. But there had been no call this time.

Outside, it was raining hard, making the roads treacherous. Perhaps he had been in an accident, just like her mother. Perhaps she would lose him as she had lost her.

Pushing the thought from her mind, she sat down on the sofa. The fingers of one hand drummed on the coffee table, as if rehearsing the piano scales she had learned as a child. There was no piano in this house, but Max had offered to buy her one when they went to Suffolk.

The phone rang. She ran out into the corridor and snatched up the receiver. 'Where are you? What's going on?'

But it wasn't him. An unfamiliar male voice asked for someone unknown to her. A wrong number. Angrily she slammed down the receiver while panic boiled inside her like fire.

A key turned in the lock.

He entered the hallway, his hair and clothes dripping, a bouquet of roses in his hand. Though close to tears, she managed a smile. 'Are those for me?'

He nodded. 'There was a ring too. I bought it from Tiffany. But I left the bag in the taxi.'

He spoke slowly, his voice a monotone that had none of its normal beauty. And his face was blank. Like a mask from which all emotion had been drained.

'What is it?' she asked. 'What's happened?'

He didn't answer. Just walked past her into the drawing room. Startled, she followed him inside. He stood with his back to her, the flowers still clenched in his hands, while water from his jacket formed a puddle on the carpet.

'Where have you been?' she asked.

'Sitting on a bench in Hyde Park.'

He wasn't making sense. 'But it's pouring.'

'I needed to think.'

'About what?'

'What I'm doing to you.'

He turned towards her, with ashen face and tortured eyes. Fear engulfed her. 'Max, please, I don't understand.'

'I've tried to believe that this is best for both of us. But I can't lie to myself any more. For once I have to face the truth.'

'What truth?'

'Of what I'm doing to you.' He sighed. 'You're young, Emmie. Your life is just beginning, and you could do anything you want with it. I'm trying to steal you away from the world before you've had a chance to know just what possibilities it offers.'

'I don't care about that. All I want is to be with you.'

'You believe that now, but it won't last. The day will come when you'll understand what I've stolen from you and hate me for it. I'd rather set you free than experience that.'

The ground seemed to shift beneath her.

'I would have gone on deluding myself, but Becky helped me see the truth.'

'Becky? What has she got to do with this?'

'I saw her today, as I was catching a cab. She didn't say anything. The look in her eyes was eloquent enough. Utter contempt for a selfish old man who was taking advantage of the misguided affection of a beautiful young girl. When I looked into her face I knew suddenly that the day would come when you'd look at me in just the same way. That's something I just couldn't bear, so I want our relationship to end while your feelings for me are still warm.'

A scream burst out of her. She flung her arms round his neck, holding on to him as if her life depended on it. 'You're all I have in this world. The only thing that gives my life meaning. Please, I'm begging you, don't do this to me.'

He dropped the flowers and took her face in his hands His touch was gentle, his eyes full of tenderness. 'Oh Emmie,' he whispered, 'I don't want to hurt you. You must believe that. But I have no choice.'

She began to sob. Deep, guttural cries which came from a place that knew nothing of dignity, only survival. He stroked her hair. 'Don't cry. I'll give you anything you want. Money. Possessions. Whatever takes the pain away.'

She clung to him, covering his face in kisses. He held her to him, crushing her so tightly that she couldn't breathe. Then, suddenly, pushed her away.

'You must leave. It hurts too much having you here. I'll arrange a cab to take you home.'

'No! I won't go!'

'You must. I'll call you this evening.' His own eyes were watering. 'Please, Emmie, help me to be strong.'

She tried to grab him. Shrugging her off, he rushed from the room, leaving her to collapse on to the floor, next to the roses, and add her tears to the puddle his clothes had left.

Half past six. Michael, who had left his mobile back at the hotel, stood at a phone booth in a crowded pub in the centre of Cardiff. The air was thick with the smell of beer and cigarette smoke.

He dialled the number of the Ash Lane flat. Rebecca had said there was no need to call, but he had been thinking about her all day and wanted to hear the sound of her voice.

The telephone began to ring. In the background Stuart and the others chanted rugby songs. The lyrics were particularly crude, but Wales was the home of rugby so perhaps people would make allowances.

A man pushed past him, making for the gents. Another stood behind him, clutching a pint and a pound coin, waiting for him to finish. He studied them both, just as he had been studying people all day. But both were strangers with no resemblance to anyone he had ever known.

The phone was not answered. Perhaps she was out, though he didn't remember her mentioning any arrangements. Not that it mattered. He hoped she was having a good time.

Putting down the receiver, he made his way back to the bar.

Seven o'clock. Emily stood alone in her Streatham flat. A bag lay at her feet. The same bag she had packed with such joy barely two weeks ago.

She looked about her, at the shabby walls and cheap

furniture. All seemed out of focus, as if she were looking into a magic mirror at a fairground.

Her eyes came to rest on the coffee table in front of the sofa. At its centre was a small china vase. A house-warming present from the office. She picked it up. Its surface felt cool against her skin as she turned it over in her hands.

Before hurling it against the wall.

She picked up a framed photograph. The one of her mother. She tore out the picture and ripped it to shreds, crushing the frame beneath her feet.

She kicked over the table, stamping on its legs, snapping them like twigs. Turning to her shelves, she grabbed books by the handful and hurled them round the room before fetching a knife from the kitchen and starting on the sofa, hacking it to ribbons, spraying its fabric across the floor. Then she turned the blade on her arms, making her skin into a work of crimson abstract art.

Until at last she had no more energy and collapsed in a heap on the floor, surrounded by the debris of her possessions. All shattered and ruined. Just as her life had been.

She lay there for some time. There were footsteps overhead, followed by the thud of rock music. Her neighbours had returned. Holding up her arm, she studied her damaged flesh. In the harsh overhead light the blood and scars seemed to fade. Her skin became transparent. Her ultimate fear had been realised. She was ceasing to exist.

The telephone began to ring. The one item she had not tried to destroy. Not when he had said that he would call.

She crawled towards it, picked up the receiver and held it to her ear, clutching it as tightly as a drowning man would cling to a lifeline.

'Emmie?'

'Yes.'

458

'There's something I have to say. Something I need you to know.'

She didn't answer. Just waited. He spoke slowly, his voice as clear and sweet as a church bell.

'You mustn't hate Becky for what's happened. I know it's hard to believe, but one day you will thank her for this.'

His voice faded away. So did the music overhead and the roaring in her own brain. Stillness enveloped her. Clarity. Peace.

She put down the receiver and sat perfectly still. Silence seemed to blanket the world. No sound, save for the steady beating of her heart.

Until a single noise began to register. A sharp buzzing.

The doorbell.

With no conscious thought, as if in a dream, she rose to her feet, pulled down the sleeves of her dress and went to greet her guest.

Rebecca decided not to try again. Emily clearly wasn't in. No doubt delayed on the journey from Max's house. Still, there were numerous coffee bars in Streatham where she could kill half an hour. If Emily hadn't returned by then she would make her way home.

The prospect of an aborted meeting disappointed her, but not as much as it would have done twenty-four hours ago. She had spent the whole afternoon agonising about the situation between Max and Emily, and had at last reached a conclusion.

Her own life had been as happy as she could ever have wished. After years of misery, Emily appeared to have found happiness too. If Max was the source, then Rebecca did not have the right to interfere. Her only right was to wish Emily joy in the future, and to reassure her that no matter what had passed between them she was and would always remain her friend.

She wanted to say this to Emily's face, but if a telephone call was the only option then so be it. Emily didn't need her any more. She prayed that she would never be needed again. That Max would provide enough love to wipe away the pain that her friendship never could.

Turning to go, she checked her purse to make sure she had some change.

The door opened behind her.

Emily stood there, hair and clothes dishevelled as if she had been moving furniture.

'Hi. I didn't think you were in.'

Emily didn't answer. Just stared at her with eyes that were strangely vacant.

She walked inside and made her way up the stairs. Emily followed behind. She tried to think of something to say but nothing came to mind.

They reached the landing. The door of the flat stood open. Rebecca entered, then stood in shocked silence, gazing at the devastation left by the burglars who had obviously not been content to steal but had also felt the need to destroy. Her heart went out to Emily in sympathy.

'Oh Em, I'm so sorry.'

No answer.

She ran a hand through her hair, her feet sliding over books whose spines had been ripped in two. She looked down at the grey carpet, almost obscured by the carnage.

And saw that it was stained.

Drops of red that looked like blood.

There were similar drops on the walls.

The hairs began to rise on the back of her neck.

There was movement behind her. The flash of metal as it caught the light.

She turned.

The knife plunged into her chest. Its blade just missed her heart, puncturing a lung.

Her legs collapsed. She tried to scream, but no sound came. In her mouth she tasted blood.

She looked up at Emily's eyes. They were as blank as those of a robot. A machine, controlled by another.

And the voice, when it came, was robotic too.

'You take them all from me. All the people I've ever loved. First my mother. Then my father, because the man I loved died with her. Then it was Michael, and now it's Max. All you've ever done is take from me. But not any more.'

Rebecca tried to rise but was too weak. There was no pain. Terror acted as its own anaesthetic. A telephone lay nearby and she reached out her arm towards it. The blade fell again, severing fingers.

Blood filled her mouth. She couldn't breathe. A multitude of images flashed inside her head. The first time she had seen Michael. Her parents on Christmas morning. Robert, handsome in his graduation robes. Sitting with Emily in a classroom, dreaming of the final bell.

And then came one that eclipsed them all. A child with Michael's looks and her colouring, screaming as its life was destroyed before it had even begun.

The blade fell again. Darkness came in a rush and engulfed her.

Emily dropped the knife.

The stillness began to lift. Sound crept back into her ears. The thud of music from upstairs, the noise of the traffic on the street outside, the ragged hiss of her own breathing and the roaring inside her head.

A rag doll lay before her, its body slashed and violated, its

461

blood flowing down on to the carpet, merging with the stains already left by her own. She gazed down on her handiwork and began to whimper.

The knife lay by her feet, its surface shiny and red. She backed away from it, crawling on hands and knees, searching for a safe place where she could hide and never be found. But it did not exist. Not in this place of carnage.

There was only one place she could go. One person who could save her.

She staggered into the bathroom. Fighting waves of nausea, she washed blood from her face and hands.

She sat in Max's drawing room, shaking as if possessed. Max sat beside her.

'Are you absolutely sure?' he asked her.

'Dead as a dodo.' A giggling started in her throat, one that she could not control.

'You're cold. I'll fetch you something.'

Her arms were stinging, the scars deep and raw. Her sleeves stuck to the wounds. She pulled one free, wincing at the pain. A single drop of blood slid down on to her hand. She watched its movement as if hypnotised.

Max returned with a blanket which he wrapped around her, drawing her close, making soothing noises. His body was warm: his skin smelled of cologne, his clothes of tobacco. His presence made her feel safe.

They sat together in a house that was as silent as a grave. Time passed, and her trembling began to ease. 'What will happen to me?' she whispered.

He didn't answer. Just stroked her hair.

'You'll protect me, I know you will.'

'Hush. Don't talk any more.'

'I didn't mean to do it. You'll make them understand, won't

462

you? You'll tell them I'm not a monster.'

'You're no monster, Emmie. All you want is to be loved. It's the most basic human need. One I've spent most of my life trying to deny.'

She pressed herself against him, putting her arms round his neck, trying to draw courage from his strength. 'Don't let them take me away from you.'

'I don't want them to. I really don't.'

He gazed down at her, his eyes full of tenderness. 'I'd like to tell you something,' he said, his voice as soft as a caress. 'A story from my childhood that I've never told anyone else.'

She didn't answer. Just waited.

'When my uncle left me at the Home, there was a woman called Miss Wheeler who supervised the younger children. I can still see her now. A small, thin woman with a face like a gargoyle who felt that life had cheated her and was out for revenge. She found it in a group of children that no one wanted, and on whom she could vent her rage.

'I became her favourite target. I could barely speak English and often misunderstood her instructions, so she labelled me wilful and in need of discipline. She beat me at the slightest provocation, but I learned how to deal with that. It was only physical pain after all. The thing I really hated was the cell.

'It wasn't a real cell. Just a storage room at the back of the house where, years earlier, a man was supposed to have hanged himself and which we were all convinced was haunted. Miss Wheeler used to lock me in there for hours at a time. There was no window, and the light didn't work. It was like being in a tomb. I dreamed about it when we were in Paris. I'll probably dream about it until I die.

'I was never allowed to cry out when I was in there. If I did she'd just leave me there all night. Once I needed the bathroom badly. I called out then, but nobody came, and I ended up soiling myself. I remember sitting in the darkness, knowing that I was just going to be punished all over again.

'So I made a vow. A promise to myself that one day I'd have all the power. I'd be so powerful that no one in the world would ever be able to hurt me again.

'And that's the terrible thing about love. It's the ultimate surrender of power. When you love someone you give them the power to inflict the most savage pain, and there's no way to make them stop. Not unless you control them entirely.'

She shook her head. 'I wouldn't hurt you.'

'I know you wouldn't. Not my Emmie.' A sigh. 'If only Michael thought as you did.'

His words were like a knife piercing her brain, damaging the nerves that allowed her to think.

His hands continued to stroke her hair. 'Poor Michael. Rebecca was his world. Now she's gone he'll need me like he never has before.'

Her arms were still round his neck. Blood from her sleeve stained his skin, but he showed no reaction. Just continued to gaze down at her with eyes that were full of sympathy and understanding.

'Poor Emmie. You deserved so much better than me. Someone who could love you the way you wanted. The way that mother on the radio programme loved her second daughter. The one for whom she would have sacrificed everything else she valued. I could have loved you like that. You could have wielded that power over me, had Michael not claimed it first.'

Her thoughts began to fragment. She felt as if she were coming apart. Losing her form. Ceasing to exist.

'I'm nothing,' she whispered.

From the street outside came the sound of cars. He continued to hold her. 'Not nothing, Emmie,' he said softly. 'Just the husband and the other three children.'

The doorbell rang.

'I'll do what I can,' he told her. 'The best lawyers money can buy. You won't be forgotten, Emmie. I promise you that.'

His words became random noise. She released her grip on him and curled into a ball on the sofa, like a foetus seeking a lost womb. Her body crashed in on herself, just as her mind was doing. She felt herself shrinking, dissolving into nothing. The thing she had always feared. But now it had come she knew that it was actually a sanctuary. The safe place that no one, not even Max, had ever been able to provide.

The whimpering stopped. She lay quite still, making no noise at all.

And when the police took her she went like a lamb.

The telephone woke Michael.

He lay in the darkness of his hotel room, senses dulled by alcohol, waiting for the ringing to stop. But it didn't. Reluctantly, still half-asleep, he reached for the receiver.

And awoke completely.

SEVEN

December. Two months later.

Brockley, like the rest of London, lay blanketed in snow. In Rushden Street, a row of shabby Victorian terraces buried behind a railway line, it lay in clumps along the pavement, slowly dissolving into grey sludge, illuminated by the glare of Christmas lights that long-term residents had hung in their windows.

There were no such lights in the windows of number seventeen. In seven weeks Michael had watched three other lodgers come and go. Currently he shared the house with a computer programmer from Tyneside called Neil, whose only topic of conversation was Newcastle United Football Club, and a council worker from Surrey called Bill who spent his leisure time listening to heavy metal music loud enough to make the walls shake. A fourth bedroom lay empty, waiting for the next arrival.

His room was at the back of the house, bare save for a single bed, a small washbasin, a decrepit wardrobe and a chair by the window where he could sit and watch the trains roll by from early morning until late at night. The grey linoleum was studded with cigarette burns from earlier occupants, and the walls were stained with patches of damp. Despite the cold, he kept the window open a fraction to reduce the smell. His *Napoléon* film poster hung above the bed, but apart from that there was little to suggest that this was where he spent most of his time.

He had not set foot in Cox Stephens since the stag weekend. Jack Bennett had phoned repeatedly, eager to tear up his resignation, but he had never taken up the offer. The recruitment consultant had kept phoning, too, with suggestions of firms that would be interested in his CV and new offers of interviews. But he had ignored those as well, and eventually the phone had stopped ringing. Since Cardiff his work suits had been left to gather dust in the wardrobe. All except the Italian two-piece that had been Rebecca's favourite, and which he had worn to say goodbye to her.

The funeral had been held in a Norman church just outside Winchester where she had attended Sunday school and later been confirmed. The place had been packed. Relatives, friends from school, college and work, neighbours who had known her since infancy. Most were in tears. He had never appreciated fully just how loved she had been.

He had sat in a front pew, next to her parents and Robert, ignoring their unspoken hostility, mouthing the words to her favourite hymns and listening to the vicar pay tribute to her talents and kindness before lamenting the destruction of so much promise. Afterwards he had stood in a graveyard bathed in cold autumn sunshine, flanked by Stuart and Sean, watching as she was laid to rest.

The wreaths lay by the side of the church. As he stared at them a terrible suspicion came to him, and leaving the others he had gone to read the accompanying cards. When he found

Max's tribute – a cross made of roses – he began to tear it apart.

People tried to stop him. Robert, his nose still misshapen from their last encounter, punched him in the face, knocking him to the ground. He had lain, unprotesting, while Robert kicked at his body until dragged away by his father and Stuart. Then he had climbed to his feet, wiped the blood from his face and finished what he had started. The destruction complete, he returned to the graveside, oblivious to the shocked expressions on the faces of the other mourners, bowing his head and whispering a final farewell.

He had nothing of her now. Her parents had claimed all her possessions. 'They belong to us,' her father had told him. 'You have no right to anything.' All he had were some photographs and those objects she had given him. It wasn't much.

But it was more than had been left to Emily.

He wanted to hate her. It would have been easier that way. But he couldn't bring himself to do so.

The police could get nothing out of her. She was completely catatonic, lost in a world of her own. He hoped she stayed there. A place where no one could hurt her any more. A place where she was safe.

No one could believe what she had done. Not Emily. Not that quiet, gentle girl. A soul so timid and retiring that she could not have hurt a fly.

Or so they all thought.

Until her stepmother came forward, dragging her husband behind, telling of a time when, for no reason whatsoever, Emily had attacked her with a knife. 'She would have killed me, too, if her father hadn't intervened. We should have told people, but how could we? She was our child, and we loved her.' A few tears. 'How could she have done it? After all we did for her.'

Others had spoken up too. Robert's friend David, generously calling himself an ex-boyfriend, described warning signs.

468

'Once I went to kiss her and she nearly clawed my face off. And only a few days before it happened she accosted me and my new girlfriend on Piccadilly, shouting abuse. Really creepy stuff. Everyone was looking at her as if she was nuts.' A hollow laugh. 'Guess they were right.'

Lorna, Rebecca's old school friend, told of Rebecca's suspicions of her supposed best friend. 'She was always a bit wary of her. Her behaviour could be really odd. Quiet as a mouse one minute and turn on you the next. She had a real go at me in a wine bar once. It was frightening. I was always telling Becky to drop her. If only she'd listened to me.'

He could have added his voice to the chorus of condemnation. 'You knew her well, didn't you?' a police officer had asked him. 'Did you notice anything odd about her? Anything that could have been a warning?' But he had refused to join in.

'She was a good person. In spite of what she did.'

The officer's eyes had widened in surprise. 'We're talking about the woman who murdered your fiancée. Don't you hate her for that?' And he, harbouring feelings that were far more complicated than the officer could possibly imagine, had shaken his head.

'What's the point? Becky's dead. Hating Emily won't bring her back.'

The closest thing to an explanation had been provided by Max, himself the only other person with a sympathetic word for the girl everyone was rushing to label a monster. 'I'd just ended our relationship. I felt that I was too old for her. Somehow I think she got it into her head that Rebecca was to blame.' A sigh. 'It's just so hard to believe. The Emily I knew was kind and gentle. However awful her actions, she deserves to be judged with compassion.'

He and Max. Emily's champions. Much good it would do her.

From his window he could see the darkness of the early evening, the train line and the backs of houses identical to the one he inhabited. Many had cracks in the brickwork. He knew them all by heart.

Christmas was only two days away. Neil and Bill would be returning to their families and he would have the house to himself. Free to celebrate the festive season in any way he wished.

He looked at his watch. Seven o'clock. Picking up his jacket he made for the door.

An hour later he sat with Sean in a pub near Leicester Square.

The place was packed. Office workers, many in party hats, toasted the forthcoming festivities, regularly spilling drinks on to the floor or over other customers. They had managed to find a table near the door. Though draughty, it was at least away from the crush.

It was the first time he had seen anyone since the funeral. All invitations had been rejected, as he had felt unable to face the sympathy and the questions. Until that morning, when he had found himself aching for the sight of a friendly face and real human contact.

'I'm sorry it's been so long,' he said. In the background the jukebox played 'Last Christmas'.

'Doesn't matter.' Sean told him. 'Sorry I kept phoning. I just wanted you to know that I was here if you needed me.'

'I did know.'

'Have you seen anyone else?'

He shook his head. 'My friend George has been phoning. Stuart, too, ever since he and Helen got back from honeymoon. They had a good wedding, apparently. I should have been there, but couldn't face it.'

Sean smiled encouragingly. 'He understood.'

470

'You've spoken to him?'

'Only to see if he'd heard from you. He's worried. We all are.'

Michael sipped his lager. It seemed weaker than usual, but he had been drinking a lot recently.

Sean looked worried. 'How much weight have you lost?'

A shrug.

'Have you found another job?'

'No.'

'Are you looking?'

He didn't answer. The draught made him shiver. He never used to feel the cold, but now it cut through him like a knife.

'You need money, Mike. You've got to live.' In the distance a jolly-looking girl with a Father Christmas hat brandished a charity box. 'What news about the trial?'

'A trial won't bring her back.'

'But it might help. Justice being served.'

'Justice?'

He started to laugh, trying to stop himself but unable to do so.

Sean watched him anxiously. Michael remembered the way Sean's eyes had always followed him when they were children. Constantly studying his reactions, searching for his approval.

He ached with the need to unburden himself. To tell Sean everything.

But he could tell nobody. The risk was too great.

The girl with the Father Christmas hat approached them, all smiles and aggressive cheerfulness, waving the charity box in his face. 'Children in crisis,' she cried, in a voice that reeked of pony clubs and trust funds. He gave what change he had. It was only a couple of coppers.

She frowned. 'That's not very generous.'

Sean gave her five pounds. 'Now's not a good time,' he told her.

The warning went unheeded. Her face shone with missionary zeal. 'It's never a good time for children in care. Tell Scrooge here to think of that next time he's asked to put his hand in his pocket.'

'And what the hell would you know about children in care?'

He rose to his feet. She backed away from him while the rest of the pub fell silent.

'You stupid bitch! You don't know the first thing about it!' He pointed at Sean. 'We could tell you something. Him and me. We know more than you ever will!' He reached for his wallet, took out what money he had and hurled it at her. 'Now fuck off!'

Grabbing his coat, he marched out of the pub. Sean hurried after him, catching him halfway across Leicester Square. 'Mike, wait!'

They faced each other, surrounded by the bright lights and the crowds who pushed past them, all full of festive good cheer. Carol singers stood nearby, holding lanterns, harmonising the last verse of 'Once in Royal David's City' while their breath condensed before them in the cold winter air.

'Just leave me alone, Sean.'

'I can't bear to see you like this.'

'You don't know what's going on.'

'But I do know that when we were kids you were always there for me, and now I want to be there for you. Tomorrow night I'm going to my parents for Christmas. Come with me, Mike. We can talk everything through and decide what you're going to do.'

A lump came into his throat. 'Too late for that.'

'No, it's not.'

'It is. Believe me.' He turned to go.

Sean grabbed his arm. 'Mike, please.'

'I'll call you tomorrow. That's a promise. Thanks for being my friend, Sean. I am grateful.'

As he pushed his way through the crowds, the carol singers finished the verse and were greeted by a smattering of applause.

He let himself into the house. The lights were on, and heavy metal music played in the living room. It wasn't as loud as usual. Something to be grateful for.

Neil called his name from the kitchen. Not feeling up to a conversation, he sought sanctuary in his bedroom.

He saw the cigar smoke before he breathed it in. Hanging in the air like clouds of poison gas.

'How was Sean?'

He stood perfectly still, feeling like a rabbit caught in the headlights of an oncoming juggernaut.

Max sat on the chair by the window, using a battered coffee mug as an ashtray. His face was gaunt. He, too, had lost weight, and it made him look old. For a split second Michael felt something like concern. He hated that.

'Nice place you have here. Makes me feel nostalgic. The first flat I ever owned was in this area. Did I ever tell you that?' The voice was as beautiful as ever.

'No one here knew that I was with Sean.' His own voice sounded weak.

'And yet I did. I know every move you make. But then perhaps you've guessed that already.'

Michael swallowed, 'And now you've come to gloat.'

'Is that what you're hoping? That I'll sit and laugh at you for half an hour, then walk out of your life for ever?' A sad smile. 'Oh Michael, if only it were that simple.'

Michael stared down at the floor. The thump of the music

was like a faint electrical current running under his feet. 'I persuaded him to turn it down a little,' said Max, 'but not too low. After all, we wouldn't want anyone to overhear our conversation.'

'There won't be any conversation. I have nothing to say to you.' He turned.

'Sit down!'

The voice was not raised, but a core of steel ran through its centre which stopped him in his tracks.

Slowly he sank down on the bed.

'That's better.' Max extinguished his cigar and lit another. 'I make all the decisions now. Please try to remember that.'

There was no shade on the overhead light. Just a bare bulb, not really powerful enough for the room. It moved with the breeze from the open window, casting shadows that crept over the walls like ghosts.

A train rattled by outside, making its way towards Kent, where Sean would soon be spending Christmas. But not him.

The cold made him shiver. Max's expression, momentarily stern, now softened. 'Put your jacket on, Mike. Don't catch cold.'

He shook his head.

'You've lost weight. We'll have to feed you up.'

'You have too. Missing Emily, perhaps.'

A sigh. One tinged with genuine regret. 'That was a terrible thing we did to her.'

'I didn't do anything.'

'Poor Emmie. So ashamed of what she'd done that she never told a living soul. Except you. The one person whose background was as traumatic as her own. She asked you to keep it a secret and you did. From everyone except me.' Another sigh. 'Now everyone knows of course.'

Michael stared down at the linoleum, its surface scarred with burn marks like the skin of a smallpox victim. The landlord should be made to change it. Perhaps the next occupant would do just that.

'Of course, we need to consider Becky's parents. Do you think they suspect?'

'There's nothing to suspect.'

'No proof, at least. That is, unless Emmie—'

'Don't call her that. You don't have the right.' He tried to put anger into his voice but heard nothing but fear.

Max stared levelly at him. 'Unless Emmie puts two and two together. Unlikely, I think. The breakdown sounds permanent. But in case she ever does I just want you to know that there's nothing to worry about. My lips are sealed. No one will know how we planned together to bring about murder.'

The shadows continued to crawl across the walls. Like demons, come to jeer at the nightmare in which he had been trapped. Weakly he shook his head. 'I told you about Emily because I thought you'd understand. I never dreamed—'

Max made soothing noises, as if reassuring a traumatised child. 'Of course you didn't. In my eyes you're completely innocent. But you must consider how it would look to others. Rebecca's parents and brother would be more than willing to believe ill of you, and they could make a great deal of mileage from the unplanned pregnancy. You mustn't worry, though. We'll survive this, you and I. Just as long as we stick together.'

'You couldn't tell anyway. By damning me, you would damn yourself.'

'Would I? You're frightened at the thought of going to prison. The only thing that frightens me is the thought of losing you.'

Strands of cigar smoke hung in the air like chains. The door was only a few feet away, and he ached to run through it and lose himself in the darkness outside. But the night was full of eyes, and there was nowhere to hide.

'It would be your word against mine,' he said.

'That's true. You might convince them. But I doubt it. Remember, I'm a thousand times better at subterfuge than you are. I convinced Emily that I loved her. Do you think I can't convince people of anything I want?'

Michael rose to his feet and began to pace up and down the room. Though small, it was bigger than a prison cell. There were no locks on the door either. But he was not free to leave.

Max remained by the window, shadows from the bulb distorting his face, turning it into a deformed mask. 'What is it you want, Mike? For this to be over?'

He nodded.

'It can never be over between us. Don't you understand that?'

Michael leaned against the wall, feeling its dampness seep through his clothes. They stared at each other in the shabby room while music continued to pound through the floor and trains to rattle past the window.

'Do you remember the evening we first met?' Max asked. 'I had a small cut on my neck. If you'd noticed you'd have thought it a shaving wound.

'I'd lain awake the whole of the night before, thinking about what I had. Money. Power. Position. Respect. Everything I'd ever strived for, only to find that my existence was an empty shell with no meaning whatsoever. That morning I stood in my bathroom for over an hour, a razor at my throat, trying to find the courage to end it all.

'And then I met you. Someone who'd come from the same world I had. Someone who had all the energy and hope of youth that I'd started out with and lost along the way. Someone whose presence made me feel young and optimistic again. Someone I could guide the way no one ever guided me. Someone who gave it all some meaning.

'And the thing you have to understand is that no one I love can be allowed to leave me. My uncle tried but he failed. If you try, you will fail too.'

A chill ran through him that had nothing to do with the cold. 'Your uncle?'

Max nodded. 'He was very much alive when I traced him. Running his taxi firm and enjoying his life, with never a thought for the nephew he'd abandoned all those years ago. But I changed all that.'

Michael was afraid to ask the next question. In the end there was no need.

'I was the one who financed the competition that sprang up around him, undercutting his prices so badly that he lost all his capital just trying to stay afloat and eventually had to go and beg a job from the very people who'd destroyed his business.

'One day he came home to find police waiting outside his house, acting on a tip-off that he was harbouring stolen property. They searched the place and found it hidden in his cellar. And they found something else too. Evidence linking him to a local paedophile ring.'

Slowly Michael sank back down on the bed. Max's eyes, unblinking, remained totally focused on him.

'He denied it, of course. Insisted that it must have been planted. But no one believed him. That's the terrible thing about human nature. We're always so willing to believe the worst of others. The police began to target his movements. His neighbours found out and started hounding him. He was beaten up in the street. His windows were smashed. Graffiti painted on his door. Friends walked away from him, and he lost absolutely everything. He hanged himself in the end.

'If you left me I might decide not to go to the police. As you said yourself, I would be damning myself as well as you. But you'd never be safe. You couldn't hide from me. I'd always be able to find you. And when I did I'd see what you valued most and take it away. Just as I took Becky.'

Michael was shaking all over. The music faded, drowned out by the pounding inside his head.

Max stabbed out his cigar. 'And now I think we've talked enough. Let's pack your things and go.'

Michael shook his head.

'It's over, Mike.' The voice was gentle. 'There's no point trying to fight me. I'll always win.'

Rising to his feet, he backed towards the door, reaching deep inside himself, past the fear, for one final show of defiance.

'I hope you burn in hell.'

A great sadness came into the eyes. 'I will, I have no doubt. But that still leaves this earthly life to get through first.'

His hand found the doorknob.

'I'll be waiting, back at Arundel Crescent. For your own sake, don't leave it too long.'

Michael fled from the room, down the stairs and out into the darkness.

He walked and walked, with no sense of where he was going. In the end he found himself back at the place where it had all started. The narrow streets of Bow.

On the outside the Home was unchanged. A square slab of Victorian grey stone, dwarfed by the council estate on the other side of the road. No longer a refuge for unwanted children, now it was simply a collection of flats.

He stood on the pavement, wrapping his coat around him as protection against the cold night air. A young couple walked past him and through the front door. A light went on in a room at the top of the house. The one he had shared with Sean all those years ago, where they had lain together in their beds, sharing their dreams of the future, with no concept of just how different those futures were going to be.

But those days were gone for ever. He was a stranger, and there was no sanctuary here.

He walked on through the streets, past the corner shop where he had stolen sweets and then, years later, tried to apologise to the owners. Past the old church with the graveyard he had told Sean was haunted. Down to the noise and bustle of Mile End Road.

Another snow shower began. He sought shelter in a late-night café: a cheerful place full of the smell of greasy food, with pictures of film stars on the wall and jazz music playing softly from a battered loudspeaker. Buying himself a coffee, he sat by the window, watching the falling flakes.

Joe Green, alone behind the counter, was feeling nostalgic.

He had owned the café for nearly forty years now. Open seven days a week save for Christmas, bank holidays and a month spent in hospital with pneumonia. It had been his whole life, but now his health was failing and his doctor had insisted he retire. He told himself that he would enjoy the lazy days and early nights, but in his heart he knew that he would keep finding excuses to come and bother his nephew Sam, who was taking the place over.

It was virtually empty now. Only one customer remained. A strikingly handsome young man with dark hair who sat in the corner, wrapped in an expensive coat, nursing a cup of coffee. Strictly speaking they didn't close for half an hour, but he was tired and saw no harm in hurrying things along. Smiling affably, he walked over. 'What's up, mate? Ain't you got nowhere to go?'

The young man looked up, revealing dark blue eyes. Unsettling eyes: troubled and desperate.

Joe felt a stab of recognition.

'Do I know you from somewhere?'

A shake of the head.

'I do, don't I? What's your name?'

No answer.

'The man with no name,' said Joe.

Then, suddenly it came to him.

'You don't know me,' said the handsome young man, his accent pure Home Counties. The boy had been a cockney. Odd-looking too.

But it was him. Joe was sure of it.

Forgetting all about closing, he sat down in the seat opposite.

'You were just a kid. On the run from some place. I would've given you a ride, but you scarpered. Thought about you for ages afterwards. Hopin' you was all right.'

The young man rolled the last dregs of coffee round his cup. The street outside was empty now, save for a lessening flow of traffic and a group of revellers in party masks chanting Christmas songs in the falling snow.

'Your name began with M.' Joe searched his memory. 'Matt?'

'No.'

'Mike, then.' He beamed. 'That was it. Mike.'

'Mike,' echoed the young man. 'That was his name. You gave him food and he was grateful.'

Joe was confused. 'It was you I gave it to.'

'No, it wasn't. The boy you met was someone else entirely. He was much stronger than me.'

The face became a mask of anguish. Joe felt touched and protective. Just as he had all those years ago.

'Why not tell me about it, Mike?' he said kindly. 'I've got time. I can listen.'

'I will tell you something. The answer to your question.'

'And what's that?'

The eyes filled with tears. 'That I do have somewhere to go.'

He rose to his feet and walked towards the door. As he passed, he put his hand on Joe's shoulder and gave it a gentle squeeze.

Joe remained at the table, watching him stand in the street, trying to hail a taxi. Eventually one approached. Climbing inside, he was driven away, swallowed up by the falling snow and the dark city that lurked beneath.

EPILOGUE

Devon: 2003

It was a wonderful day for a wedding. The May sky was a perfect blue, while a light breeze prevented the heat from growing oppressive. In the dining room of the Linton Forest Hotel, all the windows were open, allowing the air to circulate, while Henry Bellamy and his wife Eleanor gazed down from the top table on the two hundred people who had come to celebrate the marriage of their daughter Olivia to Michael Turner.

Catherine Chester, an attractive woman in her late thirties who had just been made a partner at Cox Stephens, sat with Nick Randall. Though she had not been formally invited to the wedding, Nick had brought her as his guest.

There were six at the table. Stuart she knew; his wife Helen and the other couple, Sean and Maya, she did not. But all were very friendly. Jack Bennett was somewhere among the other guests, sitting with his wife and children.

Stuart and Nick were sharing good-natured anecdotes about Michael, to which Sean added some of his own. All three were clearly fond of him, though none saw as much of him as they would have liked. He had left Cox Stephens over three years ago and was working in industry. Making remarkable progress, too, by all accounts.

A caterer, dressed like an eighteenth-century footman, cleared away Catherine's main course. On a dais, at the rear of the room, a quartet in dress shirts and tails played a Haydn concerto. While the men continued to swap their stories, she lit a cigarette and asked Maya about Olivia.

'She's an actress, but she hasn't done much yet. Just a few walk-on parts in soap operas. Sean and I liked her.' A pause. A note of disappointment. 'Though we've only met her once.'

As she listened, Catherine's eyes roamed over the well-dressed guests and up to the top table. Henry and Eleanor Bellamy sat on either side of the bridal couple, both looking tremendously proud. Years ago, Catherine had attended a wedding where the drunken father of the bride had risen to make his speech, turned to his son-in-law, and said, 'Well, lad, here's my advice. Keep her well fed and well fucked and she ain't got much to complain about.' She smiled to herself, envisaging the reaction if Henry were to give Michael the same counsel.

Olivia looked stunning. A tall, willowy brunette, with a fine-boned beauty that was typically English. Catherine had managed to chat with her in the reception line and had come away with the impression of someone who was very sweet but rather dull. But their conversation had been extremely brief, so perhaps it was unfair to draw conclusions.

She sat at the centre of the table, a vision in white silk, smiling adoringly at Michael. Impulsively she kissed his cheek. He smiled but did not return the gesture. Probably embarrassed to show affection in front of an audience.

As Olivia turned to talk to her father, Michael picked unenthusiastically at his food, looking as if he would rather be somewhere else. A typical man. Unwilling to enter into the romance of a wedding, even when it was his own. He looked just as she remembered him from his Cox Stephens days: still strikingly handsome, though there was a tension in his face that had not been there before. Pressures of work, perhaps.

Lack of appetite was not a problem shared by the best man, a chubby specimen who looked extremely constricted by his morning suit. His name was George. A school friend of Michael's, apparently. She wondered if he saw any more of Michael than the others did.

A waiter refilled her wine glass. As she took a sip, she watched Eleanor Bellamy talk to a well-built man of about fifty with greying hair and shrewd eyes. Max Somerton, the man who had become a surrogate father to Michael in the years following the tragic death of his first fiancée, Rebecca.

Catherine had never met Rebecca, but the others at the table had, and all remembered her with great affection. She had quizzed them about Max, but none seemed to know much about him, save that he was immensely wealthy. Though he didn't come out and say it, Stuart gave her the impression that he blamed Max for the fact that they saw so little of Michael. 'He's incredibly generous,' Maya had told her. 'For a wedding present he's giving them a mews house. In Kensington. Only a couple of minutes from his own place.'

Her eyes lingered over him. Though not a handsome man, he had a certain attractiveness: something she had noticed when passing him in the reception line. There was a stillness about him that hinted at contained strength. She liked that.

He was describing something to Eleanor, moving his hands by way of illustration. They were strong hands, but he moved them with extreme grace. She liked that too.

Eleanor began to talk to Michael. Though perhaps it would be more accurate to say that she was talking at him. He listened half-heartedly, nodding at appropriate moments, while Max, looking amused, gave him a conspiratorial wink, to which Michael, no doubt prompted by discretion, did not respond.

Sean and Maya, themselves recently married, had spent their honeymoon trekking in Peru. As Sean described their adventures, Catherine continued to study Max.

Later, at the evening reception, she made her move.

The tables had been cleared from the dining room, as had the quartet. A dance band stood in their place, performing cover versions of pop classics while strobe lights flashed overhead. The more energetic guests were dancing, while the rest stood in groups making small talk, picking at the buffet and taking advantage of the seemingly limitless flow of alcohol.

She walked across the dance floor, trying to spot Max. Michael and Olivia were centre stage, dancing to a raucous rendition of 'I Will Survive'. But when she drew closer she saw that it wasn't Michael at all. Just someone who looked like him.

Eventually she saw Max, standing in a corner near the makeshift bar, a cigar in his hand, locked in a whispered conversation with Michael. The light wasn't good, but Michael appeared unhappy. Max seemed to be trying to reassure him.

As she moved towards the bar, the band began to play 'The Power of Love'. Olivia broke away from her partner, gazing wistfully in Michael's direction. Noticing, Max whispered something to Michael and gave him an encouraging push.

Deciding that this was her moment, she headed for the space he had vacated.

She passed Michael in the throng. Again she noticed the tension in his face. As if the weight of the world was bearing down on him. A long honeymoon looked to be just what the doctor ordered.

Suddenly he stopped, his eyes widening as if he'd seen a ghost. At first she thought he was staring at her.

But he wasn't. His attention was focused on an attractive girl of about his own age, with short blonde hair and a mischievous smile, who was talking with friends.

He turned towards Max. Momentarily there was something like hatred in his eyes.

But the light was bad and she could have been mistaken.

And Max didn't seem to register anything. Just smiled indulgently at Michael as he had done throughout the meal.

She approached him, holding out her hand and wearing her most inviting smile. 'I'm Catherine Chester. Jack Bennett may have mentioned me. I'm a partner at Cox Stephens.'

'I believe that he has,' he said in a voice so beautiful that it sent shivers down her spine. His grip was strong and firm. Cigar smoke hung in the air between them.

'It was a lovely ceremony,' she told him.

'I thought so.'

'And the afternoon reception was wonderful. I really enjoyed it.' She sensed Eleanor Bellamy hovering in the background and prayed that they would not be interrupted.

He smiled politely, but his gaze drifted over her shoulder towards the centre of the room where the bridal couple danced together.

'You must be very proud of Michael.'

'I am. He has a wonderful future in front of him.' His eyes were penetrating. She sensed that he was a man from whom it would be hard to keep secrets.

She risked a joke. 'Now my divorce is through, I hope the same will be true for me.'

A nod. But no sign of interest. Still, it was early days. She tried another tack.

'Olivia's a lovely girl.'

He took a drag on his cigar. 'I think so.'

'And doing so well in her career.' She knew this was untrue, but flattery never hurt.

Again his gaze drifted over her shoulder. 'A shame it has to end.'

'Does it?'

'Of course. Michael is going places, and he needs a wife for entertaining. And I want grandchildren.' The voice, though beautiful, was distant. Clearly he wasn't interested, but she wasn't willing to give up yet.

She tried to be provocative, hoping that it would draw his attention back to her. 'I'm not sure Olivia will sacrifice her ambitions just like that.'

'Then she'll have to be replaced with someone who will.'

The eyes were completely predatory: following the bridal couple as if stalking prey.

A chill swept through her.

Suddenly he smiled. Warmly this time. And his laugh, when it came, was warm too.

Patrick Redmond was born in Essex in 1966. After attending school in Essex and the Channel Islands he completed a Law degree at Leicester University and then a Masters at the University of British Columbia in Vancouver. He spent ten years working in the City of London specialising in Commercial and EU law, before leaving to become a full time writer.

His novels have hit the bestseller lists in the UK, Germany, Japan and Italy, and have been translated into fifteen languages. Patrick lives in West London.

www.patrickredmondbooks.com
@PRedmondAuthor

ACKNOWLEDGEMENTS

Firstly, my gratitude goes to the usual suspects: my mother, Mary, cousin Anto, and friends, Gill, Iandra, Rebecca, Lesley, Jez, Paul and Susan, all of whom provided constant encouragement and support throughout the writing process. Thanks, folks – it really did make all the difference.

Secondly, my thanks go to Polly Edwards and Elizabeth Trott for advising on technical issues, though, of course, any mistakes are mine alone.

Last, but certainly not least, I'd like to thank my agent Patrick Walsh and editor Kate Lyall Grant whose input on both the structure and style of this book was simply invaluable, and all at Christopher Little and Hodder & Stoughton for their hard work on my behalf.

They were the PERFECT FAMILY.
He was the PERFECT STRANGER.
They should have NEVER LET HIM IN...

THE REPLACEMENT

PATRICK REDMOND

Everyone envies the Randalls: beautiful, accomplished and high-flying, their lives are almost too good to be true.

No one envies Stuart. A tough childhood has left him making his way as best he can, vowing to lose a bit more weight and become a bit more successful.

But a chance encounter sets in motion a series of events which will shatter everything. Some will think they've lost, others will think they've won, but none of them will be prepared for the final catastrophe of jealousy, betrayal and agonizing justice.

They should never have invited Stuart in –
and he should never have trusted them.

'The lurking tension and twisting cruelty in Redmond's writing and plotting make for a hypnotic, compelling read' *The Bookseller*